California Otters – Part One

California Otters - Part One

By Todd Aldrington

Edited by Emily Nemchick

Cover Design by John Nunnemacher

Book One – The Shallows

Chapter One

Four days after Trick Dixon's eighteenth birthday party, most of his friends were still 'never drinking again.' That was okay by Trick though; sitting in a bar on his own meant possibilities, not loneliness. He ordered a double single malt scotch on the rocks – Talisker, his favourite, with its hints of smoke, salt and sandy beaches. It might as well have been made here in Cali, right outside this bar, where the waves lapped the beach, the shallows looking two miles long tonight, still just about visible in the post-sunset glow. A breeze was blowing through the open door, scattering a light covering of sand over the floorboards. Tonight was surf music night. Disappointing that there was no band, but the jukebox would do. Someone had put 'Rescue at the Mavericks' by The Torquays on.

'I love this song,' Trick said to the bartender, a fellow otter whose name he didn't know.

'I know.' Fellow Otter poured Trick's drink, lifting the bottle a little high for effect. 'I loved your party the other night. And what you've done with your ears? Oh they, just cry out "Ruffle me".'

Trick licked his lips and took a small sip. 'Don't they.'

Fellow Otter kept looking at him, as if asking permission. All Trick did was keep what his mother had called 'that devil's smile' on his face. When Fellow Otter spotted a customer at the other end of the bar, Trick winked as he walked away, hoping Fellow would notice. He did. He saw a twitch of Fellow's tail.

Nice.

Trick turned around and looked at everyone sitting at tables; a quiet night but a long way from empty. He thought about an hour ago, back at the great big beach house his father had rented for him and his mother and any friends they wanted for the next four weeks.

'Style me up, Kia. Like you did on my birthday. I'm going to Winslow's.'

The snow leopard had sighed. 'Theodore, that'll take *hours.*'

'Yeah, but I'm worth it, right?' Trick got off the bed. 'Come on, just do my face then. Maybe that surf wax thing on my head too.'

'Oh, go on then.' The snep already had a comb and the pot of wax in his hands. 'As long as you get down to your pants anyway.'

His heart already picking up, Trick stripped off, pulled a chair in front of the big mirror in the bathroom, and sat down. The bulge in his pants grew as soon as his friend began to preen his fur, a suggestively naughty look on the snep's face. Kia stopped and tickled the back of Trick's neck. 'You wanna fuck? Coz if you do, we've gotta do it before I get you ready. We'll ruin all my work otherwise.'

'Nah, it's okay. Just preen me, snepper.'

'Pity. You already look as fuckable as you did on your birthday.' The snep whispered this in Trick's ear in a voice that would have done well on a drag show stage.

'Just a preen,' Trick said. 'You can fuck me when I come home from the bar still single.'

It proved an effort though, sitting there with a bulge in his pants while his friend styled his fur, giving a purr of satisfaction every time the look was right. It didn't take hours, but the snep couldn't stop at just touching up his head and face fur. Kia stroked Trick's back and tail with a heavy brush. Trick breathed deeply with every long stroke, wanting his friend's body more than anything in the world but deciding a little control now would make it all the better later.

'Don't be drunk later,' Kia said, doing up the button on Trick's surf shorts, then all the ones on his loose blue-and-white shirt. 'I want my hung otter as soon as he gets home.' The snep ran the comb between his own ears a few times. 'Kyle's going to catch us before this vacation's over.'

'Kyle's asleep right now because he worked out too hard this afternoon,' Trick said. 'When he wakes up, he's going to smoke a joint too hard too, then he'll scoff a whole seventeen-inch pizza on his own and be asleep by the time I get back.'

'Because I'm going to make sure of it, aren't I?'

'Yyyup,' Trick said. 'That thing from when we went surfing on my birthday stuck, by the way. Everyone's started calling him Dolphin. That's really not a good nickname.'

'Why not? Just because you know he's a better surfer than you.'

'Please.'

'He *does* swim a bit like a dolphin.'

'Dolphin's a sassy nickname.'

'Well, bless-him-love-him, your brother's just such a sassy otter.'

'Yyyup.'

Kia gave Trick a kiss, filling his mouth with a little too much tongue and saliva, as usual. 'But I still *do* love him. I think we should tell him.'

'You think we should tell him,' Trick said, deadpan but still grinning. 'That he's the one you love but you'd rather have sex with me.'

'Okay, maybe not tell him like that, but...how can I get him to be like you in bed? You think there's a way you can drop hints to him that I'd love it if he was just a bit more...y'know, a bit more *you*?'

'Listen, I'm always happy to share. I was a sharing-the-toybox kind of kid, and I never grew out of it. I'm just nice like that. Why don't we ask him if he minds that we both enjoy you?'

'Oh, I don't know, Trick. Because you're his kid brother? Wouldn't it be too much like...ah, never mind. But I think we should tell him what I really gave you for your birthday.'

'What have I told you?' Trick said, fondling Kia's tail and licking the tip of his nose. 'You gave me a new wetsuit, just like he saw. The rest was my present to *you*. Don't let the guilt in here.' He tapped Kia's forehead. 'You broke up with him, remember?'

'We're on hiatus.'

'And that never came with the condition you didn't see anyone else. Come on. This'll pick your relationship with him up loads when you get it back on track. New ideas. This is Cali. Loads of brothers share partners. It's not the same as fucking each other. Even if we both had you at once. Would you like that? I can ask.'

'Ooooh no! So not ready right there. I think my heart would explode.'

'Death by otter double-team. Not a bad way to go.' Trick returned Kia's kiss and then took his friend's head in his hands. 'Okay, serious time. I'll think about what to do. I promise. I've got big plans, right here. I can wake Kyle up a bit, because I want him to be part of them, because he's my brother and I love him. You'll see. Things are going to be great. Tagging along for my birthday party vacation's already the best choice you ever made. I'm going to make it even better.'

'Dreamer.'

'I'm going to make our dreams come true. I don't need a star to wish on, snepper. I'm just me. Now come on. Say what you know I wanna hear.'

Kia put his mouth next to Trick's ear, then purred softly. 'Uh-uh. You wanna hear that? Come home to me sober enough to make me say it. Why do you even want to go drinking tonight anyway?'

'I just do. I want to hear surf music and smell the bar. Maybe meet some new people.'

'Go on then. I still can't look at a drink. Have fun.' Kia pointed his finger like a pistol. 'Catch a snep!'

'Catch a snep!'

I've stolen my brother's boyfriend, Trick thought, taking another sip of scotch as the chord breaks in the middle of 'Rescue' kicked in. *Kyle never had his own quirky substitute for 'have a good night' with anyone. Whatever I do, I can't turn my brother into me so our best friend will stay with him. I'm in big trouble.*

And I love it. I'm Theodore 'Trick' Dixon, and I'm just getting started on this world. Then I want the next one too.

Fellow Otter had gone over to the jukebox. 'Rescue' ended and 'Summer at Dreampoint' by The Aqua Velvets started. What had the guy done, written down every song Trick had put on during his party?

Good. Everybody wants this otter. Trick took a deep, contented breath. Kyle was a great guitar player. Trick had always fancied learning, so he could play music like this. Perhaps it was time he got his brother to teach him properly. It would bring them together a little more. Then the rest would happen. Kyle had to come here and live this life with him. Trick didn't want this dream without his brother.

He probably knows about Kia already, Trick thought. The style the snep had put on him for his eighteenth was a copy of the idea Kyle had used for a year already – dyed ears and a dyed stripe down his back and tail and front. Except Kia had just dyed it white blond on Kyle. It was like he'd thought up the stunning blend of blue and orange on brown fur, got ready to do it on his boyfriend, and then saved it for Trick. He'd done the double stripe on the arms too, circling them in a tattoo effect that rippled while he was swimming.

Maybe he should let Fellow Otter take his ruffle and see where it went tonight. First thing was first though.

'What's your name?' Trick said, accepting another double and putting ten bucks down.

'Sanford. Call me Sandy.'

'Theodore. Call me Trick.' They shook hands.

'I already know your name. The way your mom still calls you Tadpole is adorable.'

'Don't. Nobody ever caught on to calling me Tad apart from her. But the other? I wish she'd quit it.'

'Where did Trick come from? I never heard Theodore shortened to that.'

'I played a character called that once. School play. Everyone said I was just playing myself all the time. It stuck. *Beware the Trickster in the Shadows.*'

'I never heard of that play. Who wrote it?'

'I did.'

Sandy put the bottle down. 'You wrote and starred in your own play. As a high-schooler.'

'Yep. Senior year.'

'Special boy,' Sandy said, sliding Trick's drink to him and ignoring the ten bucks.

'Not so special really. We all just had to come up with the plot for a play and write two scenes, and our drama teacher picked a winner. It wasn't really my play in the end; it was more like his. I just nagged him to change bits of it, and we rehearsed a lot of the characters together.' *Didn't we just. That story's not for tonight. Fellow Otter doesn't need to know how I worked out I was gay. Just that I am.*

'So, special otter who wrote his own high school play, you just come in here for a quiet drink, or are you meeting someone?'

9

'Quiet drink. But I think the meeting thing's just happened, huh?'

'Wanna tell me what your plot was?'

'Sure. It was like this...'

'Hey kid.'

Oh no. This wasn't supposed to happen tonight. Trick turned. He'd last seen his father a year ago. Tyler Goldman looked like he'd aged five, but he still looked healthy, and astute enough for anyone to know that it didn't matter whose conversation he interrupted. Trick had been expecting a shipwreck of an otter; now everything he'd heard turned out to be wrong. Or his father had turned things around in the same spectacular fashion he'd always been known for.

'Whisky, huh?' Ty said. 'Good boy. Enjoy it while you still can. Just remember, bit of a family weakness. Keep it in check.' He put a fifty down. 'Give the kid a bottle of that to take home with him when he leaves. I'll have a cup of coffee.'

The look on Sandy's face was one that Trick had seen a few times before, and it was best described with what he knew Fellow Otter would say next: 'Your dad's Tyler Goldman?'

'Yeah,' Ty said. 'So hurry up with my coffee. We'll have that table right there.' He pointed to the centre table, where two Labradors were having what looked like a romantic drink. 'Go tell 'em sorry, but you forgot it was supposed to be reserved this evening.'

Once they'd sat down, Trick decided he could still play this, no matter how off guard his father had caught him. 'I was just getting along well with him.'

'Yeah? Well, I'm here, and I want to spend time with you. You can meet fuckable tail some other night.'

'Except I wanted it tonight.'

'Don't play sad with me, kid. You had your party, didn't you? You telling me you didn't get at least one present from somebody?'

Wouldn't you like to know. 'Don't tell me,' Trick said. 'You didn't get my invitation. Your PA fucked up again.'

'I'm sorry I wasn't there, but strange though it may sound to you, I didn't think an eighteenth celebration full of drunk, horny teenagers was exactly the best place for a middle-aged otter who's been going to AA meetings for the last three years.'

'Translation: there's a middle-aged otter you're still scared shitless of, and her name's Shiva Dixon.'

'Your mother's an amazing woman. Always told you that.'

As close as he'll ever get to admitting it. 'You know, Dad, I'm very disappointed you're sober.'

Even his father's perpetually rock-like face changed at that. 'Excuse me?'

'I came here with a plan. I was going to be the adoring son who got you back on your feet, despite everything in the past. That was going to be 'Hello World, here's Trick.' Then you were going to go all soft and put some good words in for me while I worked the circuit. Or better, you'd get your friends to do it, so it never had to look like it came from you. I came here to use you. Now I'm going to have to work a whole lot harder thanks to you becoming a friend of Bill W's.' Trick downed the rest of his drink. 'Disappointed.'

'Well, shit,' Ty said. 'My otter.'

'Yeah. The one you didn't raise. Look how that turned out anyway.'

His father's look softened a little, but his eyes could still have bored through a wall. 'I'm not scared of your mom, kid. She and I had a good long talk, right before you came out here and brought all your friends. You think she could afford the vacation you wanted? Guess who she asked.'

'I knew she would, and that you couldn't say no.'

'She and I are still good friends,' he said. 'That's why she told me all about you. She wants me to make your dreams come true. She used everything I ever did wrong as leverage. I'll hand it to her, she was good. She really fought for you. That's why I came here to tell you I'm not doing it.'

Trick waved his empty glass and caught Sandy's eye. 'Big surprise.'

Ty smiled. 'Yeah. I think you really were that prepared. You still think you can win me round somehow. Play the game. Ride all the way to the gravy train and then ride that too. That's why I like you. So I showed up.'

Sandy refilled Trick's glass, three shots this time, and brought a pot of coffee as well.

Tyler looked at it as if to say it wouldn't do because he'd only asked for a cup. 'You enjoy your beach party?'

'Yeah. Thanks.'

'*Es nada*, kid. I might not be up for Father of the Year, but I've got a heart. So listen, take it as sincere or don't, but getting on the twelve steps did teach me a thing or two. I know I made some mistakes. I'm not that

12

good at apologies because half the time it's obvious I don't really mean them, but I'd like a chance. You came here to use me? I came here to use you too. I think we're talking the same language.'

'But I don't get a good word from you to help get my career going?'

'I'm not letting you trade on my name, and I'm not doing that nepotism crap. What would you rather have, the career Daddy helped you get or the one you got for yourself, because you actually were that good that you did it on your own name? That's why you're a Dixon, not a Goldman. That's why none of my kids have my name. Your brothers, your half-brothers, anyone I might not know about, they're their own person, like I had to be.'

'Sure. No help. Like your father never lent you your first million to start your venture.'

'Sure. Why do you think I deliberately blew it?'

'Because blowing a million deliberately got you your name known. Call it what you want. You had help.'

'There's something I just love about hearing the phrase 'blowing a million' from an otter who probably sucked cock before he walked in here and ordered his first legal drink on his eighteenth birthday.'

Nice, Trick thought. *Roll with it.* 'Let's talk about your chance, Dad. That one you want from me. Okay, you can have it. I'm not really bothered about much of it. At least you never abused me. How could you? You were never there to do it.'

His father's eyes looked deep and dark. 'I never abused *any* of my children, Theodore. There are some things you don't do no matter what else you might have

13

on your record. This business I'm in, powerful people protect their friends when they do things like that. Those of us with enough decency, though, we get it stopped. Why do you think my life became hell for several years? I couldn't just shut up. What did you want, kid? Me bringing my death threats and my drinking to the home where your mom was trying to raise you?'

'Okay, sorry, that was low. Mom told me about all that stuff you blew the whistle on. I respected you for that.' It was true, he did. *Trouble is, Dad, being that brave and honest doesn't buy your way out of everything else.* 'But let's just talk about one little thing on *your* record. I want you to say something for me. I hear it go through my head a lot, when I think about how Kyle came out to you. He was holding Kia's hand. So, would you say, "You did it with a *snep*? What the everloving fuck?" again for me?'

'Yeah, okay.' Ty waved his hand. 'Not a bad impression of me. Such a little actor. I'll make things right with your brother. As right as I can get them. I just might need your help. Before you continue your little bargain though, family reunions that mend ties aren't the same as you dreaming of topping the list of best paid movie stars. I want this for more than just me. Three years sober will do that to you. You know why I got sober in the first pla...' Trick's father looked like he was daydreaming for a moment, but Trick knew he wasn't. 'You fucked your brother's boyfriend, didn't you? The snep.'

Trick grinned. 'Yeah. On my birthday too.'

Tyler Goldman burst out laughing. The background noise of the bar just about isolated the noise of it from everyone else. Trick felt like he was caught in the perfect private moment.

'Gonna tell my brother?' Trick said.

'Course not. Are you?'

'Yeah, probably. When the time's right.'

'Was he any good?'

'What does it matter? Why couldn't you have smiled like that and just said that when Kyle poured his heart out to you? Where did this live and let live come from?'

'I told you. Getting sober makes you realise a few things.'

'Yeah, okay, I'll give you that. As long as you'll admit one other thing.'

'What?'

'You like me just that little bit more than your other kids. I'm the one you don't mind making love to other species *or* another male.' Trick waited, knowing his father probably wouldn't answer. He didn't. 'Go on then. You were telling me why you got sober.'

'Because I love this business,' Ty said. 'Producing movies. That's the life I made for myself, and I wasn't done with the world yet. I could have my life back, or I could let it run like a train with no brakes. So I put the brakes on. The films are worth it.'

'Yeah. They're your real kids.'

'Your mother knew what the deal was. She wanted five kids. I gave her that. She wanted to raise them herself, without needing a man to do anything except write a cheque. I gave her that too. She let me have visitation whenever I wanted it, but she knew I wouldn't

15

want it that much. Just as long as everything was okay, I wouldn't interfere. I gave you all a decent life. Me being there wouldn't have made it better. Don't start with "My dad never came to my plays or my sports day" either. I bought my way out of that with your little vacation already.'

'I never cared about that. Just that I knew your world was interesting since I was about five, and it took me thirteen years to get close to it. With this *little vacation.*'

'Ah shit.' Ty looked at the ceiling. 'You wanna drive to Hollywood then? Get a tour of a studio? Meet some big names?'

'No. Anybody can get on that tourist show. You know what I want.'

'And I told you already, get it yourself. I could have broken into this business even without that million I blew thirty years ago, because I'm me. You're you. You think you're good enough to make it as an actor out here? Great. I respect that. Now you can prove it. I'm going to love watching you struggle like hell. Because every time you get that little bit stronger, you'll remember the time I told you that you could do this on your own name and you didn't need mine. I look forward to the day you sit in an interview in front of me and I don't acknowledge I've ever seen you before. But here's a concession: I'll be rooting for you. I promise. You want your shot? Fine. Here we are. Your first trip to Cali. Show me what you've got, boy.'

'Show you what I've got?'

'Yeah.'

'Alright, sure. Even if you're making it sound like I'm in my pants at some porn audition and that's the cue for me to drop them.'

Ty shrugged. 'Well, seeing as you brought it up, *would* you have what it took down there if you had an audition like that?'

'It's your DNA, Dad. You really in any doubt about the "you betcha" on that one?'

His father laughed again. 'Well, here's the other thing then. You're a man now. So I wanted to tell you, man to man, that I know how this business can work. You know why you're lucky to have an old bastard like me as your old man? Look at what's on my record. So I'm here to promise I won't judge you. For anything you have to do to make it. *Anything.*'

How was he supposed to answer that? A moment later, it was obvious. 'I wouldn't have cared if you did.'

'Attaboy.' His father put a hand in his jacket pocket and took out an envelope. 'You were right about the goddamn help. Yeah, I had my million. I'm not giving you my name, my recommendation, anything else, but here. Just so long as you know that once you open that, that's it. That's all the pay it forward you get. Fatherly duties complete.'

It wasn't money, Trick knew. There was a bulge in the envelope. 'Mind if I think about this?'

'Just open the goddamn thing.'

Trick opened it, and a moment later he wondered how he hadn't worked it out before. It was a key, attached to a keyring and a tag with an address on.

'Happy birthday, kid. That oughta help get you started. Here.' Ty put another fifty on the table. 'If you can't wait until tomorrow to go try that key out, get a cab. I don't want your story starting with a DUI.'

'That's...' Trick was staring at the address. 'This is a house right on the beach.' Prime real estate. Several million. Shit, negotiation over. His father was still the master. 'Thanks, Dad.'

'Before you get up, I don't want a hug. I don't want anything. Not even a drink. Just enjoy it, and try not to burn it down or flood it before you've got insurance. I made sure there's a bed and a sofa and a TV. I stocked the fridge for you tonight as well. Why don't you stay in the bar until fuckable tail over there gets off shift and go christen it?'

Because forget him. I want to christen it with a snep. I want to think about you saying what you said to Kyle and Kia while I do it. Then I have to figure out how to tell my brother you bought me a house for my eighteenth birthday when all you gave him was...

'What did you give Kyle a year ago, Dad? Remind me.'

'I sent your mother a cheque. She put it straight in his college fund.'

He won't be going to college. Not if I can talk sense into him. 'How much?'

'A thousand bucks. I think.'

Trick nodded. 'This making things right with him's off to a good start then. Soon as I take him in that house and tell him where it came from, tell me, how many ice ages do you think it'll take before he even acknowledges you exist, let alone talks to you?'

Tyler Goldman smiled from ear to ear as he got up. 'Persuade him to. You want this life badly enough,

18

you're going to have to close harder deals than that. You're either tough enough for this world or you're not. I've got a feeling you might just survive. Have a good night, kid.'

Chapter Two

The world seemed a little too far away for Trick, and it was nothing to do with the whisky. He looked around him, found the two Labradors again, and thought that was a good way to bring himself back to Earth.

'I'm sorry about your table,' he said. 'My dad's an asshole. Have it back.'

They looked like they no longer wanted it, giving him no more than a nod in recognition of his apology.

'Believe me, I'm already paying him back for it in ways you can't begin to imagine.' *I'm going to fuck a snep in my new house later. I'm going to make so much money one day I can buy and sell him, except I'll be buying and selling his nursing home.* 'Would you two like a drink? Maybe several?'

'We're just leaving,' the female Labrador said. They gave him contemptuous looks all the way to the door, as if they'd heard everything he'd said to his father and decided he was somehow worse. Perhaps they had. Trick shrugged it off and went back to Sandy at the bar.

'Is everything covered?' he said, taking his wallet out.

Sandy put a bottle of Talisker on the bar, still in its tube. 'I'll get your change.'

'Keep it,' Trick said. 'Keep the bottle too.'

'I really couldn't,' Sandy said, trying to sound professional, but where the otter who wanted to hear the plot of his play had once been, Trick saw one who wanted him out of the bar as quickly as possible.

'I'm only going to find out where you live and drop it round,' Trick said.

'I don't drink whisky, Trick. Please, just take it. Before you tell me to swap it for something I do drink, please just don't. I'm not supposed to accept gifts from customers.'

Trick took the key and tag out of his pocket. 'Then come and see my house.'

Sandy looked like he'd been expecting those keys to be for a car. He looked like he could take the bottle between them and brain Trick with it.

'Yeah, this is why I don't tell people my dad's Ty Goldman, and I wasn't expecting him tonight. Or this key. Would you keep me company while I try and make sense of the world? I'm sorry he called you fuckable tail. All I wanted to do was talk to you about my play.'

'I really can't,' Sandy said, looking like he wanted to call Trick a rotten liar. 'I've got a shift to finish. I'm busy after that.'

'Doing what?'

'Writing a script of my own.'

'Well, I guess I can't argue with that. Night, Sandy.'

'Wait. Am I calling you a cab?'

Trick looked at the address on the tag, and another thought added to his dizziness: once he stepped outside

21

of the bar and looked along the beach, he'd probably be able to see his new home from where he stood. 'No,' he said. 'Thanks. I think I'll walk.'

* * *

Google told Trick his house was three miles down the beach. By the time he reached it, it was midnight, and the tide had come in, but Trick knew he was safe, walking barefoot in the shallows.

Growing up in Phoenix, he often imagined himself swimming out to sea on clear nights in somewhere like Cali. Since coming here, he'd found out that if you were lucky, sometimes there would be a whole party of otters on a beach doing that – just swimming together, not caring they didn't know each other, just that it was like they'd heard some sort of natural call.

Not tonight though. Trick was on his own, and from a mile away, he knew which house had to be his: it was the one with the lights off.

Some part of him told him this couldn't be it. He'd made a mistake with the zip code and just fallen into a dream. Perhaps he'd been walking the wrong way down the beach for three miles. There was no number. Only the numbers on the neighbouring houses told him he was right. He still stood and looked at the gleaming white house with its gold metalwork and glass that had a tint of blue in the moonlight, and the open porch, and told himself it was going to be okay, because the key wouldn't fit in the lock. He'd probably get a rich wolverine or pine marten come out and ask why he was trying to break into someone's place.

The key turned silently, and the door opened.

He looked for a switch and found none. Of course he didn't.

'Lights.' The place lit up like an amusement arcade with a romantic dimness to it. 'Oh boy,' Trick whispered. He'd neither lived nor stayed anywhere so clean, so new. For a moment he couldn't move, and he looked down at his wet, sandy feet on the showroom-shiny tiles. Just a deep breath of the smell inside this place made him feel like he shouldn't be here. It smelt like alpine ice in a Colorado winter and the leather of the sofas, and somewhere behind it was the sun lotion and hot sand of Cali. Trick closed his eyes, his nose twitching with pleasure, and felt like he could fall asleep standing up. When he opened his eyes and exhaled, he knew he had to make some sort of peace with this place. It was his home.

It was his *home*?

'Okay,' he said, forcing his feet to move in small, slow steps. *It's a moment in time,* he thought as he walked around the place, touching everything as if to mark it as his. *Just another moment to file away in that great big stack of stuff that creates emotions and characters and brings it all to life for an audience.*

The coffee-house leather sofas looked too good to put a crease in. The TV took up half the wall it was mounted on. The dining table and chairs were made of a wood that looked like brown-and-white python skin, probably from a rainforest tree that was close to extinction. The fridge was something from a sci-fi movie, and his father hadn't been kidding about stocking it – there must have been two months' worth of food in it.

Trick only needed a drink. He looked at the three bottles of prosecco that probably cost more than he'd ever made in two years' worth of shifts in the kitchen at Argles and picked one up, feeling like it was the least extravagant thing he could touch in this place. The glasses in the cupboard were all crystal and sparkled like someone had polished each one for hours.

About to pop the cork, Trick stopped. He couldn't enjoy this alone. He thumbed through to Kia's number, then couldn't call. Then his brother's. He couldn't do that either.

I can't live here, he thought. *What did I do to earn this?* He put the bottle down, cork still un-popped. *That's the lesson, isn't it? The same thing Dad said about Hollywood fame and fortune. It has to be earned. He bought me a multi-million-dollar house just to give me a taste of what everything for nothing feels like. Tomorrow, I'm probably supposed to beg him just to take it back.*

Well, fuck that. Let's talk lessons, Dad. Let's talk Trick Dixon's worth this house, and so much more.

Trick put the bottle back in the fridge, deciding he didn't want prosecco. That was for sharing. Kia and his brother didn't like whisky either. If he had to enjoy a moment alone, Talisker was the way. He unwrapped it, dropped two ice cubes into a heavy-based wide glass, and poured a double. It tasted better than it had in the bar.

That was when he noticed it. As he sat down at the island-shaped bar in the middle of the kitchen, he saw the copies of the deeds to the house and a fountain pen with *Mont Blanc* on its lid in silver letters. The note his father had written was underneath it. *'Only one more thing needed. Up to you. -Ty.'* The tip of the pen was pointing right at the line where Trick's signature was supposed to go, below his father's. There were two more above that – the witnesses, who weren't there. Trick picked up the pen. It was the perfect weight for an otter's light fingers.

What should his signature look like? All the times he'd imagined himself signing multi-million-dollar film deals, he'd never given any thought to what his mark would be. He traced an idea of it in the air, remembering he had nice handwriting, thinking his name in print might do. He signed a joined, calligraphy-like version instead, and next to it printed 'Theodore James Dixon.' *Always sign as yourself,* he thought. *The name you were born with. Not a character name.*

That was it. He owned this home now.

It was time to choose a bedroom and fall asleep with the glass of whisky still in his hand. There was one right next to the kitchen. When Trick saw it, he knew he wanted no other. Looking at the upstairs could wait until the morning. The level above that, the mezzanine floor, that would give him...

...a beach view in the moonlight. It had to be now.

Trick walked up the stairs, deciding not to open the doors to the rooms. When he got to the top, he walked through the one that was clearly the master bedroom to the balcony outside, an equal size. It was like he could see the whole California coast. Out to sea, it looked like a bunch of seals were swimming. Or perhaps they were otters.

Trick leaned on the balcony, put his head back, and laughed euphorically. Way out in the distance, he fancied he heard the sound of otters answering him.

Back in his room, the large sliding doors open and the breeze from the sea blowing in ever so slightly, Trick looked at his bed and knew what he wanted to do. He'd call Kia in the morning. First, he wanted to get used to sleeping on eiderdown and memory foam. The thing was so soft, he wondered if it would induce an orgasm if he just lay there for a moment and got wrapped up in the feeling. He stood on it with his paws still slightly wet and let himself flop back onto it. He stroked his own tail then stripped his clothes off until he was naked and staring out at the night sky.

Kia will love this bed, he thought, the softness of it already sending a soporific level of endorphins all through his brain. *I should never have fucked him on that bed in the vacation shack. Not when our first time would have been made so perfect by all this.*

* * *

Four days ago

'Hey Kia, will you style me for tonight?' Trick went into his friend's room, hoping the snep had brought all his kit with him. Kia wasn't dumb, he just wasn't college material, but that didn't matter, because he'd found his thing: he was amazing with other people's fur. He could

26

draw too, but his real artwork was a live animal who was open to being transformed.

'Yeah, sure I will! Happy birthday, Trickster.' Kia had put his hands on his shoulders and touched his face as though he'd been doing both for years. 'Look at you. Eighteen today. How does it feel?'

Trick stood there, enjoying it. 'Look at *you*.' His eyes flicked downward to the bulge that wasn't quite visible in Kia's pants, but Trick knew it would be there.

'You're a sexy otter, Trickster. I'm a snep who likes otters. What did you expect? Strictly professional though. I'll just give you a good thorough preen and save all that pleasure up for when Kyle gets here. When does his flight land?'

'Couple of hours. I thought you two were taking a break.'

'We are,' Kia said. 'But...man, I'm in the mood. When he lands, I want to be there looking hot. There's something about surfing with otters, and what have I been doing all day? I think I'm gonna need him tonight. Wait until he's had a few. I'm so totally up for it. Oh, come on, what am I thinking? You. Let's pick a style for you. I knew you'd ask. I brought all the latest magazines. Check out *Leisure Otters* this month; there's some cute stuff I know will just kill if I do it on you. I've got surf wax, otter musk, fur tints, scent brushes, natural oils, the works.' Kia threw himself onto the bed, where a pile of magazines was already waiting on the side table. He patted the bedspread. 'Come sit with me right here; let's pick one out.'

Trick slinked onto the bed and cozied up to his friend. 'These are all nice,' he said, looking at the covers. 'But I've already got this. Make me look like Kyle.'

'What?' Kia looked surprised. 'Sweetie, why? I want you to look like *you*.'

'I want you to make me and Kyle look like twins,' Trick said. 'Can you do that? Think that's in your skill set?'

'Woah,' Kia said. 'Okay, that's a totally *smoking* hot idea, and I *so* promise I'll do that some other time, but on your birthday? Your mom's gonna want photos. So are you when it's all over. And you want to be able to tell you guys apart in them, because this is *your* party. I *am* that good that you'd get a whole stack of memories where you can't tell who's who. Will you trust me, you sexy otter?' Kia ran a hand up Trick's tail, then kept stroking it.

'Why *do* you like us so much, sneppers?'

'Your curves, your sleekness, the way you move like you're walking and swimming all at once, what's *not* to like? Sometimes I think I only like being a snep because Kyle likes sneps. I wish I'd been born one of you guys. Not that I wanna actually transform or anything, I just get this feeling from working on you. When I open my business, I don't quite know how I'm gonna handle it. Anyone else? I'm just a pro. It's just fur and bodies and heat, and I'm an artist. You guys? I think I might need a chastity belt or something.'

'You? A fine, chaste snep?' Trick sniggered. 'With a sign on your salon door saying "Sorry, no otters"?'

'I'll hate myself,' Kia said. 'But I think I might have to.'

28

'Species discrimination lawyers might shut you down,' Trick said. 'Not to mention it's all about the social media backlash now. Can you just imagine it?'

'Are you making fun?'

Trick took Kia's tail, running a hand over it. 'Put this in your mouth and take a bite. That'll make you less horny.'

'Fuck you, Trick Dixon. Bite your own.' He took hold of it. 'Or shall I?'

The two of them looked into each other's eyes for a moment, then just laughed when neither of them could hold the staring contest.

'Come on,' Kia said, fondling Trick's ears. 'It's your party minus five hours, and here we are being a couple of dumb kids playing with our tails. Pick a style. Oh, no, wait a minute, got it. Okay. Listen.' Kia took a deep breath, a camp smile on his face, like he was about to launch into some sort of drag monologue. 'You wanna look like Kyle? You got it. I can do that, and then some. How about this: this one blue, this one orange.' He stroked Trick's ears respectively.

'I'm listening, I'm listening,' Trick said, deliberately twitching his tail and sitting up straight. 'Okay, how about the other way around?'

'Hmmm,' Kia said, now looking deep in thought. 'Maybe. Eeenie meenie miney mo…yeah, I think you've got it. It's better the other way. Okay, that's the ears.' He put his hands on the side of Trick's chest and took a handful of his T-shirt in each. 'Arms up, let's get this layer off.' Kia gave a contented sigh as Trick stretched his arms up, and he pulled his shirt off in one slick motion. 'Okay, stripe here, stripe here.' Kia swiped an unclawed finger down the centre of Trick's chest, then his back, snapping him upright. 'Just like your big brother. Now, okay, arms. I've wanted to try this on Kyle for ages. How about the same colours in a spiral snake kind of idea? Like it's a tattoo that makes a ripple effect in water?'

'Do it,' Trick said.

'If this works as well as I think,' Kia said, 'and it's gonna, maybe you should get a real tattoo. Get it right here. Make it a sun pattern or something.' He touched the top of Trick's chest on the left. 'Or maybe "Made in Phoenix" and your date of birth right here.' He stroked a curve on Trick's stomach above his belly button.

'I don't want a tattoo. It'd ruin me. I wouldn't be a pure and natural otter. Isn't that what you go for?'

'A natural look that's *not* natural,' Kia said. 'That's the skill. That's the whole thing we're going for.' He took a deep sniff, looking as though he'd rather have his nose buried in any place on Trick instead of in the air. 'I like body art on otters. Can I at least *design* you a tattoo and see if you like it?'

Trick smiled, guessing what had brought this on. 'Did Kyle already say no to this?'

'How did you know?'

'Was he really sassy about it or just a little bit?'

'We went on hiatus a couple of days later. I don't think it was connected.'

'Alright, how about this?' Trick said, sitting cross-legged on the bed and curling his tail around his lap. 'I'll *consider* the tattoo idea if you'll let me do something I've always wanted to do.'

Kia's eyes went a little wider. 'What?'

'Oh, just something harmless. Sit up straight on the bed for me.' Trick put a hand on Kia's back and guided him to the right place, slightly away from the pillows, glad his friend was only wearing shorts and no shirt already. 'Alright, now I'm just gonna get behind you and take hold of your scruff.' Trick bunched the layer of fur and fat just below the end of Kia's neck. 'There! I caught a snep!'

Kia put his head back and sighed. 'Oh, for God's sake!'

Trick burst out laughing. Copying the silly trend he'd seen online on every social media channel going lately would only have been fun if he did it on Kia, just for the reaction. Trick dug in his pocket for his phone. 'Selfie!' He held it out and clicked the camera.

'Really. Seriously. You *had* to do that.' Kia put on a pouting expression, surely knowing Trick would like it. He did. He took two more photos.

'You love it.'

'Yeah. I really love being treated like I'm destined for a zoo. Can you release me back into the wild now, d'ya think?'

Trick let go of him, and in a fluid motion, he slunk around to the front, pushed Kia back onto the bed, and finished up with his hands gripping the snep's wrists. 'I *still* caught a snep!'

Kia started laughing now, finding it as fun as Trick knew he would. 'Yeah. Fine. You caught one. Now what are you going to do with it?'

'Rug.'

'Fuck you.'

'Snep burgers.'

'*Fuck* you!'

'Hmm...maybe I'll just keep it here and keep looking at it. Until it tries to wriggle out from under me and we have a nice little playfight. Or maybe until it just lies there and gives in and tells me I can do something *really* naughty with it.'

The two of them lay there for a moment, Kia's breathing quickening until he began purring. Trick slowly lowered himself down and kissed his friend's mouth, letting his tongue slide in, releasing the grip on his wrists and rolling the pair of them over onto their sides. They broke away naturally after what seemed like several minutes.

'Trick. Honey. We can't.'

'Sure we can. You know what the best way to work on otters without giving in to urges is? You go to work when one's already gone to work on *you*. It's a great way to start yer day!' He moved in for a second lick of Kia's mouth. This time, the snep put a hand on the side of Trick's head.

'Trick, no. Come on.'

'I *am* coming on.'

'So stop. Let's just style you up.'

Let it never be said that I couldn't be told to stop, Trick thought, pulling himself up and resting his head on his hand and his elbow on the mattress. 'Let me ask you something. When was the last time Kyle took that big, wet snep cock of yours and put it in his mouth and just sucked until you came in it and then breathed like he was trying not to drown in you?'

Kia was already twitching before. Now he was trembling and hunching up, looking at Trick with a pure, guilty kind of lust in his eyes. 'Never.'

'Aw, he won't do that for you? Did *that* cause your hiatus? You told him you were bored in bed and it hurt his feelings? Silly boy. He might have liked it if he'd tried.'

'It...wasn't *just* that. I really didn't want him to get so sensitive. I think I pushed his boundaries a little bit too much.'

'Seriously? Because you asked for a blowjob?'

'He just isn't into it.'

'Boundaries. Maybe you just need a few minutes with someone who doesn't have any.'

'You *do* have them, Trick. Everybody has them.'

'Okay, yeah. I can be modest. I can also do what my brother won't. But hey, you asked me to stop. That's okay. Respect. Let's get me on a chair and do that style we talked about.' He shifted himself up. Kia pulled him back down, a soft growl coming from his throat as he took a heavier grip on Trick's fur.

'Once. That's it. Then we never do this again. Because it's your birthday. You wanna do it with a snep? I'm a snep. I can be *your* snep. Then as soon as Kyle gets here, it never happened.' This was a whispering growl in Trick's ear. 'We never talk about it. Got it?'

Trick wrapped an arm around his friend and held him there, hearing his breath in his ear, feeling the heat burning beneath his fur. 'This is *my* present to *you*. So you can work on me without that painful bulge and wet pants.' His hand moved to Kia's shorts, undid the button and slipped inside his underpants, taking hold

33

of his hard cock and releasing it from the fabric tangle. Kia sighed. Still keeping hold, Trick guided him onto his back and slid his shorts and underpants off.

'Leave them around my ankles,' Kia said, already struggling to steady his breathing. 'I want a safety word. Coconuts.'

'You *wish* this was dangerous,' Trick said, letting go of Kia's ankles and leaving his pants there. He scuttled forward, his butt in the air, hovering as he straddled the snep's legs. 'Coconuts. You got it.'

'Just watch the teeth.'

'Teeth? I'm so good at this you'll think mine are retractable. Now just lie back and take a deep breath.'

Kia took several as Trick rubbed his muzzle against the side of the snep's cock, teasing and tickling and then licking before taking it into his mouth and pushing the tip against his palate with his wet tongue. Kia gasped. Trick sucked gently, releasing the pressure every second until he felt the warm stickiness of pre-come against his cheek. He put his hands on Kia's chest, feeling it swell with the pleasure of every breath, stroking his fingers through his friend's coat.

'Trick...*Trick!* I don't wanna come in your mouth.'

Trick let Kia's cock slide out of his mouth and looked up at him, poised like he was ready to spring. 'No problem. I can let go right before you shoot. Where do you want to do it? You just wanna soak the otter?'

Kia nodded, a look of wild excitement dancing in his eyes.

'You got it, you're gonna get me *wet*.' Trick rubbed Kia's stomach, tickling him a little. 'Let's play a game. It's called Can a Snep Count to Ten? How about it?

Think you can last ten good hard sucks on that thing before you soak the otter? Count along with me.' Trick went back down and licked his friend's cock. 'Ready?'

The snep was so hard now that his tip tickled the back of Trick's throat as he took the entire shaft into his mouth, sealed his lips around it tight, and took a strong suck on it. Kia moaned, purred and then managed to count, 'One!' Trick slid his mouth up and down it, pulling harder every time, until the snep got to six and his legs became tense and shaking underneath him. Trick withdrew. 'Can you hold? You got this?'

'I got it! I got it! Four more! I can do it!'

Trick doubted it, but his own excitement was too much not to go for it, expecting to swallow, but somehow Kia counted seven, eight, then nine, his whole nether region hot and sweating and his cock pulsing inside the soft tissue of the otter's mouth.

Trick came up for air, a big deep breath of it, then exhaled, ready to suck down a second one. 'Get ready, snep! Ten!' He wrapped his mouth around Kia's cock again. This time he didn't stop. The suck just went on and on and on, and still his breath was inside him, the valves in his nose locked tight, pretending he was underwater.

'Trick...oh man...oh *man*, stop! I can't do this! I'm gonna come in your mouth! Stop!'

Trick didn't. *Safety me,* he thought. *I dare you. Coconuts indeed!* Either hold or safety me or drown me. His own cock painfully hard, he resisted the urge to hump the mattress, concentrating on the sound of his friend's fast breathing and the feel of him twitching around, ruffling the covers underneath him.

35

'My heart's gonna...Trick...let me go...let me GO! I need to come so badly!' Kia growled and arched his back.

Still Trick hung on, the suction power of his mouth and jaw pulling on the snep for all he was worth, his friend writhing and gasping with reserves he surely never knew he had. Kia started yowling, a cat's desperation call, flailing his paws at the ceiling. Only when the snep ran out of breath did Trick release him with a wet pop, and with a deft motion he grabbed his friend's cock and pointed it at himself, arching his back and pulling himself up in a curve, presenting the target.

'Go!' Trick yelled.

Kia showered him, panting and moaning with intense relief, sending a hot shower of come up Trick's chest and stomach, then squirting just below the otter's jawline with the last of the reserve.

'Trick...I'm having a heart attack!' Kia's whole body was twitching, emptied out of all strength but not wanting to stop.

'You're fine,' Trick said, still soaked and hot from his own sweat as he pulled himself along the bed so he could reach his friend's head and stroke between his ears. 'Down you come, nice and easy, steady breaths. You can fall asleep if you need to. I'll wake you up before my brother lands.' Trick picked up one of the towels from the end of Kia's bed and wiped himself off, his natural oils making the semen slide off him and onto the towel almost as naturally as water. He could smell Kia on him, a light, musky, salty scent that mingled with his own sweat. He rubbed his own cock and arched up happily, contemplating working himself until he soaked his friend back, then decided he could probably do better. It *was* his birthday, after all.

Kia didn't sleep, he just lay there breathing hard and deep as though he were consciously sedated and didn't know anything about the world except for his own unbelievable high. After a few minutes, he rolled over and opened his eyes, blinked repeatedly, and shook himself.

'Holy *shit*, Trick. What exactly was that?'

Trick took a deep breath, puffing his chest out as he stroked down his friend's back and rested his hands on the snep's backside. 'I can hold my breath underwater for twenty minutes, remember? You really never imagined what a blowjob from someone who doesn't need to breathe and just keeps sucking would be like? You made it longer than I thought.'

'God, I wish you'd warned me. Why didn't you?'

'Dumb question of the year right there.'

'Yeah. Goddamn you, you're the greatest otter alive.'

'I know.'

'You didn't come yet either.'

'I know.'

Kia put a hand on Trick's neck. 'Oh, don't worry. I know how to say thanks. Look in that drawer right there. I've got something you'll like.'

Trick reached into the drawer and found the tube of lube. He took the cap off and sniffed. It smelt like a combination of rosewater, pine wood and wet forest earth. 'Now that's what I'm talking about,' Trick said. Kia purred, flailing his arms and hands out, pawing for Trick. 'Gonna roll over and show me that snep butt?'

Kia rolled over, turning his head to see Trick coating his hand in lube and putting it down his pants, his fist making his bulge look huge. 'It's so hot hearing you say that. Say it again.'

'Shhh,' Trick said, tickling the back of his friend's neck. 'Let's see if it's as tight down there as I need.' He put a hand below Kia's tailbone and poked a finger between his butt-crack. 'Good start. That's so tight it's gonna be like we can knot.' Trick spread some more lube on his fingers and inserted two of them down his friend's crack, sliding down until he found the snep's hole, then rubbed around it, then inside. Kia gave a growling purr.

'Get a move on, otter. I want you in there.'

Trick slid onto him in a swimming motion, poking his tip under Kia's tail. 'Feel how hard that is?'

'Yes...come on! Stuff me, Trickster! Stuff till I bite that pillow and you make me wet. I'm still hard...make me come again with you.'

'Get ready, snep. I'm gonna catch you.'

'Yes! Catch a snep! Catch it!'

Trick slid inside and then dropped his whole weight on top of Kia, thrusting into him again and again, the rest of his body elegantly still as his hips did the work. Feeling his own butthole tighten up, needing his release, Trick held his breath again and took hold of Kia's wrists, holding him down against the bed, still poking him with every heaving breath the snep could manage.

His control holding, Trick wondered if he'd lost the moment, his thighs and groin aching and his friend still horny and telling him how much he wanted it, and it all just seemed to fade slightly, like all the pleasure was Kia's and none of it his.

This couldn't happen. He couldn't have sex on his birthday with his brother's boyfriend and not come. This would ruin the whole thing. What could he make Kia do? What would drive him wild like nothing else? Even re-imagining his friend's pleasure and the hot shower he'd received wasn't getting him there. All he could do was stay hard, like there was a barrier.

'What's up, Trick? You can't come?'

'Talk to me, snep,' Trick said, tightening his grip on Kia's wrists. 'Talk filthy to me. Tell me I'm naughty. Tell me something magic.'

'Okay...okay...filthy...you got it...uuuurgh this is hot!' Kia kept gasping in time with Trick's thrusts and looked like he was thinking, hard and fast. Then he grinned, showing his sharp cat teeth. 'Hey Trick.'

Trick released one wrist so he could flick sweat from between his eyes. 'What?'

'You're a selfish otter.'

'Oh *God*, that's what I needed!' Trick came, arching his back and yipping with every squirt, thrusting into Kia one final time before dropping on top of him, still inside, the pumping inside his cock refusing to stop as he repeated his friend's words inside his head again and again. Selfish otter, selfish otter, selfish otter...catch a snep.

Trick hugged his friend, the orgasm mercifully stopping, leaving him euphoric and exhausted. '*How* did you just come up with that?'

'I dunno.' Kia shrugged playfully. 'Maybe I just told you the truth.'

'Yeah, but how did you know it would work?'

'Errr...I kinda didn't. I just said it. You wanted to be dirty. I guess I just got caught up in being bad instead. You liked it. I've got an ocean leaking out of me right now. Or at least I will if you ever get out of me.'

'Oh. Sorry. You're seriously tight though. I could stay in there all night.' Trick slid himself out. *Did my brother ever do* anything *serious to this poor, neglected guy?* he thought. *Did he ever make him feel special?* He reached behind him and found the towel he'd used earlier. 'There you go. Floss your butt with that.'

'Gross!' Kia said, tossing it away. 'Selfish otter!'

They both laughed.

'Just tell me,' Trick said. 'Would Kyle really not give you a blowjob or were you just turning me on with that?'

'I wish. It was true. Kyle just likes everything clean and sweet. It's just how he is. I keep telling him, I'd really like to get naughty. I don't think our hiatus is going to turn back to anything else. Not after that. He kept telling me I was pushing him. All I wanted was a bit more...*that*. There was other stuff too.'

'Like?'

Kia rolled over. 'I can't *totally* betray him, Trick. Okay, I needed an itch scratched. You scratched it. But I'm only hot for you. I don't love you. Kyle...it's just the reverse, and a bit of personal stuff. Can you pass me that vape pen?'

Trick reached it for him, holding it away at the last moment. 'Your lungs are too good to wreck with that crap.'

'Oh, don't be a dick. I've never smoked a real cigarette in my life, and you wouldn't like me if I wasn't trendy. Admit it. It's stylish.'

'Very slightly, maybe.' Trick took a drag on it and blew it out without inhaling. 'Yuck! Bubble-gum flavour? Meh. Here you go then, fill your boots.'

Kia puffed on it contentedly. 'Once, remember? That's what we said, and we can't tell him. Happy birthday, you've had a snep. You want another one, you've gotta find a different one.'

'Why don't I talk to my brother?'

'No. Leave it. Maybe we just ought to break up amicably and I'll get back in the game with a new otter. But it's not going to be you. Even if you *are* incredible in bed. That's not the only thing I want.'

'Kyle's lucky to have you. Can I at least give him a nudge? If keeping you means all he's gotta do is get a little bit more wild, I think he'll do it. He'd be perfect for you if it weren't for that one thing. I won't push him. I'll just get him to talk to me.'

Kia looked at Trick oddly, blowing vapour at the ceiling in a great cloud. 'What makes you think he'd listen to you?'

'What makes *you* think he'd listen to me? You obviously do.'

'You're persuasive. Look what you just made *me* do.'

'What did I have to do? You were all over me from the second I walked in. That wasn't persuasion, it was reading cues. Oh yeah, and we've got a party to prepare for. Wanna shower together?'

* * *

41

<u>Present</u>

Lying naked on his brand-new bed, Trick thought about it all, his cock hard. It's never the orgasm, he thought as he got close to it. The great fucks we have are never about that. It's about the special things that come with them, the ones you remember more than just what squirting felt like. Getting called a selfish otter in Kia's drag queen voice. Talking about his brother afterwards. The shower where he'd put his hand between Kia's butt cheeks again and gently rubbed everything clean, expecting his friend to resist, but instead Kia had growled and contentedly nuzzled his head against Trick's chest, his swollen dick rubbing against his leg as if trying a third time to answer the call of pure, sinful pleasure.

Trick came hard enough to soak the top of his own chest, thinking of how Kia had done it, and how after it all, Kia's camp excitement had given way to a relaxed calm and even more attention to detail than usual. He'd been styled to be the standout guest at his own party, and hell, he'd been that. Half the attention that had been on him that night was thanks to Kia.

Trick lay there afterwards, trying to mix his breathing in time with the sound of the waves outside, wondering what his father would say if he knew his first night on this bed was spent covered in jizz he hadn't bothered to clean off himself before sleeping.

He wasn't going to sleep though. However relaxing it was, there was too much to think about. He went into the en-suite bathroom, an extravagant blend of blue marble and white ceramic, and showered off. There were fresh towels ready, and a silk dressing gown hung on the back of the door. When Trick put it on, he caught the scent of the lining infused with natural otter oil before he felt the smoothness of it against himself, one level better than the silk on the outside.

I've got to haul ass tomorrow, starting first thing, he thought as he stood on his balcony again, letting the night air blow inside the gown. *If I want to keep this place, afford to live in it, things need to happen. Fast. Just to start with I need to get a –*

Was that the doorbell he'd just heard ring? *His* doorbell? Who knew he was here?

I've made an impression on the neighbours just by jerking off? he thought. Hell, how much noise had he made without realising it?

It wasn't the neighbours though; it was an otter whose looks gave him a moment where time was out of joint. Just a couple of hours ago, he'd never have imagined such a style on Sandy, yet here it was. He looked like he was ready to pose for a surfboard commercial, and the combination of musk and spiced cologne almost knocked Trick out even from ten feet away, where the bartender was striking a confident pose.

'Hey lonely otter,' Sandy said. 'Fuckable tail at your service.'

Chapter Three

This was one of those moments, Trick thought, where no amount of studying or observing life through a movie or a documentary could prepare someone for the real thing. The longer he stared, the more Sandy's suggestive grin faded, and the more serious he knew he must look himself.

'I'm sorry,' Sandy said. 'I guess I got the wrong idea. You won't tell anyone, right? I'm sorry. I need to go home.'

'Don't go home,' Trick said. 'The joke's on me. I'm standing here like an idiot. I jerked off on my bed twenty minutes ago, and right here there's a good-looking otter who just knocked on my door and...honestly, I've never had *that* offer before. Not like this.'

Sandy looked a little relieved but still looked like he could bolt. 'Was it okay though? I wasn't out of line or anything?'

'Of course not. After what you heard me say to my dad? All you did was give me what I bargained for, and *bam*, surprise! I deserved that.'

'Yeah. You did. But I meant it though. I'm still at your service.'

'You don't have to offer to fuck me just to get inside my house, Sandy. Why don't you come in and we'll have a drink?' Trick gestured to the doorway, and as Sandy walked in front of him, trying to look confident, Trick realised the other otter was a little drunk. Maybe even a lot, but holding it. Impressive turnaround time though – during Trick's three-mile walk, Sandy had shut the bar, necked liquid confidence, changed out of work clothes and made himself look like this.

'Nice place,' he said. 'My dad never bought me a house. My parents won't even talk to me. I'm not sympathy fishing; I don't wanna talk to them either. Fuck 'em. Pair of assholes.' He put on a smile Trick was certain was forced. 'You got gin? Tequila?'

Trick stood in front of Sandy and gently put both hands on his shoulders. 'How about a cup of coffee, Sandy? A good strong one with a couple of sugars.'

Sandy sighed deeply, looking down at the floor. 'I'm a fucking idiot.'

'Uh-uh. That would have been if you stayed home tonight and did nothing. I love your courage, right here. Come on, lift this up a little.' He stroked under Sandy's chin, and the other otter lifted his head. 'That's better,' Trick said. 'I can't fuck someone who's drunk. Neither of us would feel good about that tomorrow. But we can have a cuddle with some coffee, and he can tell me why his parents kicked him out because he's gay. If that's what happened. That sound okay?'

'I don't wanna talk about Mom and Dad,' Sandy said. 'And I'm useless at fucking. All I wanted to do was

45

get my confidence up. I spent the rest of my shift feeling like an idiot for not coming with you. So I thought I could change that. But I'm not that drunk. I only had three shots.'

'That's a brand-new sofa,' Trick said, leading Sandy to it with a hand on the back of his neck. 'Never been sat on. So sit your newly confident butt on it and I'll go see if this place has a coffee machine.'

It did. It was never not going to, Trick thought. When everything else was so perfect, it couldn't be ruined by the lack of a strong, steaming cup. Making it gave him space to gather his thoughts. He chose coconut milk instead of regular and put two shots of espresso into Sandy's latte, with two sugars on top. When he put it into Sandy's hands and watched him take a sip, close his eyes and sigh, Trick wondered if he'd fall asleep right there.

'*So* good,' Sandy said. 'Thanks. I needed that.'

'So, Confident Otter, you from Cali or did you run away here after whatever happened with your parents?'

'I ran.'

'From where?'

'Maine. I hitchhiked.'

'Seriously?'

'Yeah. I thought I'd learn a bit about life, trying to walk from one side of this rock to another. I kinda did. I still don't feel like I can do anything with it. I got the job in the bar though. That's a start, right?'

'Any idea where you want to end up?'

Sandy shook his head, clasping his hands around the cup. 'I just know I need more money. You're going to think I came here gold-digging. I really didn't, I promise. I don't want your money.'

Just as well, seeing as I don't fucking have any. 'I never thought you did.'

'I just wanted to be better, cooler, get up the guts to try and get somebody decent to want to be with me. I've had two shitty boyfriends. One of them threw me against a wall and gave me a concussion. When I told Mom and Dad about it at the hospital, we had a fight for two hours, and they said they weren't taking me home or paying my bill.'

'Rough,' Trick said, deciding not to make assumptions out loud, but the rest was obvious. 'Fuckable tail' had been getting this idea since Ty Goldman called him that, and he thought he could be confident enough to tell someone who clearly had money what his going rate was. Hefty bill to pay back in Maine that he was probably getting chased for. No flight records of where he'd gone, because he'd done it in cars with strangers. Was his name really Sandy?

'I'm sorry you've had a rough time in life,' Trick said. 'But you're smart. You came to the place where you can be anybody and turn all that around.'

'Yeah. God bless the American fucking dream.'

'Listen, Sandy...I hope you don't mind, is that your real name?'

Sandy shook his head. 'I never want to hear the name I was born with again. It's dumb, and I've always hated it. I even lied on my form for the job. Didn't figure a bar like that would bother running a check on my social security number. I still go in every day worrying I'll get called in because they've done it, but it never

47

happens. I'm trying to save up my pay to get it changed legally. I always wanted to be Sandy. Like Kofax. I used to be good at baseball.'

'What surname did you pick?'

'Rickwood.'

Rickwood wasn't an otter name, but Trick suddenly wondered why not. It worked. 'Sandy Rickwood. I like that. That's cool; you're Sandy to me. You don't have to be anybody else.'

Sandy perked up, his tail twitching a little. 'Thanks. I needed to hear someone say that.'

Trick thought about stroking his cheek again, and most other parts of him, but thought a little distance would work better this time. 'Well, you're a good-looking otter, Sandy Rickwood. Even though you're strictly off limits to me until we've at least picked your self esteem up. What else do you need to hear me say? Okay, here's something. *I* need a job. I've hardly got any money. That's my dad for you. Set me up in a place like this that he knows I can't afford to live in. Just to see how I try to cling on.'

'Seriously?'

'Never mistake a rich man's generosity for generosity. But a poor man's?' This was right, Trick thought. He'd considered it while making coffee and knew it wasn't really considering. It was a first step. 'How would you like to live here, Sandy?'

Sandy only kept hold of his cup because Trick already had a hand there to help him. 'I just nearly spilt coffee on your new couch,' Sandy said, as if he'd heard nothing.

48

'Easy to save up for your name when you don't have rent to pay. Or we could share them, if you've got a no-charity principle, but I can take care of it. I've got plans. I'm keeping this place, and I don't want to live alone in it.'

'This is the...' nicest thing anyone had ever done for him? 'You only met me this week, Trick. How do you know I won't bring total misery and chaos in here?'

Trick smiled. 'When you followed me home, how did you know I wouldn't slam you against a wall like your nasty boyfriend?' A moment later, he knew he'd made the wrong choice of words when Sandy shook a little. 'I'm sorry. I won't keep bringing that up. I should have just told you I'm good, and you just knew it from the start. So, we going to be housemates?'

'I don't know, Trick. Can I think about it? I'm not used to anything this good.'

'Neither am I. I'm here on vacation. My bedroom back in Phoenix is a shoebox. I went to an ordinary high school because there aren't any pool schools in Arizona that don't cost a fortune. My mom's a waitress. My millionaire Hollywood dad pays minimum kid support. I'm the last kid to turn eighteen, and what he was really celebrating was not having to pay anymore.'

'But he bought you this house?'

'He expects me to fail at keeping it.'

'Here's to having shitty family,' Sandy said. They clinked cups. 'Sorry, I should have asked, is your mom cool?'

'My mom?' Trick said. 'She rules. Wait till you meet her.' *Your boyfriend slammed you into a wall? You should have seen my mom put my older brother Ryan against one for being a bully*. Trick almost added it but thought better of it.

'I wouldn't sweat it about the pool school though,' Sandy said. 'It doesn't matter where you go to school. It still sucks no matter how suited it is to your species.'

'You went to a pool school? Jealous already.'

'I got stuck in a tube and nearly drowned.'

Trick had to try not to laugh and failed, thanking his lucky star that Sandy was laughing with him.

'Yeah,' Sandy said.

'How do you get stuck in a tube full of water when you're an otter?'

Sandy stared into his coffee for a moment, then into space, then back at Trick. 'Before I hiked here, I was over 200 pounds.'

'Two hundred *pounds*?'

'At least your school never had to give you a written warning about your size. When you get over a certain weight for your height at a pool school, you get red flagged. So you don't do what I did. My first warning, I tried. I really did. I went to the gym more, tried to stop eating crap. It didn't work. My second, I got banned from using the tubes. So I used one anyway, because fuck 'em all. I *wanted* to get expelled; I hated that fucking place. It never even occurred to me I might drown and die. I was just mad as hell, and I got in the tube. I actually made it halfway to class.'

'*You* were a fat otter?'

'Yeah. Was.' Sandy looked confident now. Good play, Trick thought. Whatever he did to lose those pounds, he was proud of it. 'You like me now though, right? You said it.'

'You were probably good-looking even when you were fat.'

Sandy rolled his eyes. 'Aaaaand you've fucked it up. You were doing *so* well at playing counsellor to me, but let me explain something: somebody who's used to bullying and fat shaming is *not* going to take that as a compliment. I looked like shit. I felt like shit. So I did something.'

'That never meant people were right to bully you.'

'Who cares about it now? It's behind me. This is me now. Confident otter. That school and everyone in it can suck my dick. There's a water park down the road from here. I go every day to remind myself I'm a million miles from getting stuck in tubes anymore.'

'How did they get you out?'

'They had to drain the tube and dismantle it. After they'd cut a hole and got a diving mask through so I could breathe while they got ready to do it. I was stuck in there for five hours. It cost the school over thirty thousand bucks to do all that and put it right again.'

'This is an expensive otter I've just asked to come live with me.'

'Proud of it. One day I hope the world's still paying for me after I'm dead.'

'You get the expulsion paper?'

'Yeah. I never got my diploma. I'm a dropout. I thought about trying to find somewhere here so I can finish, but...I know, it's dumb, but...I want it to be the first real thing I do as Sandy Rickwood. So I need a job to save up to officially be him. No diploma, no decent job. No decent job, no... What the hell am I saying?

Yeah, I'll be your housemate. Can I pay a share of the bills after I'm Sandy?'

'You're already Sandy,' Trick said. 'I promise, I'll never tell anyone you were ever someone else. I'll never even ask what your name was again.'

Sandy went from looking grateful to looking baffled. 'How do you get this so well?'

'I had a middle brother, William. She's now my sister Willow. Believe me, I'm used to people being whatever they want to be. You should have seen how my dad reacted to that. It might take Willow quite some time to look at me again after I tell her about this place. All my other brothers too.'

'Especially Kyle.'

'Oh, you heard that part too? Nosy otter with a good pair of ears.' He let himself touch the tips of Sandy's ears.

Sandy shook his head. 'I'm sorry I turned up here like I did. I was gonna...ah, forget what I was gonna do. You've got a special person in your life already, haven't you? The snep. Even if it's gonna be a little awkward with your brother.'

'Kia's a friend who just started allowing benefits,' Trick said. 'I don't think him and me in a relationship would work. You should meet him though. Yeah, good idea, hang about down here, I'll find my phone. You want some more coffee?'

'It's two in the morning,' Sandy said. 'Normal people sleep.'

'Yeah,' Trick said. 'So they do.' He crossed his legs on the sofa and wrapped his tail into his lap. 'Go on. Tell me what you were going to do when you got here. Don't be ashamed. Even if it's what I think.'

'What do you think?'

'Well, how much does fuckable tail need to buy himself a name?'

Sandy's eyes went wide. 'I didn't want you to pay to fuck me. I just wanted to feel like somebody wanted to. Because…okay, look, I wasn't going to be a rent-boy, but I was thinking of doing something that's maybe worse. Something that'd really freak my parents out if they ever got hold of it. A great big fuck-you-world, this is who I want to be. So I've…kinda set up this audition. The kind that'll pay if I get it. But I've been thinking about it all day, and I don't know if I can. So I came here. I thought maybe if I just showed up and cut to the chase and you did your thing with me, I might feel ready.'

Trick grinned from ear to ear. 'Have I got this right, Sandy Rickwood? You've got an interview with a place that makes porn films?'

Sandy shifted around, his arms folded around himself. 'Yeah. Apparently we're an 'underserved market', if you can believe that. Everywhere wants to hire otters right now. But I can't. Look at me right now. It's hard enough to even talk about it. How am I gonna actually perform for anyone? It's not even a dignity thing. I don't care if someone else wants to watch me suck someone off, or anything else. I just…' Sandy looked at the ceiling. 'What if they say something like "It'd be better if you were fat?" These places are nuts, right? They'll say stuff that like. Fat-furs is a whole market. What if I go in there and they see straight through all this and just know who I was before and like it better?'

'Well, you won't know unless you try, huh?' Trick said. 'Can I make another of my dumb guesses? You want me to come with you. Supportive friend who doesn't judge.'

'No. You can do that if you want, but that's not it. You're an actor, right? That's what you said. What you wanna be. So act for me. I want a rehearsal.'

'Oh. Okay.' Trick thought fast. 'Yeah, we can do that if you want. But we're going to have to hold off. We've both been drinking. This might go unexpected places, and then I'll feel like I've taken advantage of you.'

'Oh come on, I was ready to go all the way with you. At least let me be naked in front of you and tell me what you think.'

Trick couldn't protest before Sandy took everything off and stood there in front of him in all his glory. He *was* good-looking. There were a few lines where Trick could tell his skin didn't quite fit him after he'd slimmed down, but anyone who didn't know that had happened would never have noticed. For someone who had likely never done that sort of audition before, he struck a good pose.

'You look good,' Trick said. 'I'd look at you in a magazine. I'd watch you on film too.'

Sandy took hold of his growing erection and looked at Trick. 'I like doing this for you. You want me to? I'm a good size.'

'Yeah. You are. Okay, go for it. Let's see you hard.'

Sandy was trying to relax and concentrate all at once, Trick thought. He wasn't naturally comfortable like this. 'Okay, compliment time: I'm getting it from this.' Trick put a hand in his own pants and adjusted himself for comfort. 'But –'

Sandy took two unsteady steps and held his arms out to balance himself. 'I need to sit down. Massive adrenaline dump right there. Is this happening?' Sandy sat down quickly. 'Too many deep breaths. Man, I must be tired or something.'

Something, Trick thought, and he'd realised what. Sandy hadn't been drunk at all when he came in. Perhaps the three shots, like he said, but that hadn't brought out drunkenness. He took Sandy's hands.

'Sandy, be honest with me. When was the last time you ate something?'

Sandy closed his eyes again and sank back on the sofa. 'Fuck,' he said. 'Is it that obvious?'

'Until you nearly fainted, no. It wasn't. What happened? One extreme to another? You just kept cutting calories and feeling good, and before you realised it you got to zero and kept it there?'

'I *do* eat,' Sandy said. 'I'd be dead already if I didn't. It's like hearing a voice, Trick. I wake up every day and it tells me I can't go back to being the otter who got stuck in the pipe. It's gotten worse since I landed the audition. That was two weeks ago. I never answered your question. Breakfast. I ate two peaches at breakfast. And I drank three shots after work. And your coffee.'

Christ, Trick thought, looking at the clock as it moved to 2:30. 'Wait right here.' He went to the kitchen and opened the fridge, hunting for inspiration, telling himself not to panic and just think. What was the right thing to give someone in this situation? *If you knew*

55

that, you'd be going to medical school like a smart person. On the top shelf, there was a box of Krispy Kremes.

'Fuck it,' Trick muttered, taking them out. He quickly poured another coffee, this time black without the sugar. Sandy was half asleep already. Trick choose the donut that looked just slightly richer than all the rest and held it under Sandy's nose. It gave a pleasurable twitch. He moved it so Sandy's jaw rose up a little in a dog-like beg. 'Mmmm,' he said.

'Wake up, silly otter. You need to eat this.'

Sandy opened his eyes. 'Oh hell no!'

'Come on. Let old you back in, just for tonight.'

'Trick, this is like giving someone who just quit a forty-a-day smoking habit a pack of Luckies and sayi...' Sandy's tongue touched the edge of the donut, then he licked.

'Open up,' Trick said, and Sandy did. Trick put the donut in his mouth. He took a small bite, then another. 'Slowly,' Trick said.

Sandy swallowed. 'Oh thank God! Peanut butter cream pie...how did you know it's my favourite?' He took the rest of it from Trick, ate it quickly, drank some coffee down, his eyes revitalised with energy less than a minute later. 'I needed that more than anything else in the world right now. You know how long it's been since I let myself do that? A year. I've been on the road a year, and I'm so tired.'

Does he even know where he is right now? Trick thought, looking at Sandy's entranced face. *Never mind.* 'No kidding. You need another one. Strawberries and cream?'

'I can't.' He was already taking it, smelling it, then biting it in two, covering his chin in jam and cream. 'You're Satan,' Sandy said. 'You're gonna wake up tomorrow to find me puking in your toilet, and that box is going to be empty.'

'No, it's not.' Trick didn't doubt it though. *I had to get him to eat something. This was the best I could do. But I'm still an idiot. Okay, do something.* 'We're going to get you healthy. First step to dealing with those interview nerves. You want to make love in front of a camera for a living? Great. But a good relationship with sex starts with a good relationship with yourself. We've got to get your good relationship with food back first. Before you lose those looks you just showed off to me and become an otter-shaped skeleton. Nobody's going to hire that. But this, right in front of me? This is a good-looking otter. You deserve to stay that way. Say it to me.'

Sandy smiled. 'What is this now, you're playing a coach for me?'

'Say it.'

'I deserve to stay this way.'

'Like you mean it.'

'I deserve to *stay* this way!'

'Good. So you're not going into the bathroom and sticking your fingers down your throat. You know why not?'

'Because you just forbade me from doing it?'

'Because you just forbade yourself. Because you said you deserve better than that. So I'm taking these back into the kitchen, you're going to take a nap, and I'm going to see what I can cook. Something healthy, where you can eat as much as you want and barely put on a gram. Can you do that?'

'Yeah. Sure.'

'You won't be grouchy when I wake you up?'

'Nah,' Sandy said, already back to being half asleep with his eyes closed.

Trick rubbed his head. 'Be right back.'

* * *

What else can tonight possibly bring? Trick thought, looking through the fridge and cupboards again, thanking himself for all the hours sweating in the kitchen at Argle's Bar as a teenager. What was in that vegan chili thing they used to serve that had always sounded awful until he'd tried it? The fridge had red and yellow peppers. There were some gourmet tins of chopped tomatoes. Onions, celery, spices, squash...or was it sweet potato? Trick found both, then just as he was giving up on finding tinned cannellini beans in the cupboard as big as a wardrobe, there they were. Hot chilli powder, cinnamon, tomato puree...this was going to need a bigger pan. He found one.

He stood in the silence of the kitchen for a moment, looking at everything set out and thinking about how at Argle's he'd wanted nothing more than just to strip those stupid kitchen porter's coveralls off and just sweat naturally. He took off his dressing gown, draped it over one of the stools, and began cooking, contentedly naked.

Chorizo. That would make this. Forget the vegan thing, his new friend needed a proper otter's diet, and

58

that meant meat. Fish would have been better, but none of the smoked packets in the fridge would go with this. Brown rice – a little fibre was good for the digestive system. A good bottle of red wine. Cilantro garnish and a little squeeze of lemon mixed into the sauce just before serving.

Still naked, the breeze cooling him as he came back into the front room, he woke Sandy up and put a plate in front of him.

'I'm not feeling so hungry now, Trick. Sorry, but I don't think I can eat.'

'Just take a taste.'

Sandy looked at the plate as if it might make him sick, but his mouth was watering so much he could only just contain it. He picked up the fork and tentatively tasted it. He ate the rest in silence, a little too fast, occasionally remembering to breathe, smiling at Trick as if to say he really had learned table manners as a child but was just caught up in a moment. That moment, Trick thought, was eternal gratitude.

Pity, he thought. *If Sandy ever does want sex with me, the selfish otter line will never work coming from him. I'd better never cook dinner for Kia.*

Trick had decided water was probably better for Sandy to drink and that one of the designer bottles from the drinks fridge was fine. Sandy had forgotten the glass, gulped straight from the bottle, then said sorry as he started to come down from the food high.

'What *was* that food, Trick? Whatever it was, I want it every meal forever. Did you really make that? You didn't order in?'

'Nope. My mom's recipe. Told you she rocked.'

59

Sandy was staring at him like he'd just discovered the meaning of life. 'You're...'

'Oh yeah. I got a little hot while cooking.'

Sandy licked his fork clean, then put it down on his empty plate. 'Come on then. How am I saying thanks?'

'You look so tired that if I let you say thanks like that, you'll probably fall asleep inside me. Besides, wouldn't you rather have your first good time tomorrow when we're nice and fresh? Or would it be your first time ever?'

'I'm not a virgin. I was when I left home. Or rather, when I left the hospital I got put in after I said no to that asshole. You ever had a brain haemorrhage?'

'Can't say I have.'

'I bet he isn't even in prison for doing that to me. I bet Mom and Dad didn't even do anything. I'm sorry, why am I bringing this up now?' Sandy sighed. 'Alright. Yeah, I've never done it, and nobody else ever made me a dinner like that. I was fat because my parents raised me on crap. I liked it. Now I don't. So are you going to come over here and fuck me or should I just go home?'

Trick sat down next to him. 'You *are* home, remember? We'll move your stuff out of your other place tomorrow and cancel your rent cheque. But by the way, how much do you think it costs to change your name by deed poll?'

'I heard it was three hundred bucks.'

'You heard a bunch of crap. It costs fifteen bucks.'

'For real? How did I not know?'

'Because you never asked anyone and didn't have time to look it up?'

'Look it up on what? I've got no phone or internet or anything.'

Trick smiled. 'If you go look in my wallet over there, you'll find the change I told you to keep. We'll go get it sorted tomorrow. Then you can fuck me as Sandy Rickwood, and whoever you've left behind can die for good. Or you can *not* fuck me, because you really don't have to.'

Sandy tried to say something but couldn't get the words out. Soon he had his hands over his mouth, tears rolling down his cheeks.

'It's alright,' Trick said, rubbing a hand down his back. 'Everything's going to be good from now on. You'll see.' He stayed with Sandy until he fell asleep on the couch, then went back to his own room and drifted off himself, listening to the waves on the sand.

Chapter Four

Trick had always been a deep sleeper, just like most otters. He rolled over and answered his phone, not thinking about how many calls he might have missed until Kia's voice almost deafened him.

'Oh thank God...where the fuck are you? I've been worried stupid all night! You've got about ten seconds before your mom grabs the phone off me. Good luck, asshole.'

'Urrrgh.' Trick opened his eyes and ended up burying his face in the pillow. The sun was midday bright.

'Trick Dixon, where in the hell have you been? Have you any idea what I felt like this morning when Kia told me you hadn't been home all night? You didn't even call anyone? I've been trying to ring you all morning wondering whether I should call the police. You absolute fucking...' Trick waited for it. His mother always ended a telling-off with half an insult when she was full-on furious, as if searching through every swear word she knew and deciding not even the worst ones fitted. 'Tell me you're okay.'

Even half asleep, he knew how to explain quickly. 'Dad showed up last night.'

His mother said nothing, then sighed. 'But you're alright?'

'Yeah.'

'I told you never to let him drag you to one of his parties. You didn't do drugs, did you?'

'No, Mom, you didn't raise a stupid otter.' *He knew not to tell you about the coke he did in the bathroom at Winslow's on his eighteenth.*

'Says the otter who doesn't call and makes his friends worry all night. In a town like this. You're *worse* than stupid sometimes, Theodore. I'd rather you were stupid than thoughtless.'

'Yeah, Mom, okay, I know I should have called, but I had one *seriously* out-there night, and I don't mean I was partying. I wasn't. I'll explain; you know I will, and I'll grovel, I promise. I'll cook you a nice dinner or something, and you can give me probation instead of grounding me now. Sound good?'

'Sounds like you think you can get off easy. Guess again.'

'Can you put the snep back on before he starts ripping up the furniture? That'll cost us our deposit if you let it happen.'

'We'll talk about this later. Eighteen now or not.'

The speaker gave him ruffled noises as his mother handed it back.

'You're getting it for this,' Kia said. 'When Kyle wakes up, I'm gonna...'

Tell him we had sex? Trick waited as Kia tailed off. *Mom's still in the room then.* He half hoped Kia would

63

finish anyway. 'That would be a very bad idea right now, snepper. Can you just cool off here for a minute? I'll tell you a story that'll make everything okay again.'

It took longer than he thought, but Kia finally sighed. 'Where are you? So I can come and punch you in the face. I must have called you twenty fucking times.'

'Yeah, yeah, we'll have make-up sex later. You want to know where I am? I'm going to text you an address; I want you to come here. You. *Only* you. You bring anyone else and I'll never touch you again. You'll be stuck making love to my brother for the rest of your miserable little leopard life.'

'You're gonna have the kind of claw-marks on your butt that mean you can't sit down for a month, you vacuum-mouthed fish eater.' Kia rang off.

Nice try, Trick thought, knowing his mother was probably still there. She wouldn't ask what the insult meant. She probably already knew about his second birthday present from Kia somehow. He texted the address. If Kia called his bluff and brought everyone around, friends and family, then this was a bullet-taking morning. So be it. Maybe it was better to get it over with.

The doorbell rang.

'The hell?' Trick said, imagining Kia in a Superman suit, doing his fastest run ever. *Kinda hot,* he thought, making a mental note for the next time he was in a cosplay shop. He slipped the silk gown on again. It smelt just as good this morning. He rubbed a hand under his tail and sniffed it. Last night with Sandy had sent his scent glands into overdrive. He needed a

64

shower, but a quick wash would have to do. The natural-scented lining of the gown would probably neutralise most of it. He used the bathroom, washed his hands and splashed his face, oiling his fur back to look slick, then went for the door.

A well-dressed lioness and girl of about his age who had to be her daughter stood there. 'Hi, we saw lights on here last night for the first time in ages. You okay if we welcome you to the neighbourhood?' As if on a cue, the daughter held up the fruit basket she was carrying.

Lions, Trick thought. The kings of the Hollywood circus. 'By all means.'

'We're the Robinsons. I'm Tia, and this is Lottie. I'm sorry Gerald isn't here, my husband. Work, I'm afraid. But he says to ask if you'll come for a barbeque later.'

Trick found his best friendly neighbour face, genuinely liking the idea of barbeque food. What time was it already? 'I'd love to. Theodore Dixon. Call me Trick. That fruit basket looks wonderful. Please, come in.'

'What a charming young man,' Tia said, giving her daughter a nudge. Lottie rolled her eyes and huffed.

'I don't want to date an otter, Mom. I've told you.'

Tia gave a wry smile. 'Excuse my daughter. She *can* be polite sometimes. I'm so glad you like the basket. I wasn't sure if otters ate much fruit. I made a lucky guess on you being otters. There were lots of them here last week moving things around.'

'They didn't want to talk much,' Lottie said. 'It's like they were the otter mafia or something.'

'Lottie,' Tia said, with a parent's warning tone.

I wouldn't be so sure they weren't exactly that, Trick thought. 'I eat lots of fruit. Don't have much of a sweet tooth. Really, you shouldn't have.'

'Oh, not at all.' Tia gave a warm smile. 'Are your parents home?'

Trick didn't know why it surprised him. Even last night, the cat didn't have his tongue like this. This was one of those tension-building stage silences, even better than the one he'd held when looking at Sandy. 'Well, the thing about that is...' *They're out doing business with the otter mafia.* 'Well, this is kind of my place. I live here. On my own.'

Lottie looked like she'd suddenly changed her mind about dating otters. Tia just laughed. 'Oh, very good, young man. You're wonderfully precocious. I knew I'd left it too late; they must be at work. What's a good time to call round later?'

The doorbell rang again.

'Excuse me,' Trick said. 'Would you both like some coffee? Give me a moment and I'll make some.' He opened the door. Kia looked stormingly angry.

'I am *exhausted* from not sleeping all night, and I am major league fucking *pissed* at you! Whoever's place this is, I'd better be welcome, and it *better* have coffee.' He shoved past Trick and into the hallway, stopping dead as soon as he saw the lions, who were wide-eyed and alert. Most likely from the heavy smell of fellow predator with claws half out.

Kia put his hands to his mouth and took a calming breath. 'Okay. I'm sorry. Errr...can we just go, Trick? Tell me that story outside. What *are* you wearing?' For a moment, the gown disarmed Kia completely. He looked as though he could fawn all over the floral pattern and spend a good hour rubbing himself against the silk. Then he was back. 'Don't tell me. Wherever your clothes are, just go get dressed. It's walk of shame time. You owe me breakfast. And these good people have probably had enough of you.' Kia looked at them, relaxing a little, his claws back in. 'I'm sorry about my mouth a minute ago. We're good friends.' He touched the back of Trick's neck. 'I'm just a *little* bit angry with him right now, that's all. Never date an otter who doesn't call.'

Lottie smiled. 'You're his boyfriend?'

'Not for much longer.' Kia dug his claws in. 'Come on, *boyfriend*, we're going.' He looked at Tia and pawed the dressing gown. 'He'll return this later. Promise.' He marched Trick out of the door and slammed it behind him. 'Start your story. It had better be good.'

Trick grinned, trying not to laugh. 'This is my house, Kia.'

'What?'

'This is my house. I live here. I signed the deeds last night.'

'*What*? You stayed out all night buying a fucking *house*? With what mon...' He stared down the street. 'No. *Nooooohohooo*. When you said your dad showed up...*this*? For your birthday?'

Trick realised he hadn't seen it from this side yet. When he'd let Sandy in, he hadn't stepped outside and looked at the street entrance. It looked like a surfer's idea of a palace from this side.

'Told you I had big plans,' Trick said.

'Woah,' Kia said, as if he hadn't seen it before storming in either. 'Surf music my ass. *This* is why you wanted to go drinking on your own. Your dad was showing up and he'd bought you a house? *This* house? You're making this up, right?' It took him another minute. 'Why couldn't you have just told me?'

'Well, y'know, I wanted to make sure I liked it first. So I didn't have to send it back and ask Dad for another one. What do you think, shall I keep it?'

Kia kept staring at it, then collected his senses, and Trick guessed which thought had brought them back. 'Now I know why you didn't want Kyle or your mom here. How the fuck are you going to tell him?'

'We'll work it out,' Trick said. 'After you've popped a couple of Valium and got a good afternoon's sleep.'

'I don't have any, Trick. I quit all that, remember? Okay, apart from the coke I scored for your party, but that was for you.'

'No problem. Wait until you try one of the beds in this place. You'll be asleep before your head hits the pillow. I'm sorry I made you worry all night. Trust me, when I tell you everything that happened, you'll know why I forgot to call. Someone else needed me last night.'

'You got laid too? Your first night here?' Kia smiled now. 'You bastard. With who?'

'Before I tell you how I *didn't* get laid, what do you say we go and ring the doorbell and have my new neighbours let us back into my house? We'll eat some of that welcoming fruit basket they brought me for breakfast.'

Kia looked at the door like his stomach was full of bricks. 'Ooooh *fuck*.'

'They'll be fine. Trust me.'

'They're lions, Theodore.'

'Come on.' He offered his fist up. 'Catch a snep!'

Kia sighed and pumped it with his own. 'You first.'

The Robinsons let them back in, still looking as surprised and tentative as they had before.

'Shoooould...we maybe...perhaps we'll call back later?' Tia said.

'Tia, I'd like you to meet Kia.' Trick said. 'Kia, this is Tia. And this is Lottie.' He looked at her. 'Kia's not my boyfriend. What he said was just a little tongue in cheek. Can we all maybe have some coffee together and I can explain what that little misunderstanding was all about?' They almost looked sold. 'My dad's Hollywood big bucks,' Trick said. 'That's why the otter mafia were here all last week. I like that name for them, by the way. It was my eighteenth on Monday. Dad surprised me last night with this house. So much so that I forgot to call the snep here. I forgot he had such a temper too.'

Tia straightened up. 'Well, it's lovely to meet you both. I'm sorry, I should be used to this sort of thing. Your father's a producer? Who is he? You *do* look so young. He should be putting your face on all his posters sometime soon. If he doesn't, we'll just have to tell him that my husband's the face of MGM and you come recommended.'

Kia was back to pie-eyed now. 'You're married to Gerald Robinson? The MGM lion?'

'Yes, I am,' Tia said.

Trust Kia to know the guy's actual name, Trick thought. How many people ever bothered looking *that* up?

'His dad's Ty Goldman,' Kia said, as if knowing he'd get a moment of smirking revenge.

He got it. Whatever look came over Tia's face, Trick saw it even though she covered it quickly. *She's probably a real estate agent or in sales,* Trick thought. Or an actress. Except a good actress wouldn't be overplaying this. 'Ty Goldman, of course. I should have guessed from all the otters. But I thought you said your name was Dixon.'

'It is. Dad wasn't really much more to my mom than a sperm donor.'

Lottie sniggered, back to giving Trick the eye already. Tia put on her laughter. 'Oh, these producers. I'm sorry,' she said, turning and offering her hand to Kia. 'It's nice to meet a snow leopard. We so very rarely see them in this neighbourhood.'

'Errr…yeah, well…guess you caught a snep!' He clicked his tongue and winked. 'I'll just go put that coffee on, shall I?'

Trick resisted a wicked smile. 'Why don't you show Tia and Lottie into the front room? I'll make the coffee. It's all just through there; it joins onto the kitchen.' So I'll be able to hear everything. Sure enough:

'Oh!' Tia yelled. 'Okay, just…hold on there a second.' Probably to Lottie. In a whispered voice: 'Did he…is that guy *supposed* to be here?'

'How should I know?' Kia whispered back. 'I didn't even know he had this place!'

'You don't know who that is?'

'Is *that* his boyfriend?' Lottie said, deliberately loud.

'I think we're going,' Tia said. 'Come on.'

70

'No, *no*, don't go! He'll be really upset. He probably just forgot he let a friend crash here. I don't know all his friends. Just…otters like to sleep on couches and not use blankets. Trust me. Trick forgets other species don't find it normal. Those guys walk around naked all the time at home. Saves taking clothes off when you've got a semi-aquatic house.'

Good save, Kia. A little exaggerated, but not bad.

'This house isn't semi-aquatic,' Lottie said. 'Why didn't his dad buy him one that was?'

'I dunno,' Kia said. 'Because he's cheap?'

Yeowch. I'm using that on Dad sometime.

'You keep telling me to try going out with other species, right?' Lottie said. 'I want to see that guy's bare butt.'

Trick sniggered.

'Don't you so much as move your feet, young lady!' A pause. 'How come he hasn't woken up?'

No sound from anyone. Damn the coffee machine, Trick wanted to hear if they were all taking a closer look.

He quickly poured the four cups as soon as the pot was full enough and took them in on a tray. None of his guests were sitting down. They were standing and pretending nothing was wrong and trying not to look at Sandy's feet and tail poking off the end of the couch.

'Oh. Yeah. Sandy. Don't worry, he *is* alive. Here, take this.' Trick handed Kia the tray. 'I'll just go get a blanket.'

'Trick,' Kia said. 'I don't think that guy's breathing.'

'Yeah, yeah, nice try. Otters are deep sleepers. We can go down to twenty breaths a minute when we're totally under. You never seen Kyle do it?'

71

'Of course I fucking have,' Kia said. 'That's how I know the difference, and in case you hadn't noticed, *I'm not joking.*'

Trick looked between Kia and the two lions, who both didn't seem to know whether they should agree or run.

'You're serious?' Trick said. 'Actually serious?'

'Actually serious, Trick. That guy does *not* look good.'

Dumping the tray on the nearest table, Trick went around to see Sandy lying eerily still. He touched his shoulder. 'Sandy?' He shook it. '*Sandy*? Come on, wake up. Wake up!' *Oh, you stupid boy, what the fuck did you do after I went to bed? I left you here feeling so happy! What happened? You didn't know how to deal with HAPPINESS, and that made you do whatever the fuck you've done?*

'I'll call an ambulance,' Tia said, now even more shaken but managing to find her phone. 'Lottie, go outside and wait to flag it down.'

'Hold on!' Trick said, touching his fingers to Sandy's neck and internally heaving the greatest sigh of relief he'd ever had. 'He's got a pulse. Okay...this is okay.' Why couldn't he be as calm as Sandy's body was right now? Trick hated any kind of adrenaline dump that wasn't brought on by surfing or a stage. He put his hand in front of Sandy's muzzle. 'Come on, Sandy, take a breath. Come on. Tell me you're just asleep and not...' Shit, did all that food put him under? Is that what starve-and-stuff can do to someone?

Trick felt air on his hand.

'Oh, thank God! It's okay, Tia, hang up.'

'He should be waking up,' Tia said. 'I'm staying on the line. What if he took something? Does he do that, drugs?'

'No, I don't...' *I don't know? How about I don't even know* him*?*

Tia held up a hand and turned away. 'Yes, 2640 New Beach Trail, please. There's an unresponsive otter here; he's breathing and he's got a pulse, but we can't wake him up. No...hold on, I need to talk to his friend.' Back to Trick. 'Does your friend have diabetes?'

'I don't know. I hardly know anything about him; I only met him last night.' *Oh Christ, why couldn't this all have stayed a joke? Diabetes? It made sense, thinking of the story he'd told. Type, 2 most likely.*

'I'll search his pockets,' Kia said, suddenly noticing the clothes that were on the floor.

'No!' Trick said.

'The fuck do you mean, "no"? We gotta see if he's got a medical card or insulin. I'm searching.'

And once you do that, you'll know the name he never wants anyone to know. That's important right now? What the fuck am I thinking? 'Okay, yeah, sorry, do it.'

'Lottie,' Tia said. 'I told you to go outside and wait. I don't want you to see this.'

'Duh, I already saw him naked. What are they gonna do, start doing surgery on him?'

'*Now*,' Tia said.

Trick sighed, feeling a second small breath of air on his hand. 'Sandy, you idiot, what did you do?' Trick tried shaking him again. Nothing.

'There's nothing in his wallet,' Kia said. 'It's just empty. Totally. Nothing in his pockets either.'

'Come on, Sandy, wake up!' Trick said, trying to force back fearful tears. He'd never cried in fear in his life, and if Sandy...shit, it was because he wasn't used to his new name. People always woke up at their name. Why couldn't his wallet have just contained something, *anything* that might have given him a clue to his old one?

Lottie opened the door down the hall, then yelled, 'Maybe one of you idiots should try tickling his feet. That'll wake *anyone* up.'

Trick and Kia looked at each other.

'It's alright,' Tia said. 'They'll be here in ten minutes.'

Trick stood up slowly, looking at Sandy's feet. He exchanged looks with Kia. 'I'll do it,' Kia said.

'Your claws are too sharp,' Trick said. 'I'm doing it.'

Kia knelt down where Trick had been, doing the same checks, as if he couldn't quite believe Trick wasn't trying to cover something up by pretending his friend was alive. 'Trust me now?' Trick said when Kia's face changed to relief. 'Alright, get ready.'

'It's not going to work,' Kia muttered.

Trick stroked a finger down both of Sandy's feet. Nothing. He tried a claw. Still nothing. He moved his fingers about a little...

Sandy opened his eyes and snatched his feet away, pulling his knees to his chest. 'Oh!' he yelped.

Kia yowled, staggering back and tripping on his own feet, his backside thudding onto the rug, just missing the coffee table.

74

Sandy's eyes bulged, and he sucked a great heaving deep breath down. 'Oh s*hit*!' He looked around himself frantically, then jumped to his feet, then looked around frantically again, realising his nakedness. 'Cushions!' he yelled. 'Why the fuck haven't you got any cushions?!'

'I don't...that's important right now?' Trick could only just get the words out. 'We thought you were dead!'

'You thought I was what? What happened?'

'You're asking *me* what happened? Why didn't you warn me you're nearly impossible to wake up?'

'Because I'm not! Am I?'

The room went silent. Everyone looked at each other, then all stares settled on the naked otter.

'Could I have a blanket, please?' Sandy said.

Lottie, who had somehow come back in during the whole scene, burst out laughing. Tia looked stupefied, then realised she still had the live phone in her hand. 'I'm sorry, it's okay, we woke him up. Call it off. Well, we just tickled his fee... no, really, this wasn't a prank call. I'm so sorry, my daughter's just...I'm sorry we wasted your time.'

'Who *are* these people, Trick?' Sandy said, seemingly no longer caring that his blanket request wasn't being fulfilled.

'Oh, for God's sake,' Trick said, trying to hide his relief shakes but knowing he could only fail. 'I'll go get your fucking blanket.'

'Or he could just put his clothes on,' Kia said, holding them up.

'Oh yeah,' Sandy said. 'Thanks.' He pulled them on, taking his time, and sat down on the sofa.

'Are you *sure* you're alright?' Tia said, keeping the same distance, as if Sandy might put her in a coma just from being in close proximity.

'Yeah, I feel fine. Little surprised to wake up to a yowling snep and a room full of shocked people, but...yeah, I'm good. What exactly happened? I was really that hard to wake up?'

'Yes, you were,' Tia said. 'Until my daughter here...'

It had obviously dawned on Tia, just like it was dawning on Trick too.

'How exactly *did* you know tickling his feet would work?' Tia said. 'Why didn't you say that at the start?'

Lottie shrugged. 'I dunno, maybe because everybody was freaking the fuck out?'

'Young lady, you watch your mouth.'

Lottie rolled her eyes, walked past her mother like she wasn't there, and sat on the couch next to Sandy. 'Your name's Sandy, right?'

'Yeah. Sandy Rickwood.'

'Well, Sandy Rickwood, it looks like you've got Underwater Sleeping Syndrome. USS. Some people call it Otter Apnoea, even though it's nothing to do with sleep apnoea and any species can get that.'

'USS?'

'Yep. It's when you go down below your usual twenty breaths in deep sleep. You don't quite stop altogether, but your body becomes so near-dormant it's like you're hibernating, even though you guys aren't supposed to hibernate. Faulty evolution at its best.'

'I've got this thing? How did I never know? You a medical student?'

'I'm eighteen, dummy. I know because my friend's got it. Sometimes you don't know because it just starts happening. Any otter can get it pretty much any time. You need to go see a doctor.'

Sure, Trick thought. *That's why I'm thinking of all the conditions Mom and our family doctor between them ever warned me we could get, and that's not on the list. Why's she doing this?* He called up Wikipedia on his phone and tried a search. 'Well, whadd'ya know? Underwater Sleeping Syndrome. There it is.' *What I'm not telling you is what else is written here besides the name of it.* 'Do you *want* to go to medical school, Lottie?' he asked, with the best seraphic smile he could put on.

'Nuh-uh,' Lottie said. 'Where's the fun in that? Mom keeps saying I gotta think about college, but I don't wanna go. I wanna be an agent to the stars. That's how you get rich without having to be famous.'

'Well, why not?' Trick said. '*And* you get to hustle.'

'You wanna be my first client, Sandy Rickwood? I *did* just make sure you're not gonna die in your sleep.'

'Oh Lottie, really!' Tia said. 'As much as I respect that you perhaps just saved the day, we're still guests in this house. And we're going. I think we've welcomed Trick to the neighbourhood quite enough.'

'Oh, come on, don't go,' Trick said. 'Don't let one naked otter with an odd medical condition put you off. We haven't had our coffee yet. I'll go make a fresh pot and make enough for Sandy too. Before I run him up the hospital and we get him checked out for this *otter apnoea.*' He couldn't resist looking at Lottie. She grinned and turned towards the sliding doors, looking out at the beach, probably hoping nobody else had seen her do it. They probably hadn't, Trick thought.

By the time he'd made a second pot of coffee, Sandy had already introduced himself and started telling his story. Trick could see Kia thinking, trying to piece together what had happened last night, until Sandy straight-up told them about the food Trick had made him after he almost fainted. He left out what they'd been doing right before it.

'Lottie was right,' Sandy said. 'Maybe I should see a doctor. Except I've got no insurance. They got one of those hospital clinics where you can get treated without it but you gotta wait for a few hours?'

'I'll take you and we'll see,' Trick said. 'First we'd better get your name sorted though, and a new ID card to go with it.'

'Won't that take a while?'

'We'll work this out,' Trick said. 'Don't worry about it.'

'My husband knows a lot of medics from the sets,' Tia said. 'I'm sure he could find someone who'd come over and look at you. All you've got to do's ask if you can't get seen at the clinic.' She'd been as taken with Sandy's story as most people would have been, almost as if it was worth all the drama that morning just to hear it. 'You guys are going to be busy today though. We'd better go.' She looked at her daughter. 'Come on, agent to the stars. Let's go talk about why you're trying college first.'

Lottie turned her head slightly and winked at all of them before they shut the front door behind them.

'I like that girl,' Trick said.

'Lottie?' Sandy said. 'Yeah, so do I.'

'She'll be a great agent,' Trick said.

'How'd you figure that?'

'Because of how she read that whole situation,' Trick said. 'Soon as I said you had a pulse and were breathing, she knew exactly what was wrong with you. Which by the way's nothing. She probably woke that friend of hers up the same way, except her friend's probably not even an otter. Just a deep sleeper.' He took out his phone again and showed Sandy the USS article, which started with *...is a medical theory proposed in the 1950s which has since been discredited.*

'That whole thing was bullshit?' Sandy said.

'And she fed it to you so convincingly, after she set herself up as a hero,' Trick said. 'She can work a routine like that at eighteen? She'll be all over celebrities right across this state as soon as someone gives her an internship.'

'Why work that whole thing on us? How did she know we'd wanna be stars? Did you tell her?'

'I barely told her anything about me,' Trick said. 'But think about it. We're two young guys in a place like this with a connection to a producer already who bought us the place. How else we gonna keep living here? She read us like a book.'

'Shit,' Sandy said, sitting back, still holding Trick's phone. 'Am I that gullible?'

'You were in a situation she knew how to make something out of,' Trick said. 'When she becomes an agent, we're so hiring her. I've got a real feeling about that girl.'

'You act on it and you go to jail,' Kia said, looking bored with all of this. 'How old is she, sixteen?'

'Eighteen. She said so. So no, I don't go to jail, and it's not that kind of feeling anyway. She needs an agency who she can tell a story about how she once hustled a couple of otters under pressure and she'll be on her way.'

'Well, this is all very nice, Trick,' Kia said. 'Nice that you're actually trying to make some sort of difference to someone *else's* life for a change. Very sweet. Even if you did just meet him last night and get him to think that gross-sounding stew of yours was fit for the president. But you've got a real problem right here. Even *if* Kyle doesn't throw the episode of his life and get on a plane back home when you tell him about this, even *if* you make up with your mom for not calling, and even *if* all your dreams are really coming true already, you've got a beach house full of your friends, and they're going to want to come over and party the fuck out of this brand new love nest until they're laughing at how it's on fire.'

'Remember the part where I told you to keep this to yourself and come alone?' Trick said. 'This is the part where you tell me you did that and let me worry about the rest later.'

'Everybody's expecting you back to go surfing,' Kia said. 'Later's gonna be half an hour.'

'No, it isn't,' Trick said. 'Because you're going to tell them enough truth to stall things for a day. I went home with the bartender from Winslow's last night and we got hammered together while I was listening to the most amazing story, and once we've slept it off, he needs my help to get a couple of things sorted in his life this afternoon. Just don't tell them we're really at *my* house which my dad just bought for me.'

'Kyle was in the kitchen when Mom started talking about Dad to you on the phone. He already suspects something.'

'Yeah? Well, you know the one thing that'd make him forget it for a few hours. I already gave you the masterclass on how to get naughty with an otter. Why don't you see what you can teach him?'

'I don't even believe I'm hearing this,' Kia said.

'Come on, snepper. For me? Think you could say "Hey Kyle, you're a selfish otter"?'

For all his sleep-deprived irritability, Kia did look intrigued by the idea. 'That'd never work on him. That's just for you. Wonder why it worked so well.'

Sandy looked equally curious, Trick thought.

'What would?' Trick said. 'You never thought of a magic line for him? Make it happen. It'll take the edge off both of you.'

Kia looked contemplative now, like he was trying to snap himself out of his tiredness. 'You know, Trick, I was saving this for a quieter moment after a bit more sleep, but I've really gotta talk to you about Kyle. You. Alone.' He looked at Sandy. 'No offence; it's a family thing.' Back to Trick again. 'This is gonna hit him real hard, Trick. I think you'd better know what else has been going on lately. When you asked me why we broke up...okay, do this thing you've gotta do today. I'll cover like you want.' He looked at Sandy. 'I get it. I don't really have a heart made of stone, and I loved hearing about how you're trying to turn your life around.' Back to Trick. 'But honey, listen, I need to have that talk with

81

you. Tonight, without you ducking out of it. Before you tell Kyle about this place. That's if your mom hasn't already called your dad and major level shit's kicked off back at the house already because everyone heard their row over this.'

'Relax. When Mom gets that angry, she goes all passive aggressive for hours while she thinks about how to *really* kick ass. You've seen it before. She won't call until tonight if she calls him at all. Know what? Tell her if you want. Just try and keep it quiet. Sleep in while everyone else goes surfing and catch her before they get back.'

'No. *You're* telling her.'

'Jeez, go sleep on my new bed for a couple of hours then,' Trick said. 'You're a bitch when you're like this.'

'Which bed did you claim last night?'

'The top room.'

'Good. It's gonna stink of snep when you sleep in it tonight.' Despite being tired, Kia still had quite a swagger in his step as he made his way up the stairs.

'Nice friend,' Sandy said. 'Real charmer.'

'Sleep-deprived cats can be unholy to be around,' Trick said.

'The way he yowled though,' Sandy said, unable to help himself from smiling. 'And the way his butt hit the floor, *bam*, like that. I thought that only ever happened in cartoons.'

'Last night I told him he could fuck me when I came back from the bar still single.'

'Aw, is a little leopard all disappointed?'

'He *is* going to cover for me,' Trick said. 'So how about we eat some donuts for breakfast and go get you your name?'

Chapter Five

'I'll never forget this,' Sandy said, his hand over the folded paper on the table that told him he was now legally entitled to his chosen identity. He'd folded it so only the blank side showed, his hand on it like a child might not want to let go of an instantly treasured Christmas present.

Or, Trick thought, *his new favourite secret from everyone. Who was he, once? He'll probably tell, eventually. The more he shares about his past, the more he'll realise people could find out with a bit of Google-fu. Or he'll share nothing at all. What does it matter? I like this guy already.* 'You want another cup of coffee?'

'I'm all good. Thanks.' He'd barely touched his first one, but it wasn't nerves or depression this time. It was endless possibility running through his head, as though touching the deed poll paper was running it through him in a smooth current. 'Do you think I should do it?'

'Do what?'

'The interview.'

'It depends,' Trick said. 'Do you *want* to do it? Or were you just desperate for money? It's not the only way to build your confidence up. There might be better ways for you.'

'That's a no, right?' Sandy shook his head and laughed. 'What was I thinking? What if I'd really gone in there and done something like I tried with you last night? That whole thing about needing to save up for my name, if I'd told them that's why I was doing it, I'd've basically told someone I'd go all the way on camera just for fifteen bucks, and I was too stupid to know it.'

'Alright, let's make the first rule of you living with me. You're banned from calling yourself stupid again. I never want to hear you do that from now on. Got it?'

'It's just a phrase, Trick. I'm not having a pity party right here. It's just that every time I think I know how the world works, I find I don't. I feel like everybody else does except me.'

'What makes you think I don't get that all the time too?'

'Oh, I don't know, Trick. Maybe all I have to do is look at you? You answer that. You know what you're doing. Big plans. That's what you said.'

Trick sat forward. 'You want to hear a secret of mine? Something I never told anyone else?'

'Right here?' Sandy said, looking around him as if expecting everyone else to listen.

'That play I told you about last night, that I wrote with my drama teacher. You remember?'

'*Beware the Trickster in the Shadows?* Yeah. What's the secret behind it?'

'My drama teacher was an otter in his late thirties. We had this one last after-school session where we ran through the finished play.' Trick lifted his chin up a little and grinned. 'I hit on him.'

Sandy looked a little taken aback, then seemed unable to resist Trick's smile. 'You really were the trickster in the shadows.' He dropped his voice. 'Did it happen?'

'No. I stopped it. I swear, he was just about to reach out a hand and touch my face. Or touch something, I don't know. I just saw it in his eyes. All I'd done to bring it out was just stand there after I'd said the last line and stare. Then he knew I'd come out of character and just stayed in the moment. I did this kind of pose. Bit like the one you did last night, and he just kept looking. I started getting a semi. He saw. Then I just snapped out of it and said I was sorry.'

'Why?'

'I don't know. I've been thinking about it ever since. The guy was married with kids. I guess I like to think I thought about lives I might ruin, and I just knew I'd nearly done something incredibly hot but totally awful. When I feel down, that's how I pick myself up. Knowing I did the right thing when a lot of people would have just gone with it. Then the other night.' He beckoned Sandy in closer so he could whisper. 'Kia called me a selfish otter while he was fucking me. It made me come.'

Sandy sniggered, sitting back in his chair, looking around like an owl again and hunching up and stroking his own arms, even though nobody could have heard. 'Trick Dixon. You're a *naughty* otter.'

Under the table, Trick slipped his flip-flops off and stroked a bare foot down Sandy's leg. Sandy's tail twitched. He stopped. They looked at each other.

'Was he alright about it? Your teacher.'

'We both promised each other we'd never tell. For both our sakes. Guess I just broke it. But you get why, don't you?'

'Totally.'

'I felt totally weird about it for weeks. Probably longer, except by then I'd gotten used to it. After it happened, we both tidied up the room for ten minutes, trying to pretend it wasn't awkward. Then he told me his family didn't know, they *couldn't* know. That he didn't get to make that choice anymore because he already made it a long time ago. I just felt sorry for him. I tried to hide it, but I think he knew.'

'You think he ever thinks about you?'

'Maybe. I don't know. At least I didn't ruin his life though. Although maybe in a way I kinda did, I just don't really know how. But I can't feel bad about it. Not really. Someone like that, something's going to tear them apart sooner or later. You deny who you really are and what you really want long enough, it's an accident waiting to happen. That's when I knew it. I told my family I was gay a couple of weeks after it happened. I got all my brothers and my sister together and Mom and just came out with it.'

'They were all okay with it?'

'Yeah. Willow gave me a hug. She was still William back then, but she wore girl's clothes, and she smelt like a girl. That's when I first noticed the scent thing too. Then Kyle had to be Kyle, he came right out and told

87

everyone he was the same, and that Kia was actually his boyfriend. I already knew. It was like this great big coming-out party. Mom was so cool about it; she made us this massive dinner, and we all got stuffed. Then Kia came round and held hands with Kyle in front of all the family and we watched TV. Perfect, right? Guess again. Dad showed up. One of his unexpected trips to town just to make sure his kid support money was being spent right. He comes "home" to two college dropouts, one guy in girl's clothes who's taking girl hormones, and two fags. And one of them's holding hands with a snep. Dad *hates* cats.'

'"You did it with a *snep*? What the everloving fuck?" Right?'

Trick smiled. A few heads had turned at Sandy's Ty impression. It was actually pretty good. 'Uh-huh. Kia might talk tough, but in front of my dad? He was scared. Kyle kept holding his hand and started crying, and he got this great big lecture, and I was a coward. I didn't stop him. Kyle was the brave one. Dad got halfway through telling Kia why he belonged down a sewer before Kyle stopped him. *Boom*, you sack of shit.'

'Kyle hit your dad?'

'Floored him, but Dad's Dad. He got back up and they started having a fight, and Ryan joined in. Mom called the cops. By the time they came and dragged his stinking drunk ass out of the house, half the place was wrecked. Mom said if he ever came back, she'd kill him. She totally meant it. If he pressed charges for Kyle fracturing his skull with the bottle that knocked him out, she'd fracture it worse next time. That's my mom. She's liberal about anything you like, but you cross her?

The only reason she's not gonna spank me this evening's because she knows I'd like it.'

'Seriously?'

'My bedroom's next to hers at home, and the walls are thin.'

Sandy shook his head. 'I can't wait to meet your family. So...your dad *did* come back, right? He was there last night, and he gave you a house.'

'You know why I think he did it? Why he likes me that little bit more? Because I'm the one who gave him a chance. Mom banned us all from calling him or taking his calls. I disobeyed. I went to a public box and called his office, and we talked. He said he was going to try going to meetings. That he'd try and make things right. He sent me money to fly out here and see him. I did it. Took me a whole day of talking before Mom would let me, and she had to go too. We sat down, we talked. Fancy restaurant near Hollywood, so it couldn't end in a scene. Not that it would have surprised anyone. I was the peacemaker. The one who helped him feel like he wasn't totally irredeemable. I'm probably the only reason he got sober. The house is his way of saying thanks. It's also a mind game.'

'Bottom line is that I shouldn't go thinking your world makes sense?' Sandy said.

'Oh, it makes enough,' Trick said. 'But you know why I won the game already?'

'Why?'

Trick beckoned him closer again. 'Kyle didn't knock him out that night, with the bottle. Kia did. Then he nearly had a meltdown thinking he'd just killed him. Kyle calmed him down by promising to say it was him,

89

and that Dad wasn't going to die. Thank God, he actually did come round.'

'And he didn't get a haemorrhage.' Sandy stared into his cup for a moment. 'Shit, enough of that already. I'm sick of being so sensitive about it.' He sat upright and ruffled his fur. 'So that's your real weapon. The truth. That your dad hates cats and he got KO'd by one.'

'Kyle tells the story so well now, I swear he actually believes it was him sometimes. Or wishes it was. Can't say I blame him.'

'What does Kia say?'

'Kia never talks about it.'

Sandy stirred his cold coffee. 'Trick, be honest. Do you think I should see a counsellor?'

'If you feel like you need to, yeah.'

'I wish I had a story to trade,' Sandy said. 'I wish I could talk about it. My parents were…actually, they were kind of boring. I don't know what I expected exactly, but then it all just happened. Then I had nowhere to go. So I just decided to get here or die trying. I nearly did die a couple of times. Dehydration. Walking along a highway hoping for another ride before my water ran out. I ran out four times. Every time I figured someone would find my body and I'd get taken home to be buried, and my parents would finally know what they'd done. Then someone always rescued me. I'd say thanks and get back on the road. One time I woke up in a hospital and had to get running before they could call Mom and Dad or stick me with another bill. Then one day I was just here, in Cali. I won. Like it was really a race with myself. I still don't feel like I'm who I want to be. But I want to live with you. Without having to dump all this shit on you constantly. Without waking up still feeling like I belong back in Maine on the streets with nowhere to go.'

'We'll find you someone you can talk to,' Trick said. 'Someone good. Right after we both get jobs and get a foothold here. Tell me one thing though. Who *is* the person you want to be?'

'I don't even know if I know that, half the time.'

'Come on. Focus. Think about when you left that hospital in Maine and just started walking. You really just pick this place because it's the bottom corner of the country, or was there something you dreamed about?'

'I was always kind of good at acting too. Plays. I liked being someone else. Always thought I'd go to Broadway or something. But probably just end up a PA to somebody bigger and better than me.'

'So why here and not Broadway?'

'Broadway didn't seem far enough away. I wanted to have a story to tell when I got here. Now it's like I don't wanna tell anything, and the last thing I ever want to go near is a stage. Apart from a couple of weeks, after I saw that ad recruiting otters for adult stuff and thought it was some kind of magic bullet. Was that *really* a no earlier? Or am I really as good-looking as you kept saying last night?'

'I meant what I said last night. I don't lie about the stuff that matters.'

'Would *you* watch a TV show with me in it?'

As good a time as any, Trick thought. 'Maybe,' he said. 'But I'd rather have you to myself first.'

* * *

91

Trick thought Sandy wanted to kiss him all afternoon. By the time they got home and Trick suggested a glass of wine and some fancy-looking meat cuts from the fridge, he was certain of one thing: Sandy wasn't into public displays of affection. This was the otter who said he didn't mind the thought of someone jerking off to him on film, but he wouldn't kiss a guy in public. Not even one who'd bought him the one thing he wanted more than anything else in the world.

On their balcony though, without having touched his wine, Sandy got closer to Trick and slowly put his hands on his hips, suggestively stroking the sides of his butt a little. 'Were you serious about letting me fuck you once I was Sandy?' he said. 'Coz I'm ready.'

Trick answered by wrapping his tail around the back of Sandy's legs, pulling him closer, and waiting for him to move in with his mouth. He did. Trick had expected it to be tentative, gentle. Sandy's kiss was firm and embracing, his tongue gliding over Trick's, inviting him to do the same, the breath from both their nostrils clouding together as they closed their eyes. They kept them closed as they withdrew for breath again and again, still touching tongues each time. Sandy stroked the back of Trick's head, his own tail wrapped around the other otter now, tying them together.

I'd love to watch him do this as much as have him do it to me, Trick thought, his cock swelling up at the thought of Sandy's naked body dancing in curved shapes with another one of their kind, the pair slicked up with natural oils and fresh, cool water. Sandy gave a satisfied sigh as Trick rubbed his bulge against his crotch.

Sandy opened his eyes and moved back from Trick a little, his hands now grabbing a firm hold on Trick's rear. 'Are we gonna fuck then?'

'Oh hell yes. How about some rehearsal for your audition? You want to play a director and tell me to show you what I've got?'

'You don't gotta pass an audition for anyone,' Sandy said, running his hands up Trick's back and neck to his head, where he ruffled his fingers as deep in the fur under Trick's chin as he could. 'You got the job. I want my first time with you. Right here.'

'Couch might be more comfortable. Or is hard on the floor what you always dreamed about?'

Sandy's eyes went a little wide, as if either possibility seemed too good to be true. 'Couch. I want music. You ever fuck to music?'

Don't admit you've never tried it, Trick thought, his next idea already picking his excitement up. 'Confident Otter knows what he wants. Can I see if I can guess?'

'Guess what?'

Trick guided him back inside, their tails still rubbing together and Sandy's hand tickling the side of his chest. 'Music,' Trick said. The stereo came on. 'Play 'Summer at Dreampoint' by The Aqua Velvets.'

'Ooooohohoho!' Sandy sighed with his head back. 'How did you kn...oh. Yeah. Right. Last night.'

'When did you first hear this?' Trick said as it started up. 'My party?'

'I've loved that tune ever since I was a kid,' Sandy said. '*That's* why I came here. I imagined surf music when I started walking. Like I needed to stay alive so I could hear one of those songs again.'

'Is Confident Otter ready to watch me take my pants off? I can dance to this music for you. Want me to?'

Sandy kept hold of him, his hands twitching, the adrenaline clearly flooding him, but his face was unmovably alight with libido. 'Call me Fuckable Tail.' He slid the tip of his real tail under Trick's, lightly tracing down the back of the other otter's pants and giving a poke where his hole lined up.

'You got it. Is Fuckable Tail still at my service?'

'Ooooh yeah.'

'So, you wanna *get* fucked or do you want to fuck me?'

Again, the impossible choice look. 'How would I know, Trick?'

'Get naked with me and I'll tell you,' Trick said. 'Nice and relaxed, just like your theme song. Just watch.' He slid everything off, the way he'd taught himself to in front of his mirror so many times. Get the angles right and you could make surf shorts and a t-shirt and your tight pants slip off as easily as the silk gown he'd worn last night. Sandy was clearly imagining it. Trick slid Sandy's clothes off him until they were back to where they'd left off the previous night.

'Know what you want now?'

Sandy smiled and shook his head, hunching up a little, trying to relax himself with deep breaths.

'What does your heart tell you?' Trick put one hand on his shoulder and slid the other down his chest until he found his naked companion's heartbeat, then pressed his palm over it. 'What does that tell you?

Despite how your fight-or-flight response kicked in five minutes ago and now you're not going to do either? You're gonna fuck. Nice and easy for your first go, have a cuddle with you on my lap? Mmmm. I like that idea. Do you?'

Sandy wasn't talking. He was entranced by the chorus of his song choice, his hand now on Trick's arm, keeping his palm pressed on his chest and looking at his eyes. 'You're so calm,' he said, his feet twitching. 'How are you so calm?'

'I'm thinking of us dancing,' Trick said. 'Without us moving.' He moved his hand and took one of Sandy's, then the other, then moved in close so they were hugging and stepping in time with the music, barely moving from the same spot. 'Don't want to run out of song, do you?'

Sandy drew his hands down Trick's naked back. 'I love this part of you best. The shape of you. It's all in your spine, your curve, those swimmer's muscles you've got. I can't be you, but I can *have* you. Tell me I can have you. Your back, your butt, your face, that grin you do...tell me I can have that.'

'You c−'

'Call yourself *my* fuckable tail.'

Oh hell, Trick thought, looking at Sandy's face. Wherever that had come from, Sandy's eyes had a wild promise like nothing Trick had ever seen before. 'I'm *your* fuckable tail, you naughty little ott-butt. What have you got? What are you going to do?' He spoke the two questions in the voice of a curious groupie, as feminine as he could make it, like the voice in a song he once heard about being a slut for a road crew.

'Will you say something for me?'

Trick was right back to asking his father the same thing. Hearing that voice come out of Sandy made the skin up his back tingle. 'Say what?'

'Will you say "Show me what you've got, boy"?'

Trick said it, still in the crew slut voice, then his father's, but more like a porn producer. Sandy liked the last one best.

'Lie down on that couch,' Sandy said. 'With your favourite part facing me.'

Trick growled, as if imitating Kia. 'Are you going to be naughty?'

'Don't make me run out of song.'

Trick lay down slowly, sprawling himself out, his chin on two cushions, his back a little arched and his neck turned so that he could see Sandy out of one eye. 'You gonna ride me bareback, or do you wanna suit up?'

'Am I gonna wh...oh.' Sandy knelt down next to the couch and put a hand on Trick's back. 'Can you promise me you're clean if I bareback you?' He smiled. 'I'll trust you. It's nicer that way, right?'

'Well, yeah,' Trick said. 'But...dammit, I could have promised you that until I fucked Kia. Cats. You never know what alley they've been down.'

Sandy looked like he'd taken it as a joke, or foreplay, or Trick's fun way of saying he'd rather be protected. He knelt so Trick could see his hard cock in full view and rubbed his sheath. 'You got a suit for me then?'

'In my wallet, in the pocket over there. Can I trust you not to dig for gold in there?' Trick rolled over, liking how he'd never thought of his next line before. 'Because if I can, you get to put something in an otter's *real* pocket.'

Sandy moved so fast, Trick was certain he wouldn't get the rubber on in time, but his hands didn't fumble. For an otter who'd once been stuck in a pipe, Sandy moved like one who could shoot from one end to the other in record time. He had his protection on and was pinning Trick into the couch cushions with both hands on his back, his boner sliding in and barely giving Trick any time to relax. Trick put his head back and gasped as Sandy penetrated him.

'Urgh...Sandy...hold on...safety!' Trick said.

'What?'

'We need a safety word. Coconuts?' It was all he could think of, not sure why he felt like he wasn't supposed to use Kia's choice for someone else, but it felt naughty when the music ended, the room became silent apart from Sandy's fast breathing, and Trick had a moment to enjoy the other otter's hardness between his cheeks.

'Coconuts. You got it.' His weight on Trick's back relaxed a little, and he began to slide out. 'Did I do something wrong already?'

No! Don't ruin this! 'Get back down there and fuck me, Sandy-paws. You're getting laid, baby! You're in the otter's *real* pocket. It's *deep*, Fuckable Tail. Feel it! Get deep in there.'

Sandy's scent glands had to be gushing. Trick could smell it, as though he'd snorted half a bottle of strong perfume. His friend thrust in and out of him with a feral energy, yipping and purring at the same time. 'You're my fuckable tail, Trick! Say it!'

97

'I'm your fuckable taiiiii*aaaaaaaaaaal...urgggh,* Sandy Rickwood, you *lied* to me, bitch! This isn't the way a virgin gets in the otter's pocket, you bitch otter!'

'Shut your mouth, boy!' Sandy's version of Trick's producer voice was scarily good. 'If you're not saying coconuts then I don't wanna hear it.'

'Well too bad, because I'm a naughty boy, and you're gonna punish me for talking back to you.'

Sandy stopped for a moment. 'Yeah? Alright. Music! Play "Rescue at the Mavericks".'

'What?!' Trick yelped, no longer in character. His posing song? Right now? 'No! Sandy, not that one...woah!' The world spun around him, and only when he was on the rug did he feel the impact of hitting it and Sandy's weight on him again.

'I'm going to ride you like a tidal wave, Trick Dixon!'

'Woah, Sandy...' *Hold it? Coconuts?* A moment later, he wanted neither, the deep fur of the rug sliding along his fur as Sandy worked his whole body along it every time he thrust himself inside, holding Trick by the wrists just like Trick had held Kia on the bed. Sandy came at the end of Trick's favourite part. Trick heard his friend above the music and held on, wanting to come with him but determined to ride this out. Tidal wave? He'd show Sandy the newly brave fuckable tail what a tidal wave was. Oh, just wait...

Sandy collapsed on top of him, hugging him as best he could and then rolling off, floppy and still panting. Trick pulled himself up and looked at his friend, spread-eagled on the rug with a huge grin on his face and stinking of his own musk.

Don't ask him how it was, Trick thought, remembering how his own first time had been partly spoiled by that stupid question. Just do something else nice. Trick took hold of Sandy's feet and rested them in his lap, looking at his pads.

'Gonna tickle them?' Sandy said, his voice little more than a breathy whisper.

'Would you like that?'

'Nah,' Sandy sighed. 'But you could squeeze them for me. Put your thumbs in the soles and work the muscle a little bit.'

Trick did it. The little bones in Sandy's toes all made a sound halfway between a click and a crack. Sandy kept sighing and stretching his leg muscles by arching his back and squeezing his butt tight with it, like he was trying to relieve intense fatigue. Trick felt Sandy's feet muscles tense up then relax, little clicks of release travelling through Trick's fingers and thumbs. '*Damn*, Sandy. How far have these feet walked?'

'You know the story. God, I needed this. You know how to rub an otter's feet.' Trick kept it going until he was certain Sandy was asleep, but then his friend raised his head a little. 'You actually take a foot massage course or something? Because *wow*. You should.'

'Willow's a physiotherapist. She did this to me a couple of times.'

'It get you off? Even though it was your sister?'

'I've never had a foot fetish,' Trick said. 'I wish I did.'

'I've got one,' Sandy said. 'Big time. Can I suck on your feet sometime right after you've cleaned them?'

'That's all it would take to drive you wild? Why didn't you tell me that while we were getting you worked up?'

'I dunno. Guess I was kinda embarrassed about telling someone. Then he let me put my dick in his "pocket" and I guess it doesn't anymore. That was hot, the whole otter's pocket thing. You wanna try mine?' Sandy pulled his feet away, sat himself up and looked at Trick. 'Damn, I didn't make you come? That wasn't hot for you?'

'Come on, don't you go getting ideas that it didn't do it for me. I liked being your surfboard. I was hard. You're a better fuck than you thought. I mean that. But listen.' Trick scooched over so he could whisper seductively in Sandy's ear. 'I've got lots of experience, and I'm *very* good at saving something special up. For some*one* special. Who was just a world-class surfer on my wave.'

Sandy took a satisfied deep breath and bristled up with anticipation. 'What have you got, Trickster?'

Trick stroked the back of Sandy's neck gently and rubbed his muzzle with the other hand before running it down his chest to his belly button, where he rubbed and poked, thinking of how he'd explained his supposedly magic blowjob technique to Kia. 'How long can you hold your breath underwater, Sandy?'

Chapter Six

They lay wrapped up in each other, under the covers of Trick's bed in the penthouse room. To get him going again, Trick had told Sandy what Kia had asked for, and Sandy had gone wild for the idea of letting Trick shower him, as if it were a secret wish he'd never known he had. Trick talked him through how to do the 'underwater' blowjob, encouraging him all the way, until he was sweating and panting from the effort of holding, and Sandy obligingly shifted back a distance, still on his knees, cupped his hands as a target, and watched Trick come. It was hotter than Trick had expected; Sandy's newly broken innocence gave him a look that Trick knew he might only have that one moment to appreciate, because after this, the amazement at watching this show would become more and more routine. Right then though, Sandy was transfixed.

Trick hit the target, squirting as far as Sandy's palms and watching the other otter catch, his eyes wide with amazement that Trick's jizz shot had actually reached, most likely wondering how far his own climax might have gone if he hadn't been sheathed up with the rubber. Sandy raised his hands close to his nose and took a sniff. Trick laughed.

'Your first go and you're such a little dirt-bag already.'

'Impressed?' Sandy said. 'How far do you want me to go?' He poked his tongue out.

'Time out, Sandy-paws. Tasting's never been my thing.'

Sandy looked a little sheepish, his hands still cupped together, as if asking himself what else he could do that Trick might like. 'Shall I just go wash off?'

'Yeah, do that. I'd like it better if you rubbed my fur with your hands clean.'

'Rub your fur? Uh...sure...so we're not done yet?'

'We can always go again later. But there's something I like. Go clean up and I'll show you.'

When he came back from the bathroom, Sandy seemed to understand. He started rubbing Trick's chest and stomach without needing instruction, his fingers as deep under the fur as he could get them. He did the same on Trick's arms, his back, his shoulders, then just seemed to aimlessly explore, sniffing and nosing at Trick's body in as many places as took his curiosity. Trick purred, telling him, 'That's it, that's good,' all the time, taking deep and relaxed breaths, showing Sandy his relaxed appreciation.

'That kind of a ritual you like?' Sandy said.

'I just like having someone appreciate my body,' Trick said. 'It's beautiful, right? But it's no good just preening myself in a mirror. I like knowing someone else thinks it. I like that you don't fake it. You really *are* hot for me. It's good just to do that when neither of us can get hard, to know it still feels good when it's nothing to do with sex.'

'It's nice just to cuddle,' Sandy said, wrapping himself around Trick. 'With the most awesome guy I've ever met. I didn't ruin your favourite song, did I?'

'Course not. It's got a whole new meaning now.'

'Can I ask you something?'

Trick wriggled a little. 'Not like I can go anywhere, is it?'

'What if the whole world appreciated your body? You're not afraid it would make it less special because everyone saw it all the time? Not just a special person?'

'I've never really thought of it like that. Is that *your* fear?'

'Nobody would ever want me as much as you. I'm not a bad pin-up, sure, not now I look like this, but you? You could win any contest going. You said it yourself: everyone wants this otter. But I want him more than all of them. I want everything that comes with him.'

Trick rolled over, nose to nose with Sandy. 'Are you asking if I'll be in a relationship with you?'

'Yeah. Guess I am. Not spoiling our night, am I? I really do feel like you're worth it. Will you think about it? Maybe, actually, I'm worth you.'

Damn, Trick thought. *From calling himself stupid to this, in one day? I did well finding this guy.* 'I've gotta tell you, Sandy, I'm not sure I'm the faithful type. I see someone I like, someone I want, I want them to want me back. Then I want everything. Kia got the measure of me exactly. That's why it was hot. But sure. We can be each other's special person. Just so long as we're a little less caught up in rules than most couples.

103

We've both got to do what we've got to do. That might mean other people. Especially if you do that audition and it goes somewhere,'

'I'm not going to do it, Trick. I was forgetting it already. But you and your movie star thing? I could deal with you having other people if you needed to. Actually...can I tell you something else? I'd...kinda like to watch that. My guy with someone else. I think I'm a cuck. An actual one. Not just the SJW meaning of it. I never wanted to do it with my last boyfriend; I wanted to watch him *get* done. He didn't like that at all. Do you?'

'Oh, totally.'

The doorbell rang.

'Oh shit,' Trick said, rolling over. 'Kia. I gotta get this. Take a nap or have a couple of drinks or something. I got a feeling this might take a while. I'll try not to let him take me out anywhere.'

Sandy tried to copy Trick's side-pose, a horny grin on his face, working his dick a little. 'Don't be too long or I'll have to sort this out for myself. Hey, maybe Kia could watch us. He likes otters, right? How about a rehearsal?'

'I'll see what I can do,' Trick said as the doorbell rang again. 'Impatient snep. I'll be right back.'

* * *

'Alright, alright, jeez, you didn't think I might be in the middle of something?'

'Oh, I dunno, Trick. After last night, I was beginning to think you didn't care about keeping appointments with friends.' Kia was smiling, but Trick knew it was to cover how much he meant his disappointment. He'd gelled his fur and used some temporary highlights on his face. The leather coat and Ralph Lauren shirt said the rest. He wanted a make-up dinner out somewhere, just as Trick had thought.

'You hungry?' Trick said. 'I've got plenty more nice stuff in that fridge.'

'I'm not going to be hungry until we've talked,' Kia said. 'Is Sandy here?'

'Upstairs. I thought you wanted this talk to be just us.'

'I do. Take a walk down the beach with me. Please?'

Trick actually was hungry, but he knew this look on Kia, and he knew it wouldn't wait.

Kia wore this worried, tired yet resolute look so well. He was an adopted snep who lived with a family of tigers – two stepsisters who didn't like him and two parents who did but could never hide how part of them still thought it had been a mistake to add him to the household. His real parents had never been traced. It wasn't until he was a teenager that he got the story out of his stepfather one night.

A garbage man had almost killed Kia Renfield and then saved his life instead in the same thirty seconds, after what should have been a regular pickup. Kia had been inside a box in a dumpster. The garbage truck driver had fished the box out just moments after he'd stopped the crusher in time. Written on the side had been: 'Please give this cub a good home, I'm sorry I couldn't.'

What had surprised Kia more? That his father had once driven a garbage truck to avoid unemployment, or that he'd admitted that the restaurant owner found him sitting on the curb, holding a snep cub, and crying for some reason he couldn't place?

Trick knew why Kia wore this look so well: his first lucky break in life had really been his last. Nothing else was ever easy for him, right down to how that garbage truck driver had named him Kia instead of Keir because he always thought the name was spelled just like the car. When Kia the car-snep needed to have a soul-searching conversation, he needed it. For someone who knew how to make other people and himself look beautiful, Kia Renfield viewed the world as ugly, nasty, and only just worth living in. Trick was leading him out onto the beach with a twinge of guilt for last night finally kicking in, even though it had all been worth it.

'I should have called you,' he said. 'No more joking around. I'm sorry. But listen, I want to make things up, so before we have this talk about my brother, I'm going to invite him to live here. I want you to live with me too. Even if you and Kyle are over as a relationship. Could you still get along if you both lived with me?'

Kia stopped walking. He'd probably guessed Trick might do this, but hearing the offer rendered any expectation moot. This was a ticket out of his tiger home, the one he'd often wished he could leave by any means he could think of, and now he looked like he was actually torn about it.

'You want *me* to live here. In Cali. In *Malibu*. With you.'

'That's what I said.'

Kia took a deep breath, head slowly tilting back to the sky, then sighed. 'You're a good friend, Trick. Even if you do keep me up all night. But I don't know if I can. It's not you. It's not that I want to go home either; I *really* fucking don't. When I came here, I wanted this vacation to last forever. It's...there's something I don't think you realise. Something awkward.'

'About you?'

'Well, yeah, kind of.' Kia shuffled his feet about and rubbed his left arm with his right hand.

'It's just you, me, and the California ocean, snepper. I can't imagine you could have done anything so terrible that I wouldn't understand. The ocean? It doesn't judge. That's why I like it. Come on. What's on your mind that means you can't eat?'

'Kyle told me something. If I tell you, I'm breaking a promise. But I think you need to know.'

Trick always loved these scenes in a play, always loved writing them the most, and now he was glad he'd been so in tune with those vibes; it meant he could walk up to Kia as if about to put a hand on his shoulder, but the seriousness meant it was better to avoid it, because such a gesture would lessen it.

'Then go on,' he said. 'What we talk about here tonight, we *never* talk about. Whatever happens.'

Kia nodded. 'Kyle and I broke up because I handled something badly. Something I've had a lot of time to think about. But I said some stuff he's only pretended to forgive me for. Heat of the moment things. I really did regret it later.' Kia looked at the ground. 'He told me he loves me, but the truth is, he desires someone else more.'

I should have known, Trick thought. The interspecies thing always had seemed a little out of place when his brother started doing it. Whatever Kyle's sexuality was, Trick had always been sure he preferred otters. 'Did he tell you who it was?'

'No. But that's the thing. I guessed. I wasn't even serious. Then I saw his face, and once I knew it was for real...shit, I thought he was going to do something stupid. Just to shut me up.'

Now Trick felt uncertain. 'You thought Kyle was going to attack you? *Kill* you? No way. Whatever it felt like at the time, I know he couldn't do that.'

'He could have to protect this.'

'Why?'

Kia looked up now, looking Trick straight in they eyes. 'Because my guess was you.'

Trick didn't realise he'd gone deaf even to the sound of the waves on the sand until they came back to him, and for a moment they were the loudest thing he'd ever heard, along with Kia's silence.

'Okay,' Trick said. 'Whatever happened between you two, whatever you said, whatever *he* said, you're sure there's no way you could have misunderstood this?'

'It was three months ago, Trick,' Kia said, looking more resolute now than he ever had before. 'I've never even questioned it. I joked that it was you, and he couldn't hide it. That's why he admitted it. He called you the hottest piece of tail alive. Then he told me it was tearing him apart. All the time he had to be around you and he just couldn't do anything, couldn't tell you. He was terrified what you might think.'

Trick looked out to sea, already in his brother's shoes, not knowing how he'd never seen it, not wanting to take it as a blow to his ego when there were more important things to talk about. But shit, *was* it a blow to his ego? Even his own brother wanted him? What was that story about the guy who got turned into a flower next to some water by a god, so he could look at his beautiful self all day?

'What *do* you think?' Kia said. 'Because whatever it is, you made me a promise. We never talk about this.'

'I need a moment with this,' Trick said. 'But that's not because I'm shocked. I should have seen it all along. Right from when he shared my coming out with me on a whim. You remember that?'

'I'm hardly likely to forget, am I?' Kia said, his hand already clenching as though it were holding the bottle that had cracked on Tyler Goldman's head all over again.

'Okay,' Trick said, glad Kia might have a bit more adrenaline pumping through him thanks to that memory. 'Did you tell me this because you want me to know, or because you want me to do something?'

'Because I wanted you to know.'

'So if I *did* do something, would you be okay with that?'

'Do what?' Kia's eyes slowly widened. 'Trick, are you seriously thinking of...'

'Thinking of what?' Trick managed not to smile at Kia's shock. 'When you fucked me, Kia, what was it? You wanting me? Or you getting a foot in the door to me and Kyle in the same room with you, and maybe you were helping him along? Remember my joke, "death by

109

otter double team"? Was that another dumb guess that was actually on the money? You were trying to help, weren't you? Because maybe it was enough for Kyle just to watch me fuck someone else. Or maybe things would happen and then we'd all make a pact of silence, and hopefully once would be en–'

'Shut up, Trick.' Kia looked away angrily, then just looked tired and most likely hungry along with it. 'Yeah. Fine. I wanted to get seriously fucked as well. The pair of you? I just wanted you to fuck me to death. You actually said it.'

Trick suppressed a sigh. 'So you're having the thoughts again. The meds aren't working?'

'I'm fine,' Kia said. 'They're working. You know what I meant. I was just chasing a high, to keep me off all the others. You two would have done that.'

'Then maybe your plan was a good one. Stay in this honest moment with me. If you watched me fuck my own brother, could you live with it? Do you really think it would help him or just make everything worse?'

'I don't know, Trick. What do you think I've been asking myself for the last three fucking months?'

'What if I found a way of just talking to him about this? Wait a little while, so there can't be any suspicion you told me, then try and get him to open up to me? See what happens. Maybe he and I just talk it out and we come to a mutual agreement, and it helps him get his feelings straight.'

'Or maybe you don't. Maybe it takes more.' Kia straightened himself up. 'I wouldn't hold it against you. Who would it hurt, if you both wanted to? It's lust, right? He's not in love with you. Not looking for anything with real meaning. I can live with being second best. *Everyone's* second best. You always think you're a special person to someone, because of the people you don't know they really desire more than you. But love? At least you always know when you've got that.' Kia took his vape pen out and took several long and relieving drags on it. 'I'm sorry I had to tell you. But I was right to, wasn't I?'

'I'm glad you did,' Trick said.

Kia looked back at the house. 'Say this goes all the way. Say I'm involved too. What about your new friend?'

Trick looked back towards his new house too. 'There's a good thing going on there. But this isn't his business. What I do to help friends and family out's its own thing. He already knows I fucked you anyway. You wanna know what the last idea he had was?' Trick didn't wait; he told Kia about the watching idea.

'Yeah,' Kia said, with a smile that Trick was relieved to see. 'After everything it took to get up the guts to tell you all that tonight, I'd like that. I'd appreciate both of you. Would you let me jerk off?'

'To your heart's content.'

By the time they reached the house, Trick knew what he had to do. 'Listen,' he said, putting his hands on Kia's shoulders. 'I meant what I offered. You and Kyle living here with me and Sandy. I think it would work. But it might not have to. I know how this is probably going to play out. Kyle hates Dad, and I just took a gift worth about five million from him. I'm keeping it. Kyle's not going to take this well. He'll try to, but he won't. If he stays calm to start with, I'll give him ten minutes before he snaps.'

Kia had obviously realised the angle, and he went tense, as if wanting to back out of Trick's hold on his shoulders but trying not to. 'You think the answer to this is making your own brother hate you? So his real feelings just go away? Then he just packs his bags and goes back to Phoenix?'

'I don't want Kyle to hate me, or to pack up and go home. I want him to *tell* me his real feelings, without him ever suspecting I already knew. That keeps you off the hook too. It's simple: we're going to have the row to end all others, and he's going to hit me with it. When he's exhausted every other insult.'

Kia looked away for a second, then looked like he was stifling his desire to sigh with relief. 'Yeah. That would probably work.'

'I know. But I need one last favour.'

Kia looked up at the sky. 'You want me to tell him about this place, right? Because you want him to feel like you didn't have enough respect to tell him yourself. So it's more likely to kick off.'

'Yeah. Will you do that?'

'The things I fucking do for you,' Kia said.

'You're doing this for *you*,' Trick said. 'If we play this nice, he'll know you told me.'

'Why don't I just *tell* him I told you?'

'Because then you'll never stand a chance of getting back on track with him. Unless you don't want to. I wouldn't exactly blame you. But I want you to live here. It would be easier if there was peace.' Trick rubbed Kia's shoulders. 'This place, right here?' He steered Kia around to look at the lights of the houses that followed the shoreline. 'This is where your career could take off. Cali.'

'My career as *what*, Trick? I haven't got a clue what I'm doing with my life.'

'The furs you'd get to style here could take you much more exciting places than most of the ones in Phoenix. They'd pay more. Look what your skills did for me already. I've got a new boyfriend upstairs.'

'You're calling him that already?'

'Why not? He's the one who said it first.' Trick tightened his hold. 'Come on. Don't move back in with those two bitches and the parents who they walked all over as well as you. So they raised you. So what? Fuck 'em. You're out in the world now. Raise yourself higher.'

'Alright, asshole otter. I'll live with you. When we're starving and calling your mom for money, I'll remind you of when you said this was all such a good idea. Trick, are you sure about this?' Kia put his hands on Trick's arms and ran them up to touch his face. 'What if you really have a fight, just like with your dad? What if Kyle ruins this?'

'My face?' Trick said. 'He couldn't. Not after what you've just told me.'

Kia came closer and kissed him on the mouth. Trick let him. It lasted a long time, the taste and scent of cat a sharp mix with the lingering smell of Sandy still in his mind. 'You want something special, snepper?'

Kia preened his ears back with one hand and smiled. 'What you got?'

'Let's get some drinks and go up and see Sandy.'

Chapter Seven

Trick waited for the doorbell or the call while cooking a spiced fish pie, Sandy's recipe. Baby vegetables on the side and a chilled chardonnay ready. He switched the oven to hot cupboard mode, almost certain he was going to be eating alone, only to see Kyle coming up the back steps. His brother let himself in without knocking and shut the door slowly and calmly.

'So this is where you've been.'

'Yeah.'

'Dad bought you this place.'

'You like it?'

'I haven't really seen it yet.' Kyle sniffed, looked at the kitchen behind Trick as if hungry, then tipped his head towards the hallway. 'Going to show me round?'

Too calm, Trick thought. He hadn't thought Kyle would manage this. Trick took off his apron and draped it over a stool, the tight top he'd chosen rippling with his surfer's muscles as he approached his brother. 'Don't do the passive-aggressive thing with me, Kyle. Kia dumped you because he was sick of all that. Seeing as I can't dump you, I can tell you to get over this shit already. Dad bought me this place and I like it.'

'Yeah,' Kyle said. 'What a happy little birthday boy he made you.'

'I don't suppose, by any chance, you let Kia get as far as saying I want you both to live here, did you?'

Kyle obviously hadn't, or Kia hadn't done it. Except his eyes didn't go wide with surprise. They flashed with everything Trick had hoped for. 'You just don't get it, do you, you dumb fuck.'

'Get what?' Trick said. 'What's there to get about me offering you something nice?'

'All Dad wants to do is own you. He didn't do this because you're his favourite. He did it because you're stupid. Too stupid to tell him to fuck his money along with himself.'

'Here we go. Sassy otter.'

'For Christ's sake, Trick, this isn't about me.' Kyle took off his jacket and dumped it on the back of the sofa. 'You *cannot* possibly be this blind to what Dad's doing. All that stuff he told you about never lending you his name, his help, he's already doing it. This is all a big disguise, a mask. You're another project to him, and it looks so perfect if he plays it from the tough love angle. You know this house is a mind game. You're playing right into it.'

Trick leaned on the bar top. 'Calling me stupid was just you being pissy about all this. You're right. I am playing a game. I'm smart enough to win. So why don't you sit down and cool off, and we'll have dinner and talk about this.'

115

'Because I'm going. You can fuck up your life on your own.'

Too soon. Damn. I've still got this. Big guns time. 'It's your fault Dad went nuts that night.'

Kyle stopped, his hand just short of the door. 'Excuse me?'

'When Dad showed up that afternoon, what did he see?'

Under his shirt, Trick knew his brother was fully bristled up from head to tail. 'How the fuck is any of that my fault?'

'What did he see, Kyle?'

'That fight was *not* my fault.'

'He saw our family watching TV. You'd brought a friend round. Mom was making us all dinner. Ordinary Friday night. That was it. Then what did you do? You had to tell him everything about our coming out. *Ours.* Because you couldn't even let me have that to myself. You had to hijack it and make it about you too.'

Kyle clenched his fists, shifting his arms back as if forcing himself not to rain punches into his brother. 'You piece of shit. You're actually pretending to be angry about this now? After two years?'

'*Pretending?*' Trick shouted in his face. 'Oh, I was angry, Kyle. Believe me. When half our house was smashed to pieces and we all thought Kia might be facing a manslaughter charge if that ambulance didn't turn up? I was angry. You wanna know how much? Let me tell you what stupid really is: opening your mouth when you know that's the kind of thing you're going to make happen. You *wanted* that fight.'

'So what if I did? God knows *you're* not going to put Dad in his place. You wouldn't have done it even before he bought you a house. You wanna keep your mouth shut? Why don't you shut it right now and listen.' Kyle slowly walked up to Trick, their noses almost touching. 'I'm not going to be a coward so that people like you can keep your peace with people like Dad.'

'People like me? There was nothing wrong with me until Kia told you I accepted Dad's gift. Or was there?' Trick tipped his head slightly, still locked into the staring contest. 'Maybe you actually *can* keep your mouth shut. So now we've got the truth. What else is there?'

Kyle broke the stare. 'I always knew who you'd decide to be would come down to a price.'

Was his brother right? As soon as Trick asked himself the question, he realised his tactic wasn't working. Kyle looked so cold towards him that maybe his angst-filled confession to Kia had lost any truth it had once had.

'You having a drink?' Trick said, deciding to skip wine and go straight for whisky.

'Yeah,' Kyle said, swiping the glass Trick had poured for himself and taking half of it down in one. 'Least Dad can stock a fridge right.'

'Kyle, what do you think that night two years ago made you, some sort of hero?' Trick poured for himself but only swirled his drink around, no sipping. 'You couldn't even win the fight you started without your boyfriend almost going to jail for you. If you hate Dad so much, why did you never tell him he nearly got killed by a cat? To protect Kia? I don't think so. You want him

thinking you owned him. But you didn't. You *don't.*
You're just faking being that tough.'

Now Kyle looked shocked as well as angry. 'Do you
even *believe* half the shit you're saying right now?'

'Why don't you tell me I'm just like Dad already? Go
on. Hit me with whatever you've got. It still won't
change one thing: I've got this house and you haven't.
Know something else? You're lucky I let you into it.
Because I knew I was going to have to put up with
another round of your whining bullshit. I've been sick
of it for months. But hey, here you are. You probably
just wanted another fight. Maybe I did too.'

Because I am *angry,* Trick thought as he walked
back to the kitchen and got the dish out of the oven, his
hands shaking as he put them inside the oven gloves. *I
had no idea how much I needed to tell him that until I
did it. Him getting gifted a house? He couldn't even
protect the one our family lived in by not trying to be
some hero of the hour. A phone call to Dad would have
done. Then Dad could have just smashed up an office,
or a bar several hundred miles from us.*

'You want some food, or are you still leaving me
alone to fuck up my life?' Trick looked around him. 'Not
gonna lie to you, things aren't looking too fucked up for
me lately. Good luck back in Phoenix though.'

Kyle wasn't leaving. He stalked into the kitchen
between his brother and the door, leaving him nowhere
to go. 'I hate you, Trick. I hate you almost as much as
Dad.'

'No, you don't,' Trick said. 'You're just hurt. You've
almost always felt hurt about life. That's how you
attracted Kia. Apart from him, I was always the one who

118

cared the most when you found life tough. Now you *want* to hate me because I took Dad's gift, but you don't. Stop the act. Stop wanting to fight everyone. Stay here and let's play Dad's mind game and show that old fuck how we can beat hi–'

Kyle was physically stronger, Trick knew. Always had been. Now that his brother had slammed his back against the fridge, both of Trick's forearms inside a clenched grip, Trick knew he was in trouble. He couldn't raise a fist, or even do anything. It wasn't a fight Kyle wanted though. Trick knew it as soon as his brother's mouth was on his, half kissing and half biting. Trick pushed against him, trying to fight back but only able to do it with the force of his neck. Only when his brother let go did Trick realise it had probably been nearly a minute since he'd taken a breath. Unprepared, even an otter couldn't go under for that long.

'Oh shit,' Trick heard Kyle whisper, under the sound of his own gasping. His brother was halfway across the kitchen now, and Trick hadn't seen him get there. 'Oh Jesus *Christ*!' He put his hands to his mouth and looked back at Trick, half frantic and half scared. 'I'm sorry.' He put his hands up. 'I'm *sorry*, okay? I never meant to...' Kyle clearly didn't know what he'd meant, or thought, or anything, apart from how he'd just forcibly kissed his own brother.

It worked, Trick thought. *It actually worked!* His surprise gave way to a surge of pleasure, a kind he'd never before experienced. *So many people have wanted this otter. Nobody's ever tried to take him by force. It shouldn't feel good. Except that I won.*

Play this.

119

Trick forced the thought on himself like it was a command, knowing that just standing there could say anything he needed it to. Kyle was looking at him, as if pleading for forgiveness. *Give him nothing.*

'Fuck!' Kyle shouted into his hands, again at his mouth. Now they were covering his eyes, as if he needed to cry but this whole situation had taken him beyond tears. He put his hands on the bar and leaned his weight onto it, eyes closed and trying to calm himself.

'You kissed me,' Trick said, touching a hand to his mouth even though Kyle wouldn't see it. He kept it there until his brother turned to him.

'Yeah, I did.'

Now Kyle was trying to be the right kind of hero. Acceptance of what he'd done so quickly? *Good. Make it real.*

'It's okay,' Trick said. 'I mean...well shit, I guess I was right about one thing.'

'What?'

'You don't hate me.'

Kyle leaned on the bar again, this time still looking at his brother, and looking ashamed. 'Course I don't. I couldn't. I just wanted you to believe it.'

'So instead of hitting me you shoved me against a fridge door and *kissed* me?'

'I'm sorry. I don't know what the fuck happened to me. But I stopped, right? I knew what I was doing was fucking crazy, and I stopped. You won't...okay, whatever I have to do to put this right, I'll do it. Just tell me what I've gotta do. Just please, you *can't* tell anyone I did that. It was wrong and I'm sorry. Just don't ruin my life, Trick. Please? Don't use this as revenge for every stupid thing I ever did. You were right about the goddamn fight with Dad.'

Trick went for the sigh. 'I didn't even care about you fighting with Dad. You were right about him too; it was about time someone gave him a taste of his own shit. After what he said, you think *I* wasn't ready to smack one right in his face? I stoked you up because I needed a fight with you. To get you to stay. I never thought you'd actually go for me. I sure as *shit* never expected that.' Trick looked at the ceiling and whistled. 'I take it back. You *do* know how to hit a guy. *And* win a fight.'

'I wasn't trying to win anything.'

Trick moved closer to him. 'Then what were you doing?'

'I...I really think I should just go, Trick.'

'You don't look like you're going anywhere. Come on. Give me a real answer. Why did you kiss me? Is this what...' *Nice pause. Nice eyes on Kyle right now. He knows you're about to figure it out.* 'Is *this* the otter you really wanted?' Trick gestured to himself, only slightly flexing his fingers to do it, relaxing his whole face to let his eyes widen. 'Kia told me he thought you wanted to be with an otter. He thought that was why you broke up with him. Something you said, some hint. So you did want that. You wanted me?'

'No!' Kyle said, neither of them realising he'd shouted until they were both just standing there, listening to the silent room. 'Yes. *Sort* of. Oh, for Chrissake, alright. I had this fantasy about you. I know you like sex. That you have it all the time, with just about anyone, because you *can* get just about anyone, with barely any more than a look. You got any idea how

121

jealous I am? I can barely get laid with a snep who's always horny. Because I'm not you. So I started…thinking about you.'

'Okay,' Trick said. 'What were you thinking?'

'I admitted you *are* seriously cute. Then I watched some stuff. Twins fucking. I find it hot, okay? It does it for me. Is that enough for you already? Happy now? For shit's sake, you're my kid brother! You're not even my twin. Why do you think I stopped? I can't have you. Ever. But I love you. So fucking much. Then you have to go do a stupid cunt thing like take a million-dollar house off Dad for your birthday.'

Trick swiped his tail and smiled. 'Five million, actually.'

'Fuck you, Trick.'

'Yeah. I would say "in your dreams", but how many times *have* you done it like that already?'

'You do *not* even wanna ask that. Could you just be my brother right now instead of a fucking walking movie? That line's a total cliché anyway. I thought you said you were good at all that stage crap.'

'This *is* kind of like a play. It doesn't have to be Shakespeare.'

'This is real fucking life.'

'Don't you think I know that after what you just did?'

'You know what? Maybe I'm not sorry.'

Trick's heart quickened. *Here we go then. You could kiss him back right now and then take him any way you wanted. But you're not going to. This moment right here? You can get more out of this than sex.* Trick struck an inviting pose, leaning on the bar top and tensing his chest muscles a little so Kyle could see them though his tight t-shirt. 'That's more like it. I took a gift from Dad, you just told me I'm your favourite twincest-type fantasy *and* you stole a real kiss. Ready to call it even yet, or shall we fight some more? Any of your fantasies involve us having a fistfight and then comforting make-up sex?'

If Kyle hadn't imagined it before then he definitely would now. Probably tonight. He sniffed and straightened himself up. 'That pie does smell good. Where do you keep the plates in your "new house"? I'm hungry.'

Yeah, Trick thought. *So am I.*

* * *

They ate in silence until Kyle asked Trick why he never cooked like this at home.

'When did I ever need to? Mom spoiled us all the time. Besides, I didn't really make this. Sandy did. He showed me how. Nice, isn't it?'

Kyle was on his second helping and drinking only water while Trick had wine. 'Yeah. Sandy, the guy who works the bar at Winslow's. Who you asked to move in with you a day after you met him.'

'Don't judge until you've heard the story.'

'I don't care, Trick. It's your house. Live with who you want.'

That's an 'I'm going home tomorrow'. He won't though. Trick put his fork down and dabbed his mouth with a napkin. 'I'm glad you kissed me.'

Kyle looked tired now. 'Why?'

'Because it got all this out of you. You know what that silence was? That was you feeling the weight lifting off your shoulders. Admit it. Feels good to tell me the truth, right?'

'Not really.'

'I don't mind that you want me, Kyle. Everybody wants me.'

'Can we just not talk about this?'

'Why are you so uncomfortable with it? I get it, you thought I'd be disgusted if you told me. Now you have, and I'm not. I could talk you through any fantasy you want right now, and you're not even excited? You think *I* never watched a twincest film?'

'Did you?'

'Sure. All those films you watched, people make them for a reason: it's hot. Guys like us find it hot. I got something better. When Kia styled me on my birthday, you know what I asked him to do first? I said I wanted to look like you. *Exactly* like you.'

Kyle stopped chewing, then after a blank moment he remembered to swallow, and he looked at his plate like he was stuffed. 'And he didn't do it?'

'*Should* he have done it?'

Kyle sighed. 'Shit, that must have spooked him right out. I told him, okay? That's why he broke up with me. Okay, he was the one who guessed I liked you. He pretended it didn't matter, but he was freaked out. You asked him to do that? You didn't make him think we actually...Trick, *tell me* you didn't make up a bunch of shit about us doing it to get Kia hot. I don't care that you

124

fucked him; he told me about it. I wasn't surprised. But did you do that?'

'Bro, relax. Kia broke up with you because you were disappointing in bed.'

'I was *not* disappointing in bed. You ever seen me doing it with Kia? He wasn't faking.'

'But he wasn't in the same place I took him to.'

'Gee, this is really making me feel good about myself.'

'Stop the pity-party and listen, bro. I'm confident about everything to do with sex. I like it. I'm good at reading people. I don't just have desire, I *get* it, in a thinking way. It's just something I'm wired to do. You're not a natural. You're nervous, you're awkward, you're a little bit prudish, and you've let thoughts you feel guilty about get in your way. I can help you get past all this. I could have done it years ago if you'd just talked to me. Loads of brothers share sex tips. People don't *know* they do it, because they're smart enough to keep it secret, but come on. You've never been on a fetish forum where someone told a story about how they jerked off a family member? A brother?'

'Now you're trying to tell me the shit people post on the internet's real? I'm not stupid.'

'So what if it's not? At least they're having a healthy relationship with fantasy. Just give me one honest answer, Kyle, right here, right now. Do you actually like the way you feel about yourself at the moment? About any of your life?'

'Like you don't already know the answer to that. Fine, you want to hear me say it? No. No, I don't. I hate my fucking life *and* myself. Why do you think I'm always in a shit mood? Why do you think I came on this vacation to get hammered at your party? I don't want to go back to Phoenix. I hate everything there too. But I can't live with you, Trick.'

'Why not?'

'After what we've just talked about, you have to ask that?'

'You don't have to let a guilty fantasy get in the way of you having a good life.'

'It might interest you to know that you're not the only thought in my head. I don't want to live here either. I want to try college. That'll get me out of Phoenix and out into the world. That'll get me distance from you. So I can just forget all this and get into a healthy relationship with someone. Kia's not for me anymore. It wasn't working. I *do* want to be with an otter. Someone so right for me that everything I felt about you just becomes a teenage angst thing, and I look back on it and laugh one day.'

'Then that's good,' Trick said. 'But you'll get over this thing about me anyway. You're not in that kind of love with me. You're my brother; you're *supposed* to love me with all the heart you've got. You do. I love you back. So I'm a beautiful otter. So are you. We really *could* look like twins with a little of Kia's magic. I've jerked off thinking about you too sometimes. I'm fine with it. It's two different kinds of love. All you got wrong is that you blurred them together, and you've done it in silence for so long that it messed up your head. You're going to go home tonight and realise it was just a great big sexy load of smoke and mirrors.'

Kyle thought about it for a moment, staring at the table as if following some pattern in the marble would solve the great puzzle that was clearly in his head. 'Yeah. Or I'm going to stay here. Then one of us is going to do something stupid and the other's going to do it too.' He looked up. 'Cut out the shit, Trick. That's what you're offering isn't it? You think if we fuck each other just once it'll burn this out of me and then it's just done.'

'I don't think it would burn it out of you.'

'But you're offering. Aren't you?' Kyle had never taken drugs to Trick's knowledge, but the look he wore right then made him look like every convincing narcotics addict Trick had ever seen, on tape or in real life. The look of knowing you were better off walking away from something but at the same time you couldn't live without it.

'This is my home,' Trick said. 'My *new* home. You want to know what the first rule I made for it is?'

'What?'

'Nothing happens in here that I couldn't live with afterwards.' He got up and slowly went to Kyle's side of the bar. 'I think you just need a hug. Come on. Let me give you a great big hug and this will all be okay.'

Kyle stood up, so tense that Trick sensed any attempt at hugging him would lead to a knock-out punch this time, not just a shove. Then Kyle took a deep breath, shook himself off and held his arms open first. Trick embraced him and hugged him slowly. His brother's muscles became tight around him as they rubbed the sides of their heads together. Kyle sighed deeply, and Trick knew it might be a while before his brother let go. He sighed again, and a third time, his chest swelling against Trick's. Trick slid a hand up his brother's back to the top of his neck and stroked it. The bulge in his brother's crotch was pushing against his own. Kyle's breathing quickened, a sure sign that he was trying to resist anything but the hug.

'Trick,' Kyle whispered. 'Ooooooh man.'

'It's alright.' Trick loosened his hug, and Kyle's loosened around him. They touched foreheads, Kyle's hand now on the back of Trick's head, fingers between his ears. The kiss they shared this time was gentle, relaxed and calming, both of them breathing through their noses, air warm on each other's faces.

'Trick, we...'

'We shouldn't? It's just a kiss.'

Just a kiss that Kyle was enjoying a second time, his body trembling slightly. When they came apart: 'So you can live with this?'

Trick smiled. 'You're a beautiful otter, Kyle. I meant it. Sure. I can live with kissing my brother. You know what?' He shifted closer to whisper in Kyle's ear. 'I always hoped we'd do it sometime.'

'What, do kissing or *do it* do it?'

'It depends. What could *you* live with?'

They separated. Kyle raised his shaking hands to his mouth and sighed into them. 'I can't fuck you, Trick. I'm sorry. I just can't let myself. You've *no* idea how much I want to. If we do this, I'll regret it for the rest of my life. I can't do it. I need a drink. You got JD?'

'Right there in the corner behind you.' Trick picked up a glass. 'Ice?'

'Yeah. This is *not* more playing around. I'm not going to get skooshed and then let this happen anyway.

128

It's not. It can't. Fine, you know the truth now. You were right. I'll just get over it. So I'm going to have a drink with you and we'll talk like things are okay and then I'll just go home and probably get into Kia's bed and not fuck him either.' Kyle filled half the glass with Jack and then only sipped from it. 'Self-control. That's what I've got to have.'

Trick nodded. 'You know what we just did?'

'What?'

'We worked this out.'

Kyle put his glass down after a moment of just holding it. 'Yeah. Guess maybe we did.'

'But listen, this doesn't have to be awkward from now on. What if we could find a way of you enjoying me as a fantasy that actually worked well for you?'

'What the fuck, first you say we worked this out and now you're trying to go back and do it differently? Can we just take a great big time out right here?' He looked around, then down at his own crotch. 'I'm still hard right here, and it's your goddamn fault for existing, and being you, and giving me that hug. So in a minute you're going to go for a night swim outside and I'm going to use your house to watch a hot channel and jerk off. On my own. Don't even think about arguing. I don't care if it's your house. I'll stop caring it was a gift from Dad if you'll just give me that.'

'Alright. Big time out. But before we have it, there's something I've gotta tell you about what I'm thinking of doing out here. Now that I know what I know, it's only fair I warn you. Whether you stay or not.'

He'll stay, Trick thought. *I've totally got this.*

'Fine. What is it?'

129

'Sandy was talking about auditioning for an adult entertainment company. I don't think that's him. But I wonder if it's me.'

'Porn?' Kyle said. 'I thought you wanted to be a real actor.'

'An actor's an actor, bro. I don't just want to act. I really like the surfing thing down here. I'm good at it. Maybe I could go pro. What if I combined it all? What if that's Trick Dixon's brand? Surf, sex and the stage.' *This is almost unfair. He'd give anything to see that, and there's always a chance none of it will come true and I'll just be selling this house in less than half a year.*

Kyle laughed. It was a relief to hear him laughing for the first time in...shit, how long *had* it been since Trick had seen his brother happy, or heard laughter without it sounding fake? 'Whatever you want for your life, Trick, you go get it and be happy. Why don't you have a drink yourself and we'll have a toast and try and forget this whole evening was so awkward?'

'Because your idea was a good one. I'm going for a swim. Load up your fav channel and make as much mess as you like.' Trick deliberately did a stop-take by the kitchen door. 'But admit one thing to me first. You don't really wanna try college, do you? *Mom* wants you to try college. You don't know how to tell her you don't want it.'

'That's because I do want it.'

He looked like he had his confidence back, Trick thought. *Either this is working or I'm playing the wrong card.* 'Okay, maybe you do. I'm not a mind reader. So what are you going to be?'

'How the fuck should I know?'

'What are you going to study?'

'You know already. Music with English.'

'So where's that going to take you?'

'I know where you're going with this. Cali is the land of half the bands I ever listened to, right? So why go to college when I could get out here and hustle?'

'Well damn. Sounds like you're in the mood to hustle already. Come on. There's really nothing about coming here on this vacation that gave even the teeniest tiniest feeling that it might be fun to try packing your bags and chasing a dream?'

'You just said it. It's a dream. You wanna chase yours? That's cool. I might look back one day and wish I'd done it with you if it works. But honestly? I'll make a bet with you. I'll give you five years of trying to make it out here before you come back and join the ordinary world and find you like it better. We'll both be working some ordinary job with regular hours and decent enough pay and that'll be fine. Just a couple of ordinary otters, and one of them tells stories about how he was beautiful, vain and daring. And mostly broke.'

Trick smiled, leaning on the doorframe. 'Snark. My favourite theatrical trope. Swim time. Enjoy the TV. Hey, it's Friday. You tried chan seven on a Friday before? There's a pretty hot wolverine who used to be a pro football player; he's in some good movies.'

'Fast Eddie Kowalski? Yeah, I've seen some of his stuff.'

'Enjoy your hand-job.'

'Wait a minute.'

'What?'

Kyle stayed silent for a moment and just stared at him, then started grinning.

'What?' Trick laughed. 'Nice as it is to see you happy about something, you look like you're about to launch yourself at me.'

'Uh-uh,' Kyle said. 'I was just thinking about what you said. You want me to enjoy a fantasy about you? In a way that works? Okay. I just thought of one. You want to do porn? Great. But I don't wanna wait for your first film to come out. Go get your speedos. I've already seen you in them hundreds of times. Now I wanna watch you put them on. I wanna see your dick. Close-up. Then I won't have to imagine it anymore. I'm gonna let you watch me get hard. For you. So you'll know what every film you're in's gonna do to me.'

Here we go. Self-control my ass. There's only one way this is going to end.

'What's the matter? Not thinking it's such a good idea now? Not sure if you can even do that audition with your new boyfriend?'

Trick got close enough to his brother to kiss him again, but neither of them moved in for it. 'Oh, I think that's a perfectly good idea. Go sit on the couch and take your pants off. I'll be right down.'

Chapter Eight

The strange thing is, Trick thought as he slowly took his clothes off, that I don't feel the slightest bit guilty about any of this.

Kyle watched from the sofa. Trick preened himself, pretending there was a mirror in front of him, standing in his pants and waiting for his brother to tell him to get a move on. Kyle only sat there staring, so Trick took them off anyway and folded them.

The look on Kyle's face sent blood straight to Trick's manhood. Kyle's pupils dilated, and he stared, his tail and feet twitching a little, his thumbs already hooked into his jeans. He shifted on the cushion, obviously trying to adjust for comfort without touching himself. 'It's a good size.'

'Yeah.'

'You've got a semi.'

'Yeah, I do.' Trick turned to the side and rubbed his butt with one hand, sticking his tail up and outward.

Kyle put a hand down his pants, untwisted his dick from them and sighed with relief. 'This is totally unfair.'

'What is?'

'That you're the hottest otter on the planet.'

'At least you've got your own private show,' Trick said. 'Why don't you jerk off? That'll cure that jealousy. Want me to do anything? Tell me what look you want.'

'The one you've got right now.'

'Okay. But you said something a minute ago.'

'What.'

'You wanted a close-up.'

'No, wait...Trick, it's fine, just stand there, I'm good.'

He was even better now that Trick was right up close to him. 'Wanna touch?'

'I can't.'

'Go on. Be a naughty boy. Touch your kid brother. I'm not a kid anymore. I'm legal. I'm hot fuckable tail. Right here. Take me inside your hand.'

'You're the devil.'

'Sandy said that to me too last night,' Trick said, still in his turn-on voice, his tip poking out of his sheath as Kyle took hold of it. Trick moaned and sighed, a slight breeze from the open windows blowing over his back. Kyle stopped and just looked at him, then took his hand away, held it to his nose and sniffed. 'I love your scent,' he said. 'I've...done something. Before.'

'Done what?'

'I've been in your room and sniffed your clothes. Your stuff.' Before Trick even knew how to react, Kyle was taking a deep sniff of his crotch, his hands on Trick's hips. 'Oh holy *fuck*,' he said, his eyes closed. 'I've never been so ashamed of myself.'

Nor have you been so powerless, Trick thought, as Kyle took another sniff, and then nipped at his tight sheath, his tongue licking over Trick's scrotum. 'Go on,'

Trick said. 'Do it. I promise not to come in your mouth.'
I'll like it better when you can't talk for a few minutes.
You'll just get on with it.

Kyle did, his breath hot as he tried to take Trick's entire erection into his mouth and only just succeeded, nearly choking himself until he remembered to breathe through his nose, hard and fast, as though he'd only just surfaced in time. Trick purred, his hands behind his brother's ears, guiding his head back and forward, until Kyle drew down a deep breath and held it while he sucked, his hands clinging tight to Trick's butt as if about to pull him with him. Only when Trick squeaked in the moment before his climax did Kyle let go. Trick's squirt hit his brother's chin and neck and the top of his chest, just above the loose collar of his shirt.

Trick let out a great humph of relief, the climax as fresh and exciting as it had been with Sandy, with Kia, with anyone.

'Oh man...I just....'

'Shhh!' Trick said, taking his brother's shoulders and gently guiding him back to the couch. 'Shhhhhh shh shh shh! You just sucked my dick off and it was totally hot, and you're wet and you're hard, and I'm your kid brother and I'm jerking you off.' Kyle only seemed to notice when he heard it, his heart pounding so fast that Trick could feel his pulse with just a stroke on the side of his brother's neck, his other hand squeezing Kyle's cock and rubbing, pulling. 'You've been a very, *very* bad otter, Kyle Dixon. What did you sniff in my room? My used underpants? My wet towels? My PJ's?'

'All of it!' Kyle panted. 'I'm so naughty! Punish me!'

'Wanna get spanked?'

'Yeah!'

'With your pants down?'

'Yeah...yeah!'

'Too late, your kid brother's about two seconds from making you c–'

The last word was cut off by Kyle's yelp of pleasure as he filled his pants, Trick still yanking hard on the bottom of his dick, digging his fingertips into the space underneath where it met his balls. Trick let him catch his breath for a moment then took his hand out, cleaned it on Kyle's t-shirt just below the wet patch he'd made earlier, then rolled onto his brother's lap and let him catch his breath between kisses. Kyle pulled his shirt off after sniffing at the stickiness and laughing at how they both smelt like semen, then the rest of his clothes with it, and they lay naked together, sometimes kissing and sometimes just laughing.

'You asleep?' Trick said after a few minutes of verging on it himself.

'Nah, I'm good.' He rolled over to face his brother. 'We're cool, right? About that?'

'Yeah, we're cool. Course we are.'

'I can't believe I did that.'

'Oh, sure you can. You've wanted it for ages. I'm sorry I had to come on strong, but let's face it, you needed it. Why do you think I took so long upstairs? I had to think about it. But I thought right, didn't I?'

'Oh yeah,' Kyle said. 'So totally.'

'Did you really go in my room back home and sniff my stuff, or was that just part of the play?'

'Yeah. I sniffed your underpants. They were still wet from when you'd jerked off. Just once. I promise. I only did it once and then the guilt just killed me. Look, I know that was hot, and I needed it, but...can we just make a promise it was only once?'

'If that's what you want.'

Kyle nodded. 'It wouldn't be good for both of us to keep this going. You've got Sandy. I want Kia back. I do. Thanks. That was exactly what I needed to clear my head. Just so long as you know I'm gonna think about that for the rest of my life whenever I need to get it up. But I love Kia too. Great big soft snep. I should have given him that blowjob first, not you.'

'He'll be waiting. You know it's not too late.'

'I'd feel so bad if I left him. We make each other happy. I feel like he needs it more than me. D'you think...ah, forget it. I'm so high right now it's like I'm riding waves like you do. I'm talking complete crap.'

'Go on. Finish your thought. You *did* just give your little brother a pretty damn good blowjob. What could I ever judge you for? I'm the one who knew you couldn't resist me. I used it. I acted.' Trick put a hand on the side of Kyle's chest and ruffled his fur. 'Share your thoughts with me. All of them.'

'I told Kia how I felt about you.'

'You already told me that. How did he take it?'

'He was cool. I think. I told him about the pants sniffing thing. I could tell him just about anything, the stuff he's told me. It's just...I think he'll know about this. When I go home, he's just going to know. What if I just went too far?'

'You didn't. Trust me.'

'Trust you? Why, what do you...' Kyle looked as dumbstruck as the silence sounded. 'Did he tell you I told him?'

'No,' Trick said, the lie effortless. 'But I've got a confession. He told me he'd imagined us both doing him. Otter double-team. Pretty sure he'd actually get seriously hot if he watched us kiss. Or do something else.'

'We can't fuck. Ever. I can't cross that line, no matter how hot Kia would find it.' Kyle rolled back over. 'You know what, Trick? This joke's going to be on you. I do want to enjoy you. Any way I can. If I could reach those pants you took off, I'd sniff them right now.' Kyle put his hand between Trick's legs instead. 'Bro, have we just done something awful? Are we going to regret this like hell tomorrow?'

Trick sat up and put a hand on the back of his brother's head. Kyle let him, looking grateful for the extra comfort. 'Listen, try not to worry so much. I'm as surprised by tonight as you are. I wasn't expecting us to be here like this either, but it happened. We both felt like it was right. It felt *great*.'

'Yeah. I know.'

'We've got nothing to be ashamed of, and this is all between us. If you'd feel better, we'll never talk about it. Not even to each other. But I've gotta admit, I'd like to do something with Kia. Maybe something with Sandy if we decide to tell him about this. He said he wants to watch someone else do stuff to me. Maybe all four of us have a go. Just remember one thing though.'

'What?'

'I'm your brother, and I'd never betray your trust.'

138

Kyle looked at him and smiled. 'I love you to death, bro.' He took Trick's hand in his. 'The rest of our family? I love them too. But you were always the special one. You always knew it. Admit it. You're the vainest otter alive as well as the hottest.'

'As if you want me not to be either.' Trick shifted his butt around on the sofa and put his hand on the back of Kyle's neck to stroke it. 'I hear you got a surfing nickname that's starting to stick.'

'Dolphin? Yeah, I kinda like it, except it sounds like a girl's nickname. I don't swim like a dolphin anyway. I need to get back to swim training. I'm starting to look fat.'

'Oh bullshit, you're fine. Do not even think about making another comment about how you don't look as much like me as you want to. You're you. If you want to feel like my twin, we can just pretend to be. The looks don't matter.'

'Okay. Fine. I'll just do me. I'll do Dolphin. But look, Trick. You're asking me to make a big decision about my life with this staying here thing. How many times have you asked me if I'll stay, in the space of one night? Just give me a little bit of space, will you? Why don't you go for that swim? I'll go take a shower and just...come down from all this a little bit. I need another drink.'

'You got it. Can you clean up and spray some scent-eater? When Sandy comes home, I don't want this place smelling like sex before we've had a chance to explain our bromance thing.'

'Urgh, you *do* want to do this again, don't you?'

As if you don't. 'Let's just see, bro.'

139

When Trick came back in, Kyle was sleepily watching TV. The sight of Trick woke him up though: he was trembling and breathing heavily from the top of his chest, his fur still half-sodden because he hadn't had the strength to shake properly.

'Jesus, Trick, you look wrecked! The hell kind of swim did you go for?' Kyle looked at his watch. 'Just an hour and...what happened?'

'The fucking tide nearly got me,' Trick said, shutting the sliding door and nearly passing out as the warmth of home rushed into him. 'I've seriously gotta start checking the tables. I got all the way out to that buoy 2K out and I started thinking –'

'Slow down. Started thinking what? Why aren't there any other otters out here? You idiot, you actually didn't check the tide board?'

'That cheetah was on beach patrol again. I think I just made a friend.'

Kyle's eyes narrowed, and he looked as though he could burst out laughing. 'You just got rescued by a Chee? *You*?'

'He didn't rescue me. By the time he'd scrambled into that pathetic rubber speedboat thing, I was already back in the shallows. What the hell does beach patrol do here, putting non-aquatic species on when the undertow's up?'

'If you hadn't made it, you'd be owing him your life. What's his name – Armando something, isn't it?'

'Armando Rodriguez. He called me "another dumb mustelid". I told him it's just because I fucked a snep the other night and caught cat-brain.'

'You're soaking. You're gonna fuck up this nice new carpet Dad's dirty money bought you. He's still an asshole. Tonight doesn't change that. I'll go get you a towel.'

'The bathroom's –'

'I know where your bathroom is.'

Trick walked through to the kitchen, ignoring the carpet, and poured himself a whisky. 'Dumb mustelid. Huh. Fucking chee-trash.' He smiled as he said it. He liked Armando; the guy had something about him. When Trick had turned around, knowing he might be in trouble, he'd seen the speed the guy could cover a length of beach at without looking out of breath. Too bad the lifeboat crew didn't scramble that fast. Maybe Rodriguez was out to teach them something.

He put it out of his mind as soon as Kyle was rubbing him with the towel. Trick let him. He'd brought two and needed the second one. Kyle left it draped over Trick's shoulders and touched his face. Trick smiled, ready to go again and wondering if he had the strength to make it, but Kyle looked like he only wanted to touch. Gone was the sass, the twitching anger, the tense posture even when relaxed. Now his brother just looked like he had peace in his life for the first time in years.

'Handsome otter,' Kyle said, then slowly touched his forehead to Trick's, licked the tip of his nose, and allowed himself one short kiss. 'I'll try it for a year. Living with you. It doesn't work out, I'll do college instead. Fair?'

141

You'll never do college, Trick thought. *Not now.* 'Good plan.'

'You really think this whole Cali being the land of bands thing can work for someone like me? Pack my bags and head here hoping for fame and actually getting somewhere?'

'It's not about being famous,' Trick said, stroking a hand down his brother's back and sliding it up his tail. 'It's being good. Any talentless halfwit can get famous for something; it's mostly called reality TV. You and me, we could be good. Better than good. We owe ourselves that. Life away from Phoenix. Where we've got waves and sand that's not just endless desert. I'm not going to be an ordinary otter. If Dad hadn't bought me this place, I'd have moved here anyway. I was ready to fuck for a roof over my head to get here. Now I can just jump straight to doing it to get a break. On camera or off, I don't care. Everybody wants this otter. You use what you've got. This is what I've got. I even got my own brother to suck me off.' Trick touched a finger to Kyle's lips.

Kyle rolled his eyes. 'Just promise me you'll be careful. Plenty of people out there probably want to *hurt* this otter just as much. You know what a mess the world is. People don't just want fun out of someone like you. Some of them like watching lives get destroyed, Trick. I'm staying here with you to keep an eye on you.'

Trick laughed. 'My big brother, the protector?'

'Yeah, you can laugh. But I pinned you against that fridge pretty good. Nobody's going to fuck with you in the wrong way as long as I'm around. You watched me fight Dad. I'd have won even if Kia hadn't finished it for me.'

Of course you would. 'I can take care of myself, bro. A brain's all I need. You know why Dad bought me this place? Because he knew I never called him up against Mom's orders just to make peace. Someone fucks with me the wrong way? I outsmart them. I want what someone else has? I take it. Whether it's the same day or years later. Dad has a production company? Great. I want a company that could buy and sell it. One step at a time. One day I'm going to gift him this house back. Because that old fuck will be begging for it.'

'Now you're talking.'

Yeah, Trick thought. *I'm talking. Telling you just what you need to hear to seal the deal. Dad will be in the ground before I get that big. Or we'll be working together to buy and sell someone in the business who's worse than him. Allies are allies. Dad gifted me this place because I'm the player.*

'Take a little time to get over how pissed you are with Dad,' Trick said. 'Let's get a little cash under our belts and we'll set up a dinner together. You might even be surprised. Dad might not be all-change exactly, but he knows he got plenty wrong. Just don't hit him with the Kia knocking him out thing. Maybe we can even get him to make some peace there too.'

'I doubt it.'

'Let me be the brain. You just be bodyguard, if that's really where you see yourself. You gonna tell Mom about staying here or do you want some help?'

'Can we just have the rest of this vacation and deal with all that after it? This was actually fun. Now you've got friends here who are all getting antsy because you've abandoned them, and they've got no idea where you are. I know you don't want your shiny new house wrecked and everything, but I think you owe them all at least *one* party here. You can introduce your new boyfriend. Who you've known for all of one night.'

'I intend to.'

'I meant what I said though, Trick. Listen, I know you're gonna tell me I worry. But so does Mom. She knows you've already got a sex life that would rival a porn star's. She's cool. But I know she worries. You wanna do "everyone wants this otter"? It's cool. But not everyone's going to want to kiss and cuddle and have hot sex. You know some people would happily get off on beating you within an inch of your life just for being this beautiful. Some people are fucked up. I know you know I'm right. I don't want to wake up to a phone call one day where I end up coming to the hospital and finding you irreparably damaged. Or...'

Trick smiled. 'Or what, identifying a corpse?'

'Theodore, is there *anything* you don't ignore by finding it funny? I'm serious right now. You never think about your own safety, do you? Because that would mean you weren't focusing on how much someone wants you.'

'Alright, I'm sorry. But being ultra-desirable doesn't mean I'm a whore. Or blind to what the world is. That story Sandy told me about his boyfriend putting him in the hospital with a haemorrhage, you think I didn't imagine that might be me too if I don't watch my back?'

'What?'

'Oh yeah, you don't know about that yet. Let's talk. Couch?'

Trick kept the towel around his shoulders, feeling a little more vitality despite his heavy limbs. After telling Kyle about Sandy, he teased his brother a little with some subtle touches and let him do it back. Trick tickled his brother's back and chest until Kyle was laughing and had a bulge slowly growing.

'Okay, serious time, before we get carried away with this.' He adjusted his own semi for comfort, the tip just under the elastic of his speedos. 'Here's what we owe ourselves. You were right about the ground rules. We don't fuck. We just have a little fun when we want to. I'll be a little bit more careful. From now on the only one I do bareback-ride with will be Sandy. He'll like that. If we're going to make this work, the first thing we've got to do is take care of our health. Agreed?'

'Yeah. Fit otters. I'd like that. I'm bored with getting drunk all the time.'

Trick rubbed his brother's stomach and squeezed the top layer. 'Hmm. You were right, you know. You are getting a little chubby. Swim training, daily. We'll start tomorrow. I've eaten so many donuts this week I don't dare get on a scale either. Sandy wants to learn to be a chef here; he's trying to work his way up at Winslow's. We're gonna have to watch the calories a little bit.'

'Uh-huh. We've got to get jobs. You first, seeing as this is your big idea.'

'I'll sort that. I bet the surf stores are all hiring.'

'Nuh-uh, I already looked.'

Genuine surprise for Trick this time. 'You already looked?' He laughed. 'You little shit, you were thinking of staying here before I even got this place?'

'I really wasn't. I just thought how cool it would be to work in a surf shack, and to actually be able to surf. How did you start?'

'Dad bought me lessons when I came here a couple of years ago.'

'Dad again.'

'Don't start; you just got on a train of thought that wasn't carrying depression vibes. Stay on it. I'll see if Javi's still giving lessons; that's the guy I went to. Mink-otter cross; you should see that guy move in water. He said I was a natural though. Bet you'd be good too. Let's both get jobs and save some cash for good boards and better guitars for you to tour the circuit with. I'll talk to Winslow's, see if we can get an open mic going or something.'

'Cool,' Kyle said. 'That's a good idea. Can we go hands-off for a few minutes? I've got such a load in my pants right now, and I need to save it for Kia.' Kyle took a deep breath. 'We've gotta talk about Kia. Can we do it without you telling me not to worry? Coz here's something *you* don't know yet. He bought a gun.'

Trick hadn't taken the hands-off request too seriously, but he took them away now. 'He did what? Why?'

'He said he just enjoyed shooting it. He's been going to target lessons, doing that shooting range thing you see cops do in movies. Then he went and got a concealed-carry permit and didn't tell me. Until one

146

night I came on to him when he wasn't expecting it, and I felt it under his shirt.'

Trick managed not to laugh, but only just. 'Damn. Snepper had a package you *didn't* like?'

'That was the night before I called the hiatus. Something's not right with him. You think I'm the one who worries? It's like...I don't know what it's like. He kept promising me he wasn't scared of someone coming after him, but a year ago he told me he hated guns.'

'And he can't change his mind?'

'Of course he can, that's not the point. What if he actually pulls it on someone at the wrong time?'

'He wouldn't. He's not stupid.'

'No. He's emotional. All the time. He's on medication to stop suicidal thoughts, and it doesn't always work. That's someone you think should own a gun? He lied on the forms to get that permit. I get it, maybe shooting targets is a good release, something for him to do that he likes. Until the day it's not.'

He's right, Trick thought. *There's no arguing with this just for the sake of it.* 'Here's what you're going to do. Go back to the bunkhouse tonight and use that load in your pants on Kia. As bigtime as you can make it. Get him one-night happy. Tell him you're staying and you want him to stay too. Get your relationship going again. His breakfast will never have tasted so good.'

'That doesn't deal with this.'

'The problem isn't the gun, Kyle. It's his mental health that's making you worry. So instead of worrying, you're going to help get him healthy, then you're going to talk to him as the person who loves him about how you both feel about guns. Then *I* talk to him and tell him

147

I don't want one kept in this house. Or maybe I think about this and I change my mind. You're the one who wanted to be my bodyguard. Your fists might not always be fast enough.'

'I already thought of that, smartass. If you pull a gun on someone, you're more likely to get shot. You keep one in your house, you're more likely to shoot a family member than a burglar. He's not keeping that fucking thing.'

'Forgive me an obvious choice of words, but don't go into this shooting from the hip. If he really likes shooting that much, then maybe this is the compromise part of you and him. You can't just give him that blowjob and say, "I've been naughty for you so now you've gotta ditch the gun for me." Couples who do nothing but trade end up divorced.' Trick sniggered. 'Or they shoot each other.'

'You're a fuck, you know that?' Kyle at least sounded happy though. 'Fine, I get it. Compromise. I've gotta go before the whole night's gone and I've slept with you instead. How do I look?'

'Like someone who just sucked his brother's dick.'

'Har har har. You at least got some fur gel in this place? Some cologne? Scent?'

'Yeah, but you don't need any of it. If Kia wants to have style, let *him* put it on you. That's what he does. He'll probably find work here quicker than the rest of us. Think he'd be an on-set stylist for us if we got somewhere?'

'I was already thinking about it.'

'Good. So was I. Go help him get back on track.'

* * *

Trick watched his brother from his penthouse bedroom, confident that Kyle wouldn't look up or look back as he walked down the beach. He didn't. Trick knew he was going to crash as soon as he hit his bed, and he looked out to sea with a sigh of satisfaction and a grin from ear to ear.

It didn't beat me tonight. Nor did Dad's little game. Nor did my sassy brother. Who's going to be a whole lot of fun in ways I'd never even bargained for. I got him to stay. I actually did.

What else can I get?

Movement caught the corner of his eye, and he looked over to see Lottie looking at him from the balcony of what he guessed was her bedroom. She'd stepped out to smoke the cigarette she held in her right hand.

'Hi, Trick.'

'Hi. Does your mom know?'

She smiled. 'I don't think so. But would I give a shit?'

There's something about that girl, he thought. *There's something about this whole place. It all feels so good.*

'Oh, I'm just saying hi to my neighbour,' Lottie said, looking behind her. Trick made out at least two voices inside the room.

'Will he buy us some vodka?' one of them said.

Trick shook his head and smiled, and Lottie was already waving her friend's comment off and shaking hers too.

149

If Kyle's conscience would have allowed it, I'd have fucked him and I'd have loved it. But let it never be said that I bought most likely underage girls a bottle. Or went to their sleepover. Dad would kill me. Especially if it were lions. Especially the daughter of MGM's face. Who could buy their vodka anyway. They just want me to go over there.

I've got to have her as my agent. Maybe not as my first, but please let her stick to her plan. There's something good in this.

'You never came to our barbeque. Mom thinks you were all embarrassed or something. Or "Oh my God, the otter next door doesn't like us!"' She put her hand to her head, palm outwards, as if about to swoon.

'Shit,' Trick muttered, realising she was right. He and Sandy had forgotten all about it. 'Sorry, I forgot. I was too busy taking Sandy to the hospital to get checked for otter apnoea.'

'You didn't actually do that, did you?'

'I wasn't born yesterday.' *I bet her mother still thinks it's a real thing.*

'You know, there was some idiot swimming on a tide night earlier; I watched him walk down the beach without even checking the boards. Looked like an otter.'

Trick shrugged. 'Wouldn't know.'

'Sure,' Lottie said. 'Night! Call me when you're famous!'

Trick went inside, pulled off his speedos, and was asleep within seconds of sprawling back onto his bed.

Chapter Nine

Trick woke up to his phone ringing. He knew who it would be.

'Kia.'

'*What* did you say to him last night?' It wasn't really a question. Kia sounded the kind of happy that meant he'd either slept like a baby or had been up all night letting Kyle find euphoria triggers on every inch of him. He took a deep breath, purred, then whispered, 'What did you do to him? Go on, tell me.'

'We had what you might call a slightly interactive conversation. I made him a promise though. Just like you.'

Kia growled playfully. 'You didn't fuck. I'd have known. I'd have smelt it. Whatever you did though...oh *God*, Trick, thank you! I've never slept like that in my life. I hate to say it, but that time with you? He beat it. There's you doing it confidently, then there's him doing it when he just goes nuts.'

'You soak the otter?'

'And then some. Just wait till I tell you what position he got me in. I don't even know how he got me there, just that he was fucking me and…it's gonna be a month until either of us can get hard again. I just slept for eight hours and I'm still coming down.' Kia took a breath so deep Trick would never have thought him capable of holding that much air. 'I switched from the bubble gum vape flavour, y'know. Know what I'm on now?'

'What?'

'Sweet, *sweet* caramel.'

Trick grinned. 'Talk dirty to me, snepper, talk dirty to me! When you take that stuff down, I bet you can still smell otter.'

Kia sucked a breath through his nose. 'Otter caramel. They should market this. Okay, Trick, seriously, can you control this?'

'Course I can. We set a few ground rules last night.'

'I know. He told me he's staying. I'm staying too. Can I move in today? I've kinda got this hot fantasy about playing snep-in-the-middle.'

'Steady on. Yeah, you can move in, but I don't quite know how to introduce Sandy to me playing *that* game if it's me and my brother doing it with you.' *He might not go for me and Kyle having that kind of fun at all,* Trick thought. *I couldn't hide it from him if he didn't. Could I? It wouldn't be right. Just amazingly hot.*

'You know, I was wrong, Trick. You *are* a kind and considerate otter.'

'Oh, stop it, you'll ruin our good thing. When you're between me and Kyle, I'm being selfish. I want the fun end.'

'Which one's that?'

'Whichever one I feel like at the time.' *Nice way to wake up,* Trick thought, even though he was now realising he must have slept until at least midday. He put his hands down his pants. 'Can I ask just one teeny tiny favour?'

'Name it.'

'Can I hear that sexy purr of yours? Do it like I'm there, rubbing the soft part behind your ears, and you can feel my boner poking at your butt.'

Kia needed no time to get warmed up. He gave Trick a good five minutes. 'My head's a little light and I need some coffee. Can you hurry up and come?'

'It's okay, I don't want to. I just like that sound. Wish otters could do it.' He took his hand out. 'Kia, there's just something I gotta ask.'

'What?'

'Ah, forget it, it'll ruin the moment. Sure, about moving in, let's get your stuff over today. I'll come help. I've gotta say hi to everyone and tell them about this place. I know how to make up for my absence. I've got an idea. You got much spare cash? We need to buy a barbeque. Party we're gonna have tonight, the face of MGM's gonna be there. But don't tell anybody. Just say I've got a special guest in mind. Get everybody stocked on booze; I'll hide the good stuff in the fridge for us when they've all gone back to Phoenix.'

What was better? Trick wondered. *The sex Kia had last night or how I've just put a brand new, life-affirming thought in his head: he's not going back.*

'If we're having a party, I need to style you.'

'Style Dolphin first. It'll help with the whole back-on-track thing.'

'Alright. As long as you ask whatever question you're dodging.'

153

Trick sighed. 'Did you buy a gun, snepper?'

'Ughhhhh,' Kia said, at least still sounding happy. 'That sassy otter, he started about all that again? I'm not getting rid of it. I finally find something else I enjoy doing and he has to get all uptight thinking it's another way for me to kill myself? If I didn't have a gun, there are a hundred other ways I could do it. I'm not going to. Things are fine now, and it's partly because I enjoy shooting. Target ranges only, I keep telling him. So just *please* can you not do what I know you're about to?'

'What am I about to do?'

'Tell me you're not having me in your house if I bring a gun in it. Before you tell me you really weren't gonna do that, I don't suppose you told "Dolphin" your little part in me getting into this, did you?'

'When I took you to that shooting range, it wasn't because I wanted to,' Trick said. 'It was just a better option than letting you out of my sight that day, the way you told me you were feeling.' *Then what did I see? The snep who grudgingly followed along came to life in the space of ten minutes and said, 'Hey, can I try shooting that too?'* He'd done it with the kind of relish he'd never had in life before. Apart from maybe when he styled someone to look good, or drew art. This was like a quick fix version of that. Kia Renfield had turned out to be a deadeye shot. Far better than Trick in half the time.

'You probably saved my life that day,' Kia said. 'I'm sorry if you didn't do it how you intended and you're not totally in control of your pet depressed friend, but this is me. I can find another place to live, if you want.'

'Don't be silly,' Trick said. 'Just promise me you'll buy a safe when you can afford one; I don't want that thing left lying around.'

'It's a gun, Trick. You can call it a gun.'

'Alright, I don't want your gun left lying around. I don't even want to see it unless you're taking it out to go to a range. Guns are for movie sets only. That whole day we spent together taught me why I *don't* like them, and if you got an NRA membership, I never want to know.'

'Actually, I didn't.'

I bet he's lying, Trick thought, *but that's fine. I'll be lied to once in a while for the sake of friends.* 'Wake Kyle up for me, would you? I wanna talk to him for a minute.'

'You'll have to wait until he gets back from the beach. He went to the early morning swim-out. He's probably stuffing down breakfast at Winslow's with a whole den's worth of otters.'

Good boy, Trick thought.

Speaking of Winslow's, where was Sandy? 'I've got to go, snepper. I don't know where Sandy is.'

'He didn't come home last night?'

'I don't know, but he's not in my bed.' Trick rang off and headed downstairs. Sandy was asleep on the sofa again, this time having put a duvet over himself. Trick reached his hand under gently and rubbed the other otter's back. Nothing. He knelt down, a little unease creeping in despite how this had turned out last time. Stroking Sandy's head caused no reaction either, or his muzzle. 'Come on, Sandy-paws, give me a breath. Let's have some oxygen. Please?'

You don't breathe out *oxygen, dummy.* It didn't matter, as soon Trick felt a deep breath of air over his hand and saw the blanket rise up. Trick sighed and held a finger to Sandy's neck. Feeling his pulse run at twenty per minute made the whole room feel like time was dilating inside it. 'My otter,' he said, quietly.

I'm going to have to tell him about Kyle. Thank God we didn't go all the way. Perhaps I was really the one who couldn't have lived with it.

Only then did Trick notice what else was in the room. Paper, page after page of it, strewn with red and black ink. Trick knew a script when he saw it. There was a laptop in the centre of the table. It was a newish HP, the fans still one decibel above silent as they ticked over.

'What you working on, Sandy-paws?' More importantly, what secrets could that laptop be holding? Sandy had barely scraped together thirty bucks for a name change but had this? It was obviously packed into a bag and brought from Maine. The last thing he grabbed from his parents' place? Because it had this script on it?

Leave it alone, Trick told himself. *If that were your privacy, you'd be furious if someone invaded it.* It probably had a password anyway. He found the title page of Sandy's script. '*Dictator Envy,* by Sandy Rickwood.'

He looked down at Sandy. 'Damn, for a nearly comatose otter, you do pick a good title out of the bag.' Trick thought about looking for the first page amongst the chaos, then decided simply to put the title page back where he'd found it. From all the red ink, Trick guessed that Sandy's laptop held the master copy. One line caught his eye:

Starvos (voiceover): "What can I possibly do?" It goes around in my head like a virus inside a centrifuge, and I keep thinking, if someone doesn't shut off the power then all my tubes are just going to shatter, before the core blows with them. One thought alone gets me to sleep: I could make sure I'm surrounded with the right people when it happens. Yeah, that's what I could do.

Another page: *Starvos: World War Three? We've been counting down to it for a long time. Let's get on with it. Whoever's left can build what we'll never have before it. Avoiding Four's easy: most of the stuff we ever fought over just won't be there. Maybe all that'll be left is some small corner of the world where there are just kids. They'll never know what happened. I hope they'll just be smart enough to survive, then forget all those questions.*

'That road to Cali took you to some *way* dark places, Sandy Rickwood.' Trick found the cast of characters page, but not before one other line:

Faulkner: We've still got a job to do, Jack.

Tasker: Yeah. Bring Anthony Starvos in. You know why he killed the president?

Pulsifer: Why?

Tasker: To make sure someone like us didn't.

Trick looked at the cast list. *Special Agent Jack Tasker - a ?wolf ?fox ?tiger. Assistant Director Mitch Pulsifer - a wolf. Special Agent Sadie Faulkner - a panther. Lieutenant (rt'd) Anthony Starvos, US Marine Corps - a ???*

'Cop saves the world from marine gone off the rails,' Trick said, sitting on the edge of the table. Not bad. A little bit *Punisher*, but every movie answered to an influence. There would be more to it, Trick knew. This was a first draft. Whatever was in Sandy's head had to be bigger than another cat-and-mouse copycat film. Why was it called *Dictator Envy*, just for a start?

Trying to decipher the rest of Sandy's notes would take too long, if only because half the pages weren't numbered. Trick decided to think about it during a walk down the beach to the surf shack. Already several hours behind with his day, the first thing he was going to do was cram some fruit from the Robinsons' welcome basket as he walked, grab a coffee on the way through at Winslow's, and try every surf shop in the bay until he came home with a job.

He stopped at the door, realising he already had the answer to the three questions. He took one of the sticky notes from the pad on the fridge door, wrote what he needed to, and left it stuck to Sandy's nose before leaving through the back door.

* * *

When Sandy awoke an hour later, he sleepwalked his way through making coffee and waffles before he realised there was a note stuck to his muzzle.

Morning! Tried to wake you but the otter apnoea had you again. Here's the first three things you need to know today:

1: I'm Tasker.

2: Starvos is a wolverrine.

3: Fast Eddie Kowalski could do with a career comeback.

Sandy sighed happily. His new boyfriend was a dreamer. Nobody was ever going to make this movie. The only directors who could ever do it justice would never work with Kowalski, however perfect a choice he suddenly seemed for Starvos. Otters didn't save the world either.

Unless, Sandy thought, *they're an otter like Trick. He saved* my *world. That's the only reason I'm glad I brought that script all the way from Maine instead of burning it. Somebody had to exist out there in this shit-heap of a world with enough hope left in their soul to play Jack Tasker.*

* * *

When Trick got in, Sandy was watching the cooking channel and looking contented. He was drinking a loaded-looking fruit-juice cocktail but looked sober enough that it was probably his first. On the table in front of him was a neat stack of paper, the title page of Sandy's script on the top.

'You haven't even read it yet and you want to play my MC?'

Trick slid the door closed. 'If something feels right, it usually is.'

'There are lines that don't work if Tasker's an otter.'

'So rewrite it.' Trick took a sip of Sandy's drink, only to find it was a straight, unadulterated fruit juice blend. 'Go on. One more draft before you go to work this evening.'

'Already did that. After the one I stayed up half of last night finishing. It better have been worth it.'

'You actually wrote a script,' Trick said, lifting Sandy's legs, sitting down, and deftly dumping them back into this lap. 'How long did it take you?'

'A year, to get to that. Mostly on the road.'

'Imagine I'm my dad,' Trick said. 'Pitch it to me.'

'Urgh, I'm not up for role play right now, Trick. I suck at pitches. You ever had to write a synopsis? It's total hell. That's why you're going to read it tonight when I'm at work and *you're* going to tell me how to pitch it. Maybe after we do one more draft together and call it both our work. You want to be Tasker, that's your price.'

'I could work with that.'

'Yeah, but let's face it, nobody's going to make it. It's just nice to see you dream. I wasn't going to show it to anybody until I met you. It's probably shit. One angry otter on a road trip trying to work the world out, for some dumb reason.'

'It's your first script. One day you're going to treasure it. It won't matter if we never make it, or if it's shit. Which it won't be. I already caught some one-liners. You already pitched me Tasker. I like the name. It sounds like Talisker, the whisky. You want a drink?'

'I can't work drunk. Or sleepy. You want to drink, you carry on. Oh yeah, did you get a job today?'

'Actually, I did. Artie Santoro's.'

Sandy sat up. 'Artie Santoro? You sure you wanna do that? Most of the kids don't last a month with him. Nobody can put up with his crap.'

'You hear that from the kids who come into Winslow's to get shit-faced because they got fired? It's because he can't put up with theirs. Half the kids on these beaches stink of entitlement before they've even opened their mouths. I've worked in a kitchen where I sweated buckets for minimum wage. I won't get fired.' Trick winked. 'Wonder if Artie likes otters.'

Sandy went wide eyed, sat up further and laughed. 'You as much as *look* at that dog's dick and I'm never riding you bareback again.'

'I'm kidding,' Trick said. *Actually,* Trick thought, *for some reason, I find it hard to imagine Artie even making love to his own wife. He's the companionship type.* 'If I ever have to have sex on set, I hope I never have to do a dog. Otters smell like something you could drink when they're wet. Dogs just smell like a rug you never washed in half a year.'

'Whatever movie that is, I'd keep that line out of your audition,' Sandy said. He shifted back a little. 'Trick, there's...something I've gotta ask. I'm not sure how you're going to take this, but...this morning when I came in. This place kinda smelt like sex, and a lot of Hilfiger to try and cover it up. I only smelt you and one other. You were meant to be talking to your brother last night, right? I'm sorry, this is dumb. You wouldn't have...right?'

Play it cool and it will be, Trick thought. Or rather he hoped. 'I don't fuck my brother, Sandy-paws. But you were right about the smell. Damn, that's one hell of a nose you've got. Something tells me you're going to learn the right trade, getting into food. What happened last night was just a bit unexpected. Thank God you're the only person I need to tell the truth to.'

Trick told him. Sandy stayed quiet and still through most of it.

'Your own brother's got a crush on you,' Sandy said. 'You made him so mad that instead of knocking your teeth out he kissed you?'

'My brother's a very emotional person,' Trick said. 'If he's not worrying about everything, he's as laid back as a sloth on Xanax. If he's not angry, he's laughing his butt off. You get it, fire and ice. If that was what it took to find that happy temperature in between, I'm kinda glad it happened. A healthy relationship with me and no more secrets means he'll have a much better one with everyone else. Kia called me this morning. What he told me? I know I did the right th—'

'Trick.'

'What?'

'I'd love to get between you two.' Sandy moved up close to him and licked the tip of his nose. 'I'd love to watch you and your brother fuck. But hey, not going to happen. Good you made the rules. But if you ever broke them, it'd drive me wild.'

Seriously? Trick thought. *Either this guy's seen it all on the road or he's as good at putting on the act someone wants to hear as I am.*

He needed to be more careful with Sandy. Something about him felt unexpectedly risky all of a sudden. Was this what got him thrown against the wall? A constant push of boundaries with someone who unlocked his daring, naughty side a little more than they'd ever expected to?

But shit, this is hot. He hooked his thumbs in Sandy's pants. 'You wanna fuck right now, with the food channel on?'

Sandy grabbed the remote and switched it off. 'I want you on my lap with you looking right in my eyes.'

Sandy was already hard enough to get inside Trick as soon as he had his pants down.

Trick came before Sandy and thought it could go on all night until his partner laid him down almost asleep on the sofa and went out to fetch some food.

* * *

When Trick woke up, the smell in the place made him ravenous. It was like his mother's cooking – heavy on meat and veg alike, with a distinct hint of booze washing the air behind it. Whatever Sandy was cooking, he'd thrown a bunch of herbs into it too. It smelt filling and rich, and Trick's nose was at work, a deep feeling of longing all through his stomach, inside his chest, a high-on-life feeling.

'There you go.' Sandy held the plate out for him. It looked like meatballs and gravy on a bed of potatoes and spring vegetables. Trick realised with the first bite that they were veggie balls instead, yet they had just as much taste as meat.

'Oh man, *so* good,' he said. 'And...damn it was hot fucking you like that. I think that was actually my best time.'

'You *did* shoot one hell of a load. And you were yelping. I've never heard an otter make that kind of noise. Seriously, *I* got you that hot?'

163

'I want to be with you, Sandy. You were right. I want us to be special. Whoever else we have to do, business or pleasure, we always come back to each other.' *What am I doing?* Trick thought. *If I had a ring, I'd be losing my head even more right now. It's a good job I don't. I've known him less than a week.*

I know he's perfect. This is a new kind of impulsive love for someone. Maybe this is how Kyle feels about me.

'Someone's hungry,' Sandy said, looking at how fast Trick was emptying his plate.

'Someone's an amazing cook,' Trick said. 'My mom would be jealous. By the way, we'd better learn how to make all that food Dad stocked me with last for a while. We're both on minimum wage right now. We've got to learn how to stretch it.'

'You'd know. My parents were rich. All I know how to do's spend money or get it spent on me. Until a year ago. I learned how to live off nothing. But I can feel all the old ways coming back like a smoker who just started again. You're right. We'd better set budgets.'

You weren't talking like that until right now, Trick thought. A simile in everyday speech? That script writing had switched Sandy's brain right on. Good sign.

'We'll be fine,' Trick said. 'Kia will get an income soon enough too. There's always someone wanting to hire a stylist. Kyle? We can carry Kyle for a bit if we need to. You need to meet him. We need a party, right here. Actually, scratch that. We need a joint party. I'll go talk to next door. We forgot to go to their barbecue. We need to invite them to one of our own and get MGM's face to

164

bring enough food to feed a whole bunch of otters. You've gotta meet my friends.'

'I've got tomorrow night off.'

'Perfect. I'll set it up. Tonight, I'm reading your script.'

* * *

By the time Sandy got home that evening, Trick was on his third Talisker and reading his favourite sections of the script though a second time, alive with the kind of excitement he hadn't felt since before his trip here. No, this was something better. This was the kind of rush you only got from seeing years of your life in advance, knowing what the perfect way to spend them would be. Trick's perfect way would be remembering this script his new partner had written every time he needed to remind himself what he was really working for.

He wanted to yell Sandy's name and tell him to get his ass in here now, but he waited, containing himself. 'This...is...*good*!' he said, putting the pages back together. 'Sandy, *how* could you have thought of throwing this away? This is your entire future, right here.'

'Oh, stop it. You want a...ah, you've already got a drink. I just want some hot tea. You want that too? You got jasmine?'

'Forget tea, and booze. Come sit down, we've got to talk about this.'

'Trick, come on, it's not that great.' Sandy went to the kitchen to make his tea.

165

Trick followed him in, whisky in hand, and set it on the bar. 'Sandy. Look at me.'

Sandy switched the kettle off and turned. 'Okay, I'm looking.'

'I know you probably don't like your own work that much right now. You've spent all year writing it and the last two days making yourself sick of it. But all the pain it took to create that story was worth it. I've seen a lot of movies. I *know* movies. I'm a great big geek for stuff that's not real. I fall in love with it. Or I think it's dreck and I watch it anyway, but I've gotta tell you, your movie might be a script, but I feel like I already watched it. Will you just trust me for a minute? Because my tail is twitching. Those pages on our coffee table in there? I think they really could make history.'

Sandy gave a disbelieving yet good-natured laugh. 'Why?'

'Come on, you can't ask me to explain it. Just like I can't always explain the stuff that turns me on. I just know when I'm feeling it, and the why really doesn't matter. If it's hot, it's hot.'

'Yeah, I get it,' Sandy said. 'But will that script be hot to anyone else?'

'You know how we're going to find out?' Trick leaned on the bar. 'We're going to make that movie. Us. You still think you suck at pitches? You don't need to worry; we're not going to pitch to anyone else's film company. We're keeping it. For when we're big enough to make it ourselves. Or for when somebody comes along who'll do it our way, no questions, no compromises.'

Sandy switched the kettle back on. 'That could take years, Trick. Years you'll spend forgetting about it, until all this excitement you got from reading that script's just become one more line of smoke in a *really* big atmosphere.'

'I won't. I promise. This is my quest for the holy grail, my *Citizen Kane*, my *Goodfellas*, my *Silence of the Lambs*; name any iconic movie you want. I don't care if it takes years before anyone else besides us reads this. But hey, you really want to test this? Let me give it to Kia. Maybe my brother. They won't just tell me what I want to hear – believe me, they're good at doing the reverse. Years is fine. I can't play Tasker yet. Not now I've seen the whole thing. I've got to grow into him. But I'm not seeing anybody else play him. Will you trust me on this? This could be our thing.'

'Well sure,' Sandy said. 'It doesn't hurt to dream, right? I'm glad you liked it that much. To me it's just a bunch of shit I wrote to try and keep living. Half of it's rage and the other half's hope, and I don't really know which one wins. Maybe neither of them does. Was the ending right?'

'When Starvos is on his knees begging Tasker to kill him? It was perfect. Why do you think you let Tasker do it?'

Something switched on in Sandy now, and Trick knew he'd unintentionally tapped into a more positive wavelength. Sandy poured his tea and stirred it, then gave the teaspoon a flick, like Starvos flicking blood from a combat knife in the scene where he dispatched a South American dictator backed by the ex-American president. 'Why do *you* think he did it?'

'Good had to beat evil. Starvos saw himself as one layer of good. Tasker was the layer above. Starvos couldn't live in the world where everything got rebuilt out of chaos. There'd be no place for him. There couldn't be a show trial either. So which one of them's the hero? Maybe that's the idea. Nobody's really supposed to know. But most people who go see it when it's made will probably think it was Tasker. Because that's the answer that doesn't require anyone to rethink right from wrong. Maybe sometimes killing a dictator or a president *could* be the right thing to do, but most of us couldn't do it even if we knew it. Tasker couldn't. He could only kill the guy who *could* do it, and secretly thank him. Then maybe hope the world would rebuild so all those questions never needed to be asked again. Killing Starvos was the last stage in a great big reset. I like to think they're both the hero. Tasker's just the one who deserved to live more.'

Sandy rolled his eyes. 'Tasker kills Starvos because Starvos was based on my crazy fuck of an ex-boyfriend. The one who threw me against a wall. Because I dared tell him his activism shit wasn't going to achieve a goddamn thing. Tasker's the guy who tries to make the world better without resorting to all the behaviour people think they can justify because they're angry enough to go through with it, but really it only makes things worse. There's only one hero in that script, Trick. Starvos kicking off World War Three wasn't a good thing.'

'The way you've set the world up, war and massive death was inevitable. No talking would have stopped it.

168

Starvos was the guy who wanted to be on the right side of history.'

'Not much good if there's no world left to make any history in.'

'But there is. You left that film with its world still there at the end.'

'We could debate this all night, Trick. What's the point? It's not real. It's just an outlet for a few things I felt about the last year of my life.'

'*That's* the point, Sandy. This has got soul. It's not just another cat-and-mouse action flick.'

'I'm happy you're so in love with it, Trick, but I don't even like it that much. It makes me feel kinda guilty.'

That much Trick understood. 'Because it's so violent? Gotcha. It's downright fucked up in places, but it's not just for the sake of it. You wrote fucked up because you felt it. You wrote angry doing as angry does...I dunno, to *stop* yourself doing it? To work out why it was done to you? I don't have to play shrink; only you know where it really came from. But this is half the reason I know it's gold. You tried to get comfortable with being *un*comfortable. That's often the start of a good story.'

'You really think Starvos could be considered a hero? If anyone could think that then I don't want that film in the world.'

'Maybe you're right. There's a bit too much fucked up to consider him a hero. When I think about it some more maybe *I'll* get a little guilt. But that's fine. Maybe there should be a more heroic side to him. That's what Draft 3's for.'

'No.'

169

'Okay, no. Not right now. I know what burnout is.' *Wait long enough and I can get your heart back in this.* 'But listen. I've spent all night having these kinds of debates with myself, until you got home. This is a thinking man's film. It's not just rage or hope; it's a great big debate you could have for years and not know a true answer to. You wrote all that. *You.* I won't throw you against a wall because we don't see things the same way. Your audience won't either. Get some distance between you and your script and it'll come calling for you.'

'I seriously doubt it.'

'Come on. All the hours you spent writing it, you never once went to sleep with dreams of seeing it actually made into something millions of people might watch? You never thought of them all seeing your name attached to something good? It *is* good. If there's any hope in this world, then it's because people keep talking. Why not give them something explosive like *Dictator Envy* to talk about?'

'Big explosive time out right here,' Sandy said, forcing a smile. 'You're in love with my script *and* me. Can we go back to just me for tonight?'

'Sure. Okay. If you'll answer one more question for me.'

Sandy sighed. 'What?'

'If you don't love it yourself, even the tiniest amount, why did you get it out again? And by the way, sorry, two questions then, how did you print it? Did Dad put a printer in one of these rooms for me? Because I didn't spot it.'

'Erm...I did it at work.'

'You went to work and left me the script right there, and it wasn't there when you got in last night.' Why would Sandy lie? Trick let it hang for a moment, then laughed when he clocked it. 'You went next door, didn't you? You asked the Robinsons if you could print a script off. I bet you even offered to pay for all the paper.'

'Errr...'

'Was MGM's face there?'

'You're going to call him that *to* his face one day if you don't start calling him Gerry instead.'

'Gerry? His wife called him Gerald the other day. Now he's Gerry?' Trick smirked as Sandy shuffled his feet. 'Oh yeah. You wanted the MGM lion to know you wrote a script.'

'Gimme a fucking break already, Trick. It was a dumb idea. I've been feeling like a dummy all evening. He's never going to be interested in it. He probably rolled his eyes as soon as I left. The guy probably gets it every day. Just another stupid dumbass boy who wants to make it look like he's dreaming of bigtime.'

'Wrong. A smart otter who dared knock on his door and ask a favour. Sure, he probably won't help us get it made. He might not even talk about it. Until we *do* get it made, and then he's got a story to tell about how you knocked on the door. Promotion. Maybe he'll even tell a few people and laugh, but we'll see if he's laughing when one of them calls us, just to make sure MGM doesn't get that movie. But hey, let's have that big time out you were on about.' Trick picked up his whisky, the ice having mostly melted into it, and drew Sandy to the back door. 'It's a nice evening.'

171

Trick let the time out last a good twenty minutes. He thought about asking where Sandy had gotten the idea for how Starvos had killed the U.S. president from and wondered if maybe he'd rather not know. The whole thing sent shivers through him as much as it had reading it for the first time.

Starvos: Morphine, right? [fills a syringe] *You think you deserve to go out on a high? Decent people go out on a high if they're lucky. Nice comfy bed in a hospital. You?* [holds the bottle under his nose.] *Sniff it, motherfucker.*

Steckler: [Sniffs] *No! No, please!*

Starvos: Every day when I clean the shit out of my toilet, I ask myself, how well could this clean the blood in a guy's veins? When it's as rotten as yours is, I'll give it an extra five minutes before it really gets to work. [Injects him] *I'd tape your mouth shut, but you know as well as I do nobody's coming for you. This isn't a silent puppet show. I want noise. Just like your presidency. Let's see how you tweet about this.*

Nothing happens for a moment, then Steckler starts screaming.

'Hey Trick.'

'What?'

'Which part's haunting you already?'

Trick suppressed a shiver. 'How *did* you come up with the injecting bleach thing? That's...a good actor could make that scene stay with an audience for life.'

'When I was in the hospital, they gave me some shot for something, and all I could smell at the time was the bleach from down the corridor. I put the two thoughts together. It nearly made me throw up. Just like thinking about how I once supported a real life Steckler.'

'You? Really?'

'Uh-huh. I was a fat otter *and* a member of Young Republicans once. But hey, that's all gone. I'm Sandy now.'

A Young Republican with an abusive activist boyfriend who reconsidered his entire values system on a road trip? Trick remembered his promise not to ask about Sandy's past. *Yeah, I can believe that's the guy who wrote* Dictator Envy. *Changing everything you ever believed in after you nearly lost your life and your parents turned out to be assholes would be as metaphorically painful as an injection of bleach. Especially if you had to admit that maybe some of the things your boyfriend said before the abuse might have actually gotten through to you.*

No wonder Sandy didn't want this film made. Whenever he worked on it, it was probably an attempt to come to terms with something different every time. Buoyed up on everything one minute, crashing back down the next. It all fitted. The great big time out was probably a good idea. It was only fair that Trick let it last months.

'Hey Sandy, listen. We can put *Dictator Envy* away if you really want to.'

Sandy didn't seem to have heard him. 'Look, there's your friend the cheetah. I think he's looking at you.'

Trick looked the other way down the beach to see Armando was indeed there, this time wearing a cowboy hat, a black t-shirt to go with it, and a necklace that looked like it was made in Arizona somewhere. *He should be chewing a cigar with a pose like that,* Trick thought.

Armando pointed a finger. 'Not again, *pendejo*! You can drown out there next time. Don't think I'm not watching your little *casa* for when you come swimming!'

'Yeah? Try scrambling into a boat as fast as you can shoot your *boca* off next time!'

'Las nutrias deben permanacer en las ciudades, Dixon. Es que no quiero verte llorando!'

'I should stay in the city? You don't wanna see me crying? Try not having a cat as a beach warden. Then I wouldn't laugh so much that I ended up in tears!'

Armando was walking over now.

'Someone's gonna get mauled,' Sandy said.

'He's fine,' Trick said. 'He came to my party.'

'You knew him before this vacation?'

'I don't know, I think so. I saw this chee watching me have a few lessons with Javi. I think he was checking me out.'

'Hey *nutria*, can't insult me back in Spanish, huh? I think you were a *maricón* even before I see your boyfriend. No offense, you both look as pretty as the tide board you don't learn to read. You ever felt cat's tongue? Rough. It's too bad you don't drown last night. Giving you a kiss of life would be nice wake up call, hmm? When you wake up and your mouth feel like full of sand.'

Trick leaned on the rail. 'Tell your English teacher "Need cover verbs again."'

'Say what you like. You're another *nutria* who's gonna go under and out to sea if there isn't someone like

174

me watching. That's California, Dixon, not just the *mar*. My boat was there. You just lose track of time.' Armando winked, tipped his hat, and walked away.

'Hey Armando,' Sandy called. 'That's your name, right? Rodriguez?'

'*Si. Y como te llamas?*'

'Sandy.'

'*Santi*? Like Santiago? You don't look Hispanic, *nutria mía.*'

'I'm not, I'm from...who cares where I'm from? It's *Sandy*, with a d not a t. Like Kofax. You ever watch baseball? Actually, never mind that. You ever take an acting class?'

'Acting? *Teatro*? No, *nunca. Porqué*? You think I'm entertaining?'

'Yeah. I kinda do.'

Armando shrugged. '*Bueno*. Tell your boyfriend "Need learn to read fucking board."' He winked at Trick again, and this time he took off at a running pace and yelled something that Tricked presumed was 'Catch me if you can.'

Sandy looked at him.

'Don't ask. I fucked up last night.'

'I don't care about that,' Sandy said. 'Well, okay, I do care that you nearly drowned out there because you didn't check the boards, but I get it, what happened with your brother probably left you not thinking very hard. Except maybe about him.'

'Why did you ask him if he took an acting class?'

'You didn't get the vibe from all that? From how he talked to you? How he looked? Come on, Trick. Forget

175

Kowalski. We'd never get him anyway. *That* was Starvos. That guy.'

'You can't be serious.'

'Just think about it. Run the script through your head again. *That* could be your hero side. He was once a chee on a beach who saved lives. Joined the marines because he figured he could up the game even higher. Then war and dumb presidents made him fall out of love with the world. Just maybe not the world, but the way it was heading. So now saving lives has a whole new meaning. Save everybody from the crazy people at the top *and* themselves. Progression. What if Tasker knew him once? What if I copied that entire exchange you two just had into their backstory?'

Trick thought on it for a moment. 'It'd be interesting. Hell, it'd be good. But I still think Kowalski. Not a chee who never took an acting class.'

'We should get him to one. Come on. Even if we *could* get Kowalski, he'd as likely wreck the whole production as make the movie gold. Have you even kept up with that guy lately? Seen what he's been in the news for? He's a brilliant actor and a brilliant train wreck all at once.'

'Exactly. So when he crashes for a couple of years and then stages a comeback, he'll need a comeback film. When there's a list of directors a mile long who won't work with him and a list of studios that say exactly what you just did, he'll have to find an unknown one. Maybe two otters with a hot idea who might be known on the scene by then. And hey, Kowalski started in porn. I've heard he likes otters. He never fucked one on film because he keeps certain species special.'

'Okay, more dreams, more big ideas to dream about. But talk to Armando for me, would you? Just run with my back-up plan. It *is* my script. You'll never be Tasker unless I say so.'

Sure I will, Trick thought. *Because you just discovered your love of that script all over again, in the space of meeting one unlikely actor. But Armando will never be interested in acting.*

'Okay,' Trick said. 'For you. I'll ask him.'

Chapter Ten

Trick's iPhone was propped up against a stack of square dessert places on the coffee table, camera pointing at him and Sandy on the sofa.

'Okay, you ready? Am I turning the little red light on? Are we gonna enter into immortality?'

'Just press the damn button, Trick.'

Trick pressed it and sat back, hoping he was really wearing the kind of smile he imagined he was. 'Hi, I'm Trick.'

'I'm Sandy.'

'We're both eighteen, and we just moved to California.'

'Yeah.'

'So...yeah, we're otters.'

'What? "Yeah, we're otters"? Everyone knows we're otters just from looking at us.'

'That might have sounded cooler if you'd called me "dude" or something before you said it. More surf-beach kinda talk.'

'I am not calling you that. So much for our first ever video; you've got no idea what to say and you go for "Yeah, we're otters."'

Trick shrugged. 'Okay, what the hell. We're *clueless* otters. We just moved to Cali, and we have no idea what we're doing. I wanna be a pro surfer and an actor, just like all the rest who ever had the West Coast dream. Sandy wants to be a chef, and he's working in a fast-food surf shack. We're making this video because it's 2010, so it's all about YouTube and livestreaming, which...yeah, we're doing right now, and...we'll probably get about five likes. Then maybe someone will say we're cute and then nobody will ever hear from us again.'

'Until you're middle-aged and washing celebrities' cars for five bucks an hour making sad videos about what might have been.'

'Dude, how did that help?'

Sandy leaned back on the sofa, obviously not faking total lethargy. 'We're also gay.'

'Oh yeah, forgot to mention that.'

'Nobody cares, Trick. Nobody's gonna take any notice of us.'

'Come on, don't insult these three good people right here. Pandaface19, Spaceotter-underscore-90 and CaliDreamin49 are spending their leisure time watching us right now. Hi guys, how are you today?'

Sandy eye-rolled but at least sounded like he wanted to laugh. 'You sound like you're about to take their breakfast order.'

'Says the guy who works in a diner.'

'Okay, sure, let's pay them attention,' Sandy said. 'We've got a guy who I'm guessing's sixty-one and stuck in some snowy climate with wife and kids, dreaming of his hippie days in LA when he liked guys. Then there's a sci-fi nerd who's probably found us by accident and is gonna click off as soon as we say we know nothing about Star Trek, and...what kind of nickname is Pandaface19? I bet you're actually thirteen.'

'*Suck my dick, asshole,*' Pandaface19 wrote. '*I wanted to find cute otters, not fat ones.*'

'Oh boy,' Trick said, as Sandy looked instantly fired up.

'Oh really?' Sandy said. 'Seriously? We're doing the fat thing?'

He'd seen Sandy in tired and grumpy moods during their first month together, and once he'd seen a door slam. Now Sandy looked like he was going to take on Kyle for the angriest otter in the world title, except somehow he held it.

Pandaface19: '*Ya rly. How did you even get a thin boyfriend?*'

'I dunno,' Sandy said. 'How rich is dunking on someone for having a bit of a fat roll coming from a panda? How is it you guys eat bamboo all day and you're still the size of wrecking balls? I've always wanted to know.'

'*OHBURN*' Spaceotter_90 wrote and put an '*XD*' after it.

The curious thing, Trick thought, was that Sandy was smirking about this. Now he believed in Sandy's past more than ever, fending off one bully after another who said things about his weight, or size, or looks.

180

CaliDreamin49 said '@Pandaface19 not cool, why did you have to be so rude to him? He was just doing edgy put-down comedy. Besides, he had my number. I live in Colorado and I'd much rather be where he is. Except my boyfriend wanted to leave Cali for ski-slopes, so I did it because I love him.'

Pandaface19: 'Blah blah blah.'

Spaceotter_90: '@Pandaface19 I bet you're not really a panda, I bet YOU'RE a fat otter who nobody sits at a lunch table with and you sink like a brick in every swimming lesson.'

'Guys!' Sandy said. 'Enough. You know what? So what if he is really that? We can't all be like my boyfriend here who's probably dying to get his kit off just to show you why everybody should be looking at him on a beach.'

'Errrrr, not exactly,' Trick said, not sure why it suddenly bothered him. He had planned to do exactly that at some point, just not like this. Something about this felt unexpectedly wrong.

'Whatever,' Sandy said. 'You know what? I'm gonna take my shirt off.' He did it. 'There you go. I was a fat otter at school. I weighed 245 pounds. I got stuck in a...okay, that story's for another day, but I've been humiliated because of how I looked. We're all supposed to be thin, right? I don't care. Take your best look.' He bunched the roll that still hung around his stomach. 'I lost the weight, but I've still got loose skin, and there's a fat roll there. I'm not really a swimming otter. I've got thicker shoulders, and my chest doesn't quite match to my stomach; I kinda look more like a raccoon. But this

181

is me. And Pandaface19 is still here even though I'm not cute.'

CaliDreamin49: *'You go, boy! I'm a pudgy old wolf, and so's my boyfriend who's watching this, and it's about time we found a guy like you in the Cali hashtags. Body positive otter. You rock!'*

Spaceotter_90: *'I'm getting some popcorn.'*

Trick smiled. 'Okay, Spaceotter right there's getting popcorn. Told you people would pay attention; it's like we're on a cinema screen already.'

'You know what?' Sandy said. 'I'll raise you that popcorn. I'm gonna get a donut. I'm gonna get the whole box and I'm gonna eat a donut right here on screen.'

Pandaface19: *Achievement of the year right there.*

'Being mean to an online stranger. Yeah, *your* achievement this year's gonna be an award for originality.' Sandy got up and went to the kitchen.

Spaceotter_90: **munch munch munch**

'Okay, I was *not* expecting this for our first livestream,' Trick said.

Pandaface19: *Hey surfer-boy, YOU'RE cute.*

Trick felt the glow inside his chest that he knew would eventually become an itch in his pants. He managed not to awkwardly shift on the sofa. 'Yeah, I know.' *Don't play this for yourself. Back Sandy up.* 'But I guess we all have a different idea of cute, right?'

Sandy came back and sat down.

'I love this donut-eating otter right here.' He rubbed a hand down Sandy's back. 'I love what he looks like. He doesn't have to have the same body as me. How boring would that be? I'd rather be with him than anybody else on that beach out there, and I'd do it even if he gained all that weight he lost back.'

'Sweet, Trickster. Sweet,' Sandy said. 'Just like Krispy Kreme.' Sandy pointed at the jam-filled donut. 'Feed me that.'

'Feed you?'

'Yeah. Like you did the night I first came here.'

'Errr...that was kinda different.' Trick looked at the camera. 'I thought he was...' *You're about to tell them how vulnerable he was that night? Just feed him the donut, you idiot.* 'Y'know what? Sure. Okay.' He picked the donut up and held it near Sandy's mouth. 'Take a sniff of that. That smell sweet?'

Sandy closed his eyes and did it. 'Mmmm. So good.'

'Go on, take a bite.'

'Mmm.' Sandy bit it, chewed, swallowed, then started licking the jam that was about to run down Trick's hand. He caught Trick's hand with his tongue, then stuck his nose right against the donut and licked the sweetness off it. 'Mmmm, yeah. That's what I'm talking about.'

'You really like donuts, huh, Sandy-paws?'

Sandy took a satisfied deep breath and then another bite.

Trick's senses were fully in action now. He knew that kind of satisfaction. He looked down. Sandy had a bulge in his pants. Being fed was a turn-on to him? Damn, had Sandy himself known about it on their first night or had Trick awoken his knowledge of it?

Spaceotter_90: *'Hey body positive otter, is that a tent you've pitched there?'*

Don't put your hands in his pants, Trick thought. *These guys might well go wild for it, but just don't. Give them something for next time.*

I just thought that?

Trick brushed a hand suggestively behind Sandy's right ear and got him to open his eyes. 'Gonna eat that last bite?'

Sandy ate it, then cleaned Trick's fingers, savouring each one. Then he looked at the screen. 'Yeah okay, well done Spaceotter, I just got a boner. But it's staying in those pants. Yeah, I like being fed. It's a turn-on. It works with fruit too. Anything sweet enough. I've learned to like what food does for me.'

Pandaface19: *'Why don't you eat surfer-boy's dick? See how sweet that is?'*

Sandy ignored him. 'You know what, guys? The diet industry is worth billions because the shit they sell doesn't work. People keep going back thinking "It will this time." Trust me, it won't. You know how I lost this weight? I took up walking. I ate more healthier foods and fewer donuts. It took a year. But forget the anti-sugar campaigns and everything you get from fitness gurus. You don't need their crap. Just get off your butt and walk, and walk *good*, I'm talking miles. You want a donut sometimes? Have a donut. Even Trick does it.'

He offered the box. Trick chose a peanut butter cream pie.

'See? That's the most calories in the box right there and he's getting it down him. Sponsor him, Krispy Kreme, sponsor him! Sugar rush before hitting the surf.'

Pandaface19: *Hey fat otter, take the rest of your clothes off.*

'Uh-uh, Pandaface. You just get to see me shirtless with a bit of a bulge and that's it. But it's nice to know you didn't just want cute otters after all.'

Pandaface19: *Yeah I do, I just wanted to see if you'd do it. I want to see Trick. Seeing as you're the boss of everything, tell your BF to get his kit off. I bet he's hard just thinking about it. Nice that he's wearing Weird Fish too. Where did your hand-me-downs come from?'*

Trick smiled. 'Okay, Pandaface19, you need to go somewhere else now. There's *loads* of otter porn you can go watch and loads of otters who'll do it live on cam for you, but we're not those guys. We're just eating donuts and talking positivity here, and my boyfriend's got his shirt off, sure, but that's it. I'm not taking anything off. Especially not for a guy who's rude to the guy I love, and probably *is* underage, because you talk like that even if you're actually *middle* aged.'

Pandaface19: *I bet you're still virgins. Stick a donut up your fat boyfriends ass then, I bet you'll think that's getting laid. *Pandaface19 has left the chat**

CaliDreamin49: *What a douchebag.*

'He's wrong too,' Sandy said. 'I *have* had sex with Trick, and he did *not* put a donut up my ass. He fed me one. The night we met. It switched *all* my lights on. I like being fed. I don't know how he knew.'

'I actually didn't. Seriously, I didn't know that did it for him. Or that he was going to reveal it on camera tonight.' *Who needs a therapist, huh.*

'Yeah. I really, *really* love food. So chubby otter. I also like exercise now too. Best of both worlds. So this

185

is what I look like, and I love this guy right here because he's the first person who ever saw me naked who didn't either bully me for being this way or do nothing while *other* people did.'

CaliDreamin49: *Sucks, right? I had the same thing all through high-school. I've gone back and forward with diet plans for years, nothing worked. Then one day I just decided I was going to like looking at myself in the mirror and I didn't care what other people thought.*

'Yeah, that's familiar,' Sandy said. 'How's the popcorn, Spaceotter? Are you actually eating popcorn?'

Spaceotter_90: *'Nah not really. Man, you just made me realise what a dick I've been to people sometimes. I used to pick on fat people. I think I've got some apologising to do.'*

'Okay,' Sandy said, and Trick had a feeling he hadn't been expecting that. 'Respect to you for admitting it.'

Spaceotter_90: *Gotta admit something else though: it would be nice to see Trick with his shirt off too.*

CaliDreamin49: *My man, that's NOT what you call backing up that apology.*

Spaceotter_90: *What? Trick's a hot guy, just saying. It's not like I was that panda guy. Was I rude to Sandy?*

'Guys, don't fight with each other,' Sandy said. He looked at Trick. 'You gonna?'

Trick smiled and curled his tail around into his lap. 'Am I gonna what?'

Spaceotter_90: *Oh yeah, here we go! That's a killer look. I bet Trick's naughty.*

'Okay, Spaceotter-underscore-90's got my number,' Trick said. 'Sandy likes being fed. I like...actually, I'm gonna keep to myself what I like. The first night we met he was...okay, can I do this?'

Sandy eye-rolled. 'Trick thought I was gonna faint, so he fed me a donut. I *was* gonna faint. I took my starve-day too far. Which by the way doesn't work either. Don't do fasting. Do eating less. I stopped that right after that night. Yes, Trick gave me a boner with a donut. It was the wake-up call I needed.'

Trick eyed the box. 'You want another one?'

'I always want another one. But y'know, moderation. One a day is enough. Okay, I had one this morning too, so let's call it two per day. Top tip of the day: don't let your boyfriend fatten you up. Come on then, Trickster, shirt off.'

'You sound like my doctor right now,' Trick said. 'First I'm taking a breakfast order from our audience, now you're giving me a physical like these guys are med students.'

Spaceotter_90: *Medical play? Holy shit, go ON, guys! Take Trick's pants off and inspect his sheath.*

Trick thought fast. 'I'm staying in clothes. Boo, right? Sucks. But here's the thing: you wanna see me in speedos? Cool, we're gonna do that next time. Sandy's gonna film me surfing. Gonna tune in?'

Spaceotter_90: *Yeah Trick my man, I'm gonna be there. I hope you really can surf. Night, I'm gonna go to sleep thinking about you.' *Spaceotter_90 has left the chat.*

'Yeah, that's not creepy at all, is it?' Sandy said.

187

Everybody wants this otter, Trick thought. *My first fan. Hell yes.*

CaliDreamin49: *I know I'm gonna sound like your dad here, but welcome to the world of online videos when you're a nice guy. You two really are nice guys, so word of advice: don't let the Cali life make you NOT nice. There are people like those two everywhere who just want you to do stuff you don't want to do. Trick: you've found a really smart guy. You be good to him, won't you?*

'Errrr, sure,' Trick said. 'Thanks, I guess.'

'Believe me, you don't sound like my dad,' Sandy said. 'And that's good. You've no idea *how* good. He doesn't know I'm called Sandy now. He didn't do anything about my problems except tell me to get thin all the time. He hated me for being gay too. I'm not just sitting here with my shirt off because I promised never to find myself gross or be ashamed of my body again. I'm doing this because he *would* be disgusted. Fuck him. I'm not a jock otter or a surfer, and I'm in a relationship with a guy who's all that and likes me because I'm not. Yeah, world. This is Sandy.'

CaliDreamin49: *Sorry guys, we've gotta go. Excruciating family dinner with the BF's parents coming up, but we're rooting for you. Make a YouTube channel, we'll subscribe.*

'Already got one,' Trick said. 'We're TrickandSandyinCali on there too.'

CaliDreamin49 exited. A minute later, two subscribes on their channel came in.

'Tell me that doesn't feel good,' Trick said, rubbing Sandy's back harder this time. 'You were awesome! How did you come up with all that?'

'Yeah, it feels good, Trick,' Sandy said, sounding tired. 'It still hurts though. Every time I hear that shit. I don't think I want to do that again. Videos are a bad idea for me. You do yours. I'll just film you surfing.'

'Hey, it's okay.' Trick snuggled up closer to his boyfriend and set the donuts aside. 'You don't want to be on film, you don't have to. But can I just suggest one thing, before we pack this up?'

'What?'

'We ought to take that video and put it on YouTube. As our first thing.'

'What the hell for, Trick? It was awkward and stupid and just crap.'

'Sandy. Look right there. You reached someone. That pudgy old wolf loved you, for being *you*. You got a bully to rethink how he'd behaved. Spaceotter. Look at that.'

'Yeah, and then what? He just wanted to see *you*. That's how sorry he was. But thank you.' Sandy kissed Trick on the head, between his eyes. 'For keeping your clothes on. For not making me look like shit next to you.'

'You *don't* look like shit next to me.'

'Not to you. But what does everybody else out there want?'

'Sandy, there are guys out there who'll think you're *way* more awesome than me, and you know how we reach them? We upload that video.'

'You're not gonna stop talking until I say yes, are you?'

'He *didn't* just want me,' Trick said. 'He spotted your bulge.'

'Am I supposed to like that?'

'If you don't then why did you get me to do something you knew would turn you on?'

'The moment just took me. I wish I hadn't.'

'That's just a little sting of guilt, right?' Trick said. *A little bit of him still being that boy who's just disappointed his parents.* 'But think of it like this: we've got sex appeal. Look at what those guys asked for. We're not actually gonna do any of that, but if people think we're hot, they'll watch our stuff and imagine it. Who hasn't jerked off to a well-known person who never actually did porn?'

Sandy looked through the comments again, obviously playing his replies back. 'Do you actually think I came off well?'

'You kicked that panda guy's ass. That's what the world wants right now: somebody who takes on those sorts of asshole people. Okay, some of those kinds of dicks might be my surfing fans, but you know what I want? To be the guy they know they can't impress with body-shaming who won't stand for it just because he could be a poster boy.'

'So you *do* just want to look good. For supporting me.'

'I want us to look good together. We do. People like awkward, because at least it's genuine. I was wet behind the ears for half of that video, but I don't care. I still like it. I want it out there. But okay, I get it, you don't right now. Will you think about it though?'

Sandy sat back. Not in tired frustration though, Trick thought. Sandy looked emboldened. Energised. 'What the hell, I've just worn my heart on my sleeve in front of strangers on the internet. I might as well wear it with my actual boyfriend. Except I'm not wearing; it's in my mouth and I'm chewing. Like Spaceotter and his fucking popcorn.'

Trick laughed. 'So you like being fed. Loads of guys probably like that.'

'Just so you know, I am not an adult baby, and I'm *never* doing diaper play. I just like the feeding thing because...I don't know.'

'Something tells me,' Trick said, putting his hands in Sandy's lap, 'that you've got a whole lot of turn-ons and I'm only just beginning to know.' He undid Sandy's belt and took his shorts off. Sandy let him. 'Every time I put my hands in these pants, every time we go at it, what are you almost brave enough to tell me you wanna do?'

'What do *you* wanna do, Trick?' Sandy put his hands behind Trick's head as if about to take him down for oral. 'Besides your brother.'

'Har har. It's him who wants to do me. He's always insisting we can't just to remind me.'

Sandy waved it away like he either didn't care or was just happy to wait for the day the rules finally got broken so he could watch. Trick thought of how he'd once said, *'I hate the word cuck. I'm a spectator, an encourager, an audience you like getting a reaction out of. Cucks are the people who either do nothing or watch because they secretly want to be sad.'*

'I'll take your deal,' Sandy said. 'But I want something added. I'll put that stupid video on YouTube if you'll let me try something on you. Something that always made me hard thinking about it.'

Jesus Christ, what else *has he got?* 'Okay, what you got in mind?

'You ever put anything up your butt?'

'Actually, no,' Trick said, deciding it would be hotter to pretend he hadn't. 'But I've always wanted to try toys. Have you got some?' Trick hooked his thumbs into his pants. 'Wanna see what they do to me?'

'I wanna...nah. It'll ruin everything.'

'Come on, otter. What do you think you're gonna do, surprise me more than you already have tonight?'

'I wanna try stuff from the fridge. I sometimes think about it at work. Sticking grapes or baby tomatoes or a cucumber up another otter.'

Trick couldn't help it, he laughed. 'Why do I just find imagining you doing that so easy? You like being fed, but when you feed someone else, you wanna feed the other end.'

'I wish I'd never said that on camera,' Sandy said. 'At least I didn't bring butt-stuffing into it. It's gross, right? But if you'll let me be gross for one night, I'll let you send out that video where I admit I like being fed.'

If this is what it takes, Trick thought, *so be it. He probably won't go through with it once we're halfway there.* 'Go see what you can find in the fridge. I'll get my butt ready.'

Sandy's eyes went wide. 'You want to do this?'

'I'm curious, yeah. I think we'll both end up laughing.' *Which is exactly what Sandy needs right now, and as often as I can make it happen.*

What Sandy found was grapes, a kebab skewer, and some string for tying up a roast pork wrap. He covered the skewer in grapes to make the holes and then slid them off it one by one onto the string, creating a neat stack of grape-beads. What made him almost frenetic with excitement was how after he'd managed to get three of them inside Trick, Trick shivered and went 'Ooooooh *man* those things are cold! How are *grapes* that cold? Brrr! Keep going. This is...okay, this is kinda...' He was hard already. He held his dick and opened his legs as wide as he dared, the pressure already building up inside, the coldness not quite painful but so odd and unexpected that he wanted more. He wanted his limits pushed by Sandy and he wanted it *now*.

'Hold on!' he said as Sandy got to seven out of eight grapes. 'Octopus!'

'Oh,' Sandy said. 'Okay. Errr...how do I stop?'

'Just don't put that last one in there. NO! Don't pull! Oh man, why didn't we get a towel under me before we did this?'

'I'll go get one.'

'No! Don't leave. I'm so hard right now it hurts. I need something to come into. We're gonna wreck the couch if I...urrrgh!'

'Stop working your dick and hold it!' Sandy said, looking afraid. 'Hold on. Here!' He grabbed a glass that had contained a cocktail they'd shared before the video.

Trick felt the coldness of it touch his cock and squirted in blissful release. Unexpectedly, he heard Sandy gasping himself and realised Sandy had filled his own pants at the sight of Trick releasing, still lying on his back with his legs up and the string of grapes stuck up his butt.

Until he realised he'd released those too.

'Urrrrgh, no!' he said, too heady to risk getting up. 'Fuck, I think we're re-covering the couch.' *With what money? It probably cost more than we both make in half a year.*

'It'll wash out,' Sandy said.

Trick sniffed. 'Okay, just tell me before I look, how bad is it? Did I actually shit myself too?'

'No, it's just the grapes. You didn't shit them out, I pulled them right before you came. That was the idea, I read it in some sex book I found in the library on my road trip.' He held them up. 'That *really* did it for you! Look at how much there is in that glass.'

'Yeah, yeah, go change your pants already, we've got a video to u...' Trick felt strange as he got back up to sitting, and then he saw what was in Sandy's hand. 'Errrr...how many grapes did you put on that thing? It was eight, right?'

Sandy looked at it. 'Oh.'

There were three missing.

Trick's stomach clenched a little, then so did his sphincter, then his butt. 'I'll be right back.' He ran for the bathroom.

* * *

194

'Did you get them out?' Sandy said, when he emerged half an hour later, showered but still feeling like he had the sweats.

'Yeah, I got them.'

'How did you do it? Actually shit and bring them with it?'

'I couldn't go. I had to take the head off the shower pipe, stick it up my ass and douche them out.'

'Oh man. Sorry. You think we should go to the hospital?'

'Oh, don't worry like my brother would. They were grapes. What were grapes gonna do up there? There wasn't any blood. Guess it's just as well you used seedless ones. I might get a grape tree growing out of my butt otherwise.'

They stood there and laughed.

'Well, I uploaded our video while you were douching out grapes,' Sandy said.

Trick kept laughing, looked at the screen with their two subscribers, and shook his head. 'My otter. This'll work for us. Sooner or later, we're gonna hit on our thing.'

'Yeah.' Sandy sat down.

'You okay?' Trick said. 'Listen, if you really don't want that video out there, take it down and let's make another one.'

'I'm fine, Trick. But I'm just thinking. By the end of this month, we're not gonna be able to waste food. We're gonna think of those grapes I just wasted, and we'd give anything to have them back so we could actually eat them when that fridge is empty. I did the math on the bills we're gonna have in this place. You and me working both those jobs for minimum wage, we're hardly gonna be able to afford to eat.'

Trick sat down and put an arm around Sandy. 'We're gonna be fine. You know how much we love each other? You just admitted you had a fantasy about sticking food up my ass and I let you do it. Not to mention you just taught me I've got another turn-on when I thought I knew it all. That's all we need. Us.'

'Turn-ons aren't gonna feed us, Trick. Except what if they could? What if we'd done what those two jerks wanted? What if we'd put a donation link under our YouTube bio?'

'Then we'd be banned from YouTube because they don't allow homemade porn, and those two jerks wouldn't have donated anyway, so we'd still be no richer, just regretting that we dropped ourselves to that because we were desperate.'

'What if we do get that desperate?'

'Then it'd be just what Tyler wants to see me do in desperation. We're not going to have to do that. We'll make this work. We got noticed tonight. It was only three people, and only one of them was even vaguely cool, but it's a start, right? We're away. We're out there.'

'Yeah,' Sandy said. 'We're out there alright.'

* * *

Sandy was right, Trick thought as he lay awake in their bed, listening to Sandy blissfully snoring away. This is not going to be easy. I couldn't even make a decent video. I resorted to "So yeah, we're otters." Stating the fucking obvious as though it was funny. It bombed.

Trick rolled over and told himself not every performance was meant to go right. He hadn't had one go wrong before, and this wasn't a terrible way to start. Sandy had rescued it. Videos where people wore their heart on their sleeve sometimes did strike a chord. It just wasn't the one Trick wanted. He needed to drop his own ego and accept that his boyfriend had owned today.

It wasn't hard to do once he reached one thought: what if they'd left the camera rolling and filmed everything that came afterwards?

No, Trick thought. *It's not my way. Mom would be so disappointed, adult making his own decisions now or not.*

But damn, those two jerks who'd tuned into the stream had wanted him.

They'd wanted him good.

Chapter Eleven

'Trick. *Trick*!'

'Hmfff! Urgh, what's happening?' Trick sat up, feeling like he'd slept far too heavily.

'Wake up! You've gotta see this!'

'What time is it?' Trick found his phone. 'Nine thirty? That's the last time I let you stick fruit up my ass. Urgh, shit, I'm already late for Artie's.'

'You're not working today, it's Monday. Get your grape-filled ass downstairs; you've gotta see what's happened!'

Trick trudged down to the kitchen, where there was porridge with bananas and raisins waiting for him. Cream and sugar too. How did Sandy know to make it like that for him?

Kyle had told him, that was how. His suitcase was in the kitchen, moved from the hotel that morning and not yet unpacked.

'Hey, bro. Nice work with your new BF. Go take a look what's been happening.'

Sandy had his laptop out, and the first thing Trick saw was a big page of stats next to their video.

'Woah,' he said. 'Overnight?'

'That's nothing,' Sandy said. 'Get a look at *this*.' He pulled Twitter up. 'Hashtag-BodyPositiveOtter. We're trending! Look at the comments we got!'

That *you* got, Trick thought, as he skimmed through dozens of versions of what CaliDreamin49 had said.

'That wolf you met last night. Good catch, guys.'

'Lottie?' Trick said, turning his head to see her.

'Morning, you cute boys,' Lottie said, a mug of steaming coffee in her hand and a grin on her face. 'Wolfie-forty-nine or whatever his name was had old-school surfer buddies right here in Cali. I watched them share it about an hour after you put it up there. That's how it started. Older guys who actually like people our age for a change, because *damn*, it's not just another jerk couple who think they can conquer the Cali scene. Its two lovable, clueless guys. Except they *did* have a clue. One of them said "No more of this shit" about his looks and the other refused to take his clothes off even though he could have *killed* it doing that. You guys are onto something, and I'm totally in.'

'Are you?' Trick said.

'Does either of you actually ever do much online, or was last night your first go?'

'First go,' Sandy said.

'Yeah, okay,' Trick said. 'I've only ever lurked.'

'Does either of you know Malibu that well?'

Trick managed to draw himself away from the likes and views that were still climbing by the minute. 'You want to be our agent, don't you?' *Like we're anything more than kids in a playground game with this.*

'I'm already Sandy's. He said yes.'

Trick looked at Sandy. One viral video was already making him do this? Yes, because he couldn't contain his excitement.

'What the hell, Trick. She's just got a job as an admin assistant in a real agency. She offered to represent me for free until we start getting some money out of this.'

Trick smiled. She was going to come into his house like this and play that angle? He was going to bait her, hard. He looked straight at her. 'Why doesn't she just pitch you to her boss who's a *real* agent?'

'Because she doesn't need to,' Lottie said. 'She's got access to all her boss's contacts and the same coms people, and she's got MGM's face and all his friends right here next door in her house. The boots-on-the-ground job is just to make her look good, and sooner or later she's gonna get fired for not giving a shit which files she sneaks into, but meh. You guys are worth it. You've got something and I know it. Let me be your first agent. I promise not to rip you off when you're worth a fortune like my boss would.'

'That's worth something,' Kyle said. 'Ask all my musician friends who tried to get agents; you should see what they usually take once you're earning. You find one you're actually friends with, you go with it.'

Trick looked at his brother, then at Lottie. For a gay guy, Kyle had always been a fool for women, and whatever time he'd started moving in, she'd already been here to move into his life. Maybe she'd even heard him play a mean guitar and that pulled her here before Sandy. Who she'd first met when he'd woken up naked on a couch.

It does have something fun about it, Trick thought.

'Sandy's got work to do,' Lottie said. 'He's just changed his accounts to call himself Body Positive Otter, and he's about to take it to another level. Tonight, he's cooking live on camera. Homemade food instead of the diet industry crap he dunked on last night. Hope you guys are hungry, coz he needs people to serve.' She looked at Trick's porridge bowl. 'Come eat that outside with me.'

Trick decided he'd humour her. They stood on the balcony, Trick's bowl on the railing. Lottie resisted smoking while Trick was eating, instead just putting a pack of Newport Green on the rail. 'You played it smart last night. But I know what that sting you're trying to hide feels like. Sandy stole your show. Admit it.'

'If I wanted my show, I'd have just filmed myself,' Trick said, pretending she was wrong.

'You *are* cute,' Lottie said. 'You've got a devil's smile, and if you were straight, I totally *would* be dating an otter already. Use what you've got. But work with Sandy on this. Don't go it alone and just film yourself next time. Two guys with different appeals who are on the same team plays well. Use your platform to get your brother a leg-up too. I've heard him; he's good. We can boost all your talents, together. Because you know what the future is?'

'What?'

'Running your own platform. Your own paywall. You get yourself fans and then you take them to your own site with its own paywall and your own content. Not a studio, no middlemen all taking a cut of your money. Except me, because you could be big enough that you'd never get time to manage all the behind-the-scenes stuff on your own. Don't wait for the big cats to discover you. Go big on your own. You could be paying all your bills and restocking that fridge like it's your birthday all over again within a couple of months.'

It could be worth a shot, Trick thought. He looked at Sandy, already setting up the kitchen, and for a moment he felt painfully jealous. 'I don't think Sandy realises something,' Trick said. 'I've got no talent for surfing yet. I can act, but what am I going to act in with just me and two other guys who aren't actors?'

'You're eighteen,' Lottie said as if she wasn't that age herself. 'That's not too late to go for pro in surfing. I've seen people do it. Get your ass on that beach as much as you can. When you're not at Artie's, be out there. Teach yourself if you can't afford lessons right now. The more daring you get, the bigger you win. I heard you already pissed Armando off with your tide-swim. You're still alive, aren't you?'

'You're telling me to risk my life. Good way to make money out of your clients, when they're dead.'

'I'm telling you to get an edge,' Lottie said. 'Do a little showing off. That won't be difficult for you, will it?' She lit her cigarette now. 'That panda guy last night said something I know you liked. "You're the boss." You *will* be. Give it time. You're the brains. Those two in there will do anything for you, and you already know it. Don't get jealous when they strike it lucky. Get clever.' Lottie nodded towards the living room and kitchen, where Kyle and Sandy were laughing about something. 'Go in there and talk to your team. Just don't call them that. Small talk only. Have fun. Encourage them.'

202

Trick looked out at the beach, where some otters were having what looked like a surfing lesson in calm water. They looked younger than him, early teens.

'Encourage them,' he said. 'Show off. Get an edge.'

'Uh-huh.'

'Okay. You got it.' He went back into the house, his plan already made. *Let's see if you like* this *edge.*

'Hey bro, listen up, I got an idea. Is Kia here? We need to get styled up for this video.'

'I already asked him,' Kyle said with a cocky smile. 'You think I'm gonna make my video debut looking like *you* did last night?'

'Ask Kia to be cameraman too,' Trick said. 'I'm gonna go buy us a good one. And bro, take your clothes off.'

'Right now? Why?'

'Coz I'm gonna do the same,' Trick said, taking all his off except for his underpants, just to tease his brother. 'From now on, no more boxer-briefs. I'm gonna go upstairs and gets us a pair of speedos. From now on, we're only wearing those around the house. We're otters. We're gonna start *living* like otters. How about you, Sandy-butt? Gonna join in?'

'I'm wearing clothes for the video,' Sandy said. 'Naked otter equals fur in the food.'

'Okay, fair enough,' Trick said. 'Strip off, bro. Show Sandy what you've got. I'll be right back.'

Surprisingly, not only did Kyle do it, but when he got back, Sandy was admiring his package. Hands on.

'Bro, your boyfriend likes my dick,' Kyle said, already responding to Sandy's touch.

'Well yeah,' Sandy said. 'I mean *look* at this guy. You never said he worked out.'

'Didn't I?' Trick said. 'Yeah, that's my big brother. He's beautiful. Backrub time!'

'Dude, right now?' Kyle said, then with no more protest he was on tiptoes a moment later, Trick's hands brushing up under his fur and Sandy's hands still on his dick. 'Oh man...you two are gonna...yeah, I'm totally letting you. Nnnnhhh! Yeah, that's it. Ooooohohoho yeah! Living like otters.'

Trick stopped. 'We've got to save this, bro.'

'Save it? Oh, come on, Sandy was totally gonna make me come. You're just gonna leave me hard?'

'If you come right now, you'll have no reason to make the best video ever later on.'

'Woah, hold on,' Sandy said. 'You don't mean...'

Trick laughed. 'No, I don't mean we're gonna do it with each other on camera. But look at us right now. We've got something cool we can use here. You saw the comments on that video. Those guys wanted to see me. But they're only gonna see this. Because we're gonna eat Sandy's food outside and we're gonna be *this* sort of otter. Both of us. Because tonight we're gonna give them double. Me *and* you. Ten to one, they like looking at you more.'

'Oooooh hell no! You wanna have me and you together like this? We'll give everything away. Look at me right now!' Kyle looked towards the back doors to see Lottie still out there looking out to sea and most likely praying she didn't finish her smoke and then turn around.

'Relax, bro,' Trick said. 'We're not gonna do it like this. We're going to eat dinner together. With butts under the table so nobody can see if you do pitch up at something. We're gonna introduce you, then give a little of what I wouldn't give last night. We'll do Sandy's body positivity thing because look at how different we all are. Come on, bro. If you do this for me, I'll finish what I just started for you, and we'll ask what Sandy *really* wants to watch us do.'

'I already know rule one,' Sandy said. 'You guys don't fuck. That's cool. But I've got something for Trick you're really gonna wanna see.'

Sandy wanted this just as much? It was a lucky bonus.

'Alright, little bro. Go buy us that camera, but don't go nuts with the money. Sandy was right with that adding up he did. We've gotta make that camera pay for itself and fast. So I'll trust you. But one thing: if this all goes wrong and we totally make Mom freak out, *you're* explaining it.'

* * *

Lottie decided that for the sake of quality. she was going to be camerawoman. She filmed Sandy making the food, two separate videos with the promise of a third when it came time to serve, giving him a break from the camera to get everything right with no pressure. Instead of the dark inside of the house from the first video, she filmed Sandy serving up Caribbean sea bass and tropical sundaes with homemade vanilla ice cream outside on the back terrace, an hour before sunset.

Trick introduced Kyle with the usual brotherly banter and a subtle amount of hand-to-arm touching to position him well for the camera. A noogie would go down well, Trick decided, and gave Kyle one, only to receive it back a few minutes later, unsuspecting, giving a spontaneous, playful squeak.

Perfect, Trick thought.

He had to wait until after they'd over-complimented Sandy's cooking for Sandy to get to the comments, then he got the question he'd been dying for.

'No, Kyle and I aren't twins. Same Mom and Dad but a year and a half apart.' That would give Kyle a bout of momentary angst, Trick knew. He'd laid it down as a rule: no mentioning Tyler's name. 'June '92, January '91,' Trick said, gesturing at both of them. 'Our Mom needed a nine-month break before carrying me after giving birth to *that*. I mean *look* at him!' Trick gripped Kyle's left arm with both his hands, feeling the strong muscle and liking it. 'He was a huge cub.'

'Bro, fat shaming me right from birth?'

'You weren't fat, dummy. What am I gripping onto right now? Look at the condition of this otter.' Trick rubbed Kyle's chest and down his stomach, liking how he tensed up, his abs showing for the camera. Just for good measure, he stroked Kyle once between his ears and down his back. It arched his brother's back a little, a real camera pose.

'Bro, I wasn't born like this, what kinda dumb thing to say's that?' Kyle said, laughing. 'I work out and I work out and I work out. Oh yeah, and I swim, because lately *you* demanded it like you're my coach or something.'

206

'Let's face it, you wouldn't get out of bed in the morning if I wasn't,' Trick said. 'You should see this guy in the morning.' He hung his hands out floppy in front of himself. 'Rrrruuuuurgh, I'm a zombie otter.'

'Bro, you're embarrassing us.'

'Yeah, okay. Let's do something cool. You *have* been working out a lot lately.' Trick got up, went behind the bench, flicked his tail, and put his hands on Kyle's shoulders. 'You had a sports massage for these shoulders lately, coz they feel tight.'

'Yeah sure, we've got no money, that's just what I'm gonna...uuuuuhhh, okay, bro...do you know what you're...mmmm.'

'Yeah, that's your guitar strap shoulder right there,' Trick said, digging in lightly, then hard, then releasing. He applied the same pressure to Kyle's right shoulder now.

'Mmmm, okay, yeah, you can do this, but really, on ca...' The word camera died away as Kyle let out a slow, relaxed breath as Trick moved closer to his neck, then down his back to below his shoulder blades.

'There you go,' Trick said. 'What are brothers for, huh?'

Off camera, on the other side of the table, Sandy looked like he couldn't stop watching, but inside he was surely squirming. Trick saw Lottie's finger on the zoom button and kept rubbing Kyle's back, working back up to his shoulders. Kyle had his eyes shut, and Trick knew he'd have to stop if his brother started making too many exaggerated pleasure noises, but Kyle didn't. He had a boner nobody but Trick could see, but he kept what the camera was streaming live to relaxed, meditative breathing.

Trick liked it. With a subtle motion disguised as working Kyle's lower back with his right hand, he adjusted his dick so it was flat against the bottom of his stomach, the tip poking at the top of his speedos, no longer pitching a tent. When he eased off and then went back to sitting down, the camera didn't see a thing, and he'd later find out that Lottie had moved the focus from him at that moment anyway and gone to Sandy, who covered it like a pro.

'I taught him that,' Sandy said with a smile. 'He was saving it for you. Good, isn't he?'

There's your edge, Trick thought. *Anyone from last night who wanted to see me in speedos also just found out they have a twincest fantasy. Will that do?*

'Well, so much for SFW, guys,' Sandy said with an exaggerated sigh. 'Look at the comments right here. We've gone from a nice, civilized dinner party to that.'

'Oh come on,' Kyle said, a seraphic grin on his face. 'All he did was give me a massage. He's my kid brother, for God's sake, it's not like we...' His face dropped, and Trick knew this could still play beautifully. 'You want me to do *what* to him?'

'Okay,' Sandy said. 'FrostRaccoon85, we are totally deleting that comment, I'm sorry.' That with a smile of his own now. 'They *are* brothers, and this is not a sex channel.'

Trick tipped his head. '*Would* you do that to me?'

'Sick, bro, do you even know what he was asking for?'

'Yeah, I know what it is,' Trick said. 'And I don't want to do that with you or anyone else. I just had to see the look on your face.'

'You're a jerk.' Kyle sat back. 'But you do give a good massage. Let me tell you something, world, YouTube, whatever this is on: we grew up poor in Phoenix, and our mom used to take us to the doctor together so she only had to bill insurance for one appointment, so I know something: what's under Trickster's speedos is really not that impressive.' He held up his little finger and wiggled it.

'Guys!' Sandy said, hands to his head. 'Family show!'

Kyle shrugged. 'We're talking about family, aren't we?'

'Sandy cooked so we're washing up, bro; let's clear the dishes.' Trick thought nothing of Kyle's comment as soon as he saw the ones coming through, all variations on the one who got to it first: *'When you're in the kitchen, I bet you're gonna prove him wrong.'*

'Maybe I will, Stinker87,' Trick said. 'You a skunk? There are loads of good surfers who are skunks, by the way. Come to Cali sometime. Yyyeeeeeeeeow!' The whip-crack of Kyle's tail against his butt came before he felt the sting, a fabulous noise that the video would surely love, but Trick couldn't help himself: he had both hands on his cheeks, hopping around on tiptoes.

Kyle was laughing like Trick hadn't heard him do for years.

'My butt! Bro, I've gotta sit on that! Arrrrgh, that burns!'

'Pay him back. SPANK HIM.'

'Talk to everyone about how nutritious that fish you cooked is, Sandy-paws,' Trick said. 'I've gotta go inside and sit on an ice pack for ten minutes.'

Lottie turned the camera to Sandy. Trick went inside with a handful of dishes, slid the door shut with his foot, dumped them in the kitchen and then turned and looked at his brother, who looked like lustful madness was going to take him anywhere.

'Okay,' Trick said. 'Do it. Right now.'

'Do what?'

'Grab me by my scruff, shove me on the couch and spank me.'

'Bro, come on, with our agent here? With Sandy still making that video?'

'The windows are shut and the place is soundproof. Do it. You know you want to.'

'Trick.' Kyle put his hands on Trick's shoulders, leaned in, and they kissed for nearly a minute. 'Later. Not now. Even if you did make me hard when you said we weren't doing it like that. You know what?' He put a hand on Trick's neck. 'You're a bad brother.' He grabbed it hard.

It stung, along with the residual effect of Kyle's tail on his backside. Kyle walked him on his toes to the couch. 'Bend over on that. Now.' He shoved Trick down. 'This is for embarrassing me.' He smacked him. 'This is for having a small dick.' He smacked him again. 'This is for lying to me earlier.' He smacked him harder. 'And this? This is for not pretending we're twins.'

Trick panted. 'For *what*?'

'One squeak and you're dead.' Kyle pulled Trick's speedos down to his ankles and smacked him, again and again.

'Bro...*please*, enough! I'll be good next time! I promise.'

'Shut your otter mouth.' He pushed Trick hard into the cushions. 'Stay here. Like this. I'm getting something else to punish you with.'

Trick stayed, resisting the urge to get working on his own cock until he came, knowing that the game would end when Kyle found what he already knew.

'Okay,' Kyle said, coming back. 'So that's not gonna work, because you two don't have any toys.'

'We improvise.'

'You...with what? Okay, actually, never mind. I've lost it. I think we're done. Did you come?'

'No.'

'Good. Okay, here we go, get up.' Kyle helped pick Trick up. 'Lie down, let's help you out.' Kyle rubbed where he'd been spanking. Trick sighed, then purred, then let himself squeak-laugh at the relief. When the doors slid open, he barely noticed.

'My work here's done,' Lottie said, looking at Trick on the couch and Kyle rubbing his bare butt. 'There you go. Make something for your eyes only. That was good tonight. Not quite what I thought you'd go for, but people are watching you two. Probably over and over with their pants down. You probably should have pretended you *were* twins.'

'See?' Kyle said.

'Bro, we don't look like each other enough,' Trick said.

'You actually do when you're styled like this,' Lottie said. 'Get Kia to fine-tune it. He's good at what he does. I'm going to get him some more clients, friends of Dad's. I want him on the team too. Why hasn't he moved in here yet?'

'Second thoughts,' Kyle said. 'But I'll sort it. He'll come here.'

'Night, boys,' Lottie said.

They waited for the front door to close.

'What did you do?' Sandy said.

'I spanked him,' Kyle said. 'So much for the video comments; they got it wrong. He's the one with a punishment-like-Mom-used-to-do thing.'

'He's still hard.'

'Tell me about it.'

'I'm going to fuck your little brother right now. I'm going to come inside him while he's begging me to release. You wanna film it?' Sandy looked at Trick. 'You wanna be filmed?'

Trick rolled onto his side. 'Sure. Why not?'

* * *

Trick was glad that they'd made that video, for their eyes only. Six months later, he thought it was perhaps the one thing that saved his and Sandy's relationship. One video after another, they gained around five thousand followers and failed to make any money. No channel would sponsor them because the follower count wasn't high enough. Donations through PayPal covered a week's worth of groceries at best.

Making the videos became a drag. Sandy was running out of recipe ideas, struggling not to steal from others. Trick wasn't getting any more attention on the beaches than any other otter, and surfing lessons were becoming an expense he'd never afford once the winter came and the heating bills kicked in.

Contrary to what people thought, big houses on the California coast were miserably cold in the winter. The evenings drawing in and the chill creeping through the house earlier every evening seemed to mirror how Trick and Sandy felt about each other lately. Kyle wasn't getting his music noticed, and his solution was to withdraw mostly to his room to work on more of it, believing the more he churned out, the more chance he had.

Kia was the only one who seemed happy. Happy that he'd broken out of that life in Phoenix, that he had celebrity clients now, even if he was secretly scared of disappointing them every time he styled them, happy that he had a little disposable income and even happy that he was the one earning the most at the moment and carrying the other three. Trick wanted to be happy for him, but one night he admitted to himself that he just wasn't. He was jealous because he couldn't get to that same place, and it burned. Like the spankings from Kyle that lately hadn't done much for him and then had stopped altogether.

One night when Sandy couldn't be bothered with more cooking and they sat together eating a bargain basement pizza, looking at the empty wine and whisky bottles that marked the last of the house's original supply, Trick pulled up their first sex video.

213

'That was us,' he said. 'We were that happy. That'll be us again.'

'Yeah,' Sandy said. 'Sure.' The last of his pizza was uneaten and clearly unwanted. 'I'm going to bed.'

'Sandy.'

'Yeah?'

'What if we uploaded this?'

'No,' Sandy said, with no strength for another argument. 'We said we weren't going down that road. I'm still not going down it.'

Trick sat there, not so much contemplating as validating his thoughts: it was up to Sandy what he wanted to show on video, but Trick knew what he himself needed to show. Because he wasn't sitting there wearing a ski jacket when he should be in speedos. He wasn't going to let this house be cold because they were rationing the gas use to only a couple of hours per day. He wasn't giving up his surf lessons either when even Artie, who never complimented anyone, had said he was making fast progress, the kind that even otters didn't usually make.

Trick was a rising star. If his boyfriend didn't want to take things to the next level, the one that was needed, then he would. He was going to show Sandy what it looked like.

He turned on the heating. He turned on the shower too. He was taking one. If he was going to do this, he was going to look good.

He switched on the camera, placed a book stack on the coffee table to get the height right, hit record, and sat back on the couch.

'Okay guys, if you're getting this, it's a special night, so spread the word. You see these clothes? I'm wearing these because my house is a fucking ice box. I've had enough of it. I need enough money to pay the bills so that I don't freeze my ass off this winter. So I'll make you a deal. I'm gonna come back to the computer in an hour. If I find three hundred bucks in my PayPal, then these clothes are coming off. That means everything. I'll do an exclusive interview for you guys where you can ask me anything you want, for an hour, and I'll be nude the whole time. If you guys can double that money, I'll jerk off. Up to you. What do you wanna make happen?' Trick put on the devil look, winked, and shut the camera off. He set his iPhone timer to an hour.

Upstairs, Sandy was already snoring. Lately he'd been working longer shifts at the kitchen than usual, seventy-hour weeks minimum to get by, and the otter apnoea would be strong tonight. Good. His snoring seemed heavier than usual, and then Trick realised it wasn't just Sandy. Kyle was asleep at his desk, open books of music and loose paper with his notes on scattered around him.

It had been rough for Kyle, Trick thought. He'd put his heart and soul into trying to get a job that was at least close to his passions, hustling around with every record store and guitar shop going, then failing that hitting up bookstores and everything else he could think of that retailed creative material. It took him two months to land a job in Church's Chicken. Kyle had never liked eating the stuff anyway, and now he came home every day smelling of it. Sandy thought he was being dramatic in saying he could never quite get the smell out of his fur, but Trick knew it was true. Chicken grease lingered.

Two's better for this than one, Trick thought. He woke Kyle up.

'What time is it?' Kyle said, looking around him as if trying to remember which of the many open books he'd been poring over.

'Half past eleven,' Trick said. 'I'm sorry I woke you up, but you'll be stiff tomorrow if you sleep slumped over like that.'

'I've been asleep since this afternoon,' Kyle said. 'I hope I'm not sick.'

Trick put a hand to his brother's forehead. 'You're fine, bro.'

Kyle laughed. 'Am I?' He got up, stretched and yawned. 'This is wearing me out, Trick.'

'I know. But listen, I want to try something, and I want you to help. I'm taking a shower. Want to share it?'

'We had one already today.'

'We're having another one. I turned the heating on too.'

'You make some money?'

'I might be about to. I offered a special promo. Come on, shower. And I need you to help style me up. If the money's there within an hour...' He looked at his timer, already down to 45. 'Okay, even if it's not, I'm going NSFW. Tonight. I want you to film it. You in?'

* * *

216

Six hundred bucks had been a pipedream. So had three. When Trick and Kyle checked the account, there was a tidy one-fifty sitting there. It would buy three more surf lessons, Trick thought, deciding he didn't really care about the gas bill. If this sort of income became steady enough, he'd get a credit card.

'So what now, bro?' Kyle said. 'They didn't pay up. You do this anyway, they'll expect it every time without you getting what you need.'

'Don't worry about it; just roll. Set it to livestream, let me work.' Kyle gave the countdown from five, the last three with his fingers only. 'Okay guys, we're halfway there, better than I thought, so I'll make you a deal: if we can get to two, I'll do it with a hundred discount. We get to three? I do the rest half price. One-time-only offer. Or maybe if we have fun, I'll run this for a little while longer. Keep hustling, tell your friends who like otters there's a cute one here waiting for you. We just need five people who can spare ten bucks.'

A couple more people joined. When they were up to one-ninety, an old memory appeared in the comments.

'Well, well,' Trick said. 'Pandaface19. Can you spare ten bucks, my man?'

Pandaface19 spared one-ten. *'Make it worth it. I was supposed to buy my mom a birthday present with that.'*

It's probably not true, Trick thought, refusing any guilt. He had his three hundred. Now for the magic part. One of them was going to ask, and thankfully he got it as soon as he was down to the speedos, having taken time to fold his clothes neatly instead of throwing them away like it was a strip club. Sophistication, he thought, played well here.

'*Who's got the camera? Is our man Sandy filming this?*'

'No, this isn't Sandy,' Trick said. 'My brother's got the camera. Sandy was a little reluctant about this whole thing, so Kyle's filming this one.' He hooked his thumbs into his speedos. 'Sandy's asleep. Shhh! Don't wake him up!' He took them down, stood up, and placed them neatly on his other clothes. 'There you go, guys. Is it like Kyle said? What do you think?' He took his sheath in his hand and rubbed a few times, exposing his head.

'*I bet Kyle's not really there.*'

'They don't believe it's you, bro. Give them a line.'

'Hey guys. You like Trickster's dick? I sure do. Yes, he's my brother; no, we don't *love* each other love each other, know what I mean? But who am I kidding, he's smoking hot. Pull that skin back, bro, show them that tip. I'm going close up.'

'*Holy shit, THIS is what you call bromance!*'

'Okay, there's my tip,' Trick said, stroking a finger lightly over his hole. 'Mmm, yeah, I got my three hundred so I'm gonna come out of that for you guys real soon, but I promised you an interview, so enjoy how hard I am and think of some questions. Seriously, you can ask me anything. No more SFW show tonight.'

'*Do a lying-down pose on the couch.*'

'You got it,' Trick said, thinking too fast to notice the names of all the people watching his show. He did the pose he often did in speedos, knowing it would hide his dick away behind his leg for a few minutes, but that was good. It was like he'd heard Kyle say about music:

tension and release. He'd thought about sex like that for a while, but tonight it seemed so much more poignant.

'How old are you?'

'I'm eighteen,' Trick said. 'Actually, I hope to God all of you are as well, but I'm gonna confess I just didn't think of that. And how would I check anyway? Ask you all for ID? I hope Pandaface19 really is 19 and didn't actually steal that money he bought this with *from* his mom.'

'Blow me, surfer boy. I sell cars and I'm fucking good at it. I worked my ass off for what I've got. I like otters, and I've been using the same nickname since I first found it out. I'm thirty-five and I like twinks. I'll give you another fifty if you'll show me your asshole.'

Trick read the comment out loud and laughed, gave his stomach a rub and slowly slid his hand down to his hidden dick. '*One*-fifty.'

'*Seventy-five.*'

'One hundred. Final offer.'

'Okay, challenge time, bro,' Trick said, shifting to sitting up and working his dick. 'Can you keep the camera on me jerking it and check the account to see if our panda's paid it?'

'Are you turned on by money?' someone asked.

'Am I turned on by money? I guess not in itself, no,' Trick said. 'But I've gotta live, right? It's hard to make a living on minimum wage here in Cali. Am I excited right now? Yeah, you bet. You guys just bought me a month or so where I don't have to worry so much, and these last six months have been worry all the time, so yeah, do I feel like doing this right now? Take a look, I'm wet now.'

219

'It's there, bro,' Kyle said, his eyes wide. 'Gonna deliver?'

'Well sure, I'd be a scammer otherwise, wouldn't I? Okay guys, let's see if my bro can film *this*.' He opened his legs a little wider. 'He made that joke about seeing my dick at the doctor's office, but here's the truth: Mom always made us both look the other way, and he didn't have the balls to defy her and take a look.'

'Yeah, okay, that's fair, it's true,' Kyle said. 'I never saw his dick until we were grownups.'

'And he sure never saw this.' Trick lay back on the couch and pulled his knees to his chest. 'Close up on that, bro, our panda *did* pay his hundred. Wonder if he'll come. Keep it there. That's my butthole, guys. Made in Phoenix, on display in Cali where it should be.'

Kyle stood with the camera in his hand, a hypnotic, fascinated look on his own face. 'Looks tight, bro. How you feeling right now?'

'I'm cool,' Trick said.

'This turning you on?'

'See for yourself.'

Kyle adjusted the camera upwards slightly. 'Mmm. Yeah. Gonna do something with that hard cock?'

'Keep talking to me, bro,' Trick said, working himself with his left hand.

'Lot of people went for our "not twins" things back when we did that, you remember? You introduced me and you said we're not twins. I kinda wish we were. I bet they do too. Gonna imagine that tip's going into your twin brother? I bet they'd love to see *that*.'

A wild thought came to Trick. 'Put the camera on the books there, bro. Where I had it before.'

'Okay.' Kyle put it on there.

'I'm still in shot?'

'Yeah, it's perfect.'

'Good. Take your clothes off for me. Down to your speedos. Throw them to me so they know it's real.'

'Man, you really DO have a thing for your brother! Admit it.'

Kyle took his shirt off, then his pants, socks, and then the speedos too, except he didn't throw them. They were soaking wet already.

'Okay, let me answer that one honestly,' Trick said. 'A lot of brothers who have a close relationship sometimes jerk off together. You'll hardly ever find a pair who'd admit it, and they're usually looking at a magazine or some videos together when they do it, but it's a thing. So yeah, Kyle and I have jerked off together. We don't mind being naked in front of each other. He's watched me have sex too. Do we have a thing? No, not like what I have with Sandy and he has with other guys. It's just brothers with more benefits than most admit to. Think about it, what's unnatural about doing something we all do just because you're family?'

Kyle threw the speedos now.

'There you go, he's naked, everyone wins. Let's go for it.' Trick worked on himself for a good five minutes, not looking at the comments but seeing the screen flicker in his peripheral vision, knowing they were all cheering him on. It was going to be tough though. For some reason he just couldn't come. Another few minutes and he might lose it.

Kyle saw. Somehow, he got it. 'Hey bro, you remember that massage you gave me?'

221

'Yeah, I remember it. Describe it to me. That'll do it.'

Kyle stepped in front of the camera. 'What are brothers for, huh?' He walked bare-butt to the couch, showing his muscled back off to the camera, and then as if he'd practiced the move, he deftly tucked himself behind the couch so that nobody caught a glimpse of the front. 'Sit yourself up, Trickster. Let's make this happen.'

Oh, this was it. Trick sat up, too late to hide his astonishment, too late not to be riding the wave. Kyle worked his shoulders and his back, letting him breathe deep and hard with excitement. He even did what Trick had avoided on the first video all those months ago and gave him a chin scratch, letting him hold his muzzle in the air so his neck and chin faced the camera, sucking down his air through his nose. He gripped his cock hard, rubbed several times, and gasped, holding his load, ready to shoot.

Then Kyle reached down and pinched his tip. 'Come for us, little brother.'

Trick shot it so hard he reached the table, squeaking with pleasure as the warm fluid spurted out of him, his brother still holding his dick, chin on his shoulder. When there was no more, Kyle stood there, holding Trick down by his shoulders as he caught his breath.

'Yeah...okay...that was worth four hundred bucks and *then* some,' Trick said. 'You guys good? Everyone filled their own pants yet?'

'Jeez, bro, is there always that much?' Kyle said. 'That's *some* mess we're gonna have to clean up.'

'Oh yeah.'

'Keep the camera rolling; I'll go get you a towel. Pass me my clothes over, would you? I'm gonna change behind the couch. They wanna see me go all in next time? It's gonna cost more.'

He's down with this, Trick thought, closing his eyes and sighing with relief and happiness. *He gets it. When Sandy sees what we've done, he'll get it too.*

Right on cue, there was a light across the room from the staircase. 'What are you guys doing?' Sandy said. 'Whatever noise you just made, it even woke *me* up. Are you alri...'

He stopped.

'Boom, FAIL, you woke his ass UP!'

'Time to say goodnight, guys,' Trick said. 'Talk to you tomorrow.'

Sandy walked slowly over to them. 'You were jerking off. You were helping him do it. You were streaming it.'

Trick put his speedos back on, and his pants, clumsily, while Sandy walked. A futile gesture, as if to suggest the show was over. 'Okay. I know how you said you feel about us doing this kind of thing. But before you go nuts, just listen to me for a minute.'

Sandy stood rigid. Trick wondered if his father had been a soldier, and part of the bullying routine Sandy might have been subjected to was a daily drill parade in his own home, because right now, he looked like a marine on parade. 'I'm listening.'

'You said you didn't want to do that,' Trick said. 'So I didn't push you. I did it myself because our fans paid me to. We've not been making the money we need. If we're ever going to actually live our dreams, we need to start now and not later. So I did want our fans wanted.

223

I asked for six hundred bucks in an hour. Then they didn't get there, so I compromised. I got us to...'

They all looked. *Four,* Trick thought as his senses came to him. *I asked for four. There's the six, right there after all.*

'Bro, they tipped us! There were...' Only now could they take a calm look at the stats, and they all were. 'There were thirty-two people watching that, bro. That's not even a fraction of everyone who follows us. If we...'

The room was silent for a moment.

'Finish your thought,' Sandy said.

'That was one night's work,' Kyle said. 'One *hour.* If we keep doing that and we get more of our daytime audience to come out after dark...' Kyle looked at Sandy, an unmistakable fearlessness in his eyes. It wasn't that he was scared of Sandy so much as he'd never wanted to fight with him in Trick's house, because Trick knew Kyle thought it felt like Sandy owned the place too by virtue of being Trick's boyfriend. 'You're always doing the math, obsessing over the numbers. We just got an entire week's shift money in one night, and that was just Trick on his own.'

'And you,' Sandy said. 'Jerking your own brother off on camera. With no clothes on yourself.'

'Except you're not actually judging, are you?' Kyle said. 'Not when you're thinking about where this could go. So you don't wanna do this kinda thing. That's you. Trick's going to make us a fortune. Look at these comments right here. That was an improvised shot in the dark. Look what happened. And look at that.' Kyle gestured to the room. 'My little brother is *not* going to pretend he didn't just have the time of his life. Lottie told him to get an edge. He just found it. So before you do what I know you're going to and start playing devil's advocate and –'

'Kyle.'

'Yeah?'

'Shut up.' Sandy broke their stare and looked at Trick, then he put his hands on Trick's shoulders. 'What did you ask me earlier?'

For the first time ever, Trick felt nervous about Sandy's hands on his shoulders. 'I asked you...I asked you why didn't we upload our sex video.'

'And what did I say?'

'You said no, we'd talked about going down that road and you didn't want to go down it.'

'Yeah. But you clearly did. So why didn't you tell me?'

'Are you going to pretend you were in the right mood for that conversation?'

'No. But I'm in it now. So let's be clear about it. I said I didn't want to upload that video because it's for our eyes only. Our private stock. It's not any good for an audience. We didn't make it for that purpose. What you just did *was* for an audience. I bet it was a good show. I'm going to like it when I take a look, aren't I? When I hear you make that noise that even woke *me* up. Just how hard did you come, Trick? That's one big mess I'm looking at. This whole room stinks of sweat and sex and you two.' He looked at Kyle. 'Did you come too?'

'No,' Kyle said, looking bewildered.

'Want to?'

'I'm good.'

'Sure? Coz I can make it happen.'

'Yeah, I'm cool.'

'Alright.' Sandy shrugged. 'But here's the deal. Next time you two want to do that, don't put the camera on a stack of books. I'm having it. Then I can film you doing whatever you want to each other. If you don't want to fuck, it's cool. That means I can. If someone has to fuck Trick, it's me. You can film that. We'll see how much they want to give us to see Body Positive Otter get sex-positive and get his partner's brother to be in on it. You want an edge? I'm the edge. These guys wanna see Trickster get spanked? I do it. Or I order you to do it and I tell you how to do it and when to stop. Do we understand each other?'

They all looked between each other.

'Yeah,' Kyle said. 'Okay. Sure.'

He looked like he'd love nothing more than to be Sandy right now, Trick thought. Alphas. Could this work?

It had to.

'Okay, guys, relax,' Sandy said. 'I'm chill. I was kinda acting. It was fun watching you two shit it, thinking I was gonna go crazy. Why *didn't* you just tell me you wanted to go NSFW though? You didn't have to let me go to bed keeping it secret. I know I wasn't in the mood. But next time, ignore my mood, okay?'

'You *are* a little bit weird,' Kyle said. 'But I like you. I like your edge. You really want to film me and Trick doing stuff? Like everything we didn't do on that first video?'

'Six hundred dollars in one night doesn't lie,' Sandy said. 'It's midnight. We just got some money. Why don't we have a drink? Tomorrow we'll tell Lottie and the world about our edge.'

'Guys,' Trick said. 'Look.' He pointed at the screen.

'More money?' Kyle said.

The money had stopped at just over six hundred. 'Better,' Trick said. 'Look right there, that like we just got. Do you know who that is?'

Kyle didn't. Sandy did. Sandy knew unmistakably, and any thought of acting was gone from him instantly.

'Woooooooaaahohohoho! *Shit.*'

'Yeah.'

'Echo Pendryl,' Kyle said. 'Who's that?'

'You don't wanna know and neither do we,' Sandy said. 'What the hell's he doing watching us, scouting younger otters? We do *not* want that kind of scouting. You know the story, Trick. Right?'

'Yeah. That's how I know the guy's got a studio. He's also the guy in a relationship with Eddie Kowalski. Our Starvos.'

Kyle groaned. 'Not *Dictator Envy* again. I thought that idea had died.'

'My man, it never died,' Sandy said. 'But it's not living like this. Trick, you seriously want to touch Echo Pendryl for anything, let alone a studio?'

'What's wrong with him?' Trick said.

'Aside from what you know he was famous for? Which I am *never* letting anyone do to me *or* you. Or even you.' He looked at Kyle. 'You know why he's got that studio? Trick, the guy got himself a billionaire sugar daddy, got written into his will, and then he murdered the poor fucking guy.'

227

Trick laughed. 'Oh come on. You believe that version? Yeah, I know the story. I've read up on it; I was following it when it first started eight years ago. It was a tragic accident. The guy was messed up for a while because it was so hard to prove his innocence, but there was no evidence it was murder. Nobody creates a setup like that and then acts like Echo Pendryl did. He was the kind of client lawyers stay awake at night thinking about, because they know he's innocent, but *fuck* are they going to have to earn their money proving it. Dany DiMatteo did. If she of all people believed him then so do I. Echo's sound. He's just a bit of a disaster magnet sometimes.'

'Then whatever you believe, that's why we don't need him,' Sandy said. 'I hope he never likes anything of ours again. I hope a like's as meaningless from him as it is from most people.'

Too late, Trick thought. *It's not. This is where it begins.* 'You had a good idea a minute ago,' Trick said. 'Let's get that drink.'

Book Two – The Riptides

Chapter Twelve

Fast Eddie Kowalski robbed his first liquor store at the age of sixteen. Whenever he thought about it now, it was as though he should have earned his nickname way back then, not as a running back for the L.A. Riders.

The two raccoons, the echidna and the pangolin all got capped. It was second bag syndrome, as Eddie always called it from that day onward. Not content with a decent haul, they went back for the rest. They'd had a good tip-off that the dumb fuck who ran the place only paid for one cash pick-up per month to cut his overheads. The tip was on the money; there was so much cash in the back safe they couldn't carry it all. Eddie Kowalski's biggest lesson that day was to always do everything in one trip.

The second was carry a gun. Don't copy the cool guy from the films who says 'I just drive.' Eddie was only looking for a speed thrill. He didn't go inside, didn't want to shoot anyone, didn't want to do anything but get away and take his cut. He got more.

When the second raccoon went down after two closed-carry heroes tried to do their thing, Eddie got away because he pulled the gun from the guy's hand. He didn't know how to aim back then, and it was luck the thing was made ready. When it turned out the closed-carry heroes survived the bullets he put in them, Eddie was glad. It made his conscience a little lighter.

His cut though, *damn*, that was what you called a lucky break. His first.

Long before Eddie Kowalski thought of L.A. as his home, he lived in New Jersey. He stuck to the plan: ditch the bags on the north side of the woods, then ditch the car and fire it on the south side. Pickup would be there five minutes after he made the call.

Pickup was the boss of the whole thing, Ginsburg, a German Shep. Eddie knew what the deal was: no bags, no pickup. He had the bags. He got to the right point. As soon as he smelt Ginsburg's scent though, his thoughts of getting everyone else's cut because he was the lone survivor vanished. Then after he'd got into the car, wondering if he'd even come out of this alive after all, Ginsburg surprised him: he split it exactly as he'd said: sixty-forty. He gave Eddie a choice: he could have the forty, they'd shake hands and they'd never known each other, or he could have the sixty, and the generosity meant 'a business agreement.' That was all Ginsburg called it.

Eddie shook Ginsburg's hand and walked with the forty. He wasn't getting his own second bag syndrome. Not that night, not any. Forty percent of what turned out to be a hundred thousand bucks was more than he needed. Turned out there was a river of dirty money running through that store, not just the takings. Whoever's it was, Eddie was glad he never got far enough into Ginsburg's world to know who else he'd robbed.

Eddie's second stroke of luck was when Ginsburg's name came up in the news nearly a year later, a report that was really more like an obituary. Heroin bust. Fifteen minutes in his company and Eddie already knew Ginsburg wasn't a man who'd ever stand trial, given a choice. Now there was nobody alive who could connect him to that first stroke of luck.

Eddie's high school teachers told him he was smart. He always had it figured it was about more than just book smarts, and here he was proving it. The cops never knocked on his door after the robbery. They didn't even have a lead, let alone know they were looking for a wolverine. Eddie knew better: what they were looking for was somebody poor who started spending money like they'd just robbed a hundred large from a place.

He waited six months, then chose to wait another six. The day he heard Ginsburg had bought it, he celebrated by telling his mother that from now on, she'd have good health insurance. Not only that, but she wasn't going to get another debt collector at her door for the last lot of bills when she *hadn't* had good insurance. Moira Kowalski had gone back to work months too soon after they'd removed that tumour from her stomach, because she couldn't afford to do otherwise, and she was still flat broke at the end of every month, working twelve hours a day with no days off.

Not anymore, Eddie knew. That was why he'd done the job in the first place. He'd never dreamed of scoring it that big for her, but now he'd done it, his mother might even have a decent quality of life to go with her new debt-free one.

Why he'd do the job again? That was a different matter. That part he was keeping to himself.

Moira Kowalski probably hadn't even seen Eddie's robbery on the news, but she was no fool. She knew where the generous tips that were getting left at the tables in her little roadside diner were coming from. Deep down, Eddie *wanted* her to catch him. She wouldn't have spent that money on designer clothes or a fur style anyway, but it was good to tell her what he'd got it for. No fool herself, she waited too, for the right night.

She leaned against the wall, one hand on her hip and a cigarette in the other, the place packed away and the lights dimmed, ready to go again in another eight hours. Her son was her only employee that day, and he'd never taken a paycheque from her in his life.

'What did you do, Eddie?'

'Do you want the answer to that, Mom? Really? Or do you want to never have to go through all that shit with money again?'

His mother fixed him with a look he now described as the only judgement that had ever really mattered to him. 'Whatever this thing was, can you sleep at night after doing it?'

That was the part he really hadn't wanted her asking. Most other guys he went to school with would have wound up with PTSD after seeing what he had, after knowing they'd nearly killed two people, stolen from somebody's business, and one look at Pickup had made them sure they were about to wind up dead in the woods.

Not him. Not Fast Eddie. He didn't really think about it much at all, but whenever he did, those thoughts *helped* him sleep.

'Yeah,' he said. 'I'm good.'

'And there's no trace?'

Of what? Eddie thought. 'Nothing. Zip.'

'Then we don't talk about this,' she said. 'We just do it. Don't make the tips as big as you have been. Do more of them, more often. Every weekend, I ring through two customers who never existed. Pay those two bills. Don't put a tip on them.'

Eddie always figured he'd have to find another crew and another store when the money ran out. It wouldn't be wise, it wouldn't even be right, but he'd do it if he had to, for his mother. Or at least, that was how he justified it. The truth was a little harder to accept. The part that eventually started keeping him awake, albeit only for a little longer than usual, was how he'd fallen asleep so easily to begin with, thinking of how he'd pulled that trigger. He didn't want those guys dead. That was what let him drift off eventually. But he'd wanted that gun, and he'd wanted to use it.

The truth was, long before he'd ever known the word 'sadist,' Eddie Kowalski knew he liked hurting people. He wasn't a bully, he didn't think he was a nasty person, but seeing someone hurt because he'd done it had always switched on a light it wasn't supposed to. He'd never lost a schoolyard fight because he'd wanted those lights inside him switched on. Shit, he'd never even started a fight; someone had always kicked off with him, thinking he was weaker. They soon learnt. If only they knew what his secret was, what spurred him on, what made him ignore his own pain.

Two years away from graduating high school, he felt like he'd found the stage he'd always thought might be beyond just having a scrap.

He might just have bottled it the night of the robbery, forgotten the plan, kept on driving until the cops picked the car up from someone's description, if the moment where he realised he had a raging boner hadn't brought him the most amazing clarity he'd ever had in his life.

This was who he was. Time to use it. It didn't matter how right or wrong it was; the reason he'd taken this job in the first place was right. This little moment of understanding with himself was just an added bonus. Eddie had never believed in God, but this certainly felt like a message from him.

What Eddie decided, around six months before the money was due to run out, was that he was going to tell his mother there would be no more tips or fake customers, and that was going to have to be it. He couldn't do that job again. This time the reasons just wouldn't be right. The diner was doing better. Moira's improved health had turned her around, and with it her business. She had more staff now. She'd even quit smoking. Hell, she had a new place too, a better location, and the place made bank, and then enough for her to buy them both dinner somewhere nice a couple of times a month. Another job would be getting greedy.

No second bag.

Eddie thought of Ginsburg, how the guy was probably on hundreds of bags by the time he went out, maybe more. That guy was the exception to the rule though. Eddie knew he wasn't going to be.

Until something else came along. Eddie's third lucky break was a longshot he only took to amuse himself. When Stanford University sent him the letter saying his application for a sports scholarship had been accepted, he almost felt ashamed of his past then. All he would have had to do was wait.

The day Eddie Kowalski showed his mother the letter, he already knew he was going to go pro.

'One thing at a time, honey,' his mother told him, but he knew from the way she'd said it that she believed him. She'd seen him play. She knew what they started calling him, just before he graduated: fast. Fast Eddie Kowalski. He loved that name already. He was going to love it a whole lot more. So was the world. His mother would never have to work again after what he was going to do.

The thing he never told her (and never would) was how she wasn't the first one he'd shown that letter. The first person to know his news was a wolf called Micky 'Lightpads' Hackford.

Everybody in the school knew Lightpads was gay. He got the nickname from dancing, and he was good at it. Everyone also knew his boyfriend was another wolf called Silvio, who went to a different school. What nobody knew, including Silvio, was that Micky Lightpads secretly loved Fast Eddie Kowalski, and Fast Eddie loved him back.

The part that Silvio *really* didn't know about was that the bruises Micky sometimes had weren't really from dance moves gone wrong. Micky loved getting it. He'd found the friend who loved dishing it out.

For a long time, Eddie felt like he'd found an outlet for that dark part of himself that was better than any robbery, or better even than taking people down extra hard in football. He didn't want to be a running back, he wanted to be a defensive end, to make that happen on every play, but they always told him no. He was fast, fast meant running, running meant points, points meant winning. So accept where you belonged.

Yeah. That was a phrase he had to tell himself a lot. Especially when reminding himself it was better that nobody, for any reason, could ever know about him and Micky. That resolve lasted all the way through college, all the way into the draft, all the way to Fast Eddie Kowalski scoring the winning touchdown of the championship for the L.A. Riders.

That would have been his fifth lucky break. He sometimes did call it that. Except it didn't feel so lucky after Micky tried to fuck it all up.

Eight years of sneaking around, of knowing Eddie had other people on the side too, and some of them were guys, and then the word got out: Eddie Kowalski, the Superbowl play winner, had a high-school sweetheart who nobody knew about, and get this: it was a guy.

Eddie always knew it was inevitable. That it was happening right now enraged him on the inside, but publicly he was prepared: deny everything. It wouldn't even matter whether people really believed him,

237

because the louder voice with the most money always got heard above all the rest.

Except Lightpads just wouldn't let it be that simple.

That, Eddie Kowalski would later tell a Narcotics Anonymous meeting, was the beginning of everything that led to where he was right then: broke, disgraced, outed, two years of his life with barely a memory to show for it, then another two lost to a prison cell, and barely alive to talk about any of it.

* * *

The real pain of it all was that Moira Kowalski wasn't there to watch her son win a championship ring. If it hadn't been for that, he might not have ended up beating Lightpads Hackford to within an inch of his life.

Eddie talked about his mother plenty in rehab, but even when he broke down sobbing, he always kept his favourite secret: the robbery he'd done for her. That was the funny thing: he needn't have done it at all. Things would have worked out fine if he'd just given it a few years, and then that NFL draft happened, and he'd scored so big, so quickly.

Within four years, he had two championship finals under his belt and an MVP title in the fourth. L.A. never traded him; he was gold. His mother was now living in a mansion in Malibu. She'd never again clear a dinner plate and say 'Thank you for dining here' to some trailer-trash cunt who never left a tip. Moira Kowalski had become a voice of influence among all the football wives, and she wasn't even married to a football player. Nobody dared make any jokes about it though. Not

238

when her son was Fast Eddie, who showed no interest in marrying anyone.

The trouble was that when her cancer checked in again, this time it was determined not to check out, and none of Eddie's money could buy her more life. She had the best medical care, no insurance companies involved, but it soon turned into the best hospice care instead. Moira Kowalski passed less than a week before the Superbowl final.

The team wanted Eddie on compassionate leave. He told them all to fuck off, including the coaches and then the owner, to whom he sent a simple message: "I'm playing on Sunday or my agent will take my contract and give it to the Dallas Bucks next year, after your team plays without me and loses."

The Riders beat the bucks in the last ten seconds of the final quarter, with Fast Eddie's touchdown.

Moira Kowalski's funeral took place the next morning. Her son stayed sober all the way through the team's celebration because he couldn't give her the indignity of attending her send-off hungover.

Two days after that, Lightpads sold his story to the press.

* * *

Fast Eddie Kowalski got away without jail time because Lightpads, for reasons nobody ever understood, stood by him during the trial. He even dropped the charges, only to find the state pressed them instead. The trial was a disaster, because Eddie's money bought good lawyers and Lightpads's dumb emotions did the rest, and the latter was down to one simple reason: the make-up sex had been so fucking hot.

Eddie knew his partner was most likely dying from what he'd done. He also knew Lightpads didn't care; he'd only sold that story in desperation, for funds to pay off a student loan for a college education he'd dropped out of because his severe depression crippled him so hard he couldn't keep up with the work.

Lightpads cried his eyes out after Eddie laid on the punch that broke his jaw, practically taking it off the hinge on one side, and told Eddie to stop. So Eddie stopped, because he knew what they both wanted. He had a boner. So did his partner, who was bent over sobbing with his head between his knees.

The EMT held out little hope for Lightpads when they arrived on the scene after Eddie called them, once Lightpads was unconscious on the bed. The surgeon held out even less. The cops described how they found Eddie just sitting there catatonic, or maybe just knowing his life was over but hey, at least he'd found some happiness before the road that would eventually lead him to suicide. Yet the trial came, and there was Lightpads, alive and understanding and telling everyone that Eddie really wasn't a bad guy, and that he regretted the story he'd sold to the press.

Eddie knew the deal though: it was time for the truth. Fast Eddie Kowalski, the hero of the hour for the L.A. Riders and one of the greatest running backs the NFL had ever seen, was gay.

The team dropped him. They said it was nothing to do with his sexuality and everything to do with how he'd beaten his ex-partner and then had sex with him instead of calling a medic. Eddie actually had to give it to them: they were right. It was his fault; he'd *made* them right. If he'd only come out without the fight, without even thinking about flying to New Jersey to confront Lightpads, then they'd probably have let him go some other way, and then he'd have been able to carry on the denial, got another contract and shown the whole world nothing was going to stop him.

That was the beginning of the end. No team would touch him now. He had his fortune, he had his championship ring, and nobody could take either away from him. Except they'd taken his life, and cancer had taken his mother's. Now Eddie Kowalski was a lone wolverine with nothing left to lose.

By the time he did his second robbery, this time high on Oxycontin and meth to balance it out, Eddie Kowalski had gambled most of his fortune into the ether, hidden nothing from the press, had a series of lovers that would put Lightpads's submission fetish to shame, smashed up every hotel room from the East Coast to the West, and forgotten he could even play football once.

They picked him up for the second robbery because he couldn't even get his first bag out of the joint without collapsing, let alone get second bag syndrome.

He couldn't afford good lawyers this time. The drugs were nothing – Eddie's real addiction was thinking he was just as fast at a poker game as he had been on the field. When poker didn't cut it, there was blackjack. When the cards were mean, there was the roulette machine. When that didn't work, he just stayed up five nights in a row feeding money into the slots. Vegas loved Fast Eddie, and Fast Eddie loved it back.

Until everything just stopped, because everything had run out.

The court-appointed lawyer did well to get his sentence down to two years. Eddie barely remembered any of them.

What he remembered was getting out of prison, being checked into a halfway house by his parole officer, going to the nearest medical centre, and asking for an HIV test. When it came back negative, the nurse told him it probably would have been the least of his problems anyway.

Prison wasn't a way to get people off drugs. Eddie Kowalski had always heard it, and now he knew it. By the end of his time there, he knew he would have been running the racket if he hadn't been its best customer. He had nothing left to pay with, so he'd paid with his body. Somehow, he'd gotten away with his life by the time they released him.

Eddie Kowalski checked himself into rehab using the one thing he wasn't sure how he remembered: the emergency 'go bag' he'd once buried behind his mother's old home. He'd gambled the place away by then and had to trespass to dig it up, his limbs shaking with withdrawal all the way through it, but he'd done it, and for a few hours he felt like he was rich again.

He wanted to die. Just like he'd wanted to collapse and give up, right before he'd run that winning touchdown all those years ago. He sat there thinking about it, the gun from his go bag in his hand, his money in front of him, and he wondered what he had left to live for.

The only answer he came up with was that once upon a time, he'd actually graduated from college, before he put himself up for the draft. He wanted that education because his mother had wanted it. English and theatre, because he'd listened to all those teachers who'd said he was smart. He read books. He appreciated the stage. The atmosphere of a real theatre, the skill, they way someone could convince you they were someone else. He'd done the football, done the money, done all the misery that came after it and somehow survived it all, and now he had a story he could use.mj

Fast Eddie *understood* fucked up, rock bottom, whatever you wanted to call it, like all the people he'd watched perform never quite could, no matter how convincing they were.

It was time to get back to being alive. Make a comeback. Show the world there was more to him than just a touchdown and a ring and a scandal. He wanted to be rich again. Rich this time meant casting the anchor away, throwing the monster off his back, whatever the counsellors and his future rehab buddies were going to call it.

Somewhere inside Eddie Kowalski was a life that was still worth living.

Especially after he met *that otter*. He switched a light on inside Eddie that had been out for far too long.

* * *

'Hi, my name's Eddie, and I'm a drug addict and an alcoholic.'

'Hi, Eddie.'

It really did start that way. This wasn't just for the movies. Eddie was going to make it count: this was his stage now. But it didn't feel like one. He just felt broken. He *looked* broken. The worst part of it was, he'd gone to this meeting expecting to need no introduction, because surely everyone would know who he was. *Everyone* knew who Fast Eddie, MVP for the L.A. Riders was.

Except they didn't. These people had all lost the years that Eddie had been famous, and they wouldn't have cared much about who he was even if they hadn't.

It really did feel like a load off his conscience, telling them everything, opening up about his life. Everything except the first robbery. He probably could have confessed to that, but he at least wanted one thing he could still call his own. One secret. They could have the rest. The bare bones of the guy who used to be Fast Eddie on display. But that first heist, what it had made him feel like? He was amazed he could still remember it, but it was just like yesterday. Ginsburg was long dead, and nobody would have cared about any agreement he made anymore, but Eddie did. A deal was a deal: they'd never met, never known each other, there *was* no deal. This meeting could have everything except that night.

'Thank you for sharing that with us, Eddie.'

They even said that too. Actually, they talked a lot. Eddie tried to listen as best he could. He thought he'd been talking for hours, but when he looked at his watch, it had only been twenty minutes. For the next two hours, he tried to make himself listen, but he was half asleep, losing track of time and always drifting off into random thoughts.

God, was his brain really this fucked? Was this worth it?

No. And yes. Because he was still smart enough to spot one thing: the gorgeous otter who wasn't talking.

For the first time in as long as he could remember, Eddie saw someone desirable who he *didn't* want to beat up. That was how he knew this meeting was worth it, for this special moment. This guy was everything Eddie wished he could be right then: a good listener, compassionate without even saying a word. Why was this guy even here? He looked so sober. He was probably a sponsor, yet nobody looked at him. Nobody named him either. He looked like he'd been clean for years and was just here because his sobriety depended on these sessions even if he didn't talk.

Eddie caught him outside. Everyone else from the circle was lighting cigarettes. The otter wasn't though. For all his vices, Eddie had never smoked either.

'Hey,' he said. 'Will you come get some coffee with me?'

The otter looked at him quizzically, and for a moment Eddie wondered if he was a deaf-mute.

'I'd like to buy you a coffee,' Eddie said. 'We can still have caffeine, right? Something's got to be there for us.'

'Yeah. Alright.'

So the guy wasn't deaf, or mute. Maybe just damaged. Or maybe, Eddie thought, not damaged at all. He'd heard about guys who trawled rehab circles, went to whatever-anonymous just to pick people up. They always had a story prepared but never said it unless someone poked them. Eddie didn't get that vibe from this otter though, as much as he wanted to. This guy was probably so haunted by something it could put everyone else he'd failed to listen to to shame. Then put Eddie to shame himself.

'I know who you are,' the otter said, after they were sitting in Starbucks with the largest cup on the menu each. 'I'm glad you're sober. You really were a great player. Let me guess though, I just killed whatever reason you wanted to buy me coffee because you were hoping none of us would say that.'

'I don't care about any of that anymore,' Eddie said. 'How do you listen so well?'

'You learn to.'

'Yeah? Well, would you listen to something else? I've got something I need to confess.'

Now he talked about the first robbery. The otter listened.

'I don't know why I did it anymore,' Eddie said. 'I don't get myself. I never have. All that stuff I talked about in rehab, about how I don't like what I am. I don't even *get* it. I just imagine myself fucking people up and it just does something. Except you. I don't want to do that to you. I want to drink coffee with you. I don't care that you probably think I should have been committed years ago.'

'You're more self-aware than most people,' the otter said. 'It might have taken you six years and forgotten memories and looking like a shell, but you know who you are.'

'I always did. I was ashamed of all of it. Too scared to be myself. But even if I was, what would it matter? Everything's such a mess. I had to do a robbery so my mom could afford to survive an illness that wasn't even her fault. That's just the start of how people are too stupid to stop fucking themselves up. Nobody needs a sadist like me to do it; we're all doing it to ourselves, and nobody knows how the fuck to make it stop.'

The otter listened again, and this time Eddie did manage to talk for almost an hour. Starbucks was getting ready to close, and the staff were probably glad to have Eddie and his sympathetic otter gone. Eddie didn't care. He'd barely cared about anything for years.

'Thanks for listening,' Eddie said at the end of it, and now he did feel something: guilt for taking up this guy's time. This guy was probably somewhere close to making peace with the world, and he'd had to sit through Eddie's verbal war with all of it. If this guy was smart, he'd go to a different meeting next week and avoid crossing paths with him ever again. Unless Eddie could keep him. 'Will you be my sponsor?'

'Eddie, let me tell you something.'

Shit, this was new. The guy was staring at him like he'd been waiting all evening to fire a bullet, and now here it was. That sobriety was really alertness, and the listening was really calculation.

'Alright,' Eddie said. 'Hit me.'

'Being mean as fuck to people is not a personality. Going to war with the world is not a solution, and hating everything is not a form of battery-powered energy for your soul. But at least you're staying alive so you can have a good complain about it all. Maybe that works for now. But if you want to survive in this world, you've got to learn to like it. To like people. Otherwise, what's the sobriety all in aid of? If you can come to a meeting and talk about just one thing you still like about the world, *then* maybe someone will want to be your sponsor. I have to go. I've got TV to catch up on.'

'Hey, don't go. Wait! I like *you*.'

The otter turned, his coat half pulled on.

'Come on,' Eddie said. 'I like *you*. I mean it. I know I'm shit. But I like you. I wouldn't have asked you out for coffee otherwise. I want another date with you.'

The otter looked at him as though he could burst out laughing. 'This was a date?'

'I paid for your coffee, didn't I? That came out of my last fifty bucks. After that, I'm broke. Like, completely.'

'Then you should have been smarter with your last fifty bucks than trying a coffee date.' The otter swished his tail. 'But thank you. I'm glad I had some company tonight and not just a TV.'

'So that's a yes then? We'll go out again?'

'I want something you like *besides* me. Next week. Don't try to convince me now. Save it up. Mean it. I'll know if you don't. If I know you do, then I'll buy you coffee here. Deal?'

It was something, Eddie thought. Something wholesome, for the first time in too many years. 'Deal. Oh hey, by the way, it's been bugging me all evening. I know it's really none of my business, but have you seen a doctor about that limp you've got?'

The otter looked like he was prepared. 'It's just a sports injury. I'm fine.'

'I was a pro football player, and that doesn't look like a sports injury to me. If you've really seen a doctor and you really don't have ALS, then somebody fucked you up. If there's a problem in your life, maybe you *should* talk to that circle instead of listening. I didn't go to Betty Ford just to learn nothing.'

The otter rolled his eyes. 'You got the wrong idea, mister. I'm fine. But it's nice to know that you care.'

Something stirred a feeling in Eddie's heart right then. He'd later find out it was a line that the otter had stolen from an old human crime-noir movie, one he remembered from his teenage years, but right then it wasn't the hint of a memory, just the way the otter said it that made him sound so fuckable, and yet the last thing Eddie wanted to do was fuck him. '*Please* will you have a second date with me? Or a first? We'll go somewhere nice. I'll buy you dinner.'

'With your last fifty bucks?'

'I'll get a job. I can still wash dishes, right? Like I used to in my mom's place. You don't have to be my sponsor; let's forget about that. Just please at least show up to the meeting next week.'

'I'll be there,' the otter said. 'I'm always there.' He winked, walked to the door, let Eddie follow him, and then as if he'd rehearsed it, he turned around. 'Oh, by the way.' He offered his hand. 'I'm Echo.'

Chapter Thirteen

The day Echo Pendryl ran away from home, he asked his mother to go with him. She said she couldn't, but she'd never tell his father they'd had this conversation.

'Things could be better for you, Mom. Come with me. We'll get a good lawyer. With what I'm going to do, we could afford one. Even if we can't, just disappear anyway. With me. Dad would never find you. He might find me, but I can take care of him.'

That's when his mother looked all the more fearful. Echo Pendryl could never have 'taken care' of his father short of simply shooting him, but right then, Echo's fantasy was stronger than ever. One night, his father, hunting the pair of them, was going to break into his property and Echo was going to pull the trigger on him without thinking twice. Right then, he really believed himself capable. Shit, he *knew* he was, and that was why he knew he had to leave in the first place. One more night in this place and he was going to murder Ray Pendryl any way he could.

'Echo, this really isn't that terrible for me. I was never going to do anything better.'

'Aren't you tired of this?' He took hold of her by the forearms, lightly. 'Didn't you secretly pray one of us would come to you and say something like this?'

'No, Echo. I didn't pray for that.'

He let her go. 'I'm gay, Mom.'

'I know,' she said. 'I've always known. So has your father, he just doesn't want to believe it.'

'You remember that trip to the hospital I had when I was fourteen? I did that to myself. On purpose.'

Cadence Pendryl couldn't have pretended she knew that too. He'd expected her to, and he'd prepared himself to say he believed her, but she just stared at him. 'Why?'

'I needed to get off.'

'On *that*?'

'I know who I am, Mom. What I like. What I want. What I'm going to do if I stay here. It wouldn't be right. So I'm going. Are you going to be okay pretending we never talked?'

'Your father just wants you to serve. What if you'd be a great soldier? You've got all the determination, all the fitness. *I'd* like to see you in uniform. Don't Ask Don't Tell isn't a thing anymore. What if you met a wonderful young man?'

'I can't, Mom. It's not me. It doesn't work like that in real life anyway.'

His mother knew he was right. That was why she hugged him. 'Send me postcards. Send them to Sheila at the library. She'll make sure I get them. But Echo, where are you going?'

Echo shook his head. 'He'll beat it out of you. Unless he knows you really don't know.'

251

'He doesn't hit women. I told you, that doesn't happen to me.'

He knew it was true. It was the same line she'd always pulled when defending her husband despite all the other kinds of abuse he could dish out. 'New York,' Echo said. 'Tell him that.' He wasn't going to the Big Apple. Maybe someday, but there was only one place that had what he wanted.

The first postcard he sent his mother was from Malibu.

Malibu was where Echo met Mr B.

* * *

Elliot Burkowski was a greymuzzle husky. He'd placed an ad for a house steward. Years down the line, Echo would tell Eddie that when he saw it, he was down to *his* last fifty bucks, sitting in a coffee house, contemplating which doorways would be most comfortable to sleep in when he told the hostel he couldn't pay for tonight.

Why had a guy in Malibu advertised for a steward in a rag like this, all the way out here? Probably because a PA had done it for him. Echo didn't care. He counted the last fifty in his hand and took a drink of coffee. The place became brighter as the clouds cleared for the midday sun. He didn't believe in the weather giving signs, but Echo felt good. Here was the edge, and he was going to save himself from going off. He checked the credit on his phone and had enough for the call.

A woman answered. She sounded young, probably a wolf or a dog. Echo introduced himself.

'Hey Mr B,' she called. 'Did you place an ad for a house boy?' Echo didn't hear the response. 'He says come over here this afternoon, three o'clock. Can you do that?'

Echo could. He did. So did a lot of other people.

The reason was obvious – Burkowski was *filthy* fucking rich. A retired hedge-fund manager and apparently only moderately successful by comparison. A billionaire at least three times over, so Echo heard later, the guy could certainly live on the East Coast in a mansion like this for the rest of his life. He must have been in his late sixties, if not seventy already. By the time Echo saw him, he wondered why he wanted a steward at all, because it seemed the role was already being filled by four stewardesses.

If you could call them that. Echo knew what they really were. Burkowski wasn't just a sugar daddy; he practically defined it. His young women were all canids – two 'skis and two wolves. The one who sounded like she'd answered the phone, Dany, sat him down with the others who'd answered the ad and asked what he wanted to drink. Everyone else had beer bottles or cocktails on the go. Echo, who had never drunk a drop back then, asked for tea.

Dany the husky looked at him for a moment, gave the kind of smile Echo thought belonged to a girl who liked to toy with innocent boys, and said, 'Tea. You got it. Green?'

Echo had never had that either. 'Sure.'

'Just plain green tea, or do you want mango and coconut? Or we've got lychee. Or salted caramel.'

You could mix those with Japanese tea? 'Mango and coconut's good.'

The others were sniggering. Echo heard 'virgin' at least twice as he sat there, deciding it was better not to try and pretend they weren't in the room. A couple of them gave nods and smiles, as if to say he didn't stand a chance but at least he was trying. They were all dressed for an interview in a fancy place like this. Echo just had on the one smart-casual shirt he owned and one reasonably new pair of jeans.

It soon didn't matter. Burkowski's women were handing out swimwear. Everyone was saying 'All*riiiiight!*' or some variation of it. Everyone got a Ralph Lauren towel too. They all got changed in front of each other, like it was an older version of the high-school locker room.

Echo Pendryl, who'd one day leave a legacy of porn footage in his wake, hid behind the largest chair he could find. He knew Dany the husky was watching and had probably just mentally eliminated him from the list, but he didn't care. His last fifty bucks had brought him here, and he was staying until he got told to leave. He wasn't in bad shape. He'd never tell the man himself, but his father's insistence on his family having a fitness regime of swimming, running and calisthenics had finally helped him have a shot at something. When he came out from behind his chair, at least everyone seemed to be laughing a little less.

'Hey, aquatic boy, can I lift that tail later?' An obviously straight hyena said that, and everyone laughed at how Echo's tail dropped and his butt tightened up. Sex with canids was supposed to be

254

hideous. A pool party with no otters? Well, there was one, and he was probably going to get touched up and pushed around all through it.

'Oh, come on, I'm just kidding. I'm Crash, this is Buster, Drax and Aldo.' Another yeen, a dingo and a fennec. They all looked like they could dress smart but were really street trash. 'I'll let you in on a secret: Mr B never hires anyone at these things. This is just how he likes a pool party. He actually got an otter here this time. He'll love that. So get that tail up and look like you're gonna have some fun. Nobody's gonna touch you if you don't wanna; Mr B *don't* like that. But if you *do* wanna? My advice, Dany already likes you, and trust me, she's sweeeeeet, sweeeeeet sugar. If she likes you, so does Mr B.' Crash rubbed his thumb and fingers together, then leaned in and whispered, 'The old man likes to watch. I think he's gonna dig you. Make yourself some moolah. You do that, word gets round. Mr B knows the whole strip. You'll never go hungry around here.'

Echo wanted to run. He also knew he had nowhere to run to.

The pool was fun. It was a proper size. Twenty other guys in the place, it was perfect for water polo. Then there was the contest on the diving board. Echo could play, scored winning points for his team, dived well, and actually felt like people were starting to like him. Crash the hyena, to his credit, wasn't a bad guy. He saw Echo watching the other guys get it on with Burkowski's girls and do nothing besides watch and sip more tea.

'Come *on*, ott-butt! You wanna earn, don't you? Coz you look flat-ass broke to me.' Crash sat down on the sun lounger and chucked back the rest of what must have been his fourth lethal cocktail. 'Alright, I'm one hundred percent hetero, but you're a good-looking guy. Mr B's just *waiting* to see you make it. You could get a tip *I'd* be jealous of.'

Where was Burkowski, anyway? He'd shown up in his silk bathrobe, cigar and cocktail in hand, told everyone to have fun, then just vanished.

'Why don't I make it with *you*?' Echo said. 'You're not a bad-looking guy either. Would he like that?'

'Are you serious?'

'Do you want me to be?'

'I told you, I'm not gay. I'm just trying to help you out. You wanna just sit there, that's fine. But look, I'd challenge even the gayest of gay guys not to get it up for Dany. She's been watching you for hours. Go say hi.'

Echo looked around, found Dany, and pointed behind Crash. 'She's helping your friend Buster be sick right now.'

'Ah, shit. I *told* him to drink water as well as booze. I'll be right back.'

Crash did come back, but it was only to smooch with Dany himself until he finally got his dick sucked and fell asleep. He was the most sober of anyone; the rest had all either gone to sleep on the loungers or been escorted to cab rides home by the notably sober females.

Echo looked around himself and felt like the party was over. He was still sitting there, watching the sunset, and thinking it wasn't such a bad use of his last fifty. It almost did seem like a waste though: he was probably going to have to fuck for money with people a lot less hot than this, in alleyways and doorways instead of in a nice place by a pool. He told himself that was a problem for tomorrow. If he was lucky, he might wake up here tomorrow before being asked to leave.

Dany was here, looking as immaculate as she had at the start. 'You okay, otter? Would you like another cup of tea?' The way she sat down, Echo knew that wasn't really the question. She put a hand on the back of his neck and ruffled. 'You're sweet. I like you. I've seen new-on-the-scene before. Would you like a good scratch? A backrub? We don't have to fuck, but how would you like to relax?'

'I'm gay, Dany.'

She smiled. 'You think I couldn't tell?' She tickled his back, and he laughed, then sighed as she worked her claws in a little and scratched. 'There, see? I know how to treat an otter right. Oh yeah. There you go. Arch that back for me.' She worked her other hand up his chest to under his chin. 'Been a while since somebody was good to you? Good boy, nice deep breaths. Let's have a purr out of you at last.'

It *was* irresistibly good, and Echo didn't resist. He purred as loud as he could, thinking, *Now at least I really got fifty's worth.*

'That's it. Who's my good boy? *Sure* I can't put a hand down those speedos? You can pretend I'm a guy. I'm pretty *good* at being a guy when I have to.'

'I'm good,' Echo said, happy that for the first time in weeks he truly felt like he was. 'Just keep doing that.'

'You got it. Mr B likes you.'

'Where is he? Watching on a camera?'

'Hah! Did Crash tell you that? That's what these dummies *think* Mr B does when he's not on the

257

poolside. He's not even here. He went to the country club to play golf about four hours ago. I think he got bored of this one.' She got behind him, ran her hands down the side of his chest, and put her muzzle on his shoulder. 'You wanna know a little secret?'

As her rubbing-scratching routine stopped and Echo came down from the bliss, he felt like he already knew what it would be. 'Go on.'

'This really *is* an interview. It's not always, but this one is. Crash was half right.'

Echo looked around himself, and for a moment, the bliss came back. Could what he was thinking actually be true? That it truly was an interview, and this was the test: who was awake, sober, and cleaning the place up with Mr B's women by the time he got back? It was probably another part of the game. An elaborate one, by a man who really was bored with the likes of Crash and Buster.

'Hey, look at me.' Dany put a hand on his check and turned his head. Then she kissed him in the middle of it. 'You're way smarter than you think. Come on.' She got up. He followed her. They cleared glasses, binned strewn food, washed up the dishes, swept and mopped the poolside, vacuumed the rooms, sprayed some air freshener, cleaned the kitchen down, and then finally woke up the comatose party zombies. Echo left Crash for last.

'Yeah, yeah, alright, I'm outta here.' Crash got up groggily and followed Echo to the front door, not seeming to realise who he was following until he got there. 'You have a good time? Listen, give me your number; we should get a drink together. Where do you live? Wanna share a cab?'

'I'm staying.'

Crash stopped, turned, his mouth open in disbelief, until he got it. Or at least, he thought he had. 'Oh! Oooooooh! Holy shit, you're an overnighter already? Man, Dany must have…oh, you're a sneaky little fucker, ott-butt. It was all an act? Damn, I bet you even got into her bedroom! Alriiiiight, I got played by an otter. *Damn*. If I kept a diary, I'd so put that in it.' He laughed, a proper laugh. At least, Echo thought, he seems to enjoy his life. 'Enjoy it, ott-butt. Just a word to the smart: don't outstay your welcome. When Mr B gives you the sugar, say thanks until next time and find the next party. I know a guy who says he can get into Tyler Goldman's place in a couple of weeks' time for something that's going down. If you're interested, call me.'

'He didn't leave a number,' Echo said, as soon as Crash's cab had left.

'He never does,' Dany said. 'Forget about Goldman's place too; I've heard that one from him half a dozen times this year. Goldman doesn't even have parties, and I don't have "overnighters." If I sleep with anyone here, it's Mr B. Just when he asks. Now how about that tea? Mr B's on his way home.'

They sat in the kitchen at the marble bar. 'So he really is a sugar daddy,' Echo said.

Dany clasped her cup between both hands. 'He's a decent man. We're all his companions, and he pays well. There's no doing anything we don't want to. He's a good find in a place like this.'

259

'Where are the others?'

'Gone home.'

'But you live here?'

'On and off.'

'Do you actually think he's going to hire me?'

'We'll see.'

'What does he expect? Any big no-nos?'

'Be polite and smile. He likes swimwear when he's here on his own. If he's got guests, wear clothes.'

'Me in swimwear as well as you.'

'Uh-huh.'

'So...would he ever want *me* as a companion?'

Dany thought for a moment, as if deciding whether to tell him the truth. 'I've never known him to have a guy. Not *have him* have him. Sometimes I've thought he maybe wanted to, but if he's done that, I don't know about it. It'd just be weird if everyone else wore swim gear and you didn't.'

'He's going to want to watch me with you? Like Crash said.'

'Forget about Crash. It's like I said, if *you* don't want it, you don't gotta do it. Relax. Talk about you. Where are you from?'

'I'm not from anywhere.'

Dany looked at him, and he knew she got it. 'Okay. You ever had a boyfriend?'

He decided there was no point in lying and shook his head.

'What do you want, Echo? For your life. Any ideas?'

'So *now* I'm getting a real interview.'

'Might be a good idea to answer the question then.'

'I want something better than being a marine.'

'Oooooh. Does that explain the whole runaway thing? Shit, did you go AWOL?'

'I never joined. You can relax this time. It's an asshole dad story.'

'Will he show up here?'

Echo shook his head and smiled. 'He's looking for me in New York right now.'

'What turns you on, Echo?'

No. Not this. Not now. He looked at her, wanting to believe it was another flirt, an attempt to crack his shell, or maybe something Mr B was looking for. He wouldn't be looking for this. 'Is the answer to this one for Mr B or for you?'

'For me.'

'If I told you, would you promise not to tell?'

'You won't shock me. I know your type. You're a little bit nervous, and whatever does it for you is just embarrassing; it's not terrible or illegal or anything.'

Echo managed to relax slightly. 'I don't have to pull my usual line then. "It's not blood, it's not shit and it's not kids."'

'Then what is it? Murder?'

'No, it's not that either. Remind me to add that next time.'

'You're still dodging the question.'

'I'd just rather not go there. Not unless you *promise* this stays between us. You can't even tell Mr B.'

'I know how to keep a promise. Why don't you let me prove it?'

'My fetish put me in hospital. It's dangerous. Like I can't even really do it dangerous, just think about it. Apart from the one time I did.' Thinking about it

261

switched lights on, and Echo knew what was going to end up happening if he told this story. Maybe Dany could put a hand down his speedos after all, at the end of this. 'Pinky promise?'

She rolled her eyes and gave the sort of laughter he knew was kind. 'Why am I not surprised you make your promises that way? Alright.' She put her pinky around his and squeezed. 'Pinky promise. Now, come on. What makes innocent Echo hit the ceiling?'

He told her.

'Boy oh boy,' she said, a little wide-eyed and looking like she wanted something a little stronger than tea. 'I've got to give it to you, I've never heard of that one. But I was still right. I'm not shocked. I bet there's others who like it. You ever looked?'

'I've never dared. I'd end up dead. Or somebody else would.'

'You ever thought about seeing a sex therapist?'

'What for? It's not a problem. It's just a part of me. I can't explain it, and I don't think I want to. What turns *you* on?'

'Money.'

'Right.'

The front door went. 'Mr B's home. Look smart.'

Elliot Burkowsi came in looking like it was first thing in the morning, and he was fresh and ready for a board meeting. He smiled, and Echo knew he was going to remember the first time he saw that smile. Nobody else had ever given him one like it.

Dany the husky who loved money had better keep that promise, he thought.

'Hey, Mr B. This is Echo.'

'I know,' he said. He looked out of the window at the spotless poolside, then turned around and offered his hand. 'Would you like to stay here, Echo?'

'Yeah,' Echo said. 'Please?'

This was happening? This longshot that had felt like a game right up to now suddenly wasn't a game anymore, but a dream coming true? A place to stay that wasn't a hostel, where his family would surely never find him?

'Of course,' Burkowski said. He took his wallet out. 'Here. For tonight's good job. I'd put it in your shirt pocket, except you're in speedos. I like that. You're a very handsome otter, and all my friends are going to like you.'

Echo managed not to put his hands to his face and cry. He just glowed so hot he could feel his own body heat and forced himself not to shuffle his feet. 'I can make a good breakfast, too. What would you like tomorrow morning?'

'Oh, don't worry. Dany makes breakfast. She'll bring you yours in bed. Tomorrow will be a nice, easy day. We'll get you used to where everything is. Your wage will be a thousand dollars a week. Plus tips. How does that sound?'

'Errr...you really want to pay me that much?' Echo realised he was already holding money and looked down. There was already a thousand bucks in his hand. Burkowski nodded at it.

'Welcome to paradise, Echo. Don't spend it all too quickly.'

'I wouldn't even know where to shop.' *Shut up, you idiot! Words coming out of your mouth will ruin everything!*

Before Echo could think of how his father had imprinted lines like that on his brain, Burkowski was looking at him like he'd noticed something. 'Dany, would you like to keep Echo company tonight?'

'Sure,' Dany said, looking like she knew exactly how to do it. 'If he wants.'

'Yeah,' Echo said. 'Sure.'

'I think it's bedtime,' Dany said. 'Let's go show you your room.'

What the sudden change in his fortune hadn't done, the room did. It wasn't big enough to cram his house back home into; it was perfect for one person. Cosy. With a TV, a fridge and a view of the bay with a cloudless starry sky outside the window.

Echo Pendryl hugged Dany the husky and started sobbing. As soon as he had the breath to do it, he said he was sorry, his head still buried in her chest.

'Let it go,' she said. 'It's alright.'

He did, for another five minutes that felt like an hour. 'He's seen this before, right? Mr B. This is what he does. Finds someone who's got nothing and gives them everything.'

Dany stroked his head. 'Yeah. Hey, look at me for a second. We can keep hugging all night if you like, but I gotta tell you something.'

He let go. 'What is it?'

'You asked me about no-nos. There's only one. You're right. Mr B did this once before. We had Leo here for two years. He was a mink. Mr B was fond of him. He

264

got hit by a speedboat and killed a year ago, on a diving trip. It took Mr B a while, but he's ready to have another steward. You're going to be perfect. Just don't mention Leo until he does. Don't go diving in the ocean either. And thank God your fetish isn't drowning.'

'Okay, Dany. I got it.'

'You want me to sleep with you tonight? I make a good teddy-bear. I bet you do too. You ever *had* anyone cuddle you, Echo? Even your mom?'

Echo remembered his father's exact words. 'Cuddling was for weak, sissy faggot boys in my house.' He smiled, wiped his face, and said, 'I can be the best teddy you ever had.'

When she cuddled him, Echo knew that if this had been his last night on Earth, it would have been a perfect one. He didn't have to pretend she was male; he still got a boner but felt too tired to do anything with it. He just wanted to fall asleep happy, for the first time in his life.

Or maybe the second. He thought of waking up in the hospital after what he'd done, five years ago. *That* was happy. That was the one time he dared do something that crazy, and boy had it worked.

Maybe from now on he wouldn't feel like he needed it.

If only, he'd later think, that had been the truth.

'So this was the real answer, when you said money,' he said. 'Mr B's your favourite teddy.'

'Oh yeah. But you're pretty good. Sure you're not a little bit hetero there? I can tell you're hot for this. You smell like musk.' She reached down and felt his hard

265

cock. 'Hello! My teddy's got a pretty good package right there.'

'I like comfort. I'm...you know.'

'Imagining I did your thing first? Now I'm giving you a recover cuddle? Told you you were sweet. We *could* pretend, if you like. How about it? *"Are you ready to play a little game?"'*

'I'm exhausted. Can we do it tomorrow?'

'Sure. Long as you give me *your* real answer. What do you want for your life?'

Echo sighed out a satisfied deep breath and thought about the thousand bucks he had no idea how to spend. He already knew that learning would be all too easy. 'I wanna be rich and famous.'

She hugged him a little tighter. 'Now you're talking. You really wanna know what I think?'

'What?'

'Under this big soft teddy-bear, there's a daredevil. That story you told me, maybe you wanna take a *little* bit more care with your life next time, but you liked the thrill. You want to be dangerous. You want to be *danger*. More than a marine. Most marines wouldn't go where I think you might. Or you might just like working for Mr B.'

'What would he think?' Echo said. 'About my thing. Should I tell him?'

She broke the cuddle slightly for a minute and shifted upright, as if thinking. 'No. My advice, keep it quiet. He's pretty good in the sack, and fit, but he's got a pacemaker. Something like that? *That's* a no-no. He can't go to Echo's fetish world.'

Echo smiled. He promised himself if he ever made a hot film, he'd make sure it got called that.

* * *

Eddie Kowalski did a surprising thing: he convinced Echo that there was something he liked besides him. He came to the next session and talked about films. Echo believed him. They had another cup of coffee.

They had coffee after every meeting for the next three months before Echo went to a meeting and said he'd like to be Eddie's sponsor. He was a senior enough member of narcotics anonymous by then: experienced, recovered and strong (or so they all thought, and Echo let them think it).

The night that Echo decided Eddie was ready for the kind of trust that formed a sponsor relationship, they had their coffee and Echo invited him back to Mr B's house.

He still thought of it as that, even though Mr B hadn't been there for three years.

The only one who lived in that house now was Echo. Dany still came by at least once a week. She called every evening. She was a lawyer now – her companionship for Mr B had paid her through Santa Barbara law school, and she was flying high on her own money.

She'd represented Echo when they'd first arrested him on suspicion of murder. She was probably the only one who still believed, more than anyone else, that he was innocent. She'd proven herself as a lawyer when the jury delivered a unanimous not guilty.

Echo knew what was coming when Eddie saw his home. It *was* his home, even if he still couldn't quite accept it. Eddie never shut up, but ten minutes in this place and it looked like he might even last hours without speaking. He didn't though.

'*You* live here?'

'Surprised?'

'What exactly do you do? You said you worked in a box office.'

'Yeah, I do. I also have a production company, but it's a little low key right now. Not found its big thing yet.'

'This is a joke, right?' Eddie smiled. 'Hah ha, you got me. Whose place is this? You borrowed their keys. Or did you steal them?'

Some say I killed for them. 'It belonged to a hedge fund manager called Elliot Burkowski. I called him Mr B. He left it to me.'

Eddie came down to earth a little. 'A late husband?' Eddie sniffed. 'You married a dog?'

It confirmed what Echo had always thought was power of suggestion but didn't want to, and for the first time in ages, he felt like the place brought him a moment of fleeting happiness. It really *did* still smell like Mr B. 'Employer. A special one. The kind most people never get.'

Eddie's eyes had fallen on the thing Echo knew he'd notice, once he was done being pie-eyed about the place. 'What's that for? You keep a taser in your kitchen?' He picked it up. It was the old-school kind, made to look like a glorified carrot peeler rather than a gun. 'You get people breaking in?'

'That's for if Mr B's daughters show up. He had two. He left them nothing. They don't like me. One of them tried to burn this place down while I was asleep. She nearly succeeded.' Echo pulled his shirt up to show Eddie the scar on the right of his chest. 'The other one gave me that.'

Echo had thought Eddie would know a bullet scar when he saw one, and he was right. Eddie stared at it, touched it, then craned his head around to check Echo's back. His reaction was just as predictable. He knew what Echo knew after it had happened: most people with an exit wound as well as an entrance one never made it to the hospital, let alone lived.

'Huskies have their heart on the right,' Echo said. 'Stupid bitch never thought most other species don't. Otters don't. If she'd thought of it, I wouldn't be here. She was a good shot. See? It's in the right place to kill a husky without them knowing what hit them.'

'She get life?'

'Twenty years for attempted murder.'

'But you still keep a taser there in case she shows up. Or is that just for Petrol Bomb Betty?'

'Her name's Louanne. She used kerosene. She got ten. Diminished responsibility. Some fucking psychiatrist helped her get off. There was nothing wrong with her. Nor's there a cure for being anything she is.' Echo took a deep breath and sighed through his teeth. 'Mr B had that taser because he didn't like guns. He never used it. He was checking it to make sure it still worked. It worked alright. On him, when he set it off by accident. He had a pacemaker for a heart condition. I couldn't do anything. CPR doesn't work when something like that goes wrong and starts firing off after you've been hit with the setting he had that on.' Echo nodded to the taser, still in Eddie's hand, and then looked down at the kitchen floor, next to a cupboard. 'He died in my arms right there.'

Eddie did the smart thing and put the taser down. 'I'm sorry. You two were close? Well, no shit, right? He left you everything.'

'That's why everyone thought I murdered him.'

That was the second time that night that Eddie Kowalski knew when to shut his mouth. A minute later, it was the first time Echo Pendryl kissed him.

'What was that for?' he said, caught as unsuspecting as he'd been at Echo's story.

'For being the first person who didn't ask me if I did it.'

'Did what? Killed Mr B? Of course you didn't, there's no way. Not you. That's when you started doing morphine, right? After nobody would believe you. After the trial where you got not guilty.'

Echo sat down at the bar. 'I was innocent. But I'm not exactly who you think I am, Eddie. I don't blame people for thinking I did it. Every morning when I wake up, I *feel* like I did it. I feel like he'd still be here if he'd never let me in his house.'

'Oh, come on,' Eddie said. 'Alright, I'm sorry, this is a big deal for you. You never talk at the meetings, and that's why I don't know this, and you're my sponsor now, right? Tell me your story. How you got past it all. Tell me how I get to where you are.'

'That's not what I brought you here for. Nobody wants to be where I am.' Now was the time to flash the smile Echo knew would cool Eddie's blood right down, maybe to near freezing. 'Except maybe me.'

Eddie stared at him for a moment, and Echo could tell this reaction from a mile away. Eddie Kowalski, the wolverine who often said he'd done it all, actually looked like unease was creeping through him. Play this right and it might soon be pure fear. 'So why am I here then?'

'What if I said I could help you in a different way? One that the people at our little meeting every week don't need to know about?'

'Oh shit,' Eddie said, taking a step backwards. 'I should have known. You're a dealer, right? You're sober but you switched from being a user.'

'It's not that at all,' Echo said, already prepared for that conclusion. 'You told me you're a sadist and that you didn't want to fuck me up. That I was the one guy you didn't want to do it to. What if I could change your mind about that? Because if I tell you this story, I bet I can. I'm a masochist. I guarantee you've *never* met another one like me.'

Eddie Kowalski had probably never been so torn between running and staying in his life. The thrill, the fear, it was everything Echo wanted to see. His own heart was in action, a thrill he'd long since thought he'd lost going through him. It had worked. Eddie really was the right person. Eddie believed in his innocence. He knew it was because Eddie wanted to, and proof didn't matter.

That wasn't going to stop this, though. Echo needed this. A last stage in his recovery. He needed to be ready to be who he really was again.

271

'Stay,' he said. 'Trust me, it'll be worth it.'

'Echo, I *really* don't want you for this.'

He did though. Echo could already tell. 'Sit down, Eddie. I'll make us a cup of tea. You like mango and coconut?'

Chapter Fourteen

On the night Mr B asked Echo if he'd ever had a dangerous idea, Echo's house duties were done, and he was looking at the drinks shelf in the kitchen. Mr B had been unusually quiet and reclusive for the last couple of weeks, but tonight he came into the kitchen like he was intent on having a long night somewhere. Echo knew how to warm him up.

'You want a cocktail, Mr B? How about a nitro-mojito? Or how about a surfin' kahuna? I got that banana and coconut rum Dany was talking about the other week.'

'I'm going to be driving tonight,' Mr B said. 'Hopefully. But you go ahead.'

Echo mixed a pina colada without the cream and charged it with a shot of Absolut red label. 'I cleaned the fleet this morning. The Maserati Quatroporte's first in line, just how you like it. Where you going?'

'The Wagyu Grill.'

'Oooo,' Echo said. Mr B was getting his wallet out tonight then. Not that he'd notice a bill like that even touch his assets. 'Business or pleasure? You want anything ready for when you get in?'

'Just out for dinner.'

'With friends?'

'With you. If you're agreeable.'

Echo set his drink down before he could drop it. 'What?'

'I'm asking you if you'd like to go out for dinner with me.'

'Well, yeah, but...why?'

'Because I want to. Because it's your birthday and you thought you could keep it quiet.'

'Aw, shucks.' Echo shuffled his feet. 'Every birthday I've ever had's been shit. Nineteen's not a milestone. I know you could give me a great one, but...are you sure about this?'

'Do I ever ask for anything unless I'm completely sure? I've noticed you never leave the house anymore either.'

'I never want to,' Echo said. 'I've got everything I want right here, and I'm never bored. What's out there for me besides an expensive steak? Not that I want to say no exactly; I don't want to be rude, but dinner with your houseboy?'

'I've told you before, you're not my houseboy. You're a companion like all the rest.'

'All the rest who aren't here. You haven't had anyone around for nearly three weeks. I know it's not exactly my business, but what gives?'

'Their time here came to an end,' Mr B said. 'For the right reasons.' He sat down at the bar that formed the centrepiece of the kitchen. 'Dany's the only one I think you really miss, and she graduated law school and now she's completely independent. Her request. She'll call, when she's finished setting up her new home in Santa Barbara. You already knew all that though.'

'I'm not a companion like the others.'

'You misunderstand what I mean by "like the others". What I meant is that you're equal to all of them even if there's a slight pay difference. What you mean is that you don't fuck me.'

Echo smiled. Mr B hardly ever said fuck, but it was always amusing rather than grating when he did. Echo sipped his drink and gently wrapped his tail around the front of his legs, leaning against the sideboard. 'I can if you want.'

'I want dinner. I can pay you extra for having it with me if that's what it takes, but I'd hoped you might do it just because you wanted to. I understand your life feels complete. That's fine. But I'd feel better if you convinced me you're not really agoraphobic.'

Echo laughed. 'I'm not agoraphobic. I just have high standards. You meet them. The world out there doesn't.'

'Flatterer. How do you know? When was the last time you went out there and tried living in it? You barely even spend your salary. Let *me* do some flattery then: you're the only person I've had here for years who wasn't greedy. You don't care about the money like the others do. Even Dany. I love her to bits, but I know exactly who I love. Greed turns me on. So does humility. Among other reasons, I asked you to live here because I thought you'd give the place a little balance. You've excelled at it. So –'

'So let me buy dinner. That's my condition. We go to the Wagyu, I pay. It's not like I can't. I'd take out some cash and splash it if I was hiding any down these speedos.' He tucked his thumbs in them. *Come on. Ask me to take them off. We can do dinner after you've had virgin otter to kick the night off. You want to flatter me, appreciate my body. Like you always try to pretend you don't want to.*

'Very well, Echo. You pay.' Mr B sat forward, his elbows on the table. 'That *is* a nice pose. Have you ever considered modelling? Swimwear, perhaps? I can ask the right people.'

'What do I need a job for?' Echo's heart sank. 'Are you letting me go? Is that what this dinner is? You don't want an agoraphobic otter who doesn't know how to be greedy?'

'Not at all. I'm just thinking about your horizons a little. Call me a good manager, if you like.'

You know what I secretly think, Mr B? Behind this nice and polite act, you were probably once a total bastard to work for. Or with. My father was right about one thing: people like you were responsible for fucking up this country's finances. Too bad his next step was thinking the military should run everything, right down to the president himself. 'I don't want to be a model, Mr B. If there's anything...alright, you know why I'm saving my money? Acting. I want to make it. I've gotta get enough pay to live off for a few years while nowhere will hire me apart from dumb commercials.'

'Well, why didn't you say so?' Mr B sat back now and looked at him with a warm smile and the kind of calm that said he already had several plans, and they'd all be good ones. 'Forget the Quatroporte. Let's get the Ferrari out and go show it off to the strip, get Wagyu, and talk about Echo Pendryl's name on the top of a movie poster. Or would you rather be a director? Or producer?'

'Producer? Hah!' Echo drained his glass and set it down. 'What does a producer even do? They've got the biggest bullshit job there is. All they are is a paycheque. If that's what you're going to tell me I've got you for, great: you're the producer who's smart enough never to call himself a producer. Or try acting like what he thinks it should be.'

A moment later, Echo got one of those moments he'd seen in many movies, where the silence had the last person who spoke asking themselves what the fuck they'd just said, only this time it wasn't reacting to the horror of the scene companion. It was wondering why the said companion was looking at them with what appeared to be total comprehension, with maybe a little awe mixed in. Whatever it was, Echo had never seen Mr B look alive with deep thoughts like this. He'd seen him switch on a brain that he knew didn't belong to a hedge fund manager, or a billionaire, or anything else he knew the guy was. It was almost like Mr B had spent his life wanting to indulge the something else that was behind looks like this, and maybe, right now, Echo had sparked it.

With a dumb couple of lines about producers?

'Echo,' he said, 'you're the one smart person I've had here for years.'

'Oh, now you're just milking it. Dany was law school smart. I'll never be that smart.'

'Dany was smart enough to read law, yes. Smart enough to be a very good lawyer. Successful. Rich. Survive in the world kind of smart? Yes. Never get stamped on smart? Most likely that too. Beneath all that, there's one reality: she hasn't been smart enough figure out that the world doesn't need more lawyers. She will, one day. I really hope I'm still here to help her pick the pieces up when she gets to that one.'

Echo's eyes had grown wide through every slow word. 'Did you tell her this?'

'Of course not. It's her journey. Shattering the great crystal boat she loves isn't my way. You, though: you won't get yours shattered. Even your father failed to do that. You ran away to stop him because you saw it all coming. One step ahead. Probably many. Now, let's get the car out. One thing though. I'll drive you a bargain. You can pay for dinner tonight as long as you let me return to one little conversation we had before. You know which one I mean.'

Echo walked slowly to the bar and put his hands on the back of one of the chairs. He did know what Mr B was talking about. 'Make it worth my while. Then you've got a deal.'

'Oh,' Mr B said. 'Your while? That, young man, I can pleasantly guarantee.'

* * *

Echo hadn't expected to feel like he was going out with a celebrity, but he'd expected people to know who Mr B was, or at least that he was a high roller, and make eyes at how he was eating dinner in a fancy place with a barely legal otter. Even if the looks all said 'There he goes again' rather than 'Look, new scandal!' Yet people seemed to ignore them, almost as if they could be father and son despite the species difference. That thought amused him.

Mr B probably thought he was smiling at the steak, which was every bit as succulent as promised and filled Echo's mouth with a taste that even put freshly caught fish to shame. This was like beef could come from the sea and was practically still alive with freshness, salt, and the charcoal taste of barbeque with vanilla and cinnamon. Echo had never drunk red wine before, but with the steak he liked it, guessing Mr B had probably picked a sweeter one, rich with blackcurrant tones and the smell of summer trees, because it would be easy for him to drink. Even the vegetables looked indulgent, garnished with leaves, cheese and saffron.

Mr B finished the last mouthful, leaving his plate almost dishwasher spotless, then dabbed his mouth delicately with a napkin in a way that made Echo think of the famous human playing a cannibal in that *Silence* movie, or whatever it was called.

'So, Echo. Have you ever had a dangerous idea?'

Echo knew what he was really asking. 'Oh yeah.'

'Why don't you tell me about the one that led to that conversation I mentioned earlier? I've been thinking about it for weeks. I even did a little research. Most psychologists and people who've been where you obviously have agree with you: your life really does flash before your eyes when you die, or *think* you're dying, but it doesn't happen in chronological order like the movies show. So, here's a little amateur psychology of

279

my own: you spoke up when you heard me and Dany ruminating out loud about what happens when you die because there's a story you want to tell, and you tried to dare yourself, but you couldn't. So, how *did* you nearly die? You said it was on your birthday.'

Echo smiled, knowing that on some level, Mr B was right. 'Uh-huh.'

'Tell me, was it really a birthday present to yourself?' Mr B picked up his wine glass and swirled it around, took a taste, then set it down and poured more wine into Echo's. 'A great gamble for that high or seeing the flash? Maybe back then you thought it wouldn't have been so bad if you hadn't woken up.'

'I never wanted to die. I wanted to see what Dad did afterwards. If he actually cared. He didn't. He didn't visit me in the hospital. My sister did. Mom did. Dad didn't want them to. He just said it was my own fault for being that stupid. He didn't even think I might have been suicidal. That was the real test. There was no concern there. No love.' Echo forced as ruthless a smile as he could, and right then he felt like he could have gone into any business meeting the likes of which Mr B always had and gotten anything he wanted. 'But I did get a pretty kick-ass flash. I woke up knowing I had stuff to *live* for. My flash was intense.'

'I think *you're* intense, Echo. In a very quiet way. That's why I'm fascinated by you. Most intense people are flamboyant. You're quiet, but behind those eyes there's a totally unique understanding of the world. Most people get a life-changing epiphany after a near-death experience. I think whatever you got, you feel like it was deeper. You don't have to be scared of it. You know what else I see?'

Echo shook his head, a flattered, glowing smile on his face, and for the first time since he'd known Elliot Burkowski, he felt like his happiness hadn't been complete until this moment. 'What?'

'I see your name on all sorts of posters, just like you want. I see a title. "Echo the Electric Otter".'

Echo's heart jolted inside him, but he kept sitting still, holding his wine glass, willing himself not to shake with nerves. 'Why do you see that?'

'Call me a detective who solved the case of Echo Pendryl.' Mr B took a sip of his drink that said the truth was just as delicious and expensive. 'Your mystery fetish is electrocution, isn't it? You never wanted me to know in case I wanted to try it, because Dany told you I have a pacemaker. She never told me your secret. I spent weeks contemplating what it must be. The only thing I got out of Dany was that it wasn't drowning. That was my best guess. Echo the Drowning Otter. So what was higher? What would most likely kill *me* if I ever tried it on you?'

Echo stared down at the table, his breath caught in his throat. Dany. *Dany* had told him. That total –

'Echo, look at me.'

After a moment, Echo managed to look up and saw the same kind eyes he'd seen on his first night staring into his scared ones.

'Before you do that shy look that I love and tell me this is too public a place, look around this room. You're probably the most normal person in it. Trust me to know the kinds of people who come here. All of them have fears, just like you.'

'Err...' Echo found his voice, perhaps only thanks to having paid attention in drama classes, to all the scenes where a distraction was needed. 'Waiter!' The weasel who'd been looking after them all night was ready before he'd said the word. 'Can we have another bottle of this please? Actually, no, sorry, could you bring us both a double Bulleit Bourbon each? Oh, wait, do you have Maker's Mark instead?'

'Yes, we do, sir. Right away. Would you like a dessert menu as well?'

'Oh yes, yes I would.'

Echo stared at Elliot Burkowski like he meant real business this time. 'On my birthday four years ago...' He looked at his watch. 'Well, shit. It's almost right on the hour. Seven PM. I took a shower and then shoved my wet tail into a socket. *Zap*, motherfucker. I'm telling you, I don't think I ever really passed out. My flash, that gave me all my most intense memories, and right at the top of them all was finally doing that. I kept living what was meant to be my final moment alive, over, over, over. I woke up with a raging hard-on. Nearly two days later. I just lay there, imagining how they'd had to keep zapping me with the defib paddles to start my heart again. How the sheer power of what's behind a socket can kill you *and* save you. It's an obsession. Ever since I found out what static shock was.

'We went on this field trip to a farm once in 3rd grade. I was the kid who touched the electric fence on purpose. Then I did it again. And again. I had to ride the bus home with my bag in my lap. Every time I ever saw a movie where someone gets whacked that way, look out downtown.' Echo laughed. 'Echo the Electric Otter. I like that. But I don't wanna die, Mr B. I can't just stick my tail into sockets all the time. All I can do's imagine it. But I always *want* to do it. It's just not fair though. I never told you because I never wanted you to worry about how tempted I might get. Eventually the worry would get too much and you'd fire me.'

'So that somebody else could worry about you instead? Not my way, Echo. I've haven't worried about it since I worked it out. However tempting it gets, a sound state of mind overrules it.'

'Until maybe I get drunk. Or high; God help me if I ever tried that.'

'I think you'd be fine,' Mr B said. 'As fantasies go, you have a rather exciting one. I did a little reading up on it, just because I get the feeling you were a little afraid to. There are actually safe levels of electricity that people can tolerate. Why else is a taser legal for police use? In fact,' he said, turning to the weasel who had brought their drinks, 'could we have the surprise now, please?'

'Oh, Mr B,' Echo said, now almost feeling like he could wet his pants in both excitement and embarrassment. 'You *didn't*.'

Mr B's present, brought out by the weasel waiter, was indeed a gold-plated taser. The same one that would kill the gift giver a few years later, but all either of them knew then was that Echo Pendryl had never received such a mind-blowing or thoughtful gift in his life.

'I left out the batteries,' Mr B said. 'Just in case the temptation was a little too much in a public place.'

Echo looked at it and thought Mr B had definitely done the right thing. His heart was racing, and he breathed slowly for calm as he held it and tried to remember where he was. Still, nobody seemed to be looking, as if this was nothing compared to what this supposedly sophisticated place had seen within its walls. Echo held it under his chin and mimed being electrocuted. 'Zzzzzzssshht! Zappy otter!' He tried to puff his fur up, wishing for once that he was a cat, remembering how puffed up he'd still been when he'd woken up in the hospital. It had taken days to go down. Mr B was obviously imagining him looking like that. He thought of the doctor who had said *'I'd say you're seriously lucky, Echo. I think you need to see a counsellor about this.'* Echo already knew the way out of that one: *'Does my insurance cover that?'*

'Zappy otter,' Mr B said. 'That sounds like a pretty good bedroom battle cry.'

Yeah. Wanna hear me say it for real later?

'Mr B, this is the only good birthday I've ever had. Besides the socket one. You maybe wanna...you know?'

'I can't be the one who does that to you, Echo. It really wouldn't be my thing, and you wouldn't enjoy it knowing I was reluctant. You need someone who'll like that.'

'Would there be anyone?'

'You might be surprised. Even if they're not so easy to find, I think you ought to find someone so you're a little less lonely. Would you like me to have another otter come and live with us? Another young man you might become good friends with?'

'You don't have to do that.'

'*Have to's* got nothing to do with it.'

'I usually think about older men, and I don't mean older otters. Maybe you were right. I should go out more. I can find that for myself.'

'Very well then. But keep imagining that poster. It's like I said, there are people out there who I know would go wild for Echo the Electric Otter.'

'Is that *your* dangerous idea? Me in a kinky porn film with a circus kinda title, getting my rocks off while some crackhead dom goes to town on me with this thing?'

'I suppose that was one thought I had,' Mr B said. 'But no. My dangerous idea is a lot worse than that. Mine means a complete rethink of everything to do with what money is. I think you're going to like it. Perhaps even as much as electricity.'

Echo sat there looking at him, as though a real, genuine leader and thinker and not just another crackpot guru or evangelist was saying words like that. Suddenly, it seemed to Echo that a man who understood and even tried to nurture a fetish as nuts as electric shocks couldn't be insane. Not when he got it like he did.

'So,' Mr B said. 'Shall we have dessert before I tell you?'

* * *

Echo had sometimes seen Elliot Burkowski do this odd thing where he blew cigar smoke into a half-full wine glass, usually red wine, presumably because the smoke changed the taste of it. When he did it this evening, Echo saw purpose in his eyes, like there was about to be a big reveal about what it meant.

'*Gattaca*,' Mr B said. 'Did you ever see that film?'

Echo shook his head.

'It's what one of the characters does as a demonstration of what Saturn's moon Titan looks like. Me, I like doing it because I think of it as the world. Smoke, mirrors and intoxicants. What do you suppose would happen if we stopped staring into mirrors, got our heads clear and then the smoke cleared too?'

'Well...honestly, how the fuck should I know?'

'What would you do if you became president? First thing. Go.'

At least that was easy. 'Pull us out of every war we're involved in with no answers given about why and then cut the defence budget by at least fifty percent. Fuck it, seventy. Just to piss my dad off and everyone like him. Then I'd make every U.S. corporation pay U.S. taxes regardless of where their head office was. Might take a few treaty changes, but hell, you can make that happen when you just took a big step towards world peace that nobody ever dared take.'

Mr B smiled, cigar still in hand. 'Very good. A little hard to work that in practice, but a nice ideological start.'

'Go on then, what have you got that's bigger? No, let me guess. Open all the borders. No more immigration control.'

286

'Actually, I wouldn't do that. In the long run, I wouldn't have to. A world with no states and no borders comes later. Once we've fixed one big problem first. Inequality.' Mr B surrounded his head in smoke. 'Go on, say it. I can tell you're dying to.'

Echo grinned and tipped his head. 'Rich coming from a one percenter.'

'Do you know why I'm not constantly surrounded by other people with my wealth, Echo?'

Echo shook his head.

'Because I'm hated by most of them. For changing my mind about everything I think money is and what we should do with it.'

'But you haven't given it all away.'

'Of course I haven't. What would be the use in that when I could spend it wisely instead?'

Echo felt a jolt of excitement. 'President,' he said. 'I should have guessed. You're going to run? Have you ever even held public office before?'

Mr B shook his head. 'I'm seventy-three, Echo. The world doesn't need another dinosaur like me keeping policies prehistoric. No, I'm not going to run, and I've never held office. I'm going to back Kalifa Sawahla. She's a wolf. I think you'll like her when you meet her next week. She's coming to stay for a couple of days to talk about her campaign with me.'

'I know who she is,' Echo said. 'Lawyer. Just like Dany. Except Dany's not a hot tip for attorney general in only her late thirties.'

'And Kali *does* get what I told you earlier: the world doesn't need more lawyers. It never needed hedge fund managers in the first place. Capitalism simply justified

287

them, like it justified all the same greed and inequality I once gave talks promoting, that were more like sermons. I've spent my life that way. I'm a very selfish dog, Echo. It's just how I am. I enjoyed it. I'd do it again, and I'm not entirely sorry for it either. But it's never too late to accept that because of people like me, the world simply doesn't work the way it should. I'd go out in search of billions again, but I'd do it with a different head on. One where I don't spend my whole life believing that anyone who's not me is poor because it's their fault for not becoming me instead.'

'What changed your mind?'

Mr B said nothing and just smiled.

'*Me*?' Echo's limbs were all so light he felt like he might just float off. '*I* changed your entire outlook on life? What the hell did I ever do?'

'You passed a test I never knew I set up. It really was a kind of interview, the party that brought you to me. I was looking for one who stood out, maybe the one who wanted it the most. You were the former. I think some of the others wanted to work for me more, but you were the one who knew that not playing the game the same way would get you noticed. Then I got the moment where it all changed. I saw how overwhelmed it made you. When I asked Dany to look after you that night, I knew you needed someone there, but what I really needed was the reverse for myself. A night alone, knowing I wasn't going to sleep, and I wouldn't want to either. I had too much to think about.'

'Why?'

'Because that was when I realised I'd chosen the person who *needed* what I could offer the most. I don't think I ever made a decision based on what someone or something else needed since I was a child. If I did, I couldn't think of it. But what I'd just done? I felt like a good person. That was when I knew I hadn't felt like that for decades. Most people rethink their lives when they screw up. I did it when I actually did something nice. When I felt like all the things I'd done that were kind were really just pretend kindness, ways to make *myself* feel better. When I took you in, we both felt like the world was a better place.' Mr B smiled. 'I know part of you is wondering whether or not you should buy a single word of this.'

'I know you're sincere,' Echo said, knowing deep down that Mr B was right: he suspected something of an act about this, even though knowing he'd had such a profound effect on someone else suddenly seemed like a better birthday present than a taser. 'Why didn't you ever tell me this before?'

'Because getting to my age and then realising you could have spent your entire life as a better person isn't exactly good conversation. Especially for someone you've just given a whole new lease of happiness.'

Now Echo bought it, and he sat there dumbstruck.

'I knew it wasn't too late to do more of the same thing I'd just done for you,' Mr B said. 'But I had to think big. Bigger than just taking someone broke and homeless and giving them a job. I suppose it's a bit like your electricity: the higher you up the voltage, the greater the rewards.'

Echo laughed. 'Yeah. Until you die.'

'Exactly. I have the perfect way to kill the old Elliot Burkowski, the selfish dog, the one who'd do it all again unless something far better came along. Or maybe there *was* a way to justify having all the money I spent my life snatching and hoarding. A way that was going to bring out the same sort of disgust in most of my one-percent peers that you fear people will give you for being Echo the Electric Otter, whose favourite thing is sticking his wet tail in wall sockets.'

'I don't care about that anymore,' Echo said, his brain now a whirlwind of inspiration. 'First thing tomorrow, I'm setting up a dating profile and I'm putting my fetishes on it.'

'Hmm, yes, dating. I did suggest you get out more. But perhaps cool your head a little, the same way I did. Take a deep breath. Have a go with that taser on yourself and get some energy out of your system. *Then* maybe the smoke and mirrors and intoxicants will clear.' He blew smoke into his wine again.

Echo took a moment to think, then picked up the taser and pressed it over his heart. 'I might need a safety-buddy. What if I can't flick the off switch while I'm zapping myself?'

'I'll advertise for a new companion. Would you like another otter?'

It was as good as he'd get. 'Yeah. Let's choose one together. A brave one who'd do that. Maybe one who knows good BDSM.'

'Oh, that too?'

'Always fancied giving it a try. It'd work well with electricity.' Echo put his hands in his lap, knowing they were trembling. 'I always wanted to try shocking someone else. I always wanted to shock a snep. I had this classmate who was one. It was my favourite fantasy. Hey, you know what? I always liked wolves too. How about Kalifa Sawahla? Would *she* safety for me? Would it risk her campaign? What if that made her like it more?'

'Are you brave enough to ask her?'

Echo shrugged. 'Maybe it wouldn't be fair.'

'We'll find you a brave snep, then. Just remember, I've never called an ambulance for a companion, and I'd rather not start.'

Damn, Echo thought, knowing it was right but knowing that thought made it all the hotter to imagine. 'You never answered your own question though. What would *you* do if you were president? Okay, no, better, what's Kali going to do?'

'What I did for you, just on a national scale. I pay you a thousand dollars per week. If I were president, I'd pay that to every U.S. citizen as soon as they turned eighteen. That's what Kali's campaign will promise. Every adult with U.S. citizenship gets the automatic right to an income. Regardless of who they are.'

Echo's jaw nearly hit the table. 'Every single person in this country? Fifty thousand bucks per year? You can't be fucking serious! Where would it all come from? That's over three hundred million of us, all getting fifty K? That's...'

'Fifteen trillion dollars. I know. Which is why we may have to be a little more realistic and maybe drop it to twenty thousand per year. Just to start things off. Before we try answering your question about where it would all come from, answer a better one: where would it all go? Where would it have gone for you, Echo? How might your father have treated you differently if he knew that you automatically had a way of defying his orders, of not doing what he planned for your life? What if everyone like you had that power, the ones who'd never have managed to run like you did? What if none of us had to work awful jobs that the world doesn't need in order to survive? What would we do instead? Maybe that's the world where we'd all get to fulfil our dreams. Someone like you can rent a home and eat while they audition for their first movie. Someone like me goes out to make a fortune, but now it doesn't have to happen through a system where a small number have it all while everyone else has nothing or fights their way through hell just to avoid poverty. Imagine if we all got rid of this ridiculous mentality where the more we work ourselves to death, the higher our self-worth is supposed to become, and then the more we deserve? I think the world we all deserve is where freedom actually *means* freedom and hope actually means hope.'

'Is that Kali's campaign speech already?'

'It could be part of it. Did you like it?'

Realising he was holding the taser, Echo put it down, feeling like his insides had taken something better than a shock. 'Mr B, do you actually think something like that could ever be possible?'

'Every century has impossible concepts that the ones after it make possible,' Mr B said. 'I think it will take Kali many rounds before she secures the candidacy. If she doesn't, hopefully someone else will take her promises up who can do it. I doubt I'll live to see it.' He extinguished his cigar. 'But I think you have a chance of seeing it. Maybe you could even do it.'

'Me as a politician? Don't be soft.'

'A kinky otter with a bold vision who's recognisable because he started as a Hollywood name. Doesn't that already sound better than what we've got now?'

* * *

Back at home, Echo changed back into speedos out of habit, but this time he was determined to finally ask the question that would either make his birthday a wonderful one or destroy everything this evening had already brought him. This, he thought, was what becoming an actor really was: pushing your luck. Saying 'I deserve this' and then saying that maybe you deserved a little more. Just because you wanted it.

'Mr B, why is it you like me in speedos as my uniform?'

'It's a natural look for you. Otters in clothes is only for modesty's sake outside of the home, isn't it? You're naturally suited to living in aquatic houses.'

'I'd like to buy one, one day.' Echo filled the teapot and put the lid back on. He turned around and leant on the bar. 'Mr B, are you lonely? I mean without Dany. Without a companion at all.'

'I have a companion here.'

'Yeah.' Echo slid one foot slightly back, slowly, and extended his lean a little. 'You know what I think, Mr B? I think this is a natural look for me because you naturally want to look at me like this. I think there's plenty else we could naturally be doing. You wouldn't have to pay me for it like the others. Not when you're going to pay the whole world my salary one day.'

293

Mr B sat down on a barstool, like someone holding an audition. 'Dany told me that even though all she did was cuddle you, there's something pretty impressive under those speedos.'

Echo tipped his chin up a little and smiled. 'Yeah. She noticed.'

'May I see?'

Echo hooked his thumbs into his speedo elastic. 'Would you like me to take these off, Mr B?'

'Yes, Echo, I would.'

Echo slid them one-handed, stepping out of them so they slid off him elegantly. He set them down on a stool and stood there, Mr B staring at his semi and nodding very slightly, a smile on his face and a kind of fascinated intensity behind his eyes. Echo knew what he liked, a pose struck slightly to the side. Not an obvious catwalk-style pose, more like a surfer's when he didn't know the camera was watching, only the ocean, like his moves should impress it more than a person.

'Mmm,' Mr B said. 'Would you run a hand down your tail for me?'

Echo lifted his tail slowly and slid his right hand down, taking a slow, deep breath as more blood filled his manhood. 'Like that?'

'That's nice,' Mr B said. 'You really do have an impressive package. Why don't you turn around and let me see your butt? You can lower your tail. Let's be elegant. Mmm, that's it.'

Echo laughed and looked over his shoulder, fascinated by how Mr B seemed to like the view of him from behind more. His pupils had dilated, and he'd sat up as if paying attention, his tail gently swishing from side to side. 'Sure you don't want to see my hole, Mr B? I can do that elegantly too.'

'I'm enjoying you just like this. You're beautiful, Echo. You're the most beautiful young man I've ever seen like this.'

'Have you seen a guy like this before?'

'Of course.'

Still looking over his shoulder, Echo smirked. 'Have you done it with a guy before, Mr B?'

'Many.'

'Damn. I wish you'd lied to me and told me this is the first time you got curious.'

'Would you like something else for your birthday, Echo? Would you like it if I lifted your tail and did more than just *see* your hole?'

Echo faked a shocked face. 'Mr B! Shame on you for being so naughty with an otter!'

'Dany said you like a scratch.' Mr B got up and walked slowly across to him. Echo switched to looking over his other shoulder, his neck relaxing a little. 'How about your back first? May I?' Echo knew he didn't have to say yes. Mr B's fingers didn't just rub his back, they danced down it, sending a great euphoric sigh rushing out of his lungs.

'You have lovely soft fur, Echo. How does it feel to have someone appreciate it?'

'It feels...' It felt like a great big sigh was enough to express it. Mr B was digging in deeper now, scratching at the soft spots at the top of Echo's back, below his arms. Echo went fully hard, gasped, then let out a groan of pleasure that echoed around the kitchen.

'Turn around for me, Echo. Let me show you who taught Dany how to treat an otter right. Mmmm. Let's start here.'

'My belly button?' Echo laughed and tipped his head back. 'What's so...eeep! Urrrrgh! Mr B, you're pressing my *belly button*?'

'Dany and I called it the Teddy Bear Noise game. Like pressing a teddy bear with a squeaker. I like the way *you* squeak, Echo. Would you do it again?'

Echo nodded, laughed, and saw how Mr B's fascinated eyes looked intoxicated-fascinated now. 'You really like my belly button, huh, Mr B?'

Mr B poked it a little with each finger, one by one, then rubbed Echo's belly. 'It's an odd quirk. Do you mind?'

'Why don't you put your nose against it and sniff?'

Mr B's eyes went wide with the kind of pleasure Echo had never seen him exhibit before. He wondered how many times he'd done this with people behind closed doors. The husky put his nose against Echo's belly button, closed his eyes and breathed deeply, for at least a minute. Echo took hold of his ears and then rubbed behind his head.

'Echo...' Mr B kept repeating. 'Oh wow.' He stopped and looked up after another minute. 'I'm sorry. I was the one giving *you* pleasure.' He rubbed Echo's belly again, then began scratching up his sides with the other hand.

Echo laughed like he was being tickled and sighed like he was being massaged all at once, not knowing how such a noise was coming out of him. He squeaked, purred and breathed in right to his toes as Mr B stroked his hands up fast to scratch under his chin. Then one hand was rubbing his stomach again, scratching, combing through his fur. Echo thumped his right foot against the floor repeatedly, his butthole feeling tight and his head light with the rush of too much oxygen.

'Ooooh, Mr B, you're so kind to an otter!'

'I know, Echo. I know. Now, would you like to be a good boy for me and let me lift that tail?'

'Anything for you, Mr B.'

'May I have that feel I was talking about?'

'You *really* wanna feel how tight my hole is? I think you're about to get your finger stuck. Go on, lift my tail, Mr B. You gonna be gentle?'

'The gentlest.'

Echo felt Mr B's fingers rub inside his butt cheeks and around his hole and gave a purr that was more like a half growl. 'You're a *very* naughty dog, Mr B.'

'And you, my boy, are a very tight otter.'

'Nobody's been there before.'

'I know. You told me.'

'Gonna be my first?'

'Yes, Echo, I'd like to take your innocence.' Mr B poked a little deeper. 'Would you like that?'

Echo breathed harder. 'Mr B...I really need you to make me come, because I am *aching* down there.'

'Me too, Echo.' Mr B slid his fingers out gently and let Echo's tail down. 'Shall we go into your room or mine?'

'Yours. Yours looks out at the pool.'

The moonlight danced on the pool water as Echo got onto the bed front-down, just like Mr B asked. He wriggled himself into the same sideways pose Mr B

297

liked, looking over his shoulder, his tail relaxed between his legs, waiting for Mr B to lift it.

'I had a test two weeks ago,' Mr B said. 'I've had no one else since. Would you like me to wear a condom anyway?'

Echo shook his head and licked his lips.

'May I put one on you? It saves cleaning the bed later.'

Echo rolled over. Mr B knelt on the bed in front of him and slid it on, pinching the rubber tip like he had indeed done this many times on someone else. Echo exhaled a deep breath through his nose. Mr B stroked a finger up Echo's muzzle, then between his eyes. 'There. Roll over again for me, there's a good boy.' He stroked down Echo's back, the other hand holding his tail. Echo, looking over his shoulder, gave a growl of satisfaction.

'Mr B, you're a very hard dog right now. Are you going to knot with me?'

'Oh, goodness yes. Are you ready? Purr for me, Echo. Just for a minute. Nice deep purr. Let's rub your back again.' Mr B did it, Echo drawing the most satisfied breaths of his life. 'Are you hard enough down there yourself? Ready to enjoy this?'

'Yes! Yes! Be a naughty dog with me, Mr B!'

Mr B lifted Echo's tail again. 'Alright Echo, take a nice deep breath. Here we go. Hold...hold...that's it...good...'

Echo felt the thrust between his legs, the underneath of his tail flat against Mr B's chest with the tip touching one side of his face. Echo's brain lit up like a super-highway. He imagined sticking his tail in the

298

socket again, the shock that had thrown him across the room, and felt like Mr B had thrown him miles.

'...and let go! Good boy.'

Echo exhaled, came, and kept coming until he was almost asleep and still emptying, Mr B's wetness inside him strange and warm all at once. His heart had never known such joy. Mr B finally lay still after gently thrusting, panting and wagging his tail, still inside Echo with the two of them rolled onto their sides.

'Are you alright lying there, Echo? This will take a couple of minutes and then I'll be able to slide out nice and easily. Do you like the knot?'

'It's nice. Keep it there.'

'Try to relax your backside and don't squeeze too tight. There, that's better. Have you ever come like that?'

'Maybe once. The morning after...you know.'

'Would you like it if I got the taser and put some batteries in it?'

Echo's heart quickened a little, then he felt too sleepy to play the game. 'You can't. It's too dangerous. Besides, with you doing me, I don't need electricity. Not when you do it like that. You were...kind. Yeah, you're a kind dog, Mr B. Not a selfish one. Not to me.'

'I wonder who else would remember me like that.'

Echo laughed. 'You just fucked a virgin otter and you want to talk about the time after you're dead? Come on, Mr B. Don't spoil it.'

'I'm sorry,' Mr B said, hugging Echo a little tighter. 'Will you be a teddy bear for me again?' He ran his hands down to Echo's stomach.

'You're my vewy vewy best friend, Mr B,' Echo said, in the silliest voice he could come up with. 'Will you be my friend fowwwwever?'

'Mmmm. Yes, I'd like that, Echo. Friends forever. With benefits?'

'Sure, Mr B, you can put extra stuffing in me fowever.'

Elliot Burkowski gave a satisfied sigh. 'Okay, nice and relaxed, out we come. There. Would you like me to clean you up or do you want to shower on your own?'

I could just not shower at all, Echo thought, then remembered how much Mr B liked cleanliness and hardly ever smelt like a dog. He did tonight though. Whatever their sex together had sparked inside his brain, his chemicals had flowed so hard they were filling Echo's nose like there was no other smell in the world. 'I'd like to shower together, Mr B. I can be a wet teddy for you too.'

'No more teddy bear for tonight. Too much of a good thing. Just be Echo for me.'

Echo rolled over to face him, then kissed him lightly on the mouth. Then kissed him again, this time with his tongue touching Mr B's. He wasn't sure how long it went on for, but when they parted, he wondered if he'd ever want to be with anyone else. 'Mr B, I'm not sure I really know who Echo is. Apart from the electric otter. He wants to be an actor. He wants to be kind. Like his father wasn't. He wants to make the world better. Apart from that...I don't know.'

'All that's not enough?'

'Well, yeah, sure it's good, but there's got to be more.'

'Well, don't forget he's gay.'

Echo propped his head on his hand, elbow bent. 'Are *you* gay, Mr B? Or bi? Or have you just never really been sure?'

'I've liked both since I was very young,' Mr B said. 'Publicly I'm straight. Because I'm selfish *and* a bit of a coward. I built my whole life around an image that wasn't entirely true. Not from now on though. Will you date me again, Echo? Will you think about being with me?'

'Like being in a relationship?'

'I think I'd like you as more than a companion, Echo.'

Echo's eyes went saucer-wide. '*Marry* you? Is that what you're asking?'

'No, it would be a little too soon if that's what I was thinking of. I was wondering about something better.'

'Like...woah, seriously? An heir?'

Mr B smiled and wagged his tail.

'You want me to inherit your estate? All of it? Don't you already have two daughters?'

'Yes, and you've never met them for a very good reason. Let's not talk about them on such a wonderful night, shall we? I know I just gave you a lot to get your head around. That's why I don't need an answer. Not right now. Maybe not ever. One thing at a time. Why don't we start with that shower?'

Chapter Fifteen

Echo Pendryl thought of his first time before and after every time. He told Eddie that, right after the story of how Mr B gave him his first good birthday. Eddie just stared at him, holding out the taser that had eventually killed the man in that story.

'He'd want me to,' Echo said. 'Didn't even take a rehab session to work that one out. Take it. My safety word is Neptune. Until then, go Pikachu on me. I can take two entire minutes of the top level on that thing. I could take more. I know it.'

Eddie looked shell-shocked already. He also had a boner.

'Echo, listen, if I can ever even *hope* to be a better person then I can't do this.'

'A sober person trying to do better has sexual needs. You're a sadist, and I'm about to be the greatest fuck you ever had. You want to keep fucking me? You stay sober. That's why I'm a good sponsor.'

'The circle won't like this.'

'The circle know that when I don't talk, they don't ask. The circle also like anything when it works.'

'Echo, I...you're disabled. I can't beat up a disabled guy.'

Echo sighed and rolled his eyes, knowing Eddie would like the sass. 'Number one, the limp probably isn't permanent even though I'm registered. Number two, I didn't get it from nerve damage from getting shocked. Number three, that's what you're doing: shocking me. Not beating me up. Although when you get into it, you can slap me if you want. Hard. Just use an open hand. No fists, no biting, no...actually, what the hell, you can gouge me if you like, just not somewhere that's going to leave a mark.'

'How *did* you do the leg?'

'If I tell you, will you do my thing for me?'

Eddie leaned back on his stool and hooked his thumbs in the top of his pants. 'Yeah, okay. How you became a crip. Go.'

'It was a skiing accident. Mr B took me to Colorado that winter, right after we became a thing. I said yes to being his heir. After he died, I went back there, same resort, thought it might help me come to terms. I jacked up before I went out on the course. I came off and hit a tree. That was the third time I nearly died. I did two more wet-tail sockets before that one. To get into the hospital so I could steal morphine. This one, they didn't have to crack my chest open; my ribs were already all broken. They just had to slice with a scalpel.' Echo took his shirt off and jutted his chest out, tightening the scar. 'That was the second tree I hit. The first one did my leg. The third broke my neck. There was less than a centimetre in it and I'd have been quadriplegic. Guess it's just as well I got Mr B's fortune. I spent nearly eight months in the hospital. Three of them were coming down off the morphine, because I'm telling you, Eddie, I didn't even *know* what high was before then. They had to wean me off because a cold turkey would have killed me.'

'Who says money can't save your life, huh? You get the best doctors?'

'They're still working on the limp. They'll beat it. But you know what I felt like, when Dany came and got me from the hospital and brought me back here? I told her I wanted to be alone. She wanted to *leave* me alone. She was starting to hate me already. I sat on the couch right there and thought about everything I had. What Mr B would tell me to do. What he would have said if he'd been there, those eight months. I was twenty-three years old, for Christ's sake. I should have been going for the stars like I promised Mr B, not rock bottom. From then on, my life was going to be what it should have if Mr B were still here to make sure of it.'

Eddie looked a little subdued by it all. 'You got back, huh?'

'Know what I did right after that moment?'

'What?'

'I jacked up again. Because I guess I didn't know rock bottom yet either. Then Mr B's daughter did her thing.' He pointed at the bullet scar on the right of his chest. 'Like she'd been waiting all the time I'd been in the hospital. Guess she couldn't hurt a crip either. It's like she was waiting to see what I did with that moment. Well, she saw. Or she heard. I don't know, she *could* have been in the house with me that night for all I knew about it. She got me a week later. Back in the hospital.

Soon as I got out, I finally attempted suicide for real this time. I did what I thought was enough to kill me three times over and swam out to sea on a rubber ring. I was still alive when the tide brought me back in and Dany was there, pulling me out. Still there for me. I've no fucking idea why. She rode with me in the ambulance. I don't know how I was even conscious, but I passed out sometime during the ride. I lost three days. When I woke up, she was still there. She told me next time, she wouldn't come. She'd take me home and she'd leave me alone again, and if I was still alive and sober tomorrow, call her and we'd talk.'

'And?'

'And I did it. I was honest. That was my first sober night for about three years. I never did heroin again. I never did anything again. Unless you count what you've got in your hand.'

'You've told the circle about all this, right?'

Echo pulled a stool close to Eddie's and sat down. 'The circle hate me, Eddie. That's my favourite truth about them. I was responsible for killing the man I loved even though it was an accident. I've been on trial for a murder I didn't do. I've *been* an attempted murder victim. I've had my miserable life saved more times than I ever deserved, and just to thank everyone who tried to help, I kept trying to kill myself. Now I'm sober. So what excuse has anyone in that circle got compared to me? There are some pretty damaged people who come and go from it, but I know what that look says every time I've shared that story. Compared to me, most of them have got jack shit.'

'That's an asshole thing to say.'

'It would be if it was my own opinion. It's not. It's the way *they* see it. They see a damaged soul who can't possibly be alive, or want to be, or deserve to be. I am. I do.'

'What about the third?'

'Do I deserve to be alive? What do *you* think, Eddie? Do any of us? We just don't get to pick. Not even when we sometimes try to. "Deserve" doesn't have any meaning in this debate.'

Eddie looked dumbfounded, then looked at the taser and flicked the button to on, making the blue warning light shine. 'Neptune, wasn't it?'

Echo took a slow, deep breath. 'Come on, Eddie. Think you've got what it takes to make me say it?'

'Where do you like getting shocked?'

'Surprise me. Where do you think it'll hurt me the most? Guess. I bet you can't.'

Eddie's pants were visibly wet through with pre-come. He looked at Echo, then traced the taser all over his chest, then stomach, then legs, and his cock and balls, then poked at his ass-crack with it, all the while trying to guess, his excited breathing picking up pace along with Echo's. He held the taser over his heart, feeling its rapid thudding beat for a moment, wondering if that wasn't the answer.

'Open your mouth,' Eddie said.

'You wanna shock me in my mouth?'

Eddie grinned from ear to ear. 'Got it! Come on then. Open it. You got a safe sign as well?'

Echo gave what Eddie would later find out was called a Vulcan salute, grinned, and opened his mouth.

306

Eddie pushed the taser down onto his tongue, his finger quivering over the button.

'Eddie.'

The name was barely discernible, but it didn't matter. Echo was laughing, the taser still pressed against his tongue, and Eddie knew what came next.

'Uh-uh!'

'What the fuck, there's somewhere worse than *that*? Why don't I just shock you right now, you asshole?'

Echo growled and gave a hysterical-sounding yelp that was more like a whoop, the thing still jammed hard against his tongue. 'Go on then! Give up!'

'Fuck!' Eddie said, pulling the taser out. He held up his hand, back outwards, as if about to backhand-swipe. 'You want this?'

'You know how you *really* wanna hit me, quitter! Keep guessing, bitch!'

Eddie took a step back. 'Alright. Fine. You can take two minutes of this?' He snapped the dial around to the top setting. 'Can you take two minutes when I find your spot?'

Could he? He could always safety. 'We'll never find out unless you find it.'

Eddie didn't trace all over him again, he just stood there looking, puzzled, until his eyes lit up with a slow, almost malevolent glee. 'Mmmm,' he said. 'Where's the tender part of an otter? Yeah, I should have known.' Now he traced down the side of Echo's chest, deliberately picking the side with the crippled leg, and found the barely visible flap of skin he was looking for. 'What's the expression? Wetter than an otter's pocket?' He put the taser inside it. 'Have I got it?'

'Why don't you give me a burst and we'll see?'

Now Eddie's eyes really lit up, and Echo knew this was going to be the session of his life. 'Because I know I'm not even warm.' He stroked Echo's head. 'Am I?'

Echo trembled. Eddie's bluff was brilliant. A slow moment later, Eddie had the taser pressed into the soft tissue behind his left ear.

'Ahhh,' Eddie sighed. 'Gotcha. Shake for me, little otter! What happens when I press this on that highest setting? It go through your jaw and down your spine and up your brain stem all at once?'

Echo laughed. 'Wanna know something, Eddie? I never tried it full pelt right there before. But I dare you. You've heard what I've survived. So what do you think? *Do* I deserve to be alive?'

* * *

Eddie Kowalski panicked. Right then, something he didn't know was inside him fired off in all directions. Shit, this had been so hot, and now he hadn't a clue what he was playing it, or what Echo Pendryl was playing at. He barely even knew where he was, only that he was stepping away, lowering the taser, and saying his own safety word inside his head, just to keep himself grounded.

'What is it?' Echo said.

'Watermelon.'

'Oh. Shit. Sorry. I never asked *your* word. My bad. Goddamn it, we really had that then. Okay, relax, we can get back in the groove. Surprise me. Mouth, pocket, they're pretty good runners up. Pick one. Hell, pick the ear. I can get back into it just like...'

'I'm not doing it, Echo. Forget it. This isn't happening.'

'What?'

'Were you actually trying to get me to kill you right then? You really don't know what that would have done, do you? That is *not* a game I'm playing. I've never killed someone. Okay, not that I know about, and even if I did, not like that.' *What the fuck am I doing even hinting at what happened years ago?* Echo Pendryl was making him do it. Like he knew it was there. Like this was still part of whatever game he was playing. 'You really *are* fucked up.'

Echo went from surprised to disappointed to angry faster than Eddie had ever seen anyone do it. 'You know what, Eddie? I was wrong. You *don't* deserve to be alive. That cure we were talking about? I found it. You're never going to. When you fall off the wagon and you try your first suicide, I hope you get it right first time.'

For all the abuse he'd ever received on a football field, or off it, or ever dished out to anyone else, there was one place Fast Eddie Kowalski had never dared go and no one had ever dared push him. Until Echo Pendryl really had proven to be as shit as the otter in that rehab story.

He drove a doorman's punch straight into the otter's stomach, his fist clenched tight and more rage than he'd ever felt before driving it in.

'You worthless bag of shit!' Eddie snatched up the taser, drove it into the same place as his punch before

Echo could even attempt to draw breath, and shocked him on full pelt.

The taser crackled. Echo writhed, his teeth clenching and no breath appearing to enter him. He staggered back to the table as Eddie pushed him, legs barely standing him up. Eddie grabbed Echo by the fur on his head, a great surge of pleasure rushing through him, pulled him onto tiptoes, and drove the taser into his neck, keeping his finger on the button for twice as long. The smell of burning fur and smoke filled the air. Echo collapsed against the bar as Eddie let go, his hands scrabbling at nothing but surface and finding the edge, with barely enough grip to hold on.

Eddie hauled him up again, eyes locked onto that patch behind the otter's ear, and then at the last moment decided it would be better plunged inside something. He grabbed at Echo's pocket, dug the taser in as deep as he could, pressed the trigger button and counted to twenty.

When he stopped, everything around Eddie Kowalski stopped. Echo dropped to the floor, barely moving enough to let Eddie know he was still alive, managing to get almost onto hands and knees and then failing, sprawling out and breathing in shallow, rapid gasps. His fur was all on end, puffing him up like a cat. The smouldering that filled Eddie's nostrils made him feel sick. So did what he knew he was going to have to do, and what he'd already done.

'Echo? Talk to me!' Eddie knelt down and got his arm around the front of Echo's chest. 'Come on, get up with me. We've gotta get you up and get you on the couch, and I've gotta call nine-one-o...'

Echo sucking down a great breath to his toes cut Eddie off. The most maniacal laugh Eddie had heard in his life did the rest. He dropped Echo and leapt back, not realising he'd still been holding the taser until he dropped that too, barely hearing it clatter onto the floor above Echo's shrieking.

'Edddiieeee! Aaaaahahaaha! My fucking wolverine! *Gotcha*, motherfucker!'

For someone who had a limp, Echo Pendryl could get to his feel like a gymnast, and through the cocktail of bewilderment and fear in his head, Eddie had maybe half a second to wonder if the otter had faked the limp all along.

'Twenty seconds in my *pocket*, Eddie? Do you know how fucking mean that is? Wooooooo! Your first go and you gave me twenty fucking seconds in my fucking *pocket*!'

'H...uhh...how the *fuck* did you just take that! There's not a cop alive who ever saw somebody take that! That fucking thing's not even legal, is it?'

Echo zapped it twice. 'Mr B had a friend who knew a friend who knew a friend. Russian black market, my man! No wonder it killed him. And you *hit* me, Eddie!' Echo rubbed his stomach. 'God-*damn* that's gonna be a bruise I won't forget in a hurry.'

Eddie held his hands up. 'I'm sorry, okay? Like *really* sorry. I never meant to...for Christ's sake, you told me to go fucking *kill* myself!'

'I'm telling you, Eddie, I've had to work hard on some guys to get them to play, but you? Look what you reduced me to to get you to do it! I *never* told anyone KYS in my life. And no, I didn't mean it, that's just how

311

much I *needed* that, Eddie. It's been *way* too long. You know who the last person to press that button was?'

Oh *God*, Eddie thought, *if you're up there, get me OUT of here!*

'Mr B, Eddie.' Echo licked his lips and zapped it again. 'Recovery complete. At last. I knew you were the one. That night in Starbucks, when you said "Don't leave, I like *you*," you remember? I liked you too. It meant something to me. I'd not heard anyone say that for real for way too long.' Echo shook himself off, smoothing his coat down a little. 'Oooooeeee! How you feeling, Eddie? Will a little love make you hot for me again, or you still wanna play rough?'

Eddie shook his head. 'I don't even think I'm a sadist anymore. You're cr–'

'Rule number one, Eddie!' Echo had never shouted before, and he wasn't shouting now, but the raised voice was enough to send a shiver through Fast Eddie Kowalski right then, together with the lust and madness in Echo's eyes and the way he held the taser up like it was a handgun. 'Don't ever call me crazy. Crazy's scared of what I am.'

Eddie nodded. 'Rule two?'

'Oh, rule two's for later.' In a fluid and practiced motion, Echo flipped the taser over in his hand so he was offering Eddie the handle. 'Take it down a few notches. You want me responsive, right? You can floor me later after I've talked you into getting hard again. Semi already? My man! Lift my tail and do the spot right underneath and stand right against me so my nose touches yours and you can see my face when you shock me.'

'So I get the shock too? Nice try. Bend over the bar right there with your feet off the floor.'

'Better idea.' Echo got on his knees. 'You want a blowjob, Eddie? Hold it behind my ear in that soft spot again while I'm doing it and tell me how you like it.'

Eddie put a hand on Echo's head to stop him. 'With those otter teeth?'

'You'll like it. I can hold my breath underwater for twenty minutes, remember? Want to feel *that* kind of suck?'

'I wanna fuck,' Eddie said. 'I'm a top. I wanna hold it behind your ear when you're face down. I want you to tremble like you did before. You're gonna get a *real* shock when I get in there.'

Echo stood up, pleasure flashing in his eyes. 'My man. You got it, Eddie.' He sprawled himself chest and stomach down across the table where he'd once shared that birthday drink with Mr B and thought of their first dinner. 'Warm me up, Eddie. Tailbone.'

Eddie worked Echo's tailbone for ten minutes, upping the setting every time, giving him time out and drinks of iced water between it, after Echo caved and said, 'I'm thirsty, Eddie.' *Damn*, this guy knew how to do the routine. Comfort breaks in all the right places, as if nobody else had dared ask him before, thinking he wouldn't do it. He stroked Echo's head as he held the drink for him, then went back to his tail until he was almost on the top setting.

How did he get this tolerance? Eddie thought. *He must have lied about not doing this for the last three years. Nobody could take this if they weren't used to it.*

313

He let Echo get up off the bar, holding the otter against him and feeling the pulse in his neck, going at a regular rhythm as if nothing had happened. Fuck, it was like this guy was some sort of lab rat, conditioned from birth to do this. He pressed the taser behind Echo's ear again. 'I'm starting to like this spot right here,' Eddie said. 'I think I'm gonna call it *my* spot.'

Echo purred.

'Can I see what it does now?'

'If you're ready, but it means you'll have to fuck me while I'm unconscious.'

Eddie shuddered. Unresponsive partners had never been his thing either. That whole routine had always felt dirty and nasty even when someone consented. Eddie needed response. 'No. I want you telling me you like it.' He took hold of the scruff of Echo's neck and jabbed the taser in, still in his favourite spot. 'Bedroom. Now. Move.'

'You got it.'

Echo was tight. He sighed and moaned with pleasure as Eddie entered, and despite all the electricity, he didn't look or feel tired. His sleek body was tensing and relaxing with Eddie's thrusts, engine running inside it so long as the taser remained poised behind his ear like it was the ignition.

'Yeah...*yeah*! Fuck me, Eddie! Deeper, get that whole thing inside me and give me that juice you got. Soon as you come...you get to shock the electric otter, bitch!'

'*Oh* yeah!' Eddie said. 'Yeah! Take it, Echo the electric otter! Take it!

'Give it to me, Eddie! You're the man!'

Eddie gave it alright, holding and holding despite being desperate for the release, not wanting it to end.

'Hey Eddie.'

Something about Echo's voice had changed. The tone felt wrong. 'What?'

'I told you *never* to hit me with a fist.'

'But you –'

If Echo Pendryl had gotten off the floor too fast, then what he did next defied any speed Eddie had ever seen. He barely saw anything. Except the twist, then the grab, then the flash that hit him. The last thing he saw before his vision went white and his whole body screamed at him was that the taser was back in Echo's hand, and he'd turned it on himself with Eddie still inside of him, zapping them both on the last setting Eddie had left it on: two down from full.

Not even the hardest of tackles and the most winded he'd ever been had stopped Eddie like this. He couldn't breathe, couldn't move, only just knew he was standing, and Echo was grabbing the back of his neck in what was more of a gouge than a grab, but Eddie couldn't feel it. The deadening pain all around his crotch and the desperate urge not to piss down his own legs took out everything else. How he was fighting, he didn't know.

'*Now* you're playing the game, Eddie. I told you *never* to hit me like that. Let's count down to your humiliation, shall we? Nobody ever makes it past five. Oh, wait, you already did. Second round.'

Eddie felt the taser against the front of his crotch.

'No! Echo, *no*! *Noooooo*!' The last time it came out as a pleading whine, through his nose and clenched teeth.

'What's the matter, Eddie? Forgotten your safety word?'

He had. Somehow, Echo Pendryl had stolen it, along with any feeling that he would ever be safe again.

Eddie Kowalski knew he was most likely dead. He wasn't going to say that word anyway, not now that it had come back into his head: *watermelon*. He wasn't giving this lunatic the satisfaction of violating it right before his death.

Echo whipped the thing around to Eddie's back and shocked him in his tailbone. Eddie screamed, his chest thudding into the floor. When the shock stopped, he realised Echo had dialled it down. Now came the rest: working back up, except Echo was going to make it last hours and laugh all the way through them. Eddie just knew it.

The taser was behind his ear.

For the first time since his mother's funeral, Eddie Kowalski felt tears running down his face. 'Echo, no, *please*, I can't take it like you do! You'll kill me! I'm sorry! I'm *sorry* about the goddamn punch, I already said it! You were *laughing* about it! I don't des...'

Wrong words, Eddie.

'Alright. Do it. Do me a favour.'

'I'm not a murderer, Eddie. You're wrong, it wouldn't kill you. It's not even really from the Russian black market. It's a cop-issue taser. Non-lethal. But it sure feels like it is, don't it?'

Eddie was rolling over, or rather he knew he was being rolled, and there was Echo with a grin on his face, climbing back on. 'But I *am* gonna shock you hardcore if you don't finish what you started. I was enjoying that.

So now you're a top, but you're not *on* top. Can you still come? Because you'd better!' Echo pressed the taser into Eddie's neck. 'Come for me, Eddie. You've got one minute.'

Eddie had no idea how Echo was timing it and didn't even think it might be as simple as counting in his head. He just knew he had to finish, and fast, and the otter had better like it. He shut his eyes and concentrated on that first night he'd met Echo, how much he'd liked him, wanted him, how pure it all seemed.

'Uh-uh. Eyes open, Eddie. Look at me. Tell me you still want me like you always did.'

'Yes...*Yes*! I want you, Echo the electric otter!'

'Tell me I'm a selfish otter, Eddie. *Mean* it.'

'You're a selfish otter! Oh *fuck* yeah you're selfish. You just want punishment, and when I next get to do it to you, I'm gonna find a place worse than behind your ear and I'm gonna....urgh! Here I go! Here I go, Echo! Ooooooh yeah!'

He'd done it. He'd actually finished despite how mortally scared he was of not being able to come ever again after this. He was inside the otter he wanted, and the whole insane game had been worth it. He blacked out before Echo had a chance to climb off.

* * *

A few years down the line, when a snep called Kia Renfield told him the story of how he'd seen the 'selfish otter' routine in a film of his and copied it to surprise a friend, Echo Pendryl felt a warm glow inside, smiled, and said, 'I don't really know where it came from either.

I just needed a sadistic wolverine to come after *I* punished *him*.'

Eddie was there. He liked it.

(What he didn't like, Echo realised later when he'd worked out what was giving him an odd feeling about that whole scene, was Kia Renfield.)

Mr B talking about being a selfish dog? A rehab circle somewhere hearing about Echo's self-pity when he realised he really *had* been selfish in how he'd tried to get over Mr B's death by going on a path that would result in his own? It didn't matter: he'd turned a little selfishness into something good.

That was all Mr B ever really wanted.

* * *

The last time Eddie woke up to find that someone had covered him with a blanket on a couch was when his mother had done it. Not only had Echo done it, but somehow he'd woken Eddie up without making him jump.

'Drink this,' Echo said.

Eddie drank, the otter holding a glass to his lips until he thought to sit up and take it from him. When he stopped, realising he'd tasted nothing, it turned out to be iced water, and it had rushed to his head almost as keenly as alcohol used to. He caught his breath for a moment, a rush and a slight headache cutting off his thoughts, until he saw Echo, dressed in a bathrobe and a pair of expensive-looking pyjamas, sitting on the couch next to him in what looked like some kind of yoga position, his feet tucked under his backside yet completely relaxed about it.

'Watermelon?' Echo said.

Eddie nodded. 'Neptune?'

Echo nodded back. Eddie had never known any partner of his do a reverse-safety to indicate the game was over before.

Eddie gave a great sigh of relief and lay back. 'Never call you crazy, right?'

'You can call me crazy when we're on safe,' Echo said, playfully tipping his head back and to the side. 'But honestly, am I?'

'I thought you were going to kill me.'

'I'd have a hard time disposing of a corpse with *this* neighbourhood always watching. Besides, what would be the fun in killing you? We couldn't have a searching conversation if you were dead.'

'And I guess not having anyone left who'd play your little taser game had nothing to do with it, huh? You just want a deep conversation with me. Did you miss the part where I'm totally shit at that side of relationships?'

'I didn't miss the part where you've never really tried to be good.'

Eddie still felt too bewildered by the memories of last night (he realised he'd had a night's sleep, registering the bright morning light around him for the first time) to bother arguing. 'So what's Rule 2? One's don't call you crazy and hit you with a fist, or maybe that's one and two...are we on three?'

'Two's the fist thing,' Echo said. 'Three? You're going to love three. You may be the dom, but I'm *always* the one in control, Eddie. No exceptions. You've

319

seen what happens when I get a little *out* of control, and I didn't even start. This is control. Crazy's we'd be going round two right now. Just to start with.'

'So I'm your sex hostage,' Eddie said. 'Nice. Don't fuck with Echo or it's a dark room tied to a chair with the mains plugged into it for a week next time.'

'Too many people have tried to take advantage of me, Eddie. So I lay down a few rules now. You get your kicks, I get mine, nobody gets carried away. Let's face it.' Echo shifted up. 'I had the measure of you right from the start. You're the guy who needs someone in his life to tell him, "You won't do this; that's where the limits are." I need someone tough enough to satisfy me and with enough conscience to know enough means enough.'

'Look, I know I kind of fucked last night up,' Eddie said.

'Nah,' Echo said. 'Last night was fine. From now on, I don't have to tell you to kill yourself and you don't have to use me as a punch-bag. Last night set the rules.'

'*Your* rules.'

'Don't argue, Eddie. We work. Admit it. You liked it last night. That little shock you weren't expecting? Me being a bit of a maniac when I get going? That was the fun part, but we get each other. Do you still like me as much as you did that first night?'

'Yeah. Totally. Did me saying that really mean that much to you?'

'I stopped and looked back, didn't I? Yeah. It did. Can we have a cuddle now and just be two normal people for five minutes?' Eddie didn't have time for an answer before Echo pulled up right next to him and put his right arm around him. Eddie tried to copy him awkwardly, feeling rigid and embarrassed, until a deep breath seemed to sigh out of him without him forcing it, and he relaxed into it and turned his head to look at Echo, and their eyes met.

'You're a good person,' Eddie said. 'You're not crazy.'

'You know what you are, Eddie?'

'What?'

Echo put his head on Eddie's shoulder and hugged him tighter. 'Soft and fluffy.'

'Oh come on. I thought you said you had the measure of me.'

'Of you, yeah. You's an asshole. Your *body's* soft and fluffy. Take something literally for once.'

'*You're* an asshole. Or at least you've got a tight one for an otter who's been around the block and done electro-porn. Seriously, I think there are people who'd die just *watching* you do what you do. How are you still alive?'

'Remember those rules we just set? I've got a set of my own, just for me. They keep me alive.'

Eddie pulled the blanket back over the two of them.

'We need to both get healthier, Eddie. I don't just mean sobriety; that's not enough. We need exercise. A focus. Let's work together. Do a film with me.'

'Porn?'

'You up for it?'

'Do what we just did on camera?'

'Maybe not exactly like that. Our private stuff's for us. The two of us going on display for other people though? I think it would be hot. Not too prudish to be

321

Fast Eddie in a whole other sense of the term, are you? You *did* come in under a minute for me. Did you really think your life depended on it? Coz that's actually pretty hot.'

'No shit,' Eddie said. 'Except I want the roles reversed next time. You're the one who comes for his life. With that taser right behind your ear.'

'You got it, Eddie.' Echo rubbed a leg against his. 'Go on, touch me. See how just talking about that's made me feel already.'

Eddie slid his right hand under Echo's pyjama pants and purred with pleasure at the hardness of his dick.

'Give me some pleasure, Eddie. You said you didn't want to fuck me up to begin with. Am I actually the guy you also want to be nice to?'

Eddie answered by rubbing Echo's sheath and then teasing him with a finger on his tip. 'You like getting your neck tickled? Huh?' Eddie said. 'Who's a happy otter?'

'Mmmm, that's the stuff, Eddie. Nice. Make me arch my back for you. Give it a scratch right down my spine. *Ooooooh yeah.*' Echo tapped his foot for a minute, then relaxed, still not wet but surely on the verge of it, Eddie knew as he continued working him. 'Talk to me, Eddie. How does that hot little plan sound?'

'One thing I've gotta know,' Eddie said, his chin on Echo's shoulder, claws working his back and the other hand still rubbing, squeezing. 'How does this whole porn thing fit in with your whole Mr B's legacy thing? How's any politician out there supposed to take donations from a guy who does what you do? They'd get burnt alive during a campaign where their main backer's a maniac porn otter with a taser fetish.'

'Everyone having a voice *means* everyone having a voice, Eddie. Inclusion. Diversity. When you say everyone deserves Universal Wage, you mean everyone. I've got a fortune, and hey, I'm still working. I still bring people pleasure. I think about others even if I *do* get my kicks doing what I do. Selfish otter, kind otter.'

'About to come in his thousand-dollar pyjama pants otter.'

'Keep it going, Eddie, and I just might.'

'You might not be crazy, but this great big dream of yours is. People are going to ridicule the whole thing, and you, and I don't just mean call you a cuck or a libtard or an SJW, or any of that shit, I mean try and publicly shame you for everything that you are, everything you've ever put on film. Don't tell me there's no such thing as bad publicity. There fucking is; I've dealt with it.'

'You know what we both are, Eddie? Honest. What can they dig up on us that the world doesn't already know? Politicians, they *deny* they get off on their partner giving them one minute to come before they get a shock behind the ear. Tell the truth about that, what could you ever possibly lie about? I don't want to make America great again like those fucking caps that people like my dad wear tell us to. I want it honest again, Eddie. Like right now. Uhhhhhh, yeah, work the otter, Eddie!'

'You want a little shock to get you going?'

'Nah, chill, we're on comfort time. Don't worry, I'll take care of you too.'

'What was that twenty-minute thing you talked about last night?'

Echo breathed deeply, the size his chest swelled to impressing Eddie. 'Make me come while we're talking politics and I'll tell you. You ready to get behind me and Mr B?'

'You always talk about him like he's still alive?'

'He might as well be, the money he left me to do this with.'

'Until it runs out.'

'It won't. Not when our honesty gets more people like him in on this. Not when it's not just the USA that starts thinking this is a good idea. The most powerful country in the world wants to stay that way? All it's got to do is lead on making the world *truly* free. Free to spend less time working bullshit jobs that don't need to exist, imposing rules on each other that we all hate more than celery, and....aaaaaah, that's hot, Eddie. Rub that spot.'

'I like celery. Give me sticks of it and some sour cream any day.' The place behind Echo's ear again, this time with a gentle stroke. 'How can you talk politics and be this horny all at once? Was this you and Mr B again?'

'Yeah. I taught him this one.'

'Okay, Mr Future President, squirt for me.'

'Ooooohoho, nice touch, Eddie!' Echo came with as much strength and pleasure as he had the previous night, Eddie knew, even without the electricity. Thinking of a better world just turned this decent otter's lights on. Finally, for the first time in years, Eddie Kowalski felt like he'd made something good happen. It was happening inside him as well. Echo was on his knees already, between Eddie's legs. 'Okay, Mr future chief of staff, let's have your pants down.'

'Hah! If I'm working for President Pendryl, I want secretary of state. *Then* you can blow me.'

'Shut up and drop 'em, Eddie. Before I make you press secretary.'

Eddie did as he was told, a great big grin on his face as Echo nipped the tip of his cock. 'By the way, that little robbery you confessed to me about? Better keep that one between us from now on. And next time, don't pick Starbucks, where someone else might hear. You got any other stories like that? Tell me one now. You were right, I'm a good listener. I'm even better like this.'

Eddie made up a job based on one he almost pulled in Vegas but didn't and knew Echo would know it was bullshit, but it didn't matter. Ten minutes later, Echo swallowed without Eddie asking him to, too late by then, because the almighty force sucking on his cock had cut off the end of the story and the rest of Eddie's senses with it. With Eddie sprawled on the couch and panting, Echo sat on the floor looking proud of himself and wiped his mouth.

'We're gonna take on the world, Eddie,' he said.

Chapter Sixteen

However much fun Echo was, Eddie knew two truths that morning. The first one was that Echo's political fantasies were never going to become reality.

When he was close to being wrong, a few years later, Eddie was actually happy.

They did everything the way Echo described it: exercise, good diet, the films, the campaigns, and then Eddie landed his first role in a serious, mainstream film. It was only twenty minutes of screen time as the villain's henchman, but it got him noticed. A few reviews mentioned his college education as well as his past disgraces and his apparent reformation. He got an interview with some British magazine called *Empire*. The overseas audiences started to like him. Hollywood saw a way of expanding its reach. A studio cast Eddie in a cop flick as a tough-talking good cop, not just another villain role or another sadist to mirror his real life. All the way through it, Echo was next to him. So was the campaign to secure the democratic nomination for Kalifa, which was a mere three votes from success.

'It was always going to take more than one round, Eddie.'

'That's the second now,' Eddie said. 'The whole thing's becoming exhausting.'

'There's nothing either of us could do instead that *wouldn't* end up being exhausting,' Echo said. 'We're going back for a third.'

'Four more years of this?'

'You don't want it, Eddie? No problem, all you've gotta do's break up with me.'

Eddie hated it when Echo gave it to him as bluntly as that, because the otter always knew Eddie wouldn't do it. The way Eddie felt about Echo by then was something he'd come to privately call 'swapping a thousand other dependencies for one'. He kept it to himself. The circle (who still seemed to understand between little and fuck-all about him) didn't believe in relationships curing everything.

When Eddie hit his first relapse, he felt like that proved it, because that was when he nearly lost Echo, after the second truth he'd known on that morning finally came true: Echo's body was not going to take having that fetish literally zapped through it forever.

The day Echo's body zapped him back, Eddie had the set medics to thank for him having made it to the hospital at all. He knew the worst thing he could do was handle that situation drunk, so when he left the hospital to hit the bar during Echo's emergency surgery, he limited himself to just two. Then it became just four. Then he managed to switch 'What-the-fuck-am-I-doing Eddie' (another private name just kept in his head) back on and go up to hold Echo's hand, with nobody knowing exactly when he might come around.

It took three days. Eddie kept a four-drink limit on each one.

The night the doctor asked to see him before he saw Echo, he went back out for two more after the resulting conversation, gave himself two hours to sober up, ate half a packet of extra-strong tic-tacs, and went in to tell Echo what was going to happen. The doctor, Eddie decided, was one of the few he'd ever met who wasn't a total asshole, because he was letting Eddie deliver this.

'I told you you were sick before this happened, you dickhead.' He said it with a smile, holding Echo's hand.

'Enjoy your moment, Eddie.' Echo looked past him to the doctor. 'Are you going to tell me, or did Eddie bully you into making it him?'

'I didn't bully anyone,' Eddie said, knowing full well Echo had already guessed this, or the doctor had told him already and was just doing the damage limitation on Eddie as well, setting all this up. 'They had to give you bypass surgery to save you. You were out for four days afterwards.'

'No shit, Eddie, you think I don't know surgery on my chest when I feel it?'

'Congratulations, dumbass. You've got a pacemaker now. Just like Mr B. There were no other options, and it's for life. You know what it means already, but we both know you need to hear me say it. There's not going to be any more Echo the Electric Otter. Not for real. There's just Echo now. You might find it odd, but I'd rather like him to be alive even if it comes at a price.'

Echo looked down at his lap, then towards the window, then anywhere in the room apart from at Eddie, who already felt like it was his fault. 'A price like me not being able to *be* me. Yeah. Nice of people to ask me if I wanted to pay that.'

Eddie was glad of the drinks now, his guilt about them vanishing in a second. For once in his life, that slower headspace made him keep his cool instead of flash. 'You were unconscious, and you were going to die before that changed. What was anyone supposed to do differently?'

'You don't get it, do you?'

Spoken like a true junkie, Eddie thought. 'Here's what I get, Echo: a fetish for electricity is not who you are. It's a part of you. A part you always knew that one day somebody was going to tell you you couldn't have anymore. Nobody's body can take what you do to yours for a lifetime.'

Echo's furious looked said, *'What WE did.'*

'You're twenty-five years old and you've got a fucking pacemaker,' Eddie said. 'How old was Mr B before that happened to him? Fifty? Sixty? Wake up, you dumb motherfucker. A fetish isn't worth dying for. I *do* get it, because that's all there is to it.'

Echo straightened up in a way Eddie wouldn't have thought possible for someone who'd just been through another round of hospital treatment like that. 'How many drinks did you have, Eddie?'

'What?'

'Don't what me. Tic-tacs? You fucking amateur.'

Eddie let go of his hand and managed not to bunch his fists. 'You've been out for four days and you just...*know* this?'

'So your relapse was all four ago, was it?'

'I'm not the one in a hospital bed because of something that usually kills people three times our age.'

'Go home, Eddie. Let me deal with this on my own.'

'No.'

'What was rule three? You remember?'

'Shut up and fucking listen to me,' Eddie snapped. 'Everybody on that set saw how shaky you've been, how exhausted, how you've tried to hide it all. I told you I thought you needed to see a doctor. What did you do, Echo? Huh? You knew what was coming. You carried on. You want control of everything? Try convincing anyone you're in a good state of mind right now.'

'Try convincing anyone *you* are. How many drinks, Eddie? You start with two? Then you make it three? How many tonight?'

'I can get back on the wagon. I can go back to the meetings. What meetings are there for someone with a suicidal addiction to electrocuting himself? I leave you in control of your life, you'd be dead before you even got to one if they *did* exist.'

'I don't want you in control of anything, let alone my life!' Echo shouted. 'Get out!'

'Fine. You wanna play hardball?' He took out his phone and held it up. 'Dany.'

'Fuck you, Eddie. She won't come.'

'I know,' Eddie said, putting on the best nasty smirk he could and meaning it. 'Because I'm gonna tell her how the last few weeks have played out, then I'm gonna *tell* her not to come when you call her later because you know I'm right. You don't want to be alive, Echo? Break up with me and then go climb up a fucking pylon!'

Eddie slammed the door, went home, and waited another two days before Dany called and said Echo was staying with her, and Eddie wasn't to come near either of them unless he wanted a restraining order slapped on him.

Eddie knew how to stay away: he hit the bar with no limits that night, withdrew ten thousand from the account Echo always fed the campaigns through, and got on a plane for Vegas.

A week later, he somehow came back with six grand more than he started with, and the worst hangover of his life to back it up. Not hungover exactly, he'd realise later when he pulled up in his car to go to AA still drunk. He stumbled into the meeting, took a seat, let the circle have a minute of silence, and then felt worse for all the years he'd looked down on them for being right all along.

'You've gotta help me,' he said. 'I fucked up. I think Echo's gone.'

Echo wasn't gone. He was late to the meeting and saw Eddie arrive. He sat outside the door without anyone knowing he was there.

After making the session last so long that two of the circle were actually asleep, Eddie was determined not to check into a clinic. He was going to go home and get sober, for Echo, and risk getting the order slapped on him when he went round to explain it all.

Three evenings later, Echo came in the door, his limp more prominent than ever and his walk slow, but a smile on his face. Eddie was making clam chowder and on his second bottle of grape-flavoured Gatorade.

'Thought I told you to get out,' Echo said.

'Yeah,' Eddie said. 'But what would be the fun in that? You can't have a searching conversation with me if I'm gone.'

'You had a pretty good one with the circle. I wasn't gone. I was outside the door.'

Eddie sat down at the kitchen island. 'Should have known.'

'The restraining order thing was a test, Eddie. I wanted to see if your sobriety could stand me rejecting you for a while.'

About halfway through Vegas, Eddie had said, 'Should have known' about that too, when he'd clocked it.

'You still can't deny I was right,' he said. 'You were one stupid decision away from dying. My body can still take a round or two of stupid behaviour. Accepted yours can't yet?'

'Eddie, let me tell you something.'

That line from their first coffee date again. This many years down the line, Eddie still knew he was in trouble when it came out.

'I always *did* know that day would come. You got that much right. You know what I also knew all along? That losing me would make you do exactly what you did. Like it was the worst thing that could happen to you, and that made any kind of relapse you wanted okay. It's your mom dying all over again, but this time it's worse. Your mom never understood you like I did. I

332

get it, I get why you needed a drink. Or many. Or that whole week.'

'Echo, look, it wasn't that. Alright, it *was* that, but are you still pretending I'm the only one who's got a problem in this room right now?'

'No,' Echo said. 'So let's go to a truth we both share: neither of us can be with someone right now when there's this level of complete dependence involved.'

'Oh, that's just great. It's painful when the people around us fall apart and get fucked up and die, so let's just not love anyone because it's too much like hard fucking work.'

'You're still not escaping rule three, Eddie. We need a hiatus. You need to know that your sobriety can stand being apart from me. I can't get healthy and deal with what's in my head right now by being a nympho, with a partner who's as hooked on the fetish that'll kill me as I am. Face it.' He took the taser from his pocket. 'We *both* needed this. It's not just me it's gone for. You said it: it's just Echo from now on. I don't think you're going to want to be with just Echo.'

Eddie Kowalski almost burst into tears. He had a moment of staring into the pan of chowder, looking away from Echo, wanting the tears to come, and they didn't. He turned around. 'You're wrong. I can't even begin to tell you how wrong. I told you: a fetish isn't who you are. It's not who we are together either. Everything else we've done and you think I'd leave you over that?' Eddie brought his hand down on the table a little too hard. 'Will you just show me a little respect and put that fucking thing down?'

Echo looked at the taser, still in his hand.

'What happened the last time someone stood in this kitchen holding one of those and knowing it could kill him? Oh wait, it fucking *did*.'

Eddie hadn't intended for it to do anything but start a row, but everything about Echo went floppy, his tail and ears drooping first and then the rest of him. 'I'm sorry,' he said, putting it down on the bar. 'I wasn't thinking.'

'You weren't even thinking about Mr B?'

'No,' Echo said. 'Because you were right: my head's a mess. That's why we need a hiatus. Remember what you said about meetings for people with fetishes that'll kill them? There *is* a rehab centre that specialises in the kinds of people we both are. I booked myself in already.'

'Where is it?'

Echo smiled. 'Nice try.'

'I'll check in too. Come on. You want a hiatus, you got it. Big time out. I've done that before, I can do it with you. *With* you. Not apart. Don't do this to me.'

'Don't do it to yourself. Don't make this your excuse to fall apart. I'm going away for a while, Eddie. That's what I need. What *you* need is to keep working, keep going to AA, keep up with the circle, keep helping the campaign. Keep living the life we made. When I get back, we'll see if we really do both still want this.'

'Stop it.' Tears were rolling down Eddie's face now.

'Eddie.' Echo came over and put his hands on both his shoulders. 'I want us both to stay alive. This is what it's going to take. You *are* doing this with me. We don't have to be in the same place at the same time to be together.'

Eddie closed his eyes and felt the world turn around inside him like he was drunk again. 'Alright,' he said, nodding several times before he opened his eyes. 'But will you at least eat dinner with me? I hate fucking chowder, you know I do. I made it for you.'

'You didn't know I'd be here tonight.'

'So what? I still made it for you. I was never going to eat it. Unless you came back.'

'We're going to have to be quick. Dany's picking me up in half an hour.'

It was good enough, Eddie thought. *This* was the best he could get with the person he loved now? Half an hour to eat a nasty, salty bowl of fish-flavoured puke? It brought a smile to Echo's face though, because Eddie cooked it just how he wanted it, and how he wanted it was better than any fancy restaurant had ever cooked it for him.

'The cod's a little bit dry,' Echo said.

Eddie knew the line, from hundreds of dinners like this. 'So's your pocket.'

They both smiled. Neither of them laughed. Neither of them said anything else, even when Dany's car pulled up. All they had was a hug, and Echo was gone.

* * *

That night, Fast Eddie Kowalski went to a different AA circle because he knew he wouldn't hold out until Friday, when his met.

He stayed sober for nine entire months, all of them spent mostly with himself for company in the home Echo had inherited. He tried working on his own movie script. Nine months of sobriety, and all he had to show for it were a bunch of shit scripts he'd probably never show to another living soul, but he didn't care: it was a focus. He might get good if he gave it another nine months of this.

The only word he ever had from Echo was through Dany. It had become a joke of a routine that he went through every Monday, right before his AA meeting:

Dany: Yeah, he's still alive. Doing fine. What do I tell him about you?

Eddie: Tell him I'm still sober. *Doin' fine* too.

It was every bit as catty as it sounded, and Eddie had come to like it. No info for no info. If Echo wanted to do politics so bad, here was their stalemate: neither of them budging.

Until the night he got his phone out to call Dany for the weekly routine, only to have the doorbell ring because she was there, outside.

'Don't worry,' she said. 'It's no different. He's alive. Doing fine. Can I come in?'

Eddie stepped aside for her. 'You sure you wanna see this place again?'

Dany smiled, looking around her, obviously taking in how different it was. Eddie had changed a lot of it himself, because when he wasn't writing, he'd secretly fancied himself as an interior designer. 'Yeah,' Dany said. 'I like it.' Now she turned to him with a friendly yet poised look. 'You still think I don't really believe in his innocence, don't you?'

'I don't care who believes what,' Eddie said. 'I believe he didn't kill Mr B. I'd be with him even if I thought he had. What are you here for?'

336

'To tell you to put this place back the way it was,' Dany said. 'He's coming home.'

Eddie's heart felt like it had turned a somersault inside him. 'Tell him if he gives me a house to live in, then I'll live in it however I want. He doesn't like it? He can get his ass back here and put it all back himself.'

Dany shrugged. 'Okay.' She walked for the front door. 'Don't be late for your meeting.'

'You can't leave me hanging on this, for Chrissake,' Eddie said. 'Give me a date. A time.'

'Next Monday,' she said. '9 PM. So you can still go to AA before he gets back.'

* * *

Eddie only went to the meeting for fear of Echo walking straight out the door again that night if he said he hadn't. He heard the car pull in and sat waiting with his usual grape Gatorade, the flavour he chose because Echo didn't like it and he wouldn't have to worry about it disappearing. Echo always had fruit punch. Half the fridge was stocked with it. Eddie refused to make the chowder. Tonight he was either ordering in or taking Echo out.

Providing he didn't get the kind of surprise he didn't want. He was prepared for another of Echo's tests, any kind of test, so long as it turned out to be one. Because if there was no more Echo, Eddie Kowalski no longer cared about his life. That was the way it had been nine months ago, and that was the way it was now. It had been a peaceful, reflective nine months, and at the end of it, nothing about the way Eddie felt for that gorgeous,

337

lovable maniac of an otter had changed. There was never going to be a second Echo, no matter how long he stayed sober for.

Yet he wanted to be sober. He wanted to be alive. But he'd have a hard time doing anything but just existing. That's what he was prepared to tell Echo if it came to it.

Please, do anything but let it come to that, Eddie silently pleaded, to gods he didn't believe in and fate he believed in even less. Echo controlled everything. He was really pleading to Echo, hoping telepathy was somehow a thing.

Echo wasn't walking with a stick or a crutch. That was Eddie's first relief. He looked like he'd gained a little weight, but it seemed more like muscle than fat. His fur was trimmed shorter, his face more streamlined. He actually looked healthy, not the walking corpse who'd ignored Eddie's pleas to go see a doctor. Eddie's memories of that Echo were even worse now that he saw what Echo was meant to look like.

'I leave you for nine months and give you a little money and you do *this* to my house?' Echo said. 'What the fuck are those curtains?'

'You leave me for nine months, you won't tell me where you are, and *that's* the first thing you're worried about? That I like blue-and-white stripes? I'd tell you to go fuck yourself if you hadn't already been doing that all the way through rehab.'

Echo put his bag on the table and went to Eddie with open arms. Eddie took him. God, he could even hug like the Echo he'd first met all over again. He smelt the same – natural otter oils with coconut, warm car seat leather

338

and jasmine. A hint of something else…was that tea tree oil? Lemon grass?'

'Surfing wax,' Echo said. 'And salt. You still sniff me like you're doing coke.'

Eddie sighed and hugged him tighter. 'I'm never relapsing again. Promise. You done punishing me now?'

'I wasn't punishing you, Eddie.'

'I know. You did it for you. It worked. I can already tell. You learn anything important?'

'I learned how being done with being the Electric Otter isn't as hard as I thought. How did you do without a BDSM partner?'

'How do you know I didn't have one?'

'Because you told Dany the truth, and she said you spent most of your time in here alone apart from meetings.'

'I did. I liked it. I wish life could just be you and me and we didn't have to bother with other people. Just give them all your Universal Wage and let *them* sort their own shit out. You and I could just have our own world. Maybe we'd have Dany and a few others there for when we get lonely. Okay, maybe we should go out tonight. I think I *need* to get out. See some people after all.'

'Me too. I'm back. I want people to know.'

'Your agent kept calling. No matter how many times I said I've no idea where you are or when you're coming back. You didn't even tell Brandine anything? That woman's been a pain in my ass.'

Echo smiled. 'I fired her before I left. Nice to know that she cared though. I think I might rehire.'

'Please, she's an agent; she cared about her cut.'

'Let's not talk money. Not tonight.'

'What *can* we talk about?'

'Coming back. Both of us. I've got something. Something you'll like the sound of. Take a walk with me.'

Eddie leaned on the bar, picked up Echo's Gatorade and offered him the bottle. He took it and had a drink. 'Where have you been? You wanna talk about coming back? How about I know where you've been first.'

'Oh, yeah. Sorry. England.'

'You're kidding, right? England? "Bad food, worse weather, Mary fuckin' Poppins."'

'*Snatch*. Denis Farina.'

Eddie pointed his finger like a pistol and clicked his tongue. '"Anything to declare? Yeah: don't go to England."'

'Yeah, well, I went. It's actually pretty good.'

'The Priory?'

'You got it. So you Googled rehab centres and even thought to go outside the USA, huh? You call any of them, ask if I was there?'

'I didn't even do the Google thing. I heard about it from someone in the circle. Never figured *you'd* go to England. I've heard the surf's shit.'

'The cinema isn't. Nor's the TV. England's hot stuff right now, Eddie. You know why I really wanted the Priory? Film stars. I spent three months there. The other six I learned how to make films.'

'You were a *student*? Your rehab was only rehab for six months?'

'When did I even tell you it was rehab? I only said I was going away. I said there was a centre for people like us. Did I tell you I was going there? Okay, I was. Then I changed my mind. I got on a plane for England, and I didn't even tell Dany I was there until I was. You really didn't try to find me, this whole time?'

'I meant what I said. If you wanted a hiatus, you had it. Privacy? I respected it. I even did exactly what you told me to, apart from the socialising bit, but you never said I had to do that. I tried learning to write films. I sucked. I don't care. There's gotta be eight different scripts of shit in this place for you to try your new director skills out on.'

'I'll read them all. Promise. I bet they're not as shit as you think. But I might already have one. Gerry Robinson called me. Said he saw something lately, an amateur script, but it got his attention. Apparently, there was a pretty hot bad guy role in this, and your name came up.'

'Me? With you behind the camera?'

'I'm not attached as anything yet. Apart from maybe a cheque, if this thing turns out to be any good. How do you like the name *Dictator Envy*?'

'*Dictator Envy*,' Eddie repeated. 'That's hot. *Is* it hot?'

'Dark. I don't know if there's much sex, but I think we've both learned how to live without much of that lately. I've been clean too. Completely. You know what I really learned? How to use my imagination for other things. How do you like the tagline: *'Nothing says "We're not going to take this anymore" like a dead president.'*

Eddie's eyes lit up so fast he could almost feel his own eyeballs glowing. 'I'm gonna play a president killer? Holy Jesus yes, I *would* like to kill the fucking president half the time. This is gonna be a World War III flick, right? You don't kill a U.S. president without that happening.'

'Something like that.'

'There a studio attached yet?'

'I'm going to start one. Mr B always said I should think about it. Go on, make the joke: soon as I do this, it's gonna *really* look like I killed him, because I just couldn't wait for the cash to do it.'

'He'd've given it to you.'

'I know. But listen, Eddie, there's something you've gotta know before I even make the calls that are gonna start this thing. I've read this script, *Dictator Envy*. It's incredibly hot stuff. It's gonna be even hotter when it's gone through a couple more drafts and this guy behind it's had a little coaching. Which we're gonna give him. Names are talking. A lot of people are gonna want this. It could be huge. So what I'm telling you's this: some people are talking about you for this thing. Others aren't. I can't necessarily give this to you just because it'll be my studio. I have to be a studio that negotiates, plays, does the business. Me being attached to you? This whole thing has to be bigger than that, if that's how it turns out. Can you handle that? That it might not be you?'

Eddie had one of those moments he usually got in the circle, where there was just silence and someone didn't so much contemplate a profound idea or an epiphany, but just let time stand still and accept they didn't quite know what to make of anything, and that was okay.

342

Two minutes inside his front door after nine fucking months, and Echo Pendryl was already bringing a moment like this? Eddie loved him more than ever.

'Yeah,' he said. 'I'm good. I know what kind of world this is.'

Long before the real unravelling of his life began, where all the shit he'd been through felt like a mere rehearsal, Eddie knew he wasn't sure that was the true answer. Just that it was what this wonderful, ambitious and beautiful otter who had come back to him against all the odds needed to hear him say. That otter needed to believe that was the truth, and right then, Echo Pendryl did believe it. Eddie almost did too.

Just not quite.

But it could *come* true. He wasn't going to fuck this up. Not when it was Echo's life attached to it as well as his.

That was what he told himself. Right then, he meant it.

'Gerry Robinson, huh? He forgiven you for burning his house down yet?'

'What? Oh Eddie, you didn't wake up yet? Gerry paid me a million bucks to take the blame for that. He torched the place himself. He was sick of that house, sick of the whole neighbourhood, and his shit-for-brains starfucker wife wouldn't move. You didn't pick that whole thing up from that party? She was giving him the daggers all night. She's still too clueless to know that he showed her who was boss.'

Eddie laughed. Half a minute later, he was laughing like he actually wanted to laugh, nearly spilling his

Gatorade. 'Man, it's good to have you back. Don't ever do that to me again.'

'Don't make me.'

'So, how are you with the whole electricity thing? What's it like having to totally leave a fetish untouched? Not scratching the itch. Are you really used to it?'

'Yeah,' Echo said. 'It's weird. I think it's like smoking. You know it's bad for you, you know it might kill you, but *damn*, right? You just can't stop, so you find reasons not to that always seem like good ones. I should have quit for my health a long time ago. You finally wanna hear it, Eddie? You were right about the whole thing nine months ago. I should have seen a doctor when you told me to. I should have been more understanding that you found the whole thing with me in the hospital so shit that you hit the bar. I wasn't a good partner. I learned that too. So from now on, there's no rule three. If that's how you need this to be. I need to give you some control too. I said I had it because of people who'd tried to take advantage, remember? You're not going to do that. Maybe all along I was the one taking advantage of you.'

'It never felt like that.'

'It did to me. It's part of why I had to call time out. I knew how dependant you were on me. I used it all the time. It wasn't fair.'

'You're blaming yourself for nine months ago? It wasn't you. Not *just* you. It took both of us encouraging each other to nearly kill you. I only worried about your health when you looked sick. I was an asshole too.'

Echo rubbed Eddie's left arm. 'Let's go out, Eddie. Dinner. Somewhere nice. Then we can make a toast about how all that's the past, and the future and our studio are going to be better than all of that.'

'*Our* studio?'

'Yeah. You wanna be a partner, don't you?'

Again, that moment. At least this time Eddie knew the right answer. 'I always wanted to be an actor, when football was over. I never even thought about owning anything, let alone something like that. I don't think that's me, Echo. It's you. So it's what I'm attached to, but it's not me. But yeah to dinner. That's a good idea.'

Chapter Seventeen

They shared pizza, salad and waffles with ice cream, two cups of coffee each. Echo was quiet, Eddie thought. Nine months of no electricity seemed to have made him sedated yet sober all at once; the pace of everything was slow as soon as Echo slowed down, as though otters were supposed to be placid and chilled. It verged on surreal. For some reason, Eddie liked it.

Now's the time, he thought.

'There's something I was thinking about,' Eddie said. 'Before it all happened, before you started to look sick, you remember what was in the news?'

'I remember a lot of things in the news,' Echo said. 'Which one were you thinking about?'

Eddie smiled. 'I think you know. But okay. Gay marriage became legal in California state. Before it happened, I was going to ask if you'd marry me.'

'Ah,' Echo said, with the kind of smile that Eddie knew meant something unexpected.

'What am I supposed to deduce from that?'

'That I'd wondered. Go on, keep talking.'

'Let's not make this a game, Echo. What you really mean by that is no, but you want me to try to convince you. No more tests. I love you, and I've wanted you back here since the night you left, and now that you're back and you're looking so well, I'm happier than I've ever been. But I've been patient enough. You either want to marry me or you don't. Yes or no?'

'No,' Echo said. '*But*. And I mean this, Eddie. Can you patient for two more minutes? Because I thought about this too. I thought about it when that news broke just like you did. So there's a but, and it's this. Here's what marriage for gay people is to me: the chance to be as equally shackled and tied and eventually unhappy as most straight people get. But there have been two people in my life who could *maybe* make me see another side to it. One of them's dead, and I'm talking to the other one. I'm open to listening, and I'm open to thinking. But not committing, Eddie. Not at the moment. I'm happier than I've been in a long time too. Here's another little bit of wisdom we don't get from a circle: happiness is responsible for wrong decisions too. We need more time to cool off.'

This wasn't Echo, Eddie thought. This was nine-months-to-find-myself Echo. He should have asked before Echo looked sick. Hell, *during* might have worked, might have made him stop and get grounded in reality a different way. Anything but this.

'You'll have us cooling off forever,' Eddie said.

'So what if I do? We'll probably share a great life together, and it will be better for not having done the same things everyone else feels like they have to do. You want me to be committed to you? Look at everything we

347

promised we'd change about the world, the things we promised each other we'd work for. Those are better promises than "I do" and a ring.'

'We're in the public spotlight all the time with Kali, with *everything*, and we're about to take it to a whole new level. Us being married could play well. What's the worst that could happen, we get a divorce someday? That could play well too.'

'I don't want it to play at all, Eddie. If we do it, I want it to be something *we* have, not just another roll of the dice and a move on celebrity snakes and ladders.'

A thought flashed through Eddie so fast he wondered why he hadn't thought of it months ago. He knew Echo had seen it in his eyes before he said it. He put both elbows on the table and put his head in them. 'Alright. Say that Kali actually becomes president. Say that Universal Wage becomes a thing, regardless of how much it is or how exactly it works. Say we get there, and it maybe feels like just half of what we want the world to be. Would you marry me then?'

For the first time in as long as Eddie could remember, Echo looked like he was caught unprepared. The otter looked around him slowly, obviously trying to disguise it as finding the nearest waiter. 'If I say yes to this, are you going to interpret it as me not really believing we can achieve all that? Because I just said no, so that means I think that saying yes to those terms amounts to the same thing?'

'Stop treating this like a movie. Just have a line that's you and not the scripts in your head for once. If you want this to be about us, then we get to be about us once we've changed the world, right? Come on, don't tell me that wouldn't be change enough. Don't tell me you don't secretly doubt we'll ever see it. You wanna make it happen? Why don't you give me a little extra motivation? If I can help you deliver this, I get to marry you. Is there a better way of keeping me sober? Keeping me working? Even getting out of bed and doing half the shit involved in this? Because I do it for you. Okay, and me. And sometimes, on my absolute worst of days, I even think I care about other people. Just a tiny, tiny bit. But it's for you. So will you think about doing this for me?'

For a moment, Eddie hoped and prayed that Echo really did mean that he was open to thinking about this. A moment later, the otter answered his prayers.

'Yes. Never mind Kali being president; it might not have to be her. Just someone we're backing. They give the USA our Universal Wage, it rolls out, it works, then I'll marry you, Eddie. Deal.'

Eddie took Echo's hand across the table. 'Thank you.'

'If we're still together.'

'What? Why wouldn't we be?'

Echo didn't look away and gave no sign of guilt, but after a moment, Eddie still let his hand go.

'Were you seeing someone else?' Eddie said. 'I won't be mad. Just tell me. Is this all because you were thinking we might be better off as just friends?'

'It's none of that. There was nobody. It's just a reality check. Did it ever occur to you there might be someone else you met one day who you'd want more than me?'

'There's nobody else like you.'

'I know. But who says it would have to be another me?'

'What is this talking right now, Echo? Is this your way of saying you don't just want to be with me? Like you want our relationship to be open?'

'Look at our lives,' Echo said. 'Our living's all about sex. We're surrounded by hot people, we openly fuck other people because it's work, but we both like it. I like fucking other people besides you, sleeping with other people besides you, and now that I've gotten over being obsessed with the electricity thing, people are actually starting to come to me without being scared shitless of the real me. They actually do that outside of the safety of a set where we know what we're going to do. I like it. I didn't want the marriage thing because I'm not monogamous, and I know you don't want to think of me as belonging to anyone else. You're possessive, Eddie. That's not a criticism of you, it's just who you are and it's a fact. It's one of the things I wanted us to talk about while we cool off. If you still want to be with me, you've got to find a way past that, let me enjoy other people without me always knowing it's going to secretly piss you off.'

It hurt. It hurt enough that Eddie caught himself looking at all the bottles behind the bar. He knew Echo would have noticed, but it didn't matter. What mattered was what he did next, and tonight, he was keeping his promise of sobriety.

'Okay,' he said. 'You got me. Being less possessive about you? It'd be a good thing, and you want it. Don't ask me how exactly, but I'll work on it. I'll try a counsellor if you want. The two of us together doing that? You want that?'

'I'd go with that,' Echo said, taking Eddie's hand again. 'Don't be all unhappy for the rest of tonight, Eddie. We were doing fine. We just needed a little serious talk right there, but we're fine. I came back because I still love you too. I didn't have anyone else during those nine months because I *did* have a sense of loyalty to you. I just don't want it to work that way forever.'

'You don't get even the tiniest bit jealous when I'm fucking other people?'

'No, I don't.'

'What does that feel like?'

'It feels...well, when I'm watching it, it feels hot. When we do it, I get to see most of you. When I watch you do it, I get to see *all* of you. I get to choose the angle. You look amazing from all of them. Watching you fuck makes me hard, Eddie. I've got a semi right now. Because you know what? It was always my favourite thing after electricity. Warming up by watching you take someone else, thinking about how you were going to do that to me, only better, because I'm your favourite.'

They rubbed legs under the table. 'What if,' Eddie said, 'you had to watch me do more than fuck. Actually date someone, hold hands, kiss, treat them like they were as special as you. Still no problem?'

'Still no problem. Why don't you actually try that? Date another otter. Bring him into our home. Spoil him, be nice, ask if he'll do a little BDSM so I can watch, maybe join in. More than one special person's a good thing, Eddie.'

'Because I might forget about marriage?'

'You might have a little more perspective.'

'You really think we're both going to go poly? By experimenting? Turn Mr B's old house back into a love nest?'

Echo looked like he'd indulged enough in conversation. 'I'm looking forward to you fucking me tonight, Eddie. On my knees on the edge of the bed. You can handcuff me if you want. Hell, do my feet too. Muzzle me, blindfold me, spank me, take your pick. Just so long as you do one thing I've really missed.'

'What?'

'Put the taser behind my ear and count to a minute. It won't have any batteries in it. But there's your challenge right there, Eddie: can you still make it feel real?'

'You bet your ass I can.' Eddie felt like he'd been shocked himself, and this time he found it as pleasurable as Echo always had. 'So...you think that's how you can make up for the buzz? Get as close as you can to the beast in the cage without touching it?'

Echo grinned and licked his lips. 'Yeah.'

'This is why you came back. Because if it's gotta be simulated, then nobody plays the game like me.'

'I came back because I love you, Eddie, and I missed *you*, not just the sex. But yeah. I've gotten a lot of pleasure from a lot of dominators, but you're the master. Nobody else gives me that feeling deep inside me like you do.'

Now Eddie felt better. Not as good as he'd wanted to feel – as good as a yes to his proposal would have made him feel – but this was enough. He didn't need to worry about feeling jealous. He needed to worry about taking it to such heights that Echo simply wouldn't want anyone else. Not for real.

'You wanna know how far that game can go, Eddie?'

'Go on.'

'I'll get the cheque. Let's take that walk we talked about. I want to show you something.'

* * *

The walk started with a drive, out to the city limits. They parked at a picnic bench and started walking. Moonlight walks in a city like this were unheard of, Eddie knew, but they were far enough out that it felt like moonlight, an odd kind of glow Eddie hadn't experienced before, somewhere between the California glare and something a little romantic.

'My favourite view,' Echo said. 'I never brought anyone here. Not even you. I thought about this all the time I was away, how much I wanted to get back so I could see it again. With the man I love this time.'

They stepped out of the trees, and there, down a slight slope, was a sight that made Eddie both thrilled and fearful.

'I love looking at this,' Echo said. 'Natural and manmade beauty. A perfect balance.'

'A perfect place for a bonkers otter to feel awestruck and tranced out and...' Eddie knew that whatever this was doing to Echo now, he probably didn't get it. He put

353

a hand on Echo's shoulder. 'What *do* you feel right now?'

'Powerful,' Echo said. 'Just like this. It's like a siren call, but I can resist it.'

Eddie laughed. 'Your favourite place in the world is a California power station.'

'It's beautiful to me, Eddie. I don't expect anyone else to quite get it. You know why though? I used to go to sleep back in Wyoming dreaming of a place like this. This is exactly what I dreamed about. Right down to the fine details. Don't ask me how that can happen, but it did. I saw this place without ever having seen it. I didn't even find it; Mr B brought me here. We made love together right there, under that tree. I was on his lap looking over his shoulder so I could see this all the way through it.'

Eddie grinned. 'We can do that.'

'I don't wanna recreate it,' Echo said, taking Eddie's hands and kissing him on the mouth. 'I wanted to tell you you're a genius. You gave me my best idea ever.'

Eddie kept his face close to Echo's, slid his hands down to the otter's backside, and said softly, 'What was it?'

'You remember what you told me that night in the hospital, when you stormed out?'

Eddie laughed. 'Oh, yeah. "Go climb up a fucking pylon." You didn't actually come here and do it, did you?'

Echo shook his head, a wild grin on his face. 'It hit me one night. I was sitting on my bed in London, just drinking green tea, thinking, and I thought of that.' He put a hand on Eddie's back and turned him. 'You remember much about physics from school, Eddie?'

'A little bit,' Eddie said. 'Usually the stuff I could apply to football, somehow. What's that got to do with anything?'

'Imagine I did climb up one of those pylons.' Echo stroked down Eddie's back, sending a chill right through him. 'Now imagine I jumped, and I grabbed hold of a zipwire handle and slid down one of those cables, with all forty thousand volts switched on. Know what would happen?'

Eddie's blood began to chill inside him as it all fell into place. 'Echo, *no*. Tell me you're not actually thinking of setting that up as some kind of stunt.'

'What happens is I ride the line just like any other zipwire. Unless you're earthed, you're just like a bird sitting on the wire.'

'Then you hit the next pylon when you run out of wire. You *cannot* do this! No TV station in history would let you fucking do this!' Eddie was glad that sounded right as soon as it was out of his mouth.

'Maybe not with lines like this. But if you custom-build a great big circle of them, with a setup where you slingshot yourself around each pylon to grab the next zipwire, then hell yeah they're gonna let me do it! We've gotta build that, Eddie. I've given plenty of Mr B's money to the Universal Wage campaign. Now I want a little of it for myself. I wanna do that stunt. I *need* to.'

'Why?'

'To do what you said: climb up and feel the rush, the buzz, the *everything* this place makes me feel. Get as close as I can to God. If I can't have the real thing, I've

355

got to get as close as I can. I want to surf those lines, Eddie. Imagine what it would feel like to someone watching. Imagine what publicity like that does for a campaign. For *us*.'

'Echo, I'd be pissing my pants and crying. Seriously. Please just get your head down off this one and cool off. I care about you. More than anyone or anything else in the world. I don't care if you don't want to marry me, I don't care if you say no to me about *anything*, just so long as you don't make me have to watch that.' Eddie wanted to get out of here. Anything to make Echo stop thinking about this. If it took a fight, now was the time to have one. 'Your life isn't just about you. Not when you've made someone love you like I do. I don't care who else wants to watch you do that stunt. I don't.'

Echo looked away for a moment, and for a moment Eddie was certain his next words were going to be the final goodbye. Then he turned back, looking as sober as he had on that first night Eddie met him. 'Okay,' he said. 'If that's how you feel, then okay. I won't do it. I won't even think about it. It ends right here. Just so long as you don't tell me I can't come here anymore. With or without you. I need my favourite place. But no climbing, no stunts. You got it.'

Eddie stared at him, wondering how it had been that easy. It probably hadn't. It was just words, but right then, Eddie was convinced, and that was all he wanted to be. 'Thank you.'

'Alright,' Echo said. 'Here's what we need to focus on instead then. I've heard about an otter down in Malibu who's looking to be a pro surfer. I've been following him online. Apparently he's "got what it

356

takes". He's been funding everything with a pay-per-view AD account. We're gonna go see him. If he checks out, we'll sponsor him. Our studio's gonna get him to the next level; we'll film some proper adult stuff and get it on a real channel. His boyfriend's the one with the *Dictator Envy* script. We need it. We need *them*. Come with me to Malibu tomorrow. You're taking up surfing.'

* * *

It was early when they hit the beach, and Echo had already told Eddie not to be a 'stinkbear with a sore head'. And 'For a guy who fucks on camera, you sure are weird about sitting on a beach in just shorts. Why are you looking so awkward?'

'Echo, have you checked what species I am lately? Now look around you and tell me what this beach is crawling with. You blend in like...I don't even got anything clever to say right now. Everyone's looking at me.'

'Then give them something to look at that's not a guy who's half asleep and half looking like he never saw bare fur in his life.'

'Uuuurgh.' Eddie rolled his eyes, genuinely feeling like he was back at school and didn't want to take swim class. 'Why did you have to bring me anyway? You could have just...' What had stopped him was one otter, rising up on a board out in the distance. Eddie didn't know surfing, but he knew some of these guys were good, and that the storm last night had brought in waves that only the experienced would brave, and there was plenty of show here, but only now did he feel like watching it. 'Holy shit, tell me that's our guy!'

'I dunno, I don't know him yet.' Echo was looking too though, as if it had to be.

'He can just...I don't know, pose? Why's he different to the others? They're all doing the same but...I don't get it. I think I got a semi though.'

Echo put his hands down Eddie's speedos. Eddie let him. It felt good. The coffee was kicking in too. Or at least that's what watching this one surfing otter felt like. 'He got in the centre,' Eddie said. 'That's what this is. He set this up like a movie shot even though it's not one.'

'And he got up that quickly,' Echo said. 'If that's not our guy then maybe it is now. You're thinking about me, right?'

'Sure,' Eddie said. He wasn't. 'You thinking about me?'

'Who else?'

'What if he gets up close and he's actually *not* smoking hot?'

The closer the guy got to the shore, the more Eddie doubted that. Part of him wanted to. The same part that knew the last thing Echo was thinking about right then was him. This was the guy everyone was supposed to hate, who even carried a board like a poser, a total bigshot who probably had Hollywood money but had never earned a cent of it, Daddy's boy who'd bought his way into a gang.

Until he fell off. Eddie saw it as clearly as Echo did: the movie-pose otter lost his balance because one thing had made him do it: he'd seen the two of them.

'That's our guy,' Echo said.

'Might just be a fan,' Eddie said. 'Or maybe a guy who's seen your stuff and he's gonna swim all the way back out there just in case you get a little zappy.'

'Eddie, *look* at that guy. I wouldn't even need to think about electricity to get it up for him.'

I bet you wouldn't, Eddie thought. The posing otter was at least getting some taunts for falling off his board early. Everyone around him seemed to like him, but they loved the excuse. There was a cheetah who looked like he dished out good banter. Hispanic, Eddie thought. There was something about the way that guy carried himself too, and his board. Now the other otters around the pair of them were looking their way too. The poser had told them what had made him fall, and now they were looking like they *all* might swim back out to sea.

Except the poser. He was grinning all over his face, his turn to take the stage back now. One of the others looked like he was trying to talk him out of what Eddie knew would happen next. The poser brushed it off. Everyone else thought it was going to be his funeral.

Eddie wasn't so sure he didn't wish for exactly that. Because if this guy came over here, red-hot movie deal in the making or not, Eddie knew something was going to happen, and something just told him it wasn't going to go his way. It was going to seem like it was, and he'd jerk off later thinking about the stunning piece of tail that clearly wanted to talk to him, but there was something. Just that hunch. Like this was some different version of that second-bag syndrome he'd

359

learned about before he'd even become a man. This wasn't like meeting Ginsburg, or anyone else like him.

None of that had bothered Eddie. Eddie got bad people. He didn't get this guy. This guy seemed split between good, bad and just impossible to tell. This guy bothered him on a level he'd never experienced.

But Christ was he cute. If this guy had been in that rehab circle years ago, Eddie knew he might never have given Echo a second look. He didn't love this guy, but wanting him was enough, and great, he was still hard from Echo's half a hand-job. It could play well enough. If he got to fuck this guy, he'd probably get over that inhibition about not feeling like he knew what his game was. This guy was barely even legal, knew how to work the boyish good looks, and probably didn't know who the real boss of a good session was yet. He'd probably never been spanked hard yet, never done anything that wasn't 'nice', never been on a wild ride but thought he could boast about plenty.

Yet what bothered Eddie was that he felt, somehow, like none of that was true. *That* was what he didn't like about this: this was what it felt like to know you might get taken to school by a kid.

'Hi,' the poser said. 'Trick Dixon.'

'Eddie Kowalski.' Fuck, it was already happening. Trick had shaken hands with him first. 'Big fan, right?'

'Actually, I'm something better. But yeah, I'm that too. And this is Echo the Electric Otter.' Trick shook himself a little, flicking water out of his coat but looking more like he was getting a shock just from the handshake. 'I'd try stroking my tail and saying you could stick that taser behind *my* ear any day, but

360

honestly. it's not my thing, and I heard you don't do that anymore.'

'I don't,' Echo said. 'But for the record, I'd *love* to shock you.'

'Believe me, that's a compliment,' Eddie said. *Like he doesn't already know that, the smug little fuck.* 'So what's better than a big fan? A big fan with money, wanting a private show? We don't do that either.'

'No, no,' Trick said, like he'd expected Eddie to pull any one of a hundred responses like that one. Like it should have been Eddie wanting the private show with him. 'What if I told you two that for one zap behind my ear, I'd give you the rights to a script a lot of people are going to want?'

'I'd say you were making a fool's deal,' Echo said. 'I've read *Dictator Envy*. It's good. It's better than good. Why don't you sell it to a real studio instead of making a deal that I know's too good to be true?'

'Because I want to show my father who's boss.'

There was a deal, Eddie thought, and there was a *deal*. How did Trick Dixon know about the history with Echo's father? Most of that had somehow stayed off the public radar, mainly because Echo had evaded all those sorts of questions in every interview. This guy had already closed this. This was good. Better than good. Schooling from a kid and then some.

This guy could have convinced Echo to marry him any day of the fucking week.

'Where's the guy who wrote that script?' Eddie said, deciding to pretend he'd read it. (And there was the other thing, why *hadn't* Echo given him time to read it

361

yet? Or even given him a copy at all?) 'Sandy...what was his name? I gather he's the real brains behind this.'

'Oh, Sandy's not here. He's more of an off-camera presence in all this,' Trick said. 'I'm the guy in front of the camera. I'm Jack Tasker in that film. I want *you* for Tony Starvos. How'd you feel about that? As big as what's downtown right now? Yeah, I do that to people.'

Eddie laughed. Strange, he felt like it was genuine. 'I'd say you ought to be worried about who's gonna steal your show. I'm in.'

'One thing,' Echo said, like he'd seen this all before and he was going to sit them down for a realistic talk. 'Jack Tasker's an experienced FBI agent. Tony Starvos is a grizzled veteran.' He looked at Trick. 'You're barely legal.' Then he looked at Eddie. 'And you're not quite grizzled enough. Maybe on the *inside*, but look at the pair of you. Neither of you can carry this movie.'

Trick smirked. A fuck-me kind of smirk, Eddie thought. '*Yet*. That's the beautiful thing about this. We're sitting on a great movie for the sake of the movie itself. We're going to grow into it. Until then, I've got something else in mind. Something to help you set up the studio I wanna ask if you'll set up.'

'Go on,' Echo said.

'*Otterotica*,' Trick said. 'People have been using that for years as a term for otters going at it, but I want to give it a whole new meaning. I don't just want porn. I want an otter talent show. Half of it's more like family stuff, good influences, the wholesome stuff we do. I surf. Sandy does cooking. My brother Dolphin does music. Eddie does football, coaching; we can have an honorary otter; people will love that. *Then* there's the

362

adult stuff, the after dark, the NSFW, the part that shows we're honest about everything we do. Just like your campaign always says. Oh yeah, I love that stuff. Universal twenty-five thousand bucks for every citizen? My old man would shit *bricks* if I put my name to that, and that's before how I think it'd be a seriously good thing anyway.'

'So what do *I* do?' Echo said. 'You want me in this, right?'

'You bet. Out of retirement and on the cameras again.'

'To do politics.'

'Uh-uh,' Trick said. 'Film making. I want you to direct everything. Your talent is the "behind the scenes" day. Think about it, five of us, that's Monday to Friday. We get two more otters we're gonna hand-pick, there's your weekend. I'm hoping you'll give me Saturday though. Five, six, seven years time? We think about making *Dictator Envy*. When we've already got a platform to shout about it from.'

'Well, you had my interest,' Echo said. 'Now you've got my attention. Eddie?'

'Yeah, I already said I'm in,' Eddie said. 'But I want my own show. I don't think I'd make a good "honorary otter". Or whatever you called it.'

Trick shrugged. 'Fair enough. But you're gonna love Starvos. Honestly, I think there's an Oscar there in just playing yourself. Maybe on a little crack.'

Or a lot, Eddie thought. *You've no idea what kind of bad guy you make me want to be.*

He told himself to cool off, get to know the guy, maybe find him not so different to that circle he once

363

thought he'd never have a good word towards. This was something good, meaningful, probably the best thing to keep Echo going, and as long as that was happening, Eddie was keeping going to. He was just going to have to get used to taking that step back and not being old Eddie anymore for the sake of it.

Because what he knew right then was that however good this was, however little Echo would like it, and however ashamed of himself he might be later after he'd done it, he just really, *really* wanted to fuck Trick Dixon up.

'Hey otter,' Eddie said. 'That father you want to show who's boss. Is it true you're Tyler Goldman's kid?'

Echo replied before Trick could. 'I'm sorry about him. I told him not to bring that up. Not because it bothers you, just because it's not relevant.'

'Whaaaat?' Eddie said. '*He* brought it up when he mentioned he wanted to show his old man who's boss, right? Which was blatantly a ploy to get you on board because you hate your dad's guts and the whole world knows about it, but I respect the effort.' He got up and put his hand on Trick's shoulder, hoping Trick would hate it. It was even better that he didn't. This was going to take work, Eddie thought. This guy had something. Eddie didn't know what, just that he didn't like it, and this guy wasn't having Echo.

Yeah, that was it. Trick Dixon thought he could have anyone he wanted and deserve them. He wasn't having Echo. Nobody deserved him apart from Eddie.

'You're alright, otter. Is your name actually Trick? That what Tyler called you?'

'My real name's Theodore, but the only person who calls me that is my mom when I've fucked up bigtime, and Tyler didn't name me. He just liked my mom, so he gave her five kids and paid her a special kind of child support. Now he won't give me any help getting an acting career off the ground, but hey, he's actually right. Nepo-babies suck. Just look at any royal family or heir to a massive fortune; they're all a fucking mess. Getting the world handed to you does that. Echo probably told you not to mention it because he already got the measure of me. When I'm in that spotlight, I want the world asking, "Tyler who?"'

'You've actually got it wrong,' Echo said. 'Although don't *get* me wrong, you're on point with everything you just said. I told Eddie not to mention it because I know the real reason you don't want it talked about.'

'Oh you do, huh?' Trick said, smiling and looking like he was humouring Echo. 'Go on then, what is it?'

'It's obvious, and I know loads of people say it. Put you next to Tyler and anyone can state the obvious.'

'Which is?'

'You sure don't look like him.'

Trick laughed, and instead of getting out of Eddie having his hand on his shoulder, he put his own arm around Eddie's shoulders. 'That's not an original thought, Echo. You're right, loads of people say it. Here's the thing: put me next to my mom and you'll see where I get *all* my looks from. Not every guy looks like his dad.'

'That's your get-out?' Echo said. 'Tyler Goldman is *not* your father. That's why he won't lend you his name. He'll do anything else for you apart from that. It's a

365

mind game, and it's more for your mom than you. She knows the truth. He wants you to know *he* knows, because she doesn't think he does.'

'Now who's being an asshole?' Eddie said, playing along. 'You meet this guy for five minutes and you think you know all that?'

'It's fine, Eddie,' Trick said. 'It's like I said: Echo's not the only one who's ever said it. Tyler's tough love thing is because I'm his favourite. You don't do what he does for a favourite who's not yours. If I'm not his then he really doesn't know, but I totally am, because my mom's the straightest talker there is, and if I wasn't his, she'd have told me so by now. Then told me to pretend I never knew the truth, because she's a gold digger. She'd want me to dig for anything else I could get too. But that's not what she did, so I'm Tyler's.'

Echo shrugged. 'I guess that's good enough logic. You know your life better than me.'

You don't believe a word of it, Eddie thought. *Neither do I.*

'Do you two surf?' Trick said. 'Because this is the longest conversation I've had on dry land in months.'

* * *

Eddie waited until Echo was in bed that evening and snoring uncharacteristically early before he got to work. Whoever Trick Dixon really was, he wanted to know. He'd scoured the internet for dirt on people before, mostly to blackmail them to get drug money, but after several years sober, he fancied that his Google-fu was better than ever. He could spend hours on Trick Dixon,

366

looking for everyone in his and his family's life for possible fathers. Someone who dumped their entire life on social media was easy to do this with. Shit, this otter was doing it before he even knew what a computer was, always getting in photos knowing where his mom and anyone else he could get the attention of would put them. It was such a rich history that Eddie was still going at 2:30 AM.

Right when Echo got up to take a piss and Eddie didn't even hear because he was so into everything he'd printed off.

'Eddie, what the fuck are you doing?' Echo laughed, because even sedated with the kind of sleep you got when always sober, he knew the answer. 'You're obsessed with that otter already. Give it up; you'll never find the truth. It's there in plain sight that he's not Goldman's kid, but that's the beauty of it. Hundreds of journalists are gonna chase this once our new studio makes him big, and nobody's gonna find it, let alone how you're trying to. It's buried deeper than your corpse would be if you ever found the truth and Goldman knew about it.'

'I'd *love* to see that motherfucker try coming for me,' Eddie said, sitting back on the desk chair, a smirk on his face even though he felt like Echo was right: he really wasn't any closer to discovering who Trick's father was.

'That's what I'm afraid of, Eddie.' Echo put his hands on Eddie's shoulders. 'Leave this one alone. I planted a seed. It'll grow, trust me. Trick will follow this up. It might take months, it might take years, but he's the one who can get the truth. Then when he does, it'll play well for us. It might even be *good* if it waited years.

Let's get him big, famous, rich, anything else he wants. Then when it's all there, we start to get the *real* story. D'ya see?'

Eddie saw alright. He loved Echo more than ever for being the brilliance and thought behind his driving emotions. Echo breaking his hours-long train of thought had done one extra thing though. Playing tabloid journalist had led Eddie to what he realised was an odd place indeed: the one where he realised that everyone hot on the trail of a lead eventually began to harbour a secret doubt about it once their head cooled off and they realised they were no closer than when they started.

Echo was right: too many possibles effectively meant none. The real one was buried so deep it was going to take a much bigger shovel and way more time. If it was even worth it and not just a flight of fancy.

'I was just humouring the idea,' Eddie said, looking around him and realising he'd spent way too much time on this already. 'Were you actually serious about everything you said, or did you just want to have a laugh if it got me to do all this?'

'Both,' Echo said. 'You're a great big dummy. What fucking time is it? You've been here for way too many hours already. Come to bed. But I meant it all. Tyler Goldman is a sea otter. You've seen Trick up close and personal now as well as on film and in pictures. There's not a drop of sea otter in him. His mom's a river otter, but hey, you already know that because you've been ransacking her online life like every good amateur PI.' Echo picked up all Eddie's printouts. 'Take it from me: his dad's an Asian short-claw. *All* the cute otters are

368

mixes of those two, and then there's Trick. Daddy is or was a smoking *hot* ASC. Like the kind photographers come in their pants over because they never take a bad photo from any angle.'

It stumped Eddie: he'd never thought that he might be looking for an otter who was no longer alive until Echo offered both tenses up for consideration.

'Mom was a pretty hot looker in her prime years as well,' Echo said. 'Then five kids and two packs of cigarettes a day added the weight and the gravel. Once upon a time, she was in love with a guy who was none of *these* guys, and definitely not Tyler Goldman.'

'In love?' Eddie said. 'Fuck that; look at her in her twenties. She was a slut.'

'Maybe she was. But she loved Daddy.'

'Do I even wanna ask "how d'ya figure"?'

'You don't create a con like she has unless you're really protecting someone. I bet Goldman himself doesn't even know. I think Trick was right about that much. Goldman's the smartest man in movies, but on a creature level, he's still dumb enough to see what he wants in his "favourite". Now come to bed and let our boy Trick take this from here. And Eddie?'

'Yeah, what? I'm gonna hate whatever punchline you've been waiting for, aren't I?'

'Don't think I didn't see that look on you earlier. I know just looking at Trick Dixon burned your ass, and that's the other half of why you're doing this.'

'Oh for God's sake,' Eddie said, pretending it wasn't true. 'You told me to work on my jealousy issues and I'm doing it. Tell me who *wouldn't* get that whole vibe about Trick. He knows it. He was playing it. He knew if he

369

flirted with you, it'd burn me like I swallowed napalm, and that's why he did it. That guy's out to fuck with me already. But I did nothing all day about it, because I promised you I'd make an effort. Good enough, or are you going to give me one of your lectures?'

'No, Eddie, it's fine. So long as you make me a promise. Call it a new rule three if you want: you don't unleash the side of yourself that's kept you up for hours doing this right here on anyone we have to work with professionally. You wanna dig dirt on other people for kicks, I'm not gonna police you. Spend your free time how you want. But don't mix it up in the business. That won't go good places. Especially not with our golden boy.'

Our golden boy fuck, Eddie thought. *That otter will burn out as fast as his self-admirant little mouth can run.*

Somehow, he didn't quite believe himself.

'Okay, I promise. I won't fuck up our business. I need a shower before I come to bed. They call us stinkbears for a reason. I think you're right too. Me and Trick Dixon on screen could have chemistry.' *Like I upstage him. That's chemistry enough for me.*

* * *

There was something Echo admired about Eddie's dedication to investigating Trick's life, but what irked him was the motivation. This was Eddie with his hackles secretly up, the ultimate passive aggression replacing what he used to be like while drunk, high, or

370

just sober and in full-on goblin-mode. This wasn't him playing PI; it was a precision asshole-strike.

It didn't matter though, Echo decided. If Eddie was doing this, then he wouldn't do anything worse to Trick face to face. That would keep the partnership Echo wanted to form going. Trick and Eddie could be brilliant on camera, regardless of what Eddie thought of him off-set. Half the great partnerships in the world were built on managing animosity, and Echo felt like Eddie knew that, deep down.

Just keep him tame, Echo thought. *That will be enough.*

That's also easy. He could never deal with me leaving him. He'll do anything to avoid that. All that time I spent away, I realised I'd played that fact from the wrong angle. It wasn't his sobriety I should have been testing at all. It was his obedience.

It was with that feeling of victory and control that Echo sat back and then saw the name that sparked a feeling he couldn't place. There were names everywhere in Eddie's articles, the pictures of possibles muddled around with them, but for a moment, clarity seemed to come through the chaos as Echo re-read the name he'd just seen, over and over.

Eddie hadn't looked up a picture of this guy, but Echo knew what he looked like, even if only vaguely. He hadn't seen a picture of him for a while, but he was looking now, using his phone instead of Eddie's computer, even though Eddie had left himself logged in and unlocked, giving Echo full trust with his life.

What Echo thought he saw was everything Eddie had been looking for.

No, Echo thought. *That guy couldn't be connected to Trick in any way, let alone secretly his father. That would just be too cruel, for both sides.*

And too thrilling for the likes of Eddie if he ever got hold of it.

Echo listened to the sound of the shower running in the background for a moment, then dug a little further. He scanned several articles and found nothing that gave him a lead, until he got to one that placed his possible in Phoenix, AZ, around the time Trick would have been born. An obscure reference to a little-known fact.

Echo checked Trick's profiles. It took a few clicks, but he found what he wanted: Trick had been born in Phoenix, just like he thought.

It was one link, Echo thought. Millions have been through that city and lived there. Especially people like this guy.

Still, he couldn't get over the pictures. Especially not when he found one of the possible in his youth.

It wasn't a possible now, Echo thought. This was *it*. This was the man.

He covered the printed article with that name, knowing Eddie was too tired to notice he'd been looking and rearranging. Even though he gave Eddie no access to his most personal stuff, he wiped the search history from his phone.

One thought cleared his head and told him what he had to do: this guy couldn't possibly know Trick Dixon was his son. If he did, the world would know already.

But say he did know, Echo mused to himself. *Would he actually want the world to know too? Given everything I know so far? Maybe not, and if that was*

372

the case then there were people who'd go to pretty big lengths to keep that *truth quiet.*

Echo felt sure Trick didn't know. Trick couldn't use Tyler Goldman's name, but the ways he could use this one, if Echo's hypothesis was right? That was sensational, dangerous, and potentially huge fan-bait, which all translated to irresistible to someone like Trick. He'd soon fall foul of it though; it would get him embroiled in lawsuits or killed or maybe worse than both. It could wreck his mental health with identity issues. Then would come the revenge he'd want on the liars.

For a moment, Echo wished he'd never said what he had to Trick in front of Eddie. Then he reminded himself of Eddie's compliance with every rule he laid down, and how Eddie had so obviously missed what Echo had seen, and decided he could contain this.

If he slept on it for a while, he'd probably realise he was seeing what he wanted to, because he wanted to know what Eddie didn't, beating him at his own game.

Still though, he let himself go back to bed with one thought: how could this play one day if it really did turn out to be true?

Made in the USA
Columbia, SC
07 October 2024

43796748R00207